AIRY CASTLES

ALL ABLAZE

GEORGE PHILLIES

ACKNOWLEDGEMENTS

I must specifically thank Richard VanHouten for his careful line edit of the final manuscript. The remaining errors are, however, mine.

The cover art is the beautiful work of Brad Fraunfelter.

The author would also like to thank Kiralee McCauley, Bill Roberts, Collie Collier, the gangs at Interregnum, WAPA, and The Wild Hunt, and most especially Dani Zweig for their most welcome suggestions on This Shining Sea, the earlier version of this volume, and Dani Zweig and Edith Maor for their comments on an earlier draft of this volume.

Discover other novels by George Phillies

Minutegirls
Mistress of the Waves
The One World
Against Three Lands
Eclipse: The Girl Who Saved the World

and coming soon

Stand Against the Light
Volume 3 of Eclipse, the Girl Who Saved the World

Of Breaking Waves
Volume 4 of Eclipse, the Girl Who Saved the World

POEM

Till setting sun her golden rays
  Strikes tow'ring cloudy casements high,
Sets airy castles all ablaze,
  Draws fiery shades cross twilit sky,
  Gives burning sign that night creeps nigh.

excerpted from The Sacred Ode to the Most Glorious Namestone
as translated from the High Atlanticean by Alfred Lord Tennyson

GEORGE PHILLIES

WHAT CAME BEFORE

Meet Eclipse.

She's twelve. She's hardworking, bright, self-reliant, good with tools, vigorously physically fit, tough as nails, still young enough to disguise herself as a boy.

She's also a superhero—persona, they're called on her time line. She flies, shrugs off bullets and artillery shells, and shatters fortifications with a glance. Her timeline is almost like ours, if you ignore hordes of superheroes, the IncoAztecan Empire, the League of Nations, and a long list of past technological civilizations.

In Eclipse-The Girl Who Saved the World, Eclipse solved the Lesser Maze. Her prize was the Namestone, which gave her unlimited power to remake the world, bringing Paradise to Earth. She says the Namestone would better be named The Quintessence of Evil, and explains why. Her other prize, within the Maze, was getting beaten most of the way to death. She spends half the book by herself, recovering.

We soon meet Eclipse's friends, the three Wells children, Trisha (Comet-superfast flier, does all the housework), Janie (Aurora-mentalist, brilliant chess player), and Brian (Star-heavy-duty combatant, prefers building models). They've met Eclipse in disguise. They think she's Joe, the boy who plays the strategy game City of Steel with Janie. Trisha is suddenly in very deep trouble with her parents, and has no idea why.

The great game is full of players. The Great Powers. The League of Nations Peace Executive. The mysterious Lords of Eternity. Kniaz Kang's Shanghai Marco Polo restaurant. Spindrift—the girl Eclipse's age who does not live in linear time.

All the world is changed by Eclipse's deed. Wars erupt around the world. The Lords of Eternity try to assassinate her. The Lords of Death try to kidnap Janie, because they think she knows Eclipse's secret identity. A high-power aerial battle follows. The Aztecans attempt to kidnap the three Wells children. Mysterious persona and their indestructible giant flying jellyfish attack White Bluffs, Washington. Spindrift summons and destroys a long-gone ancient tower; she then dies in Eclipse's arms. Manjukuo and the IncoAztecan Empire invade America. Eclipse destroys the Namestone by flying it to the core of the Sun, almost dying in the process.

Finally the Wizard of Mars speaks. Eclipse and the three Wells children must fly across the universe, find the Two Dooms and destroy them, or everyone in the world will die. They agree to go. Trisha, who has spent the entire book being rejected by her parents, invokes the

Heinlein Act to divorce them. The four take off, leaving their Earth behind them.

And now we reach the beginning of Airy Castles All Ablaze.

CHAPTER 1 MARTIAN LANDING

Comet dropped feet-first through the thin Martian air, arms above her head, her flight field slowing her descent. She landed on the balls of her feet, knees flexing slightly, arms snapping down to break her impact. The red sands of Mars crunched under her sneakers. She staggered slightly under the weight of her duffel bag, then straightened gracefully. Inertia, she thought, not weight, here it's really light. Moments later, faint thuds marked first her twin siblings Star and Aurora and then her good friend Eclipse setting foot on the ground.

Not too bad travel time for me from Earth to Mars, Comet thought, especially hauling everyone and their sea bags: A minute and a bit to solar escape velocity, a minute faster than light, and a couple minutes for a gentle landing. She could remember when, not that long ago, she'd needed half an hour to fly Earth to Mars. You're a persona, she thought, but not any old persona; your gifts make you the fastest flier in the world. StarStreak paid off on his bet last fall, even though he for sure couldn't believe he'd lost a here-to-Alpha-Centauri race to a not-yet-thirteen-year-old girl, namely me. She'd been entirely polite to him, carefully not mentioning she also had superspeed and vision that let her see with naked eye the planets of nearby stars, while he mostly flew fast.

"We're here," she announced. "Welcome to the Red Planet."

Star turned to face her. He was not quite a year younger than she, and a good half-a-head shorter. His usual grin had faded to a somber frown. "Good flight, sis," he said. "Thank you. We'd have been in a real jam if you hadn't joined us."

"I got what I wanted," she answered. "It was a fair deal." Her hands started to shake. She pressed them together, hoping her brother and sister didn't notice the tremors. They were barely twelve; she was their big sister, always covering their backs. This was not the time to frighten Star or Aurora.

She'd been fine while flying, but last few days had caught up to her. She'd always been a polite, obedient girl, she thought, no matter how much her resentment hurt: Grounded, no explanation. Thirteenth birthday party—cancelled. Volunteered to save the world, and mayhaps die trying, or stay at home and die for sure. Eclipse? Eclipse had saved her life, several times; Eclipse was still the world's leading war criminal. At the end, she'd had to stand up first to dad and mom and then to Speaker Ming, First Citizen of the American Republic, telling them what they had to give her, or else. Divorcing her parents had been terrifying, even with Eclipse at her back.

"You were utterly frigid, Trisha," Star said. "I'd have been totally terrified, but you were calm as a rock. And I have to thank you for sewing Janie and me new garb." He shook out his cape.

Comet smiled as she inspected her seamstress work, one more time. It had already passed muster with Speaker Ming, with the woman who her siblings had not noticed was the Immortal Morgan Le Fay, or, most demanding of all, with her former parents, but it was her work so she would check again.

They had the same cut to their garb, with loose trousers tucked into short boots and long-sleeve pullover tops. Light jackets, open in the middle, had broad sleeves tapering at the wrists. The long capes appeared to be affectations, until you noticed their supplies of pockets. They'd each chosen their color and sigil. Star's garb was great sky blue, the seven-pointed star of his name covering half of his chest, with seven arrows radiating out in all directions. Aurora's garb was black with silver trim, the sigil on her chest being the pyramid, lidless eye, and radiants seen on old-style currency.

"Yes," Aurora said. "And I'm really sorry you mayhaps never sew for us again," she added. "Except, Brian, we're wearing our public persona garb, people expect me to read minds and you to blow holes in walls, so we should be real careful to use our public persona names. So I'm Aurora, not Janie, and Trisha is Comet."

Brian gritted his teeth. Aurora was right, but did she have to go on for so long about it? "Sorry, Trisha, err, Comet," he managed. "It's just, this is the first time we've been using our gifts for real, not in lessons, while wearing garb."

Comet, why are you talking? Aurora asked. *Every other time we've been here, we just let me use telepathy.*

"I was curious," Comet said. "There's a little air. We seem to hear each other." That was a lie, she admitted to herself, but it was a totally solid excuse for keeping Aurora out of her mind. Almost until the end, her dear sister had been completely oblivious to the tension between her older sister and their parents. Now was not the time to have Aurora blame herself for missing some of the clues.

Sort of, Comet, her year-younger brother answered mentalically, his twin sister's telepathy carrying his thoughts to the four of them. Then he remembered what his sister had just asked. "Except our voices sound strange. Soft and low-pitched."

Aurora, looking at Comet, wrinkled her brows. Her sister, Comet realized, hadn't fallen for her evasion, or was too busy thinking about some game to notice it. "And Heinlein...that was a bit upsetting. I'd rather it settled before you hear me think about it." Aurora smiled wanly.

"We don't have company," Eclipse announced as she finished her pivot, delicately balancing on one toe as she scanned the distant horizon. "In a few moments your host will give us breathable air. But stay ready for vacuum."

"Thanks for checking, Eclipse," Comet said. "We were a bit busy with family matters." She turned her attention to the last member of their party. Eclipse was almost her height. Her curly platinum-blonde hair complimented the brilliant white of her garb. The clothing masked her figure, but Comet knew from hauling firewood with her that Eclipse carried almost as much muscle as she did. Surviving Aurora's teaching of City of Steel, and coming up in skill level as fast as she had, said that Eclipse had real brains on her shoulders.

"Habit," Eclipse answered. "It helps me not get killed." Comet nodded agreement. Eclipse had to be very careful. In much of the world, she would be attacked on sight by the local persona corps and national armed forces, all hoping to be the first to capture the Namestone from her.

"Now that it's too late," Star asked, "did everyone check their duffel bag?"

"We're good," twin sister Aurora answered. "Dad and Mom only checked what we were packing three times." She stopped, suddenly embarrassed. "They checked yours and mine, I mean, Star." Her twin brother nodded.

"Dad told me I should for once try not to embarrass his family by forgetting too many things," Comet said, trying unsuccessfully to force a smile. What had she packed? A week's changes of fall-weight clothing. two dozen pairs of socks. Smallclothes. Multitarp. King-size ultra-R blanket. Shelter half. Long coat, parka in side pocket. Extra pair of sneakers. Survival rations. Water. Deionizing life straw. Camping knife. Heavy-duty multitool trio. Work gloves. First-aid and trauma kit. Sewing kit, with thread and patches to match three sets of garb. Small fishing kit. Slingshot and ball bearings. Carefully sealed change of formal clothing. LessonComp. Three solar recharging cloths. Fresh-made sandwiches. Two one-pound French Imperial milk chocolate bars, sealed. She had paid for those, though the storekeeper would wonder where the money on his register came from. Small folding fry pan holding dishes, cup, bowl, eating utensils, sealed tin of wax-sealed strike-anywhere matches, one plasma-UBS lighter. Soap concentrate. Baby wipes. A roll of paper towels. The duffel itself was air-core; it unfolded into a small air mattress.

"And that was before, before I said 'Heinlein'." She shuddered, clenching her fists, trying to convince herself she had not made a terrible, irrevocable mistake. The Heinlein Divorce Act had let her sever her ties to her family, but there were no take-backs. Her parents were gone forever. She even had to choose a new family name for herself, one more problem she didn't need.

Comet? The voice in Comet's head was Eclipse, carefully shielding her thoughts from Star and Aurora. *We need to talk. Now. Could you please crank up your superspeed, all the way, just the two of us?*

Sure! Comet hesitated. *No! When we did this before, back at home—it was home then—we did telepathy at superspeed. I could feel how much it hurt you.*

It hurt. It wasn't hurting me, not frying my brain or anything. It just needed a lot of power. Eclipse knew she had to reassure the older girl, before her self-confidence collapsed. *It's real important. Please?* Eclipse begged, then watched as the world beyond the two of them slowed to a stop. Aurora had been turning to face her brother. She was now all but motionless.

Here we are, Comet said. *A five-hundred-to-one speed-up.*

Comet, I have your back. 100%. It ends up well, Eclipse promised.

How can it? And I can't take back, what I did. Heinlein divorce you can't take back. Comet clenched her fists again.

I have a couple memories for you. Please don't let anyone else see them. They'd help people find me. Eclipse felt Comet nod assent. She let Comet see images. [A sprawling house, somewhere in the woods, Eclipse's big, sunny bedroom with several rows of Captain Infinity Atomic Soakers on one wall, a long-course swimming pool, Eclipse stir-frying chicken and vegetables, the Manjukuoan sauce simmering in a separate pan.] Comet was sure. Just outside the sounds she could hear, Eclipse and her Mom were talking to each other in...that had to be High Goetic, didn't it?

There was a break in the memories, then a swirl of light. [That was Eclipse, teleporting, not so much as a half-year ago. She appeared a few feet off the ground, at what should have been one end of the swimming pool. The pool was gone. A trio of large walnut trees rose where the house had been. What? had been Eclipse's startled thought. Her force fields slammed to full power. She had to be in the right place. The trees across the lane hadn't changed. What was going on? Right where her bedroom had been, a tree stump pointed skyward, a small cherry-red box sitting on its top.

[Very briefly, Eclipse summoned ultravision. This was no invisibility trick, no puzzle from her Mom. The ground was undisturbed, with no sign of buried chambers or reinforced basement walls. In fact, the street utility pipe carrying power and datanet lines was seamless, missing the

T-link leading to the house. Eclipse, Comet remembered, occasionally mentioned that ultravision was unpleasant for her to use. As usual, Eclipse had understated her suffering. Comet knew that if she'd felt that much pain, she'd have dropped half-stunned to her knees.

[Memories flashed forward. Eclipse opened the box. Inside were two U-Pak-It keys, a U-Pak-It receipt, and a missive in her mother's crisp notehand.

[Eclipse:

You are not being punished. However, you are now on your own. Don't bother trying to find me.

Good-bye.

Mom

[Eclipse's sharply active mind crashed to a stop. It was late afternoon. When she'd left in the morning, everything had been perfectly normal. Not quite in shock, she'd walked back and forth across the property, looking vacantly for further clues. None were to be had.

[Memories flashed forward: A new house, with huge den and study, a wall of bookcases, a big computer screen next to plenty of writing surface. It was even better than the old house, especially one key difference: It was her house, not her Mom's house. Paying cash, modestly more than the asking price, had made the real estate agent entirely uninterested in asking questions, especially when the client was a very expensively dressed if somewhat short older woman. A big bedroom, large bed, the same Atomic Soakers lining one wall. A windowless room with weight machines, a sweat-soaked Eclipse happily doing bench presses. Eclipse riding a horse bareback, knees clamped around its sides, feet nudging the horse toward a gallop, laughing in delight as Snapdragon took a jump over a fence.]

You see, Eclipse said, *for me it started pretty awful, but it ended up fine. And I was alone. You have folks at your back. Me. Professor Lafayette. You start out with money. I didn't. You'll be fine, no matter how rough it was a few minutes ago.*

Your parents dumped you? No warning at all? That's terrible. I can't imagine it! You couldn't ask for help? Comet stared at her slightly-shorter friend.

Real, real bad idea. Eclipse shook her head. *Even before I grabbed the Namestone.*

Comet pivoted and hugged Eclipse. *But I don't even know how to open a bank account, let alone buy a house. How...*

Scripting. Rules Engines. I'll give you them later. It's a solved problem. You'll be fine. Eclipse hugged Comet back, projecting firm reassurance. *There are things to worry about. This isn't one of them. I promise.* *

Comet looked at the ground, swallowed, squeezed tears from her eyes, and took a deep breath, her gifts supplying the air she needed. **OK. I'll be all right in a bit. Let's not keep our host waiting.** Eclipse survived her travails, she thought. I can pass my vale of tears, too. I think. She released superspeed.

"Are you two ready?" Comet forced a smile as she looked at her brother and sister.

"Sure," Star said. "What was that between you two?"

"Nothing," Comet said. "Nothing. Me getting the pep talk I needed." She nodded at Eclipse, and now had a genuine smile on her face. How, Comet wondered, had Eclipse survived what her parents had done to her? Most kids her age—Eclipse hadn't been twelve yet, had she, when she was dumped?—would have rolled up and died. But here was Eclipse, bright and cheerful, helping her friends, when she should have been hiding in a corner, too depressed to move.

Aurora looked skyward. **That was the Wizard of Mars, talking to me. He says the three of us should come in and get our StarCompass. Since Eclipse won't talk to him, she should wait out here and guard our luggage.**

Deal with the Wizard, Eclipse thought? Mayhaps to save the universe. Dealing with the Wizard was incredibly dangerous. You asked him a question and he might give you an answer. He would always give you a bill, though, sometimes an impossibly high bill. Supposedly the Pragmatic Empire, the mainland competitors of Gaia Atlanticea, had been presented with a bill, refused to pay, and soon thereafter ceased to exist. She was not about to give the Wizard a chance to claim she had asked him a question, so he was giving her a bill. She wouldn't put it past the Wizard to try replacing her three companions with illusions, but supposedly the Wizard's illusions could be identified; they were not that carefully made.

She looked carefully at her three companions. Comet? Eclipse realized she'd been too distracted to think about Comet's new garb, even though she'd never before seen Comet wearing it. Comet's old garb had been cut much like Star's. Her new garb was a tight-fitting green body suit that left absolutely no doubt that she was vigorously physically fit. The comet of her name was gold, starting almost at her throat, its tails wrapped around her torso and legs and reading down to her sneakers: Her black sneakers, the color no American girl would consider wearing. From the way she walked, the suit had to be one of the modern stretch fabrics that didn't restrict movement.

Several lines of thought came together in Eclipse's mind. Something that revealing was surely not what a proper Cantabridgian girl wore. The design must have annoyed Comet's parents no end. Perhaps that had been one of the garment's purposes.

OK, Eclipse thought, with some luck I can spot a fake if the Wizard fails to copy their designs perfectly. Now I guard the luggage, not that there's anyone here to steal it.

Time to go in, Aurora said, gesturing up the vast staircase toward the gates. The Scarlet Castle, she thought, had originally been the largest volcano in the solar system. The Wizard of Mars had sculpted the whole of Olympus Mons into a dwelling, a palace so large that in a single lifetime you could only see a small fragment of its endless halls. They'd landed on a plaza halfway up its side, two dozen stairs taking them to the front door. Of course, she considered, the lowest stairs, miles behind and below them, were a good mile wide, but they narrowed toward the five hundred foot width of the Great Gates. This was not quite the moment to wonder what the point of it all was. The Castle seemed more than what was needed for its purpose.

The Gates shimmered and vanished. The three walked forward, footsteps echoing dully in the near-vacuum of the Martian atmosphere.

It's the simple entrance, Star said, *even if there's that weird twist on the inside stairs, where we drop back in time and walk through ourselves.*

"An exceedingly simple manipulation of time, space, and natural law," the Wizard of Mars announced, his voice seemingly coming from the sky above. "Someday, Star, your older sister will be able to duplicate it for you. If she lives through this unfortunate event. But this time it's the straight staircase."

The receiving room was lined with pale blue stone. The Wizard sat behind a simple round table. He gestured for the three siblings to sit. "Greetings. Brian Wells. Jane Caroline Wells. Jessamine Trishaset Wells. And this," he pointed, "is a StarCompass." To Star's eyes, the starcompass looked like a three-dimensional astrolabe. He'd made an astrolabe for the MIT History Museum, but his had just been flat plates. This one was a sphere, circular plates sticking out in all directions, discs connected by odd eccentric gears whose shape somehow shifted when he leaned sideways. Gold, Star thought, that looks to be solid gold, and incredible detailing on the engravings. And those gears turned motion in three normal dimensions into motion in a fourth dimension. The StarCompass was not merely quadridimensional, extended in four spatial directions; it was quadrudimensional, all dimensions linked by those gears. He told himself not to be jealous about the engravings. He was seeing a standard of craftsmanship that he could duplicate, given time.

Comet shook her head vigorously.

"You doubt my claim?" the Wizard asked.

"No! No! It's wonderful. It's lovely." For a moment Comet smiled. "It's quadrudimensional, isn't it? I've never seen anything quadrudimensional before, just read about it. It's really neat! No, my 'no' is that I am not Jessamine Trishaset *Wells*. Heinlein Divorce means I need a new last name."

"Ah. Of course." The Wizard nodded. "And now, instead of searching for a new last name, you will set sail across the cosmos, crossing it twice in the span of a single day. No other persona of your world could do that. You will be as great a navigator as Admiral Anson, the Hero of the Republic, who set sail from Marblehead, circled the world in his cockleshell sailing ships, and returned in glory. You've heard of Anson?"

"I read his diaries. He was brave." She looked up sharply and stared at the Wizard. "You've solved my problem for me. Without me asking. Thank you!"

"Pick the StarCompass up! The chain and wrist clasp are a lanyard. It wouldn't do for you to drop it in midflight." The Wizard waited. "When you picked it up, you learned how to use it. That's a simple third-order trick. And now you, my four volunteers, are prepared for your journey, across the universe to the Tunnels, and back to Earth, and the same trip after you defeat the dooms. Unless you die first. Of course, if you fail, you will all die, and you will take eight billion people with you to the next plane of existence. The StarCompass serves for passage for whichever of you are travelling with it. You present it to the Keeper of the Tunnels, wait thirty minutes, and you're allowed to pass. All four of you, unless some of you have died first, or under the rules more of you, if you recruit supporters before you reach the Tunnels. Remember, no flying or teleporting inside the Tunnels."

Comet shook her head again. "They're volunteers. I'm not. I'm doing this because people are paying me. A lot. I'm a persona for hire."

"And if Speaker Ming had refused to pay you?" The Wizard sounded genuinely curious.

Comet's backbone was ramrod straight. "I would have reminded him of the collapse of the Third Republic, when no compromise was possible, because all sides knew that yielding was political suicide. Did he want the Fourth Republic to join the Third? And did he think I wouldn't go to the press?"

"I see," the Wizard said.

"But I was positive he's a good man, and would give me what I wanted," Comet answered.

"You were right. And you knew I already knew all this," the Wizard said.

"I'm sure you had a reason for this back and forth," she answered politely.

"Which you may learn in due time. However, mentioning time, it is time for the three of you to be on your way." He stood and pointed at the stairs.

~~~~~

Eclipse waited patiently on the Great Stairs. If she waited long enough, she might glimpse Phobos rising in the west. What had the Wizard's last words meant? she wondered. No one else was here to steal anything...no, that was backwards. Wizard was giving a clue. Someone else was here. Whether he was a thief was unclear. None of her senses found anything. She couldn't hear the thief thinking. Vision, even stretched well outside the visible, showed nothing untoward. If there were footprints in the wind-blown sand, she didn't recognize them. She looked over each shoulder. Nothing seemed to be there. Perhaps the Wizard had made one of his obscure jokes.

"Hey, Comet!" A boy's voice interrupted her thoughts. "Fantastic new hairdo. Super dye job. And the color works great with your new garb."

Eclipse tensed. The voice came from directly behind her, and not far away, either, all in a direction she had just finished checking. She whirled on one foot, gifts already half-called shimmering about her. Facing her, a dozen yards away, was a boy a bit older and taller than she. He wore persona garb, pale blue with a huge thunderhead rising across his stomach and chest, lightning bolts showering down from its base.

He stared. "You're not Comet!" he shouted. "Who are you?" He took in Eclipse's garb. Recognition dawned. "You're, you're Eclipse, aren't you? I thought you were gold blonde. And a lot older. No. I'm only here because Morgan Le Fay brought me. Please don't summon the Namestone and kill me."

Eclipse smiled. "I'm just guarding all this luggage. There's mayhaps supposed to be a thief here someplace. That wouldn't be you, would it?" He shook his head vigorously. "And I don't randomly kill people."

"Northern Illinois? All their aldermen and judges?" he challenged.

"It was hardly more than half, OK, two-thirds, of them," Eclipse answered. "The Namestone knew what lay in men's hearts. The honest ones slept in peace. The corrupt ones? The Namestone let me weigh and measure them, find them wanting, corruptions upon this earth, and slay them without salt, all in a single night."

13

"But if you could do that, you could make yourself Empress of Earth, and no one—well maybe the Lords of Eternity—could stop you." Cloud shuddered. "But you didn't. Yet. Or was that a test of your powers?"

"There were rules in the Namestone," Eclipse explained. "How to take control of it. You performed deeds. Smiting evil was one of them. After all, North Illinois had made telepathic evidence inadmissible, so no one could catch their crooks. I did."

"All hail Eclipse, Empress-to-be!" Cloud muttered.

"Not! Whoever had the Namestone could do that. But there was a totally sure way to prevent that. I did it," Eclipse said. "It only almost killed me, but I did it. It can never happen."

She ransacked her memories, trying to find mention of his sigil. "So? Who are you?"

"You don't know me?" he asked bewilderedly. "I'm Cloud, friend of Comet and Star. I'm going with them to save the world. Morgan le Fay told me so."

"Cloud? Oh, right, Aurora mentioned your name a couple times. We just never met. You're coming with us?" Eclipse smiled. "Great to meet you, then. Yes, I'm the real Eclipse. No, I don't randomly kill people. But why did she drop you here?"

"She said she'd be meeting with Comet's parents. She knew. It would be seriously bad to have anyone ask me about my parents." He looked away from her. "Dad said I should go. That's weird. I was in suspended animation for a day, since when she brought me here. You met Le Fay a few minutes ago. But I remember seeing you all in Comet's living room. I was standing behind her, at her left shoulder. I heard everything you said, even Comet invoking that Heinlein thing. But I was here and asleep."

"Mentalic trick," Eclipse explained. "Morgana is very good with those. You're here. Your parents aren't. I care about you, not them. Did she mention how she hid you? You didn't seem to be here, and then you showed up."

"No. Sorry. Do we have to wait for the Wells kids to come back out?" he asked.

Eclipse shrugged. "No choice. Comet has to fly us. Hopefully we don't wait too long. What did Morgana tell you about the dooms?"

"The Wizard of Mars knows everything," Cloud answered. "Morgan said the Wizard says the world is doomed, everyone in it will die, unless we stop the dooms. There are two dooms. He won't describe them. Except we stop them, or eight billion people die, which is weird, because the whole world only has a billion people in it. And he says it has to be us. If someone replaces us, a bunch of teenagers, with adult personas, people like Starstreak or Morgan Le Fay, the dooms win." He looked carefully at her. "You are a teenager, aren't you?"

"Star and Aurora just turned twelve," Eclipse answered. "And replace Comet with Starstreak is a lose. She's faster, and has better other gifts. No secret, Morgan doesn't like high power combat."

"Then she said that we fly from Earth to the Tunnels, fly back to Earth, beat the dooms, fly to the tunnels, and then fly back to Earth again," Cloud continued. "We get back four minutes after we left. Except some of us may die first. What are the Tunnels?"

"You fly out ten billion light years," Eclipse said. "The tunnels are a rock wall in space, two light years long. No, it's not real rocks, it's some sort of higher order construct. You go in, and it's like a cosmic subway station with lots of destinations. Each destination is a different universe, or a different place in our universe, or something like that. It also does some sort of time travel. You can come out before you enter. I don't get why we fly there just to come back."

"The Wizard knows everything and is always right," Cloud said. Eclipse gave him a thumb's up. He started, then finally returned the gesture. "Girls don't do that," he said. "Are you sure you're a girl?"

"Of course I'm sure!" she snapped. "And that 'girls don't' line is totally retarded! Except you only repeated what you learned, so I'm not mad at you." Yet, she added to herself. Her smile was sincere. "That boy-girl thing is silly."

He smiled back, started another thumb's up, then gingerly extended a fist. They exchanged gentle fist bumps. "Don't tell anyone I did that! The rest of the gang will never stop ribbing me down if they find out."

She giggled gently. "You'd be surprised. OK, there weren't any hints about the dooms? Or which of us get to die?"

"No," he answered. "Just we do this, beat dooms that the Lords of Eternity can't, to save the world, or all die if we fail."

"OK. You got exactly the same message we did." She thought for a few moments. "Do you fly faster than light?" He shook his head. "Then Comet or I live. Even if we beat both dooms, if Comet and I both die, you-all can't fly to the Tunnels again. And perhaps the Lords are one of the dooms. They won't beat themselves."

"How did anyone talk you into doing this?" Cloud asked. He stepped through the sand until he was a few feet from her.

"Duty, heavier than worlds," Eclipse said. "And least bad choice. Besides, the Namestone is no longer an issue. Tell you later."

"That's what Dad said, too" Cloud responded. "Life, lighter than atoms."

15

GEORGE PHILLIES

CHAPTER 2 FROM MARS TO INFINITY

The Great Gates shimmered and vanished. Three Wells children passed through the Gates' arch and came down the stairs.

"How'd it go, guys?" Eclipse said. It was strange to talk on Mars, but you could do it. Her mentalic screens were at high power. She hoped those were the real Wells siblings, but on Mons Olympus strange things happened.

"Hi, Cloud!" Star shouted, his voice muffled by the thin air. "Great to see you! The Wizard said you'd be here."

"Great to see all of you, too," Cloud answered. "That goes double for you, Comet! Sorry about what happened to you!"

"I'll live," Comet said. "I think. And this is a StarCompass." She held it up so Eclipse and Cloud could see it.

"Frigid!" Eclipse said enthusiastically. "Quadrudimensional. Like the sky octopus. Except the octopus is weirder, somehow. Do you mind if I do an ultravision scan?"

"When you...," Comet grimaced. "No, that's up to you."

Eclipse did the scan, not mentioning to her friends that she'd included them in her field of view. She hadn't spotted anything wrong with their garb, and she didn't see anything wrong with them. They were the real Wells siblings, not some Wizard trick.

"Did you guys learn anything new from the Wizard?" Eclipse shook her head, trying to clear her new headache.

"It was kind of weird," Star answered. "All he did was give Comet a StarCompass, which only she can use. He wouldn't tell me about the menaces. He said...self-defeating prophecy. No, for some reason I know that you can use the StarCompass to fly us across the universe, Eclipse, if you have to. And he promised you will be Athena's shield and spear, whatever that means. How do I know that? I don't remember him saying it."

"Wizard put facts in your mind," Aurora said. "He tried that on me, too, except I think he failed."

"Wait," Star added. The Wizard told me to tell Cloud: Whatever Eclipse told you, when you two were talking out here, it's true."

Eclipse swallowed deeply at the Athena reference. That was not quite a death sentence for her, but it was respectably close. "Me? Fly across the universe? By myself?" Eclipse asked. "That's a desperation move."

"He kept not knowing things about me," Comet added, "like my Heinlein divorce and my deal with Speaker Ming."

"When...?" Aurora asked. The three siblings exchanged memories, lightning fast. "Strange," Aurora continued. "We had three different conversations with the Wizard, like we split into three time lines and then merged them back together again. I talked chess with him. Star tried to get clues about the menaces. Comet learned about the StarCompass. And each of us thought we had the only conversation."

"Let's get the show on the road," Comet ordered. "Eclipse, this time, please let me do the climb to orbit. I want to feel the load on my flight field while we're still close to the ground." Also, she thought, I want you to recover from using ultravision.

Eclipse nodded agreement. "OK, I've got my flight field up, enough to keep us together if anything goes wrong. Not that it will with you, Comet." She smiled at the older girl. "And I'm snagging enough Martian air—no, you can't breathe it but you can use it to talk—that Aurora doesn't have to keep mindlinks up between all of us."

"Belt and suspenders are good. Does everyone have their luggage?" Comet asked. "Off we go." The five of them soared skyward, their acceleration increasing with every instant. "This part takes a bit. I need like 500 miles a second for galactic escape velocity and a safety margin. Figure fourteen minutes before we go faster than light."

"Comet," her younger brother asked, "would it distract you too much if we four talked?"

"That's fine," she answered, "it'll keep me awake."

"Except first," Star said, "the Wizard gave you a lanyard on the StarCompass. He must think you need it, even though you're absolutely always supercareful not to drop anything. Well, except those letters from your dresser. I knew this was an adventure, like in Creatures and Catacombs, so I brought along the most important thing for an adventurer."

"The rulebook?" Aurora suggested.

"Food? Water?" Cloud proposed.

"Nope. The mile of rope. Well, a couple-six hundred yards of high-test polymer twine." Star nodded vigorously. "And a few tools. I chose those myself. I mean, we don't need the ladder, when two of us can fly, and a raft would be heavy. But twine means we can tie ourselves together." Star pretended not to notice his sisters rolling their eyes. After all, bringing the rope had been his idea, and it was so obviously what they needed.

"Makes sense," Eclipse inserted. "It's like a safety line and helmet when rock climbing. You don't need them at all, until you really do. Do you know the Seyforth knot?"

"I tug hard on the line between us and it's secure at your end?" Star gestured, pretending to pull on a rope. "You tug on your short end and it releases all at once? Know the name, can't tie it."

"I know it," Cloud said. "It's tricky. Aurora, please share my memory." The younger girl passed to the four of them Cloud's muscle memory of tying a Seyforth knot.

"Except I want to talk about what's going on," Star said. "What are we supposed to be doing? Why fly across the universe, just to turn around and come back? What are the dooms? Oh, one thing, Eclipse. You get to say I'm prying and not tell us. I know what my sisters can do—and, no, Comet, I don't understand that Heinlein thing but you're still my sister. Just don't tell Dad or Mom I said that—but it's hard to be a team if you don't know what gifts your team-mates have. Except the Wizard gave away you can fly faster-than-light, Eclipse. And we know you can pound on people and shrug off attacks."

"Star likes these simple questions," Aurora said. "Except I agree on asking every bit of that one."

"Start with Heinlein?" Comet asked. "Let me answer. I might feel better afterward. I can hardly feel worse."

"Sure," Cloud answered. Star nodded agreement.

Eclipse could feel the aching void in Comet's heart, the void that only time might fill. "Your choice, Comet," she answered.

"OK, back to the beginning," Comet said. "Heinlein was this Navy Admiral. He was wounded fighting pirates. We had two aircraft carriers. They had six, until everything was over, and they were down to one, but his two were banged up pretty thoroughly. He knew he'd be retiring, so he read law and became a divorce attorney. Divorce, like Mister and Mrs. Amico across the street."

"One day, they weren't married any more," Aurora explained to Eclipse.

"This is before he started writing science fiction and won the Fiction Nobel Prize," Comet explained. "So one day this little girl appeared in his office. She'd read the new California divorce law. She wanted to divorce...her parents. She had real good reasons why. They were terrible people. The letter of the law said she could. He took her case. His appeals finally reached the Supreme Judicial Court of the Republic. He won, got her a divorce. She became her own family. She did get a guardian, she being short of money. There was a big foofaraw. The Speaker, not Ming, two guys before Ming, asked Heinlein to write a law, so Heinlein divorce would be the same for everyone. That law is the Heinlein Divorce Act. There are rules. I satisfied them. So I'm not part of my old family any more, like Mr. and Mrs. Amico aren't part of each other's family any more."

Star's mouth was a large 'O'. "And Dad blamed you, Eclipse, for all this?" Star asked. Cloud looked baffled.

"Your parents, Star," Eclipse explained, "were dead certain your sister was a wanton roundheel carrying on with a boy. To be precise, your dad thought she was carrying on with Aurora's old City of Steel opponent Joe. After all, he'd gone cloud-diving with Comet, which for sure proved it."

"But you're Joe. Dad thought you'd been carrying on with Comet?" Star was baffled.

"Just because you dropped from the sky? That doesn't make sense," Cloud added.

"It's some stupid romance novel thing," Eclipse explained. "I never heard of it until recently. Except there are romance novels where the couple goes cloud-diving, and then...oh, yuck."

"Eclipse! That's impossible!" An outraged Aurora interrupted. "You couldn't have carried on with my sister. You're a girl!"

"I was in disguise. Your Dad and Mom thought I was a boy," Eclipse said. "They may still think I'm a boy."

"So if I go cloud-diving with a girl, I might...eeuw. That's gross. OK, I won't do that," Star observed. "Not ever! Is it even true?"

"No!" Comet snapped, glowering at her younger brother. "It's total nonsense. I went cloud-diving with Eclipse, when I thought she was a boy, and that idea never entered my mind! Not ever! Not even a tiny bit! Is that clear!" Star wondered if his sister was about to take a swing at him. Perhaps several swings. Or a firm kick to the head.

"Absolutely!" Star answered. "No! Really! I believe you, Comet. I mean, ugh!"

"Besides," Comet added, "to cloud-dive with someone you have to be able to fly. Bouncing when you hit the ground doesn't count as flying, so you can't."

"Oh, good." Star said. "I'm safe."

"I went cloud diving with Silver Knight, but we never did anything we shouldn't," Cloud added. "We were going to go to an Edison theater, but the line stretched around the block."

"You went on a date? With Silver Knight?" Comet asked in amazement.

"You went to an Edison theater?" Star chimed in. "With a girl?" His face squinched in horror.

"No!" Cloud answered. "No! We, we just have the same hobby. We like English Regency Romance edisons."

"English what?" Eclipse asked.

"Have you ever heard of Jane Austen? Georgette Heyer? Edward

Bulwer-Lytton?" Cloud was greeted with head shakes. "They're these great English authors. They wrote novels about the early 1800s. The French turn them into Edison theater films. They're wonderful. Color. Fabrics. Dances. Plots."

"I can see why you didn't tell us," Star said. "I thought European films were illegal."

Cloud shook his head. "Perfectly legal. But they're like detective movies. Almost no one watches them. That was the only showing in New England."

"Dad and Mom dumping on me for what I didn't do, refusing to say what they thought I did, was only the last straw," Comet said. "Even before that, no matter how hard I tried, I couldn't get on their good side. It was terrible. Enough of that for now. Back to your question for Eclipse, Star?"

"What gifts do I have?" Eclipse asked. "I won't tell you them all. Too many people want to kill me. Some of my gifts are surprises that might save my life. But there are a whole stack of times people watched me use gifts. Those gifts I'll describe. I fly, way slower than Comet. But I don't have your super vision, Comet, and I can't turn invisible. I sort of have mentalics, my levin bolts being way less powerful than your death glance, Aurora, and I'm a middling and clumsy telepath, not powerful and subtle like you. If I do telepathy with someone, they get a headache. My mindscreens might be better than yours, Aurora, or I've had more training. I've got several energy attacks and a strong force field. My plasma torch? I've been rigorously trained on putting power into it, for a very long time. When you've had as much practice as I have, Star, you'll probably be better. How strong a force field? Last week I flew to the core of the Sun. By myself. And made it back. Barely. But I did get back. Oh, I teleport."

"How did you manage to escape Tibet," Star asked, "when whoever dropped the lithium bombs on you? You had no warning. You got away before you were vaporized. That was so totally frigid!"

"I didn't teleport," Eclipse answered, "not before the bombs went off. The bombs went off, and my force fields cranked high enough to protect us both. That's presets, same as yours, Star, except faster than light, and a crash drop to power the force fields."

"But if you can always crash drop, Eclipse," Star said, "and shrug off lithium bombs, what are the rest of us doing here? I mean, you're totally invincible. Whatever these dooms are, we might as well just sit around and cheer you on. Oh, I get to cook for you."

"Cook for me is fantastic! I've had some of your cooking. It's great!" Eclipse paused. "That goes for your cooking, too, Comet, and yours,

Aurora, the one time I had anything you baked." At the mention of Aurora's cooking, Star looked doubtful. " But me? Invincible? Not hardly," she answered sadly. "My gifts are like anyone else's. There are things I can't do. I may not be the key that unlocks whatever door we need to open. When doom almost came to Sarnath, the High Combatant beat it because he was an incredible wine-taster. Oh, yes: Rule zero. Crash drops court death. No matter how good you are, you do a crash drop and you're rolling the dice. A bad roll means you die. Do you follow?" Star and Aurora nodded agreement. "Comet?"

"Should I care?" she answered. "Not that I can crash drop. Okay, I might care tomorrow. I'm just dropping smoothly through my levels to speed up."

Eclipse blinked to hide her tears. Poor Comet had had a totally ghastly experience, and no time to recover. Now she was down to not caring about herself. "When I flew to the core of the Sun," Eclipse said, "most people don't know that yet, I spent two weeks powering down first, ever so slowly, down to levels most people never see. On the way back to Earth, I still almost died."

"You flew to the Sun?" Aurora asked. "Why?"

"That was the other Copper Book, wasn't it?" Comet interrupted, "the one Dad doesn't know I read off his desk. Did it work?"

"The True Copper Book?" Eclipse asked.

"Yes," Comet answered. "Is that thing as horrible as the book claimed?"

"Worse," Eclipse answered. "Worse."

"What are you two talking about?" Cloud asked. "Or is it a secret?"

"I promise I'll tell you later." Eclipse nodded.

"Let's please put this off," Comet asked, "say until after we take care of the two dooms?"

"Deal," Star said. "Do you have any weaknesses, Eclipse? I don't know. Are you deathly allergic to mustard?"

"If I really crank down my power levels, like fighting the Lords of Death, I start to toast myself," Eclipse explained, "I need recovery afterwards. That's days of rest, not a few minutes to catch my breath."

"OK," Star said. "And you just said you have ultravision. But wait. You fought that Aztec guy. That was you killing Popocatepetl, too, wasn't it? Video said it was 'Joe'. And you flew to the Sun. Are you recovered from everything?"

"As much as I will be," Eclipse answered, fatigue for once showing in her voice. "I did what I had to do. Needs must. The fellow today wasn't very good. Not as good as me, anyhow. Popocatepetl was weird. His shields were fuzzy, easy to chew up. His energy attacks were all spread out, diffuse, easy to block. I don't get it. You could have beaten him, Star, if you stayed calm."

"Thanks," Star said. He decided he liked having Eclipse say good things about his gifts, that being more than his sisters or Professor Lafayette ever did. "No, really, thank you. Except, this Popcat guy, he spent his time beating up peasants. He never had to be real good, never needed strong shields or great attacks. And focused attacks, they leave the target dead, meaning the target can't be a human sacrifice, so he didn't want focused attacks."

"Hadn't thought of it that way," Eclipse said agreeably. "You're right, Star." He was right, she thought, and she had never thought of the explanation.

"Come back to dooms, Star." Aurora nodded at her twin brother. "Popopatecetl, I mean Popocatepetl, is dead."

"We don't know anything about the dooms," Star said resignedly, "except the Wizard of Mars said there are two of them. They destroy the world and everything in it. Unless the five of us beat them. And one or the other is strong enough to kill us, at least some of us, but mayhaps not all of us."

"That's so helpful," Aurora grumbled.

"But it's true," Comet interjected. "Brian, Star, I mean, you did a super good job of summing up what the Wizard told us. But those menaces sound so silly. What can destroy a world? Why do we need this incredible long round trip? It's going to go on forever."

"I don't know, sister," Star answered. "But everyone, Dad, Mom, Speaker Ming, Professor Lafayette, they were all sure we should believe what the Wizard of Mars was telling us, even if it didn't make sense. So here we are, thanks to our great sister, flying across the universe. Four times. In the middle, we get to see time travel in action. We start our return trip before we left Earth."

"I'm missing something," Eclipse said. "There was some clue I heard, and now I can't figure out what it was. I never, I usually don't forget things. Not like this. I can't find the memory."

"Mind control?" Cloud speculated.

"Through her screens?" Aurora challenged. "Not hardly."

"Time travel?" Comet suggested. "You remember having the clue, Eclipse. Someone went back in time, just a bit, and tweaked history, so you never heard the clue? You just have a memory of learning it, but it never existed?"

"Could be," Eclipse agreed. "I've been used as a puppet by a time traveler before, well, Spindrift didn't live in linear time, so to her some things happened in different order than they did for me. She apologized afterwards. But she rigged a whole bunch of coincidences so I'd grab the Namestone and be up to flying into the Sun."

"Different question?" Star asked. "How did you manage to take the Maze? That's just so incredible."

"This is a bit embarrassing," Eclipse said. "And I'm not sure I'm right. It was a setup, and I was the mark, the dummy being led by the nose. I don't know who did the leading. The Maze had all these challenges. I was exactly prepared for each one. I could have died. If the challenges had been a teeny bit different I would have died. I did get three ribs broken, bone bruises, internal bleeding, little things like that. I was just a tool. Someone used me to get the Namestone out of the Maze. But I gave one hundred percent, and I had the tools I needed. Like your City of Steel move, Aurora. So I won."

The younger girl thought carefully. "You know, it's strange. I swore to myself, up and down, I'd tell no one about that move. And I didn't. Except I told you, and then almost forgot I'd done it."

"If someone was playing with time," Comet began, "they could have been playing with time for all of us, so you were set up, Aurora, to give away your move, Dad and Mom were set up to be mean to me, and, what happened to you, Eclipse."

"Yes," Eclipse agreed. "Except Spindrift, when she hopped back and forth in time, she never rearranged things. I think. She just remembered what happened in a funny order, so sunrise was after mid-morning."

"Mentioning playing with time," Comet said, "this is a twenty hour flight. You're all on deep space breathing? But at least twice we stop for ten minutes, and I take a nap."

"Is ten minutes enough, sis?" Aurora asked. "You're doing all the work."

"Ten minutes for you." Comet smiled. "I'll be at superspeed. That'll be a full night's sleep for me. And each of you is breathing for all of us, in case I forget while I'm sleeping."

"I never thought of something," Star said, "not until now. We could share superspeed with you, Comet. We could do all our studying for class in ten minutes a night."

"Professor Lafayette warned me. Study at superspeed is a real bad idea." Comet shook her head. "But a full night's sleep in ten minutes, study all night, sleep again, and be fresh in the morning? I started doing that."

"Of course! That's it!" Star said. "That was how you suddenly started rolling though lesson segments like they weren't there, wasn't it?"

"Yes," Comet answered. "I was piling up near perfect scores faster than anyone else in the history of Franklin Tech, by a lot. That's twelve hours of study a day, not four, and the extra eight weren't interrupted. Except Dad and Mom didn't care. They didn't even look up what my grades meant. They thought a Q was some sort of failing grade, when it meant that I had Qualified for a grade level. When we left I was officially an eleventh grader. Oh, we just passed 500 miles per second, so we now go faster than light."

Around them the star field shimmered. More and more rapidly, near stars appeared to drift across the heavens. Comet rolled up, taking her flight perpendicular to the galactic plane, soon leaving behind the dense star fields of the Milky Way. "If you look behind us, in a few minutes you'll see the whole galaxy. Once we're in deep space, I can really turn up the speed, so after a bit everything around us becomes the silver sea."

"Across this silver sea of suns," Eclipse said, quoting from Tennyson's *Sacred Ode to the Holy Namestone*, "I flee on blackened, limping wings. My erstwhile foes are cosmic huns, who fondle gauche, bejeweled rings. So long I'm free, they're would-be kings. Except, Comet, your wings are anything but limping. Your flight is just so incredible."

"There's one thing the dooms could do to kill us, well, you, Eclipse. And the mean people back on earth could, too." Star hoped he understood things correctly. "Keep making surprise attacks. Make you crash drop. Wait for the dice to kill you."

"Of course, first they have to find me," Eclipse said. "That's why I hide. For the dooms, we find them, not the other way around, and they get taken by surprise. Anyone on Earth who tried that on me," Eclipse said, "they get traced. Then I take the war to them, like the Austro-Hungarians burning Berlin to end the Summer War."

~~~~~

"Another hour," Comet said to her companions, "and we reach the Tunnels. Those naps on the way really made a difference. Thanks for covering for me, gang."

"It was the least we could do," Star said.

"You're our sister," Aurora added, "we take care of you. No matter what all the silly grownups say."

"Eclipse, are you awake yet?" Cloud turned to the last member of their party.

"Sort of," the older girl answered. "Sleeping helped. A lot."

"Wait!" Aurora interrupted. "There's something following us. I can feel its ultravision scan. It's getting closer."

"We're doing a billion light years an hour," Star countered. "How can anything be gaining on us?"

"I can't go any faster," Comet answered. "I just can't. I'm trying as hard as I can."

"We lend your our strength," Star proposed. "Then you'll go way faster. We've done that before. It's easy. All you have to do..."

Stop! Eclipse's peremptory mentalic shout cut Star off. "Just wait. Let me check something first. Comet? Please?" At least, she thought, this time Aurora told us we were being scanned.

"I trust you, Eclipse. I always have. Even when I didn't know you were Eclipse." Comet shuddered. "Go ahead. Whatever it is."

"I'm using my healing matrix on you. You shouldn't feel anything." Eclipse reached out with her healing gift. Her rules engine flashed glyph after glyph, bright blue with flickers of deep violet. "Comet," she said, "You really have to ease off a bit on flight. Please? You said you trust me."

"Easing off," Comet said. The glyphs shifted to blue-green. "What was that?" Comet asked quietly.

"I did a scan; it's part of my healing gift. You were pushing yourself so hard you were hurting yourself," Eclipse explained. "Hurting yourself enough that you were killing yourself. Now you aren't. I can try helping you repair some of what you did, while we're flying."

"I think they're gaining on us faster," Aurora said.

"Can you find them mentalically?" Eclipse asked. "My ultravision, it's strictly a short range thing."

"Like all the way through the sun?" Cloud grumbled.

"Cloud, this is intergalactic. The sun is teeny-tiny by comparison," Comet explained.

"Fair enough." Cloud nodded.

"I'm trying," Aurora said. "Following ultravision back is hard. Except they aren't exactly following us. We keep dodging galaxies. Their path. It's sort of straighter."

"Yes!" Star said. "That's how they can be gaining on us, when Comet's the fastest persona in the world. They have some sort of a map with shortcuts. The StarCompass just gives us the straight line direction."

"Great! All I needed," Comet grumbled. "I'm giving one hundred ten percent, and it isn't enough. No matter what I do at anything, I'm not good enough."

"Comet," Eclipse said. "Think back at your school grades. Think back at lapping the boy's base ball nines team, day after day. You're plenty good."

"We did volunteer for this," Star said. "The Wizard of Mars said some of were likely going to die on this trip."

26

"No," Comet said. "You four volunteered. I named my price, and Speaker Ming paid me what I wanted. I'm a persona for hire, a, what's the word?"

"Mercenary," Eclipse answered. "Mercenary. Except what you asked for, you were entitled to have." I hope, she thought, you won't regret being paid the price you asked. Invoking the Heinlein Act and divorcing your parents is something you can't take back. I was your champion, so I saw your facts. I could tell: It wasn't a spur of the moment decision. For sure, what you wanted was a fair request. Your parents were absolutely wonderful toward Star and Aurora, and completely terrible toward you.

~~~~~

Across space loomed an enormous rock wall, stretching out forever in both directions.

"How can it do that?" Star asked. "We're in outer space. That thing must be light years across. It's impossible."

"It's a symbol," Comet said. "The Wizard of Mars told me. I think. It's the West Edge of the Universe, but it's actually not in our universe, just close, and there's universe on all sides of it. It's not made of rock. In any event, that circle is the entrance. The Wizard showed me a picture. We walk in, no flying or teleporting. I show the Guardian of the Tunnels my StarCompass. We wait thirty minutes. No, I don't know why. Then I get to fly us back."

Aurora peered into the heavens. "Do we have a half hour?" she asked. "Whatever it is, it's getting way closer."

Comet stared into the sky. "Yes, I see it. But I don't get it. What am I looking at?"

Comet! The mentalic message came from the void behind them. *Turn around. Go back to Earth. That was not a suggestion. You are a child, and you will do as you are told.*

"Who's that? Star asked. "I hear him but I don't see him. Where is he?"

"Aurora, please show me what you are seeing," Eclipse said. Aurora did as asked, forwarding what her mind-scans revealed. Aurora blanched at the words Eclipse used next.

You will turn around, or you will all be punished as the disobedient children you are! the voice announced.

"They're way closer," Aurora said. "They'll be here before that half hour is up."

"Who's back there?" Comet asked.

"A bunch of folks who want us to turn around," Eclipse said. To be precise, she thought, most of the Lords of Eternity.

CHAPTER 3 ECLIPSE VS SOLARA

This is just wonderful, I thought. I may be Eclipse, bearer of the Namestone, recently back from the core of the Sun, but buying Comet the time she needs is going to be a bear. It couldn't be just Solara by herself. No, there's a whole pile of her friends with her. They even pulled poor Corinne out of hibernation and insisted she wear the Ambihelicon. At least we've reached the Tunnel entrance. That makes things a lot simpler.

Child! The voice echoed across the cosmic void.

I'm an adult, Comet answered. *Heinlein Act. You have a complaint, me being here, take it up with the Wizard of Mars.*

Little girl, I am Solara, the Eternal Supreme. The voice rose to a roar. *Return to Earth! Return to Earth at once! Return to Earth or be destroyed. This is your only warning.*

"What do we do?" a panic-stricken Comet asked her friends.

"There's only one way in," I said. "You four get inside, find the Guardian, and get the clock ticking. I buy you the time you need."

"What about you, Eclipse?" Star asked. "Should I stay to help?"

"No." I shook my head. "Later on, your sisters may need someone with firepower to deal with the Wizard's dooms. You, too, Cloud."

You cannot outrun us, Solara warned. *You cannot escape us. Turn around, or before you can cross the Tunnels, we will catch you, and then you will surely die.*

"You four head down the Tunnel!" I ordered. "I stay here, bar the way until the thirty minutes are up."

"You're going to fight Solara by yourself?" an unbelieving Star asked. I could say 'nothing like having confidence in your friends', but realistically speaking my odds left something to be desired.

"No, I'm going to stomp her into the ground!" I answered.

"There has to be another way, " a desperate Cloud insisted.

"Star, the Wizard warned us. Some of us may die on this trip." I tried to smile. "This may be where I get to die. But I will bar this entrance, as long as I can. Get moving! The longer I have to hold, the more likely I get killed."

Comet hesitated.

"Go!" I screamed. My four travelling companions faded into the Tunnels. Grimly, I dropped through level after level, powering my gifts as rapidly as I could. I'd flown to the core of the Sun, and held on while the Timeless Ones were doing their best to blow up the Sun and me with it. If I have to, I told myself, I can hold here for thirty minutes.

Being realistic, there is no single persona in the world who would like these odds. Mum has a certain weakness that they know. She stays away from fights with them. Morgan Le Fay by repute is not fond of high-power combat, no matter what she did to the Imperial Manjukuoan Grand Fleet and its persona host. However, if you're a grown-up, you play the cards you were dealt. The odds were only close to impossible. My iron determination damped out waves of fear. I summoned the strongest force wall I could muster, blocking the entire tunnel from side to side.

Solara landed on the portico outside the tunnel. Her garb today was a loose-fitting mix of white and lemon-yellow panels. The bejeweled Mask of the Sun, a golden plate wider and taller than her head, hid her face. Her body screens burned sun bright.

I am Solara, the one and only. You are ordered to lower your defenses and return to Earth.

I am Eclipse the Invincible, I said. *You and which army? I've been here before. Last time it was the Peace Police, Valkyria, and one of your people, all demanding I hand over the Namestone. You may have heard what happened.*

That time, Eclipse, Solara said, *you fled as soon as you could, going where you were not followed. This time, you cannot flee. You must stand until you yield or die.*

I must stand until you quit, I countered. *You know, I did destroy the Namestone, as promised. Or mayhaps you didn't know that. I saved Starsmasher's life. Doesn't that count for anything?*

That's why I'm giving you a chance to run away, rather than killing you on the spot, Solara answered. *You should take advantage of my generosity.*

What's the issue, anyhow? I asked. *The Wizard of Mars, himself, asked us to do this.*

You are disrupting the Great Plan, the Plan that has lasted far longer than you would believe possible, Solara answered. *You do not have a need to know what the Plan is. You only need to know you must remove yourself from my path, or you will surely perish. Your whole life is ahead of you. Please don't throw it away.*

The longer we talk, I thought, the less time she has to pound on my force wall. *You get to quit,* I countered. *Or you get to die. I don't care which. You shall not pass.* I was inside the Tunnel, so the Guardian's teleport block kept them from going around me.

You cannot win, Solara announced. *Yield now, or I'll beat down your every defense, and paddle your backside raw.*

That, I thought, was at least a unique threat. Stupid, but unique.

Solara, I didn't know you were a child molester. I thought you preferred guys. Of course, you're stuck with the second-raters the Silver General leaves you, but they are guys. Well, sort of. I guess. Being generous.

I command the stellar fire! Solara screamed. *You cannot stand!*

You only command the stellar fire? I giggled. *Is that all?* Solara sounded really upset. She's a bit sensitive about the Silver General lifting her better boyfriends. There's a line here from one of mom's really old story books. *Wimp! I command the secret fire, the fire that underlies all the world, before which your stellar fire is a cool summer breeze.* Solara, I thought, was starting to sound like Valkyria. If you get under someone's skin, so they get angry, they become several bales short of a full load. Angry opponents make stupid opponents, and, the stars know, I need every advantage I can find.

I see several of your fellows aren't here, I continued. *Plasmatrix? Starsmasher? You know, folks with brains as well as flabby muscle? What's wrong? Did they figure out how totally stupid you are, going toe-to-toe against me, the invincible Eclipse, Bearer of the Holy Namestone?*

I reached farther into my levels. Here was that impossible geometric object, the Straight Circle. The Solid Rainbow came almost unbidden, its surface comfortingly warm against my skin. There was the Well of Infinity, a cerulean blue pool that went down forever. I figuratively stepped forward, dropping straight down into the well, down to the place where ideas are solid and material objects are the palest of palimpsests. Once again I saw the Nipponese gentleman, sword drawn and held high, seemingly bowing in my direction. In the distance, the girl from atop the burial mound nodded at me. I scrabbled for the full width of every level I could reach, shoving all that power into charging my force wall.

We share our powers, Solara announced. *You face the combined powers of a dozen Lords of Eternity, and the limitless power of the Ambihelicon.* Supposedly that 'limitless' adjective is a gross exaggeration. I was about to find out. In any event, they were working through Solara, not standing next to her. They are a bunch of cowards, after all. The attacks they could send through her were way limited, enough that the folks I wasn't seeing would be farless strong than Solara by herself. Solara chose the moment to strike at my force wall.

For an instant, the impact took my breath away. Solara's attack was brighter than a lithium bomb, more penetrating than the radiation at the starcore. Can I do this? I wondered. She's tearing away at my defenses. I have to reinforce it, faster than she's destroying it. I yawned affectedly.

Solara launched a half-dozen attacks, each as powerful as the first, each different from all the rest. Gamma ray pulse laser burst. Plasma torch. Neutron beams. That's all her friends, I thought, each with his own attack, all passing through Solara, so I can only target her. All at once is a multiple attack, way more effective than them just lending Solara their levels. All the time we'd been talking, I'd been charging up the wall. Now I had to see if I could hold.

I felt Aurora's null links trigger. Now what? She should have been at the grand junction of the Tunnels, someplace safe and quiet. The null link said Aurora was pushing some of her gifts as hard as she could.

Help! Her agonized cry for aid rang in my ears *She's crushing my mind screens. It's a mind control attack. They want to make Comet give up and turn around.*

Mind control? From outside the tunnels? Someone had to have an absurd amount of power behind that attack. I was putting every bit of power I had into holding my force wall, and somehow I had to find even more to help Aurora. We'd never practiced sharing levels, she and I. Now I had to lend her the power she needed to keep her screens up. My fists clenched so tightly my fingernails bit into my palms. Medico's glyphs flashed in my head, burning from green, to blue, to the violet that warned I was doing lethal damage to myself.

What could I do? I stood squarely at the bottom of the Well of Infinity. I could feel myself decomposing into ideons made real: Will. Determination. Duty. Down here, they were the material objects, and my physical body was a ghost made of words. I'd reached the limit of my gifts, and that limit was not enough.

Bottom? What if there were another level, further down? I imagined the abstraction I stood upon cracking, like the ice on a frozen pond when you whack it hard with a sledgehammer. That was a figurative image, but down here figurative images are physical reality.

Suddenly I was through. The new power level made no sense. It was a circle that was a square. Someday I might understand what I was seeing, but not now. That didn't matter. The level supplied me with astronomical amounts of power. Medico glyphs flashed deep violet. I was killing myself. If I'd spent weeks easing into the new level, I'd've learned how to handle the power it was giving me. I didn't have those weeks. I was taking the power all at once.

The draw from Aurora changed. She was drawing vastly more from me, much more smoothly than a few moments earlier, yet so smoothly that I hardly felt the extra load.

A medico glyph flashed flat black. That was the death glyph, my final warning. I was sliding from mortally injured into death itself. I couldn't control the power I was drawing. The Lords of Eternity were still leaking damage through my shields. I needed a better answer than holding my force wall. Aurora's words rose to the surface of my memories. If the situation is hopeless, use desperation attacks.

Solara was in front of me. Her friends were way back. I had no way to target them. I couldn't tell where they were. OK, Solara, you're the target. Mum had taught me a cute trick against an attacker drawing on friends' levels. I had to get the timing right, way harder when I didn't have Mum's picosecond time control and precision targeting.

I dropped my wall. Much of their attacks now passed through empty space. I'd have to hope my personal force field stayed up. I fed a huge pulse of power into Solara's gifts. That pulse needed instants to pass through her. Before I fed her the pulse, I'd already maxed out my plasma torch, which needed instants of its own to travel from me to her. Medico? Glyph after glyph flickered between violet and black. I hadn't died yet, but I would, soon enough.

Things took place so rapidly I really didn't see what happened. My personal force field flared red-green-blue into the far ultraviolet in next to no time. Some of that was Solara's attacks. Much of that was me boosting Solara's attacks, incidentally frying her ability to control her gifts. In particular, frying her ability to reinforce her personal force fields. Tiny stars, red and green and blue, crawled across my field of vision. My plasma torch smashed straight through Solara's defenses. She would have died on the spot, except one of her friends teleported her out before she was actually dead. I didn't have another target for the torch, so I eased off on it, smoothly easing back on how hard I was drawing on my power levels. Now I was standing above the Well of Infinity, but I could remember, all too clearly, how to reach the Square Circle if I needed it.

It would have been frigid, I thought, to have had a teleport block in place, so Solara died instead of disappearing, but I was already using more power than I could control. My medico glyphs had been flaring between blue and violet. I wasn't really scared until I saw one after another flip to black. That's the death color. Solara and friends had been killing me through my own screens, driven absolutely as hard as I could. Perhaps they had succeeded.

Eclipse! Time! Aurora's mentalic message was a shout. I turned and ran. Not being able to fly or teleport inside the Tunnels was a nuisance. I had a solid mile to take at a sprint, or as close as I could manage. The tunnels were symbolic, but they provided a very real one gee of gravity. Pressure on my shields had stopped, but surely that wouldn't continue. Soon enough, another eternal would be hot on my tail. Gasping for breath, my heart pounding, I reached my friends. The Guardian of the Tunnels was nowhere to be seen.

Guys! I shouted. *No time! They'll be on us in an instant. Comet, where's the exit? Get us out of here!*

On it! Stand close together! Comet answered. *All five of us!*

Aurora staggered. I caught her by one shoulder. Star moved to take the rest of her weight.

Aurora? What's wrong? I asked.

Don't know, The younger girl answered. *They kept trying mind control on us. I blocked them, but it was so hard. Then it got easy, and I got dizzy. And I feel strange.*

Please don't block me, I asked. I touched Aurora with my healing gifts. Every glyph came up gold—good health. *You're fine,* I announced. *Except you powered your mentalic shields way way up.* Way more, I thought, than I would have guessed you could. I could feel the personality behind the attacks she'd blocked. *If it makes you feel better, that was Corinne and the Ambihelicon trying to break your mentalic defenses. She failed.* Blocking the Ambihelicon qualified as totally amazing. How did Aurora do it?

That was Corinne herself? Aurora shook her head *Now I feel all right,* she announced. *I was just dizzy for a moment.*

The present was not, I decided, the moment to solve this little mystery. Aurora was not a casualty, which was just fine with me. She also wasn't a whiner, so I'd take her at her word on having been sick and now being all right.

All luggage has to be off the floor, Comet said. *Orders from the Starcompass.* I looked for my bag, saw Comet had its straps, and the straps for her own bag, over her shoulders. Cloud had his own bag in position.

Two off, Star announced, pointing where he had his bag and was helping Aurora with hers.

Comet straightened her legs, hoisting both bags clear. Goddess, I thought, those two bags weigh well more than she does. And she's hoisting both of them clear of the ground..

Comet rotated two of the StarCompass's disks. *Exit is inside the Starcompass.* The StarCompass's golden plates spread like a peacock's feathers until they were enormous pale images, yards and yards across, into which I found myself falling. My sense of balance is fine, I decided. The room really is spinning wildly around us.

Everything went black. For a fraction of an instant, my eyes saw nothing, not even phosphenes. Starfields snapped back into view, still, silent, and beautiful.

Where are you? Comet thought. If sister Aurora wasn't here, she realized, the rest of her party couldn't hear her call.

Right behind you, Aurora answered. Aurora followed with an image, five travellers in a tight bunch, Star carrying his and Aurora's duffel bags.

Comet, I asked, *Please get us out of here before those people get here. Beating them up once was plenty for me.*

Luggage check? Comet asked.

All here, her brother Star answered. *Sis, thanks for grabbing Eclipse's bag. It was way too heavy for me.*

Any time. Comet reached out with her flight field. *OK, I've got all five of us, and equipment. We're out of here.* Her flight field flared a brilliant tangerine. *Homeward bound.*

I shook my head, trying to clear my thoughts. *When I ran in, I could hear you guys having an argument. What's wrong?*

Cloud says Morgan Le Fay, Aurora explained. *But he has images in his mind. That's not Morgan Le Fay. It's Professor Lafayette from RTI. So something is way wrong.*

Is this a hoax? We can't go back, can we? Star asked. *What do we do?*

Go back? After I just nearly killed myself so we could get this far? I wondered. *Wait. Could I please see this image?* Aurora did as asked. The image Cloud remembered was indeed Professor Lafayette in a white and red body suit, the Orb of Merlin spread across her chest.

Comet? I focused my thoughts, so only Comet heard them. *You know perfectly well what's going on. Morgan and Morgana are the same person. Why didn't you just say so?*

Give away someone's persona identity? Comet shuddered. *Like telling people your private persona, Eclipse, not that I know who it is? I can't do that. It's not gift-true.*

I thought for a few moments. *OK, guys, this is tactical necessity. If Lafayette complains I gave away her persona identity, she complains to me. The rest of you, you tell no one what I'm telling you. Is that clear?* Four heads nodded.

Lafayette and Le Fay. They're the same person. That's why Comet, back at your house, said Lafayette was a country, all by herself. I waited, expecting to hear denials. Comet smiled and nodded. Her fellows stayed quiet. *I just broke one of Morgan's personas. She has every right to get really angry with me, but that's strictly between the two of us.*

Aurora? Comet said. *I don't see them behind us. Can you hear any of their minds?*

No. Mayhaps they gave up. Aurora answered. I hoped that was true.

Why are we bothering to be here? Cloud asked. *You're Eclipse. You have the Namestone. You're infinitely powerful. Whatever needs

35

doing, you can do it with a snap of two fingers. *

She doesn't have the Namestone here, * Comet said. *The rest is her story to tell. We all have to do our best, or the world ends.* *

If she could have done this herself, the Wizard wouldn't have sent the rest of us, * Star observed.

Why's she just lying there? * Cloud asked again. *Eclipse doesn't look very powerful to me.* *

I was looking over her shoulder, * Aurora said, *while she was keeping our pursuers out of the Tunnel. She went one on one with Solara, a dozen other eternals lending Solara their levels, and Corinne herself with the Ambihelicon right behind them. In the end, she got so much power from someplace, she smashed straight through Solara's force fields. Solara would have died, if her friends hadn't rescued her.* *

Not quite that bad, * I added. *Eternals are cowards. They all hid behind Solara and sent their attacks through her, so they were really weak. It's just that multiple attacks are bad for the target.* *

Aurora looked carefully at me. I was soaked in sweat. I hardly needed a mirror to tell: My usually-immaculate curls covered my scalp in mangy clumps.

Who has a blanket? * Aurora asked.

Ultra-R, * I answered. Now my thoughts blurred so much I was groggy. *Top of my duffel bag. Pull it out. But you shouldn't be cold, Aurora.* *

Star, get it out! Now! * Aurora looked at me. *I'm not cold, but you're about to be. You way overpowered.* *

Everything is so fuzzy, I thought. I'm not thinking clearly. Now I was cold, colder than cold, just like Aurora promised. I have to stay alert, I told myself. I can't let them down. No, I corrected, I was too tired for that.

Bundle her up, * Star said. *I'd say use a sleeping bag. But mine is already small on me. She'll never fit inside.* *

Use her blanket. It's big. And bundle me inside with her, * Aurora announced. *She's freezing.* *

I distantly recognized that Star had rolled me in my blanket. The wonderfully warm patch on one side of me was Aurora, not my barn cats. I fell asleep.

What was that about? * Cloud asked.

When you overload enough, you get terrible chills, * Comet explained. *Enough to kill you...Morgana warned me. Eclipse went through that, when she saved Aurora and me, two years ago. Aurora and the blanket is first aid.* *

She saved your life? * Cloud asked.

Several times. Aurora, Star, could you tell the stories? I'm busy flying. Oh, Aurora, I'm speeding up time for you two, so Eclipse gets more zees before we get back to Earth. Shout if anything starts going wrong. Comet's mind dropped out of the conversation.

~~~~~

Half-way through her headlong flight, Comet yawned and enjoyed the sight around her.

Light. Silver-blue light. Light from a hundred years' full moons, beams scattered by rolling wave and foaming surf, flooded vision in every direction, so all was transmuted to shimmering curtains of coldest brightness. Through the glow passed the tangerine ball of her flight field, its steady brilliance in stark contrast to its flickering surroundings.

Shall I take over flying for a bit? I was now sort of awake from deep sleep.

Eclipse? No need. You did plenty. Catch your breath. Comet wished Eclipse would go back to sleep.

I ought to do my share, oughtn't I? I said, not quite insistently.
The others have different gifts. But I could cover for you, so I should.

Really! There's absolutely positively conceivably no reason at all for you not to join the three sleepyheads, Comet answered.

There is too a reason! I could be using my gifts. I responded, trying to stifle another yawn.

Oh, really! And what would I do? Please, let me? You do so many things, and all I do is fly fast. Join Star asleep! I yielded to slumber.

I'm not sleepy, sis. Only resting the eyes. came a third voice. Star really had been awake, Comet told herself, reading to her from a girl's adventure novel.

Well, don't let me stop you, Comet answered.

Aren't we there yet? Star queried.

It's a long way. Why don't you rest your eyes again? Comet said, slightly tense at another repetition of the same question.

Sorry. I won't ask again, Star said. *But I will stay awake to keep you company.*

She says she's okay now. Only Comet could hear Aurora's thoughts, referring to the somnolent Eclipse. **She's not. She was hurt back there. Enough to kill you or me. Don't let her do anything.**

More than overdid things? Comet asked.

You see she's so quiet? Aurora pointed out.

**She never said a word! She just insists it doesn't matter she got shook up a bit. But it's not much farther and we'll be home. Why don't

37

you doze off, too, sister? ** Comet said.

Cloaked again in silence, a solitary pastel-orange gleam raced across the shining sea.

CHAPTER 4 REACHED EARTH

Guys, an exhausted Comet said, *we've reached the Solar System. Time for everyone to wake up. Yes, Star, I know you've been awake all this time, pulling your first all-nighter ever, to help me stay awake. That was so good of you. And I know it'll be rough on Eclipse but, Aurora, you'd better see if you can wake her up.*

You're my sister, Star said. *For you I'd do anything. Ummh, can I fall asleep now?*

Star? Aurora asked quietly, *weren't you supposed to wake me up so we took turns with Comet?*

You were sleeping so peacefully, Star answered. *Besides, you shielded us in the Tunnels.*

I'm here, Eclipse finally answered. She called her Medico rules engine. The dead black glyphs had turned to violet tinged with blue. *I seem to have missed dying. Barely.*

Where's the Star Compass pointing? Star asked. *Is it pointing home?*

It shouldn't be, Aurora answered. *We haven't done anything yet. But where'd those people go? We got out of the Tunnels a different way, but they didn't ambush us on the way back.*

Merlin be thanked for small favors, Eclipse said. *Fighting those idiots once was enough.*

You really wrecked them up, Star said. *You were incredible. Mayhaps they think fighting you once was enough.*

For sure, I won't complain if you're right, a tired Eclipse answered.

I'm getting a sharp direction from the StarCompass, Comet said. *Does anyone see a reason not to follow it? What did you say, once upon a time, Eclipse? Recon first or regret later?*

That was one of my mom's lines. Eclipse then wished she'd kept her mouth shut. *It's about bargain basement shopping.*

Soon they were a few thousand miles above the earth's surface.. *OK,* Comet said. *It's after dark across America, Hawaii approaching nightfall. The StarCompass is real sure this is where we're going.*

Comet, Cloud said, *Could we possibly land now? Please? I'd like ground under me. I don't care that I fly, I just want to be standing on something solid. No, you've been fine, but flitting between galaxies is just weird.*

Can you do invisible on us? Star asked. *Enough we don't set off the air defenses? I'd rather not be shot at.*

39

Will do, Comet responded.

Mayhaps I handle everyone's weight, Comet, that's one less thing for you. Cloud tried to sound apologetic about asking more of Comet.

Sure, she said. *OK, let's try the switchover.* There was a momentary feeling of weightlessness. *Thanks, Cloud, that helps me a lot. I see where the StarCompass is taking me. That must be state forest or something. I see a nice clearing where we can set foot.*

Comet brought the five in for a gentle landing. The night sky was clear, every constellation sharply visible. Dense woods on all sides shielded them from the wind.

"Where are we?" Aurora asked.

"Oregon, near the coast. I think," Comet said. "There was a river. It had to be the Columbia. But there should be a huge city just north of it, right on the ocean. Cosmopolis, Pearl of the Pacific. Dad took me there, once upon a time. That city, it wasn't there."

Wherever we are, Eclipse thought, it's cold enough that I see my breath. Comet, Star, and Cloud are drawing on their gifts to stay warm. I can tell. You can see the air flicker. Aurora is drawing, too, I think, but she never gives anything away. Me? I have my Ultra-R blanket, so I can lie back on this nice stone slab. Star pulled out my under tarp for me. The rock is a little hard for sleeping. It's good enough, though, me being this tired.

"Eclipse, may I please share your blanket again?" Aurora asked. "Like we're seventh grade friends at a slumber party?"

"Sure," Eclipse answered. It's a big blanket, she thought, enough for her and me, her being barely twelve and shorter than me. Besides, I never had a slumber party, never had friends my own age who'd do that, and two of us under the blanket warms me up lots faster. My gifts should be taking care of all that, but I really toasted myself when I fried Solara. Sometimes my gifts work, and sometimes they're a bit iffy. Aurora took off her boots, slipped back between the blanket halves, and leaned up against Eclipse. She's smart enough, Eclipse realized, to realize she should be absolutely terrified, so I get to play big sister protecting her. She's even careful to lean her head back on my good shoulder, not the one where the ribs and stuff got broken in the Maze.

"I could tell," Aurora whispered to Eclipse, "your gifts weren't keeping you warm. Besides, this way we can pretend to be asleep, so we don't have to get involved in the stupid argument."

"I could try to draw on my gifts." Eclipse whispered. "But you're right. I wasn't toasty-warm. I've taken photos on Pluto and Mercury, never felt the least bit hot or cold. That's gifts. I can take getting cold. I froze in Antarctica, first time I did something actually dangerous. I was nine. I teleported to Antarctica, the Deep Waste. That had to be me by myself, and Mom knew she couldn't know where I was. Anyone else close, I couldn't've listened hard enough, even gifts damped. Hid out of the wind, dropped all my gifts to zero, and listened. Listened with my mind, listening for the Currents of the Earth. After a half-hour, I was chilled to the bone. Then I heard them, singing ever so softly in scales and rhythms not our own, songs of Rome and Atlanticea and Marik and the Goetic Knights. Singing of memories never fading. I 'ported home. A pint of Mom's hot cocoa later, I was warm. And a bit dizzy, Mom having spiked the cocoa with a shot of chocolate brandy. But I'll always hear the songs. Sorry, I'm wandering a bit." And distracting her, Eclipse thought to herself. She stopped in wonderment. "Wrong! Can you get senile at twelve? I'm not hearing them, not at all. I should. And I didn't notice, not until I thought about them."

"Eclipse," Aurora said, "Not senile. Distracted. Tired. Lots of ways, you're the smartest person here. OK, Comet might be smarter. But she's my sister."

"She's smarter," Eclipse said. "And you focus way sharper than I can."

Star leaned back on the ground next to them. "Aurora, mindlink us three, please?" he whispered.

Done. Aurora answered. To Star's inner eye, Aurora's mind always focused sword-sharp. He could tell that Eclipse was there, listening distantly, except behind her conscious thoughts she felt as though she had the worst case of the flu imaginable, with aches and pains in every bit of her body.

I'd like to be doing something, Star said, *except I don't know what, and I think we have to wait for those two to stop arguing.* He pointed across the clearing at Cloud and Comet.

I wasn't paying attention, Aurora confessed. *Right after they got started, I found this really neat Territories strategy, and was trying to see why it doesn't work.*

I keep falling asleep, Eclipse added.

What are they arguing about? Aurora asked.

Who runs our team, Star answered. *Cloud said it should be him, because he's a boy and only boys can see the big picture. Comet said it should be her, because she's a girl, and only girls can get every detail right. They think it's them leading, because they're both most of a year older than me. Then Comet tried doing something with her lessoncomp, and it didn't work.*

Merlin preserve us, they're doing the stupid boy-girl thing, Eclipse commented. *They're like two cats snarling and hissing but never *striking. I guess this teamwork Comet keeps talking about means they don't try to kill each other. But Cloud couldn't just stop with saying 'I think that command is only for ClassLink.' He had to say 'only girls are so dumb they think that command is for SPS.' They both learned the boy-girl thing from their older friends: Only boys/girls choose one have brains, common sense, or experience. That's wrong, you two. You both have brains and common sense. Goddess be thanked, I wasn't brought up that way.*

So they're standing there slamming each others' lessoncomps as second-rate cheapo models, Star added. *I happen to know: They have the exact same model comp.*

After a while, Aurora grumbled, *they'll get tired of it, and start whining the 'when I grow up' thing, on account they think when they grow up they'll do whatever they want, or other reasons, all equally dumb.*

Don't we all want to grow up? Star asked. *They want to change, because they know change is better.*

Do I? Eclipse asked. *Me? No. I don't want to grow up. I know who I am. I'm comfortable being me. OK, I'll be more a lot comfortable being me when I recover. Getting older is changing. I don't want to change.* And if I'm very careful, she thought, I can hold my age almost constant.

"Guys?" Aurora shouted across the grass. "Comet? Cloud? I get to decide who tells me what to do. You don't. Please argue about something intelligent. How to win with the Horns of Hattin opening comes to mind."

Praise the highest, Eclipse thought, Aurora is finally tired of the sniping. Of course, she's a Gamesmistress, well, 'Highly Esteemed by the Lords of the Hexagon' is not quite a Gamesmistress, but your list of 12-year-old Highly Esteemeds in all history is real short. Not zero, but real short. So she remembers, half the time, Comet and Cloud are only boys and girls, but she's a Highly Esteemed.

Star turned his back on Comet, rolling his eyes at a particularly choice bit of Comet's invective. Comet, Aurora thought, was in rare form this evening. My brother is a boy, but oft times he thinks the sniping is really dumb.

"Is there food?" Star asked. "I think mine is packed at the very bottom of my duffel bag."

"I have ration packs in my duffel," Eclipse said, "near the top. Did you guys all pack water?" Heads nodded. "It's dark. We're tired. Let's eat, go to sleep, talk about it in the morning."

Star powered up his force field, very slightly. "Enough light to see," he announced. "I didn't think to pack food where I could get at it."

"I did," Comet announced. "Sandwiches. Apples. Chocolate bars. Better eat the sandwiches first. Sandwiches won't last. Near the top, right under my blanket."

"Chocolate?" a shocked Cloud asked.

"Yes, chocolate. Super dense calories. You're a persona," Comet said. "You're immune."

"If my dad finds out...," Cloud continued.

"He won't," Star said. "But since you aren't hungry, I'll eat yours for you." Cloud stuck out his tongue. Five tired travellers happily laid into Comet's sandwiches.

"Do you all have sleeping bags?" Eclipse asked.

Star and Cloud nodded. "My blanket matches yours, Eclipse," Comet said. "And I have a tarp matching yours, to go on top so we stay dry if it rains."

"Me, no. Mom and Dad," Aurora announced, "said that their little girl would always sleep in a proper bed."

"You packed a bed?" a dumbfounded Cloud asked.

"Well, no," Aurora answered. "I mean, that's impossible." Mom and Dad had told her exactly what to pack. For the first time, she wondered if perhaps she should have thought for herself about what she was packing. That was silly. Mom and Dad had told her exactly what to pack, and Mom and Dad were always right.

"Now I'm cold," Comet said, swaying on her feet, half-drunk with exhaustion.

"Aurora!" Eclipse said, "Your sister. Overload shock. Help me get Comet inside her blanket and mine!" You really want to roll over and collapse yourself, Eclipse thought. You don't get the chance. A minute later the three girls had bundled together, a shivering Comet in the middle.

"So cold," Comet said. She passed out.

Eclipse, Aurora asked. *What do we do? Is she dying? Perhaps Star helps?*

I'm right here, he answered, looking over the top of his sleeping bag.

Eclipse forced her healing gift to pass over Comet. *Comet just needs to sleep,* Eclipse announced, *and be kept warm. That's us two. Star, you stayed up with her. Just fall asleep.* Star's thoughts faded into darkness.

Eclipse? Aurora suddenly asked. *How did you get into such a jam with the League and everyone?*

Okay, Eclipse answered.. *'Become world's leading war criminal' was not my best twelfth birthday present. My two ponies were the greatest present a girl could imagine.* Eclipse decided she was not quite ready to fall asleep, not when Aurora needed to talk. Aurora might sound calm, but behind the words Eclipse could feel Aurora's emotions. She was utterly terrified. *I bought all my birthday presents myself, every one. For the appaloosas I paid silver cartwheels. For 'love and kisses, The League of Nations. P.S. We're choosing between flaying you alive and crucifying you', I paid three broken ribs, black eye, bone bruises on both thighs and left arm, various sprains, and 'wrecked up my garb something fierce even if it's his blood and guts'.*

You got the Namestone, too, Aurora said.

At least the Namestone didn't whine, not even when it knew what I was about to do to it. Perhaps the last part I shouldn't say. When the League of Nations finds out, they'll be so heated they'll invent a whole new crime, just for me personally. But I did every bit of it, on purpose. I knew exactly what I was doing. I knew what the League would say about me.

Was the Namestone that bad? Aurora asked.

It was a mind control amplifier. A very powerful mind control amplifier. Eclipse answered. *That's how I killed the corrupt judges of North Illinois.*

Eeuw! Mind control. That's terrible. Aurora shuddered. *That was the Lords of Eternity after us? You said I faced off against Corinne.*

After us all? Eclipse wondered. *Solara has a plan. I don't get that part. I've never heard of this Great Plan thing. Going toe-to-toe with Solara was a bad trade for me. But I couldn't find an out. Not without letting Solara into the Tunnels. And you did go toe-to-toe with Corinne and the Ambihelicon, and beat her, which is really super. I somehow seriously peeved the Lords. That's after I saved Starsmasher's life. Now I have them on my case. They get to stand in line, taking numbers with the League and half the world's persona legions, for a chance to kill me.*

Could you have talked to Solara? Aurora asked. *I couldn't hear that part.*

I tried. She was only interested in telling us what to do, Eclipse said. *I don't care she's four thousand years old, gets politely called Solara the Obliterator, and thinks 'first melt a planetary hemisphere' is a truly frigid way to start a barbecue, she doesn't own the universe. I told her 'This way is closed', just like in Mum's old book. But I made it stick. She even tried the 'I am fire's mistress' line on me. I really shouldn't've said back 'I command the secret fire', even if it was in Mum's book, especially not when it's true. That talks about my gifts.*

You beat her. How? Aurora asked.

I think I surprised Solara, Eclipse answered. Though I won't, she thought, mention where I found the power I needed. *She thought she would stomp me into the ground in nothing flat. Yes, I'm twelve, not four thousand. I'm also my mom's daughter, no matter how Mum treated me. Push comes to shove, my feet stand where Mum's do. Solara hit me with everything she's got. I was still standing, afterward . Sort of. Then I hit her back, good and hard. I flattened her. I'm as tough as I have to be, tougher than her. Yes, she is Solara. But I'm Eclipse, the Mistress of the Maze, She Who Held the Namestone. And I bake better brownies, too. Not as good as Star's, of course.*

Eclipse, Aurora said, *thank for everything you do for us. Without you, we wouldn't be here. We'd be dead.* Eclipse shifted uncomfortably. Being praised didn't happen very often. *We can't do what you do. But you can let us do what we can do, not try to do everything yourself.* What did Eclipse mean, Aurora wondered, 'how her mom treated her'? This isn't the time to ask.

Sounds good, Eclipse said.

That means my weather screen heats the air for all three of us, so you and Comet can sleep better, Aurora explained. *I'm up to doing that.*

Thank you! That's very kind of you. Eclipse realized she was at the edge of tears. It was so rare for her to get help with anything. She shifted closer to Comet and Aurora. *Shall we try to sleep? I think your sister's chills are ending.*

Good night, Eclipse. You're my best friend, Aurora said.

Good night to you, too, Aurora. You're my best friend, too, Eclipse answered. *You and Comet and Star.*

~~~~

The sky was the bright blue of early morning. With the three of them wrapped in blankets, Aurora thought, they hadn't gotten too cold. Weather screen or no, she wished she had had a scarf to breathe through. Comet was still dead to the world. Eclipse's mind, Aurora realized, was like a cat's. Eclipse was sound asleep, but someplace a piece of her mind was wide-awake alert. Across the way, Cloud was sound asleep, but Star had awakened and was glaring at his lesson comp. Her own lessoncomp was being uncooperative, refusing to talk to the world.

"Star?" Aurora stuck her head up from her blanket. "Would you do me a favor?" she whispered. "Please? You've got a better comp than me. Ask it the datanet carrier signal strength."

Star winked at his twin sister. His fingers rustled against the touchpad. He looked puzzled and tried it again. Eclipse, now awake, looked carefully at what Star was doing. He's twelve, she thought, not a mind-reader, but he's real good about 'I don't know' when he doesn't know something. So he knows what he's doing, but he got the wrong answer.

"Aurora? It says there's no signal. None at all. The CommLink signal is zero, too." He tapped more keys. "And I'm talking to your unit—that's a frigid Territories position you were studying last night—so our lessoncomps are working."

Suddenly Aurora was much more alert. "That's impossible! How can there be no signal? We're out in the open."

Eclipse snapped from drowsy to brightly alert. That's my cue, she thought, to wake up and try thinking. I was dead to the world, pretty nearly. Solara and I got down to the 'seriously bad for local solar system' power level. I paid for that. But I'm not totally dead, not when it matters.

Eclipse leaped to her feet, platinum white curls shimmering, body screens flaring toward full power. She pushed locks of hair from across her eyes. Her body screens were up before her feet hit the ground. "Is something wrong, Eclipse?" Aurora asked.

"Guys? I think we may be in a T-R-A-P." Eclipse waited patiently for them to notice her. Cloud and Comet took a moment to wake up. Eclipse decided that later she'd have to brag up Star. She'd barely reached "P" before his force field came on. "You block CommLink and SPS with a force wall." Last night, Cloud had been ranting to Comet about some claim that girls have fewer brain cells than boys, and they didn't work as well, either. Comet had not restrained herself in saying whose brain cells were actually "fewer" and "poorly". Eclipse hoped that Cloud had run out of rant.

"Talk elsewhere?" Aurora suggested.

"Grab your stuff, everyone!" Eclipse shouted. This would not, she thought, be the moment to point out who was actually giving orders. "I'll teleport us out. Cloud? Are we sure we're in Oregon? I think we are."

"You don't have an SPS?" Cloud asked.

"Of course not," Eclipse snapped. "You think I'm a total idiot? They can be backtracked. I daren't carry Satellite Positioning anything. Not unless I want League of Nation goons tracking me. You guys all have SPS in your lessoncomps. SPS should say lickety-split where we are."

"They won't," Cloud said. "Our comps agree. There's no signal, none at all."

"I watched landmarks as we flew in." Eclipse said emphatically. "The Pacific is just west of here." Not, she thought, that I'm telling you how I happen to know the Oregon coast so well.

A freshly awake Comet briefly faded into a blur of motion. "Everything's picked up," Aurora announced. "thanks to my super sister's super speed."

"Time to teleport," Eclipse said. Of course, she thought, someone could be trying a teleport block on me. Key word, for me versus teleport block: 'try'. Light, blue as cornflowers. The chimes of distant bells. Freezing wind and bright white ice from horizon to horizon. The Great Sky. A ringing cascade of sound. Warm air, the sun not quite peeping over the horizon. A mile below were ocean waves, rolling from horizon to horizon.

"We're where I meant to go. I think. Everyone!" Eclipse shouted. "Check I 'ported all your stuff?" She pushed more curls back from across her ears. Force field and teleport and holding everyone aloft, she considered, all at the same time, was a lot of anvils to juggle at once, not to mention she was being ready to break something if she needed to. I'm way better at breaking things than at being clever, she admitted to herself, but sometimes breaking is all you need.

"Eclipse? I grabbed your blanket. And Comet's, too. And the two tarps." Aurora started folding them.

Eclipse smiled at Aurora. That was truly thoughtful of her. She is thoughtful, Eclipse thought, when she puts her mind to it.

"My flight field is ready." Comet bathed herself in the orange flecks of light that marked the most powerful flight field in the world.

"Passing across—don't worry, there's plenty of room if we drop someone," Eclipse answered. Mind you, she thought, I will not drop Aurora, because she can't fly, shows no sign of learning, and trusts me implicitly. The flecks of light surrounded the five of them. The load on Eclipse's flight field, her supporting five people and three hundred pounds of equipment, rose to zero.

Cloud looked around. "OK. Where are we?"

"Pacific," Eclipse pointed at the waves below. "A tad north of the Kingdom of Hawaii. By way of Antarctica. What's your SPS signal now?"

"Zero!" Cloud answered. He dropped a long antenna from his LessonComp. "Ditto CommLink is zero. The only links I see are to our four LessonComps. No SPS. No Global Time."

"No satellite video feeds, even too weak to read," Comet added. Star and Eclipse looked meaningfully at each other, nodding in unspoken agreement: Once Comet and Cloud forgot to be telling each other off, they really worked well together.

"Are the lessoncomps working?" Star asked. "Mayhaps they cooked themselves?"

"Eclipse?" Aurora whispered. "I shook out and folded your blanket and tarp and put them back in your duffle." Eclipse nodded her thanks.

"My comp brings up my history lessons," Cloud announced. "And it'll talk to Comet's. It's working. Mayhaps we didn't have to 'port out so fast?"

"Better safe than sorry," Star said, closing down the debate before Cloud could start complaining again. Eclipse gave Star a thumb's up. That's a boy's gesture, she thought, but Star had her worked out: She was totally outside that boy-girl silliness. He was happy to treat her as a person, not a boy or a girl, because she treated him as a person. They both knew: Cloud would only take being told to hush if another boy said so.

CHAPTER 5 COMET IN ORBIT

"Comet, can you see any SPS satellites?" Cloud asked politely.

Comet stared at the sky, which was more than a bit hazy. Yes, Eclipse thought, she has this extra vision, so she thinks stars are like planets, but with smaller disks. Seeing through glare has limits. "Don't see any," Comet announced. "But it's way after first light. Cloud? Would you please hold everyone up for a bit?"

Cloud's flight field, the puffy white carpet of his name, appeared beneath the five of them.. "Thanks! That's lots better for repacking duffel bags, too," Comet added. "Are we OK to shift?" The twins nodded. "Dropping my flight field on three. One. Two. Three." The scatter of orange sparks faded, everyone and their camping equipment coming to a rest on a decidedly solid patch of white cumulus.

"No, wait," Comet said. "Something first. About last night. I apologize, Cloud. I got overheated. It was stupid."

"I shouldn't have said," Cloud answered, "what I said. I'm sorry, too."

Comet stepped to the edge of the cumulus, raised her hands, and did a back dive, falling oceanward. "Show-off," Star mouthed.

"Just a bit," Eclipse whispered her answer. She was happy that Comet was having fun. She'd certainly gone through enough in the last days. Comet's flight field appeared. She rocketed skyward. No, Eclipse told herself, Comet does not go supersonic instantaneously. She just pulls her sixty gees. She needs most of a half second.

Star industriously began repacking camping equipment, first his pack, then Comet's. He and Comet and Aurora, Eclipse noted, were real good about taking care of each other, for all they sniped at each other on occasion. Then Star looked over twin sister Aurora's shoulder, found her lessoncomp screen filled with game notes, and grinned. Eclipse could tell his thoughts without reading his mind. When Aurora wasn't studying Chess, it was Stones. Or Territories. Or City of Steel. Or... Star shared a smile with Eclipse, who nodded approvingly. He's really proud, she thought, of having a sister who was incredibly good at games.

"Eclipse," he asked hesitantly. "Do you have any idea what's going on? What should we do?" To her ears, his tone wasn't quite hero worship. It was very respectful.

"It's a puzzle, isn't it?" Cloud asked. "Like the Maze?"

"OK, I solved the Maze," Eclipse said. "I beat traps that defeated armies and persona leagues for millennia. I've spent months not being arrested by the League of Nations, their best tries notwithstanding. But I need at least a few clues. I'm baffled."

"The StarCompass," Star said. "It points vigorously at exactly where we should go. When Comet gets back, we can ask her where that is."

"So I should tell her she's going to follow the StarCompass?" Cloud said. He didn't quite make that a question.

Star, his back to Cloud, rolled his eyes. "I'll ask her," he said, "politely. She's my sister."

"Good idea," Cloud agreed. "you lead your sisters; they follow."

"We're doing what the Wizard of Mars said." Eclipse lay down on Cloud's flight field. Her back was very grateful. "That's much better than the rock. Thank you for the cloud, Cloud."

"Is something wrong?" Cloud asked.

"My combat throw in the Maze," Eclipse answered, "something the last defender didn't expect, meant I tossed someone half again my weight, fast and hard. That's 'threw hard' while my free hand pulled the sharpened shank from one of my boots. I slit him open from guggle to zatch. I didn't wreck my shoulder up permanently. I hope." Cloud nodded. "But why fly in a circle? Why not just fly here in a straight line? I'm sorry, guys, I don't understand."

"That's a good 'why' riddle," Cloud agreed. "We're missing something."

"You're always so good at solving puzzles, Eclipse," Star said. "You did the Maze. You can solve anything."

"Anything?" Eclipse gave a weak laugh. "I'm really a lot better at breaking things than solving puzzles. I wish! I know a few tricks. The lesson from the Maze is 'be patient, hints may be here soon'. Mentioning which, it's been a couple minutes, Comet should be a thousand miles up. Aurora? What's the word from her?"

Aurora frowned. A rainbow flicker passed over her head. Eclipse winced. I could kick myself, she thought. No one asked Aurora to keep overwatch on Comet, so Aurora didn't. There's no classical game based on persona tactics, so Aurora never thinks about what her gifts should be doing.

"She says 'hi' to us." Aurora smiled. "She's way up there. She says there are lots of satellites, but she doesn't recognize any SPS satellites. She's closing on something strange." Aurora flashed a mentalic image, something white with huge gold wings.

"No, not wings," Eclipse said, "they have no thickness. What is it?"

Aurora linked the four of them to Comet's mind. *That's the biggest thing in orbit,* Comet announced. *I'll see what it is. It's not a skyhook, for sure. They're missing. I checked. Be there in a few minutes.*
Comet's flight field ramped up toward a hundred gees. Her gift for

matching orbits cut in.

To his credit, Eclipse thought, Cloud saw Comet's mistake before I did. His mentalic shout carried through Aurora's mindlink. *POSSIBLE HOSTILE.* Comet made her emergency turn, fast enough she felt hard acceleration though her flight field. Aurora cranked her mentalics way down, as much power as she could handle, if Comet needed help.

"That thing has windows," Aurora announced. "It's way too far for a mindscan, but mayhaps I can just look inside and see crewmembers." The silver pyramid and eye appeared above her head. "Yes, found several. And if the SPS satellites are missing, perhaps they're the thieves." She spent a little time examining their thoughts. "OK, they call that thing 'Space Station Liberty'. It's not armed, not even with a grav lance. The folks inside seem to be nice people."

Eclipse pondered what Aurora had just told them. She'd looked much more carefully than was even marginally polite at the minds of the Space Station Liberty crew. Of course, there is no such thing as a Space Station Liberty, Eclipse thought, and several skyhooks are to Comet's eyes obviously missing, so these Liberty people must be space pirates. Taking notes on their thoughts is defensible.

"This is weird," Aurora said. "These people have never heard of space piracy. One of them knows what a skyhook is, except he has some funny name for it, but he's sure no one has ever built one. How did they get up here? Oh, dear! Giant skyrockets. And how does Liberty stay up there?" Aurora passed her companions the answer to her question, an answer she didn't understand.

"That's ridiculous," Star said. "This so-called 'Space Station' is a complete crock. It doesn't even have engines. It flies in circles around the earth because it is stuck in orbit, like it's some dumbwit rock."

"I don't care how big a bribe you offer," Cloud added. "How could anyone persuade even the Chicago Board of Aldermen to pay for something like that?"

"OK, I'll tell Comet they're friendly," Aurora said.

Comet returned to the space station, parked outside a space station window, knocked politely on the neighboring hull, then waved 'hello' at the people inside. . Her companions clapped approvingly. It was clearly a really frigid way to introduce herself. Eclipse wished Comet had spent a bit more time looking around before sticking her neck out.

Is this where the Starcompass is pointing, Comet? Eclipse asked, trying to sound polite. *There was a reason we came here. I somehow have the impression we've gotten sidetracked.*

"You'd rather be at your base?" Cloud whispered in Eclipse's ear.

I never say anything about where I hide out, Eclipse thought. Not that

Aurora would peek, but I have lots of mentalic screening around those issues. Some secrets are worth keeping, given the League of Nations warrant for my arrest, not to mention Manjukuo offering a hundred tons of gold for my head, preferably after it's been neatly boxed and gift-wrapped.

"I'd rather be lying back in my hot tub," Eclipse answered wistfully. "With a book. And a cup of hot chocolate in easy reach. Or sleeping. For a day. Or two days." She pretended to ignore the shocked look on Cloud's face when she mentioned cocoa. Sometimes, she thought, he's a real prude. "Most of a day flying in a big circle I did not need. Not to mention the violent bit in the middle that we still need to talk about. Especially when my sense of direction keeps saying we didn't fly in a circle, and are off someplace else, way far from home, except StarCompasses are perfect. But I volunteered for this." Cloud nodded.

Am I part of Cloud's team, Eclipse wondered to herself? 'Team' means different things to boys and girls, of course, but if I'm with his team he's sure to think I'm OK. Eclipse realized that Aurora was reading the mind of the Space Station Liberty computer, a truly feeble mind but a mind, so she could hear them talk on their radio.

"...Houston, I have a medical emergency. I am having hallucinations...please clarify...outside the station #7 port...and she's kind of cute...this is Kondratieff...I see, I think, the same thing...I have the minicam and am transmitting...please, please tell me there's nothing there...Liberty, this is Houston. We have some good news and some bad news. The good news is we see her, too. The bad news is we see a human female, dressed like a comic book escapee in green spandex and wraparound gold comet, floating about three feet outside the window. That's in vacuum. Okay, how are you guys pulling today's practical joke?"

Aurora could feel Comet's miffedness. She'd dropped by to say hello. They didn't believe she was there. Not waiting, Comet backed away from the station.

"The people inside have never heard of personae lifting spaceships into orbit," Aurora added. "Make that, they've never heard of personae except as the literary gimmick 'comic book super hero', whatever that is."

Eclipse winced at what Aurora did next. She looked really impolitely closely at their thoughts. Eclipse told herself to be reasonable. If someone doesn't know what personae are, Eclipse thought, and these guys don't, they must be mind controlled, or crazy, and we can help them find their right minds. Well, Aurora can. When I try mentalic stuff on people, I tend to wreck things. I get the facts I want out, or shove a message in, but there are these side effects.

"I'm waving good-bye," Comet announced. "They for sure are not where the Star Compass points. I'll be down in a couple minutes."

CHAPTER 6 PERSONAS TO THE RESCUE.

"Guys," Aurora announced, "I just found a memory. These people have friends on a space plane stranded in orbit. And no way to rescue it, none at all. Can we save it? Please?"

Eclipse, frustrated, gnashed her teeth. Again. A rescue, she thought, had like absolutely nothing to do with the Starcompass directions. Or stopping the flying jellyfish.

"I'm sorry," Eclipse said. "The five of us can't solve all the world's problems. That's why there are persona leagues by the score. They should have rescued this space plane way before now."

"Except I looked carefully," Aurora answered. "None of these people have ever heard of personae."

"Why isn't League America rescuing these people?" Star asked. "Or Stars Over Boston?"

"Eclipse, you could use the Namestone," Cloud announced. "Why don't you?"

"Not an option," Eclipse snapped. I'm sure, she thought, we've already told him I didn't bring the Namestone with me. But Cloud's question explains why I did the Maze. To make sure I had the Namestone. The other choice was giving it to a group of halfwit politicians who'd try using it. Yes, it could convince everyone they'd reached utopia. Half the time it would be telling the truth. After all, I did give the North Dakota Goetic Knights and their Shelter for Homeless Orphans solid diamond windows and structural gold trusses for their one-room school houses. The other half the time? It would mind control people so they'd prefer eating library paste to chocolate or rose preserves. "What it does? It's not what you think."

Aurora winked at Eclipse and closed her eyes. Only Eclipse heard Aurora's mentalic message. *Someone might try peeping while I'm looking.*

Eclipse nodded understandingly. Aurora has clairvoyance, Eclipse thought. She sees what lies in distant places. There are people who could tap Aurora's mentalic link and see what she was seeing through her own eyes, like Eclipse lying five feet in front of her. That would be really bad, Eclipse allowed, if I didn't want unexpected hostile visitors, but anyone trying that on Aurora hits her first-line mentalic screens and then, well, her eyes are closed. Aurora put up a hand 'Wait!'.

"They're gone. Nothing there." Aurora mumbled, so terrified she was scrambling consonants and vowels. She shuddered in fear, terrified half out of her wits. "I tried remote viewing: Boston, Philadelphia,

Washington, Cosmopolis—which by the way is a small suburb of someplace I've never heard of. I can't find personas. Not one. They're all gone. We rescue that plane, or no one does."

"Wizard of Mars trick," Eclipse announced calmly. Mind you, she thought, I have no idea which one, or how he pulled it off, let alone why. But when you deal with the Wizard of Mars, things get seriously weird, like his pet whale. That's the blue whale that lives inside his dining room table, only its tail visible as it swims through the polished mahogany. "Deal with it later."

Star and Cloud glared at Eclipse. "You aren't afraid to do the rescue, are you?" Cloud asked.

"Do I sound afraid?" Eclipse answered. She supposed crossing her arms across her chest and frowning was not her mark of approval. "I've flown to the Starcore. I took on most of the Lords of Eternity, toe-to-toe, one me against a bunch of them. It's just that it's a good bet it's a trap. But I'm completely grounded in my powers, know who I just trashed thoroughly, and wouldn't mind teaching some League bullyboys what 'respect' means. Well, the survivors, if any, might learn something about respect."

"Please?" Aurora asked. "None of these people in that space station, let alone their bosses on the ground, have heard of you or the Namestone, so it's not you show up and get attacked."

"Makes no sense." Star shook his head. "How can all these people not know who you are, Eclipse?"

"Another Wizard of Mars trick," Eclipse said. "One time. We rescue this plane. Then we follow the Star Compass. The plane is nothing Comet can't do by herself. Wouldn't hurt, Cloud, if you came along and killed the plane's inertia first, so she doesn't have to push so hard. She's still tired. Flying across the universe does that."

I could argue, Eclipse thought, that we shouldn't rescue these people, whoever they are. The time wasted arguing would be longer than the time needed to find one space plane and deposit it on the ground. There's no problem, except Comet's mind is an open door. I really ought to fix that. It wouldn't be hard, just two days fasting for me. She's a really nice person and does not need the bother.

"Aurora?" Eclipse asked. "Screen Comet's mind during the rescue? So whoever sees her can't read it? It would be totally inconvenient for everyone chasing me to find me through her."

"Did that already," Aurora announced. Eclipse beamed at her. Aurora just needs encouragement, Eclipse thought. She's a Highly Esteemed of the Lords of the Hexagon. I'm just a kid who knows a few tricks. She can use tactical thinking other than for Games. She just doesn't.

"I learned where this stupid plane is," Aurora continued. "It's trapped in orbit because the rockets it uses to slow down are broken, so it can't ram the atmosphere. At full speed." She followed with mentalic pictures.

"Oh, wow," Star said. "You actually meant 'it lands by ramming the air at 18,000 miles an hour.' This space plane doesn't have a flight field, either. On the way down it's a fancy glider that flies like a brick. For a spaceship it's the most incredible bunch of random junk I've ever heard of."

"Eclipse?" Cloud tried to sound as polite as he could. "Could you please teleport us there? If it's in your envelope?"

Eclipse grinned. For once Cloud was doing things as a team. While he was doing that he was all team, no stupid boy against girl nonsense. He even remembered 'envelope'.

"Envelope?" Star asked.

"When we teleport into orbit," Eclipse said, "all that energy and momentum comes from someplace. Me, to be precise." She nodded to Aurora, who reported the where and how fast. She sent another mental image, Comet rapidly closing on the space plane.

"OK. Two jumps," Eclipse said. "First is North Dakota, ground, taking the luggage. Star and Aurora stay there. Nothing to fight. In mentalic range. Doesn't give away to the dooms where we are looking for them. Then we two join Comet?" The three nodded agreement.

"Cloud? Ready for vacuum?" Eclipse asked. He nodded. Light, the horizon at noon. Rolling ground. A xylophone's melody. Black sky sprinkled with stars and distant galaxies. Eclipse spotted the space plane. There it was, two miles out, looking like something escaped from a Goetic Knights space opera. A comic opera.

~~~~~

Aboard space plane SP-7 Lemuria, Flight Captain Randolph Peters, RAF, sank deeper into a drowsy near-sleep. This had been the first flight of a space plane with a non-American as co-pilot—the Yanks of course insisted on the title 'pilot' for his position—a circumstance conditioned by details of the Lemuria's funding. After this disaster, it might be the last such flight. Not that he'd had anything to do with the errors that had stranded the ship in its gradually-decaying orbit. He willed himself into a deeper slumber, breathing more and more slowly, staring into the darkness in front of him. He told himself that oxygen was not the critical consumable, then let his mind drift, gradually becoming aware of the equally shallow breathing of the ship's mission commander, Janice Svoboda, asleep in the other acceleration couch.

Cabin lights were off. Illumination came from a few key instrument panels reporting the status of absolutely critical systems. Beyond the cockpit windows, the brightest constellations were marginally visible. Suddenly, a cerulean glow illumined the cabin, sending shadows down and forward. Peters snapped to consciousness, sleep restraints preventing him from tumbling heels over head into the ceiling. Svoboda's reflexes, just as fast, wakened her. The instrument panel showed no warning indicators.

"I'm sorry I had to wake you." The voice was female, apologetic, unfamiliar—and located dead aft. Svoboda hit the cabin lights. Mission Commander and Pilot looked over their shoulders and stared in surprise. Facing them was not a mission specialist—all three of whom should have been sound asleep—but a person assuredly not on the crew manifest: an eleven-year-old girl wearing ornate white tunic and trousers, ankle-high boots, and a full-length, deeply-hooded cape which flared over square shoulders and hung firmly deckward in seeming ignorance of the lack of gravity.

"Houston, Houston, do you read?" Svoboda's voice chanted the mantra into the radio.

"Lemuria, we copy," the voice in Svoboda's headphones answered.

"Houston, we have acquired a stowaway. Repeat, we have a stowaway. Over," Svoboda continued.

"I am not!" Eclipse interrupted. "I came on board just now."

"Lemuria, this is Houston. Please clarify 'stowaway'? Over."

"Young lady," Svoboda asked calmly, "Might I ask where you've been hiding all this time? How did you manage to stow away on board?"

Peters looked befuddled. "Why haven't we noticed all the air you're using?"

"Air?" Eclipse was baffled.

"You breathe," Peters said. "You pull oxygen out of the air, which shows up as an extra load on the Air Processing Unit. But there's been no missing oxygen on this flight, certainly not a person's worth."

Peters' eyes strayed sideways. The cabin air pressure and composition were nominal. Hallucinations based on some gross anomaly in the air supply seemed excluded. For an illusion, the girl appeared to be remarkably matter-of-fact, albeit not quite the age or state of dress of the woman he might have hoped to meet in a hallucination. But how could she possibly have smuggled herself on board and hidden for the past weeks?

"I'm Eclipse. I haven't been hiding anyplace. I just got here. I'm a persona. We're here to help you," Eclipse said. "I'll show you how I got on board. Look out the window."

"Houston," Svoboda answered, "Stowaway. A person on board, not on the crew roster, who we didn't know about until now? Caucasian female, apparent age ten or so. Grey eyes, five feet and a bit tall, perhaps a hundred pounds, dressed like an escapee from a comic book, cape and all."

"Lemuria, this is Houston. We read your cabin oxygen as nominal. Please confirm. Dressed like what? Over."

"I'm not using your air," an offended Eclipse countered. "It's not like I have to breathe. And I'm not ten! I'm twelve!"

"Houston," Svoboda continued. "Confirm air nominal. Dressed like UltraGirl, from the Sunday evening kiddie show? Cape? Tunic? Only no 'U' on the chest, and no gold blonde hair? Distinctly, ummh, distinctly younger than UltraGirl, with a significantly larger materials budget for her costuming. Are you receiving her voice? Please advise. Over."

"Watch you?" Peters asked Eclipse. "What am I to see?"

"This," Eclipse answered. A swirl of indigo, the tinkle of distant chimes. She vanished, wondering as she did what Svoboda meant. Who was UltraGirl, and what did 'materials budget' signify? She had to remember that name. Finding a persona might explain everything.

"Lemuria, this is Houston. We heard a female voice in the pickup. We also heard bells. We can't identify her. Is it a mission specialist? Over."

"Houston," Svoboda said, "this is Lemuria. Negative. Negative. I am not repeat not speaking to a mission specialist. The girl is not repeat not a mission specialist. The mission specialists are all six inches taller and twenty years older. Over."

"Lemuria, this is Houston. We copy you have a stowaway. We're examining this contingency. There is no plan for this contingency. Over."

"Where'd she go?" Peters asked. He slipped free of his restraints and pushed himself slowly toward the rear bulkhead, waving his hands through empty air. "There's no one here. She vanished in a flash of light."

"Houston, this is Lemuria," Svoboda reported. "The stowaway is no longer in sight. She vanished, repeat vanished like we were on television and someone beamed her up. Over."

Eclipse hovered above the nose of the ship, the two astronauts looking away from her.

Eclipse? Aurora asked, *Did your speech go OK?*

Not very well. A dismayed Eclipse described her conversation. *I guess it's hard to explain personae. Harder than I thought. I figured I'd say we were personae, and that would take care of everything. Except they think I'm dressed like some girl persona I've never heard of, and they were too distracted by my garb to listen to me.* She surveyed her clothing. It was all in place. What was wrong with it? Was something off with it, so it offended? That would be really bad. *They wouldn't watch me teleport.*

They're looking the wrong way, Aurora said. She turned her thoughts to the flight crew. **Guys? Look out the window? Please?**

The astronauts jerked, searching for the new voice.

"Houston, this is Lemuria." Svoboda spoke slowly into her microphone. "We seem to have a second stowaway. Also female. Except we can't see her, only hear her."

"Lemuria, this is Houston. We have powered up the control deck television camera. We see you two. We don't see anyone else. We don't hear anyone else. Over." The television gave Ground Control a sharp view of the control deck. To Ground Control's extreme dismay, only the two astronauts could be seen.

"Houston, this is Lemuria," Svoboda said. "I don't see anyone either. Only Peters and I are on the control deck now. Did you hear the second female voice, Houston? Over."

"Lemuria, that's a negative," Houston answered. "We do not hear a second female voice. We heard Svoboda, Peters, and one repeat one unidentified repeat unidentified female repeat female voice. We have the voice identifying itself with an eclipse. Is that solar or lunar? We don't show an occultation for twenty-nine minutes. Over."

They can't hear me on the ground, Aurora explained to Svoboda and Peters. *I'm doing telepathy from outside the ship.*

"Telepathy?" Svoboda asked.

"Telepathy," Peters answered. "That's what she said. Whoever she is. But where is she? I hear her, but don't see her. Where'd she go?"

No. I didn't go anyplace. I'm Aurora. I'm down on the ground. It was Eclipse [mental image of Eclipse in garb] who teleported inside.

"Let me get this straight. There are two of you? And your UFO, too?" Peters asked.

Four of us. Comet's gonna fly you down. Cloud's gonna make your ship not have inertness, so it's easy to fly. Eclipse is checking you're ready to land. I do mentalics. We don't need a spaceship, Aurora answered. *Now you know everything.*

Eclipse decided not to mention she could simply teleport this space plane to the ground. That wouldn't, she thought, be Comet's team approach. Also, the space plane weighed like a hundred tons and was travelling five miles a second. I can handle that, Eclipse told herself, but momentum really takes a lot out of you. Besides, these people are broadcasting to ground and I'm really curious how long it takes for some persona league to get its act together and try arresting me. Note, she thought, I said *try*. I am not in the greatest mood, right at the moment. In fact, I am in a really, really bad mood, and beating up on people mad because I saved their friends might make me feel better. It might also make them feel deader, but that's what you get for having bad manners.

"You're going to deorbit us?" Svoboda asked. "With a comet?"

"Lemuria, this is Houston. Lemuria, this is Houston. Are you receiving on another band? We're only hearing your half of the conversation. Please clarify 'UFO'. Are you reporting an ET event? Over."

"Negative, Houston, negative. We don't see her now," Svoboda answered. "Can't you hear the girls talking? They said they're outside the shuttle, using telepathy. Does telepathy make it an ET event? Over."

On the ground, panic replaced pandemonium. Had the flight crew lost their minds? Was the Shuttle Lemuria being contacted by extraterrestrials? Controllers sent wake-up calls to the mission specialists, asleep on the flight deck. Supervisors began ringing their superiors in Washington. On international flights, downlinks were not enciphered; Television Nippon was carrying the picture and conversation live.

Eclipse, flight fields providing feather-light impulses, drifted up to the bow window. The two people inside were still looking rearward.

OK, now what? Aurora asked. *I told them where to look. I can hear their minds hearing me. Telepathy made them all confused. Why aren't they talking with their minds?*

They don't know any telepaths. They must not know how you do telepathy, Eclipse pointed out.

"Lemuria! Lemuria!" The voice of ground control had lost its accustomed calm. "What's, ummh, there is a foreign object visible outside the shuttle. Directly toward the nose. Please confirm immediately. Over."

Peters and Svoboda turned. Eclipse, manifestly not wearing a pressure suit, peered back through the window, waving politely. Around the globe, the thousands who had always known that space travel was an utter fraud, all broadcasts from space being faked in a New York City television studio, saw the ultimate confirmation of their beliefs. Someone in street clothes had finally walked on camera, on the wrong side of the mockup spaceship window, just like in that 1950s TV show.

"Houston, I confirm." Svoboda hesitated. Was this really happening? Or was she hallucinating both the girl and the conversation with Mission Control? "Houston, this Eclipse person we reported earlier. She appears to be outside the forward port. She does not appear to be wearing a pressure suit. Please advise. Over. Recommendations, Peters? Do you recall a 'man overboard' drill?"

Peters smiled at the moment of levity. "Man overboard? Not since sea duty. Might we invite her on board again? A trifle hard to chat her up, there being vacuum between our selves and her ears," the imperturbable pilot answered.

Svoboda began a charade, smiles and waves and pointing hands, to be interrupted by Eclipse's reappearance inside the cabin. "Hi, again," Eclipse said. "We're here to rescue you. OK? You do want to be rescued. Don't you?"

"Lemuria, this is Houston. We now show the foreign object now inside the ship on the control deck. Please confirm."

"Of course we want to be rescued! Please?" Svoboda answered. "Pardon me, Eclipse. Houston, she's back inside the ship now. Stop calling her an object! She's a person. A friendly person. Even if her friends do have transporter rays. Over."

Eclipse? She's busy, Aurora thought, but this is important. *No one in their ground base station recognizes you.*

"Lemuria, we copy. Houston says over."

"Lemuria copies, Houston," Svoboda answered. "Are you really there?" she asked Eclipse, gently flipping a monogrammed clipboard at her. That was Marge Koster's clipboard, she thought, to be updated with consumables notes.

Eclipse caught the clipboard and returned her questions. "What are transporter rays? We're flying you down. We were afraid you'd be frightened. If we didn't warn you first, I mean. If you were startled, you might turn your weapons banks on Comet."

"Weapons banks?" Janice Svoboda asked. "Comet?"

"Disruptors. Neutron cannon. Whatever you're armed with." Eclipse tried to sound innocent. It occurred to Eclipse that the Lemuria's weaponry was remarkably well hidden. From the outside, there was not a sign of ship-to-ship missiles, disintegrators, or any of the other accoutrements of a competently designed orbital spacecraft. I couldn't spot anything, she thought, and Aurora read their minds, but that's silly. No one builds unarmed space ships. Don't these people know anything about spaceship design?

"We're on a peaceful scientific mission," Svoboda said stiffly, "not a military operation. We are not carrying weapons. Honest! Cross my heart and hope to die!" After she said the last, she hesitated. That seemed to be the wrong hope, given her situation.

"Comet?" Peters asked. "I think I have not had the fortune of an introduction."

"She's outside with Cloud. I'm Eclipse. That's my public persona name. Comet flew up here. I teleported." Eclipse wished she knew how to get control of the conversation.

"And I am Flight Captain Randolph Peters, Royal Air Force," Peters answered.

"Persona?" Svoboda asked.

"Lemuria, this is Houston. We copy your guest says she arrived on a comet. Please confirm." On the ground frantic telephone calls were being made to Washington. The airlocks had not been cycled. There was no way for a human being to have boarded the ship. The creature visible in the monitors was therefore an alien intelligence. To judge from her costume, her people had gleaned human customs from an eclectic choice of children's television programs.

"Not a comet," Eclipse said. "Comet. Comet is her name. Comet's a persona. She has gifts. She flies. Like I'm doing."

"Persona?" Svoboda asked again. "Is that the name of the planet you came from?"

"Not quite," Eclipse answered. Now she at least had the conversation going the right way. "A persona is a human being, like us three. Personae have gifts: telepathy or teleportation or flying. A public persona is someone who's gifttrue, who uses their gifts in a virtuous way, the way Cicero said you should."

"Quite," Peters interjected. "Quite. Marcus Tullius Cicero?"

Her smile confirmed his guess. "The Essay On Duty," she responded.

"Naturally." Peters had had a properly classical education. "However, to float in zero gravity is not to fly."

"If I couldn't fly," Eclipse said, "I could only float in straight lines. I couldn't keep station, and I couldn't do this:" The slightest urging of her flight field moved her in a semicircular arc around the cabin. "You see, I fly. Like Comet."

"Quite. Quite so!" Peters complimented Eclipse. Gingerly, he reached out to touch her. After he was committed, he realized that he might have been wiser not to hazard his dominant hand. An inch from her skin, he encountered a flat, invisible surface. A firmer grip showed the surface to be completely unyielding, as hard and smooth as a block of glass. "Janice," he remarked casually, "You can tell Houston that she's solid. And wearing an invisible pressure suit."

"Screen," Eclipse corrected Peters. "That's a screen. You don't need one for outer space. But you might have shot at me, so I called a screen as well as a body field. Body field is what protects me from the vacuum."

The two looked at each other. "Houston, this is Lemuria," Svoboda spoke. "Are you getting this? Over."

"Affirmative. We copy, Lemuria." Mission Control was completely non-committal. Washington had informed Mission Control that the flight crew had lost their minds, and rigged a clever hoax. Washington-Houston phone lines filled with impassioned discussion.

The rear hatch opened. A female head, hair salt-and-pepper grey, pushed its way forward. "Sorry for the intrusion, guys, but Mission Control thinks you've both..." Marge Koster, by ten years the oldest of the three mission specialists, took in the presence of Eclipse. "...taken...leave...of...your...senses?"

"Hi," Eclipse said cheerily. "Sorry I startled you."

"Oh, no, not at all," the older woman answered blandly. Several of her children had pulled bizarre stunts, but stowing away on a space plane had to qualify for the Book of Records. The other two mission specialists, heads 120 degrees apart, appeared at the same hatch.

"Oh," the first began.

"Wow," completed the second.

"Peters," Kara Sellers, at 32 the youngest of the three specialists, said, "I've heard of sailors smuggling women on board sailing ships, but isn't she a trifle young?" She grinned. Peters pouted.

"They didn't smuggle me on board," a miffed Eclipse answered, not quite sure how to interpret the reference to sailors. "I just arrived here. Like this." She teleported again, this time directly behind Sellers. "See?" She touched the specialist's shoulder. Sellers jumped through the hatch, shying away from an impossibly-placed voice. Svoboda caught her before she hit forward windows. Sellers maintained her grip on a large, gleaming wrench. If it were necessary to immobilize the flight crew, she thought, she was now admirably positioned to do so.

"Hi," Eclipse said to the other two mission specialists. She teleported back to the flight deck. "I'm Eclipse," she put out a hand, screens damped below the wrist.

"Janice Svoboda, Mission Commander." Svoboda said, taking Eclipse's hand.

"Randolph Peters, RAF, Pilot." Peters noted that Eclipse definitely did not have a little girl's soft grip. Perhaps, he thought, she was also a gymnast.

"Kara Sellers, Mission Specialist"

"Anne Reischauer, Mission Specialist."

"Marge Koster, Senor Mission Specialist."

"Pleased to meet you all," Eclipse said.

"You teleport, fly, and ignore hard vacuum," Marge observed. "Can you teach someone else to do that?" There had, she thought, to be a Nobel Prize in there. Perhaps two Nobel Prizes. Perhaps even something good enough to earn a faculty position.

Eclipse cringed. Koster was asking to be engifted! "Would you settle for being teleported outside your ship? You'll be in my body field."

"Body field?" Svoboda asked.

"It lets you breathe vacuum," Eclipse explained. There really couldn't be any personae here, she decided. These people didn't know even the simplest things about gifts.

"Go for it!" Koster answered. The experience would be worth a letter to Nature. At worst she would be decompressed. Surely Eclipse would get her back inside the Lemuria before that proved fatal? Besides, unless Eclipse was real, she really didn't have a life she could lose. Eclipse put her hand on the specialist's shoulder. Too late to protest, Peters realized what was about to happen. Koster and Eclipse dissolved in an azure haze.

They were outside the shuttle. Marge Koster froze in shock, tried to inhale, remembered that inhaling vacuum was an incorrect response, and noted that she was not short of breath even though she could not inhale. She forced herself to calm down. She wasn't short of breath. She pressed her hands together. There was the faintest peculiarity where they touched, as though her hands were wrapped in microscopically thin plastic sheaths.

Stars burned impossibly bright. A glance at the Pleiades revealed not four or six but dozens of points of light, utterly sharp in the absence of atmospheric twinkle and background light. "Incredible," she whispered. She decided not to look at the Sun. "I'm not out of air. Is that plastic-wrap feel why?"

That's it, Eclipse answered. *We'd better go back. They're upset in there.* The crew could be seen through the cabin window, pointing excitedly at Eclipse and Koster. The world's tens of thousands of saucer cultists saw absolute proof of their faith. Koster, clearly visible through the deck camera, was obviously calm. She must therefore have known in advance that she would be taken outside by these extraterrestrials. That foreknowledge proved beyond all possible doubt that she, and therefore the government, had always known the truth about UFOs. The government must have been in contact with the space aliens—Eclipse, Comet, and Cloud—all along, the public space program existing only as a deception.

A flash of light, a faint jingle of bells: Koster and Eclipse were back inside the ship. "See? Nothing to it!" Eclipse said. Koster was at a loss for words. "We're ready to rescue you guys," Eclipse announced.

"Wait a moment," Svoboda countered. "Let's not be hasty. How can we re-enter? Our retro-rockets are dead."

"We know. We know. Comet's going to stop you first. You'll be doing a couple hundred miles an hour, tops, when she brings you down." Eclipse said.

"She can do that?" Peters asked.

Sure I can, Comet answered, Aurora passing the message into the minds of five astronauts. *Here, watch.* A pastel luminescence the hue of vanilla-orange ice cream engulfed the skin of the Shuttle.

Eclipse dropped her own flight field and grabbed for a bulkhead. **Comet, go easy. I'm inside!**

You can fly, Comet answered. **You can keep up, right?**

Yeah. I could catch up. Carrying whichever section of wall I go through. This thing's just a big aluminum bubble with a little ceramic armor. Remember? Not a real ship at all. It doesn't even have armor plate, let alone inertia dampers, Eclipse responded.

Oops. Comet's chagrin at her oversight was self-evident. **But I wouldn't have started, not without asking you.**

You're right, Eclipse answered. **I'm sorry. This is all so weird, these people not knowing what we are.**

"Should something be happening?" Svoboda asked. "You seem lost in thought. Who are these friends you mention?"

"I was speaking with Comet," Eclipse answered. *By telepathy. Like this.*

"Is this an inertialess drive Comet has?" Koster asked, noting the absence of perceived acceleration. Her doctorate was in Physics; her thoughts were firmly concentrated on her chances for the all-expenses-paid winter trip to Stockholm. "Like a TV spaceship?"

"Inertialess? Teevee?" Eclipse repeated. She wished she knew physics. She knew what inertialess must mean. Sort of. Comet would know exactly. Any time science was important, Eclipse thought, Comet could think circles around her. But what was the other? It named a type of spaceship, so 'Tivi' must be a country, one that hadn't existed before. The name sounded like a group of Pacific Islands. Might the place be some Atlanticean remnant, transposed from one ocean to the next?

"We don't feel any acceleration," Janice Svoboda remarked.

"When she starts, she'll be very gentle. You won't feel a thing," Eclipse said blandly.

"Gentle?" Svoboda asked.

"For her. If you could only do five gees, you'd need forever to go translight. She can do that in a quarter-hour." The astronauts noted that Eclipse didn't appear to be boasting. Each calculated silently how many gees corresponded to Comet's alleged 0.07c per minute.

Svoboda surveyed the control deck. "This certainly was not covered by operations planning. Eclipse, could the five of us consult privately, please?" Eclipse nodded agreement. Svoboda bowed slightly and retreated to the lower deck.

"Well, folks? Do I hear recommendations? That includes you, ground." Svoboda waited for her crew to respond. Ground control was silent. Transmissions were now being carried live on all six American television networks. Telephone calls from Washington had completely disrupted higher administrative headquarters.

"The situation does appear to be a mite sticky," Peters observed. "It can't be said we'd be throwing our lives away. Trusting them, I mean."

"A mite sticky?" Koster questioned. 'Is that Brit for 'totally hopeless'? You're right. What could we lose?" The other specialists gestured their agreement.

"Okay, folks, is there anything we need to do before we land? We're all stowed? Let's go for broke!" Svoboda raised her voice. "Eclipse, go ahead. Stop and land us," she asked, challenging her crew to demur.

"I need a landing site," Eclipse said. "Not your big base. Look. We don't understand how you and your ground people can not know who I am. It makes no sense. But someplace there are personae who do know. When they catch up with me, things get seriously violent. So we land someplace not expected, and I make my getaway before something bad happens." Something violent, she thought, like a troop of League Peace Police getting vaporized.

Svoboda hesitated. "OK. The best place for that is..." Eclipse put a finger across her lips.

I should think it, Svoboda continued, *and you hear me?*

You have it right! You caught on! I can tell when you try to broadcast! Aurora said enthusiastically. *Your other thoughts, they're private.*

Svoboda envisioned a location. *That's upstate New York. Northeast of Buffalo. Close to Marge's home.*

Eclipse stared at the image of the planned flight path and aerial view of the landing site. *They let you overfly Canada?* she said in surprise.

Sure. World's longest unfortified border and all that. Somehow, Svoboda thought, she was missing a subtext to Eclipse's question.

And that's Buffalo now? This time, Svoboda caught Eclipse's flash image of Buffalo, the premier industrial city of North America, its hundred-story skyscrapers marching from Eden north to Lake Ontario.

Svoboda answered with her image, a familiarization flight into their destination landing strip, with flat farmland and orchards replacing Eclipse's towering office spires.

Aurora tensed. *Flight Leader. Can you envision the approach, what you fly over?*

I dream of them. Here's where we're going. Svoboda realized she was somehow getting an aerial view of Ontario, Lake Erie, and finally their landing point.

Thanks, Aurora, Eclipse inserted. *That was great. OK I have the teleport destination locked. Comet, can you generate an orbit for that?*

I already have. We need about a quarter hour to get there, the older girl answered.

Need more than that, Svoboda objected. *We're over Mongolia now.* She suggested a landing path.

That path is all coasting, Comet said. *I do powered flight all the way.*

"This is all impossible," Svoboda said, "except all of us see and hear you. OK, do it." Outside, the tangerine glow intensified. A gentle pressure appeared within the cabin, slowly forcing everything to the floor of the ship.

"Eclipse, dear? Be so good," Peters asked, "if you would, as to advise Miss Comet that we are accelerating the wrong way. Outward from Earth, not the direction that would kill our velocity."

"That's not acceleration," Eclipse explained. "That's gravity, so everything settles before you land. Oh, can you lower landing gear?" Eclipse asked. "Now, I mean? Whatever else you do to land? If I must, I'll teleport your ship down. If I do that, you're on the ground all at once."

Comet, Eclipse added, *if I teleport, kill your flight field? Or we reach the ground, and you pull three gees until we hit the first line of trees.*

OK! But mayhaps I should keep my field on and hold us still, so if we come in a little high or moving a bit I protect you and the ship from dropping?

Oh, right. OK. Don't worry. I have a destination locked. Eclipse wished she'd had more practice using her gifts with her friends.

WAIT! Comet shrilled. *You teleport us? All? I mean, this thing must weigh a hundred tons and some and we're orbital.*

You said you wanted a backup, a confident Eclipse answered.

You can do that? Comet's intuition sounded warnings. The power involved sounded too much to be reasonable.

Sure. Well, mayhaps I'm a little hazy afterward. Why don't you get on with it? Eclipse said to Comet.

"Are you talking to your flying saucer again?" Svoboda asked.

"Sort of. But she's not a saucier, though she does cook. Star is better at cooking," Eclipse answered. She told herself that Svoboda couldn't possibly have meant what she had just heard Svoboda say. "After all, he's a boy. He's supposed to know how to cook. Comet's giving us energy and all that stuff." She told herself that when she got home, she had to get those details straight. *Did I say that right, Comet?* "You can't feel it, because she pushes everything at once. Just as well. We're doing several gees." *Right, Comet?*

Barely three? This thing is awful fragile. I have to be gentle. Comet's mind betrayed a determined concentration on her task.

"Houston," Peters announced, "says we're changing velocity. At thirty-four meters per second squared. They want to know why our IGS doesn't confirm."

"Inertialess drive!" Sellers supplied.

"Ask them," Eclipse said, "ask them to tell us when we reach dead stop. Comet's very good at flying, but... It'll make them feel useful. People stop worrying if they think they're being useful."

"Did you say 'teleport'?" Reischauer asked. "The blue glow and the carillon effect when you took Marge on her EVA?"

"Eeveeay?" Eclipse asked. Every so often, they simply stopped speaking Modern English.

"Extra Vehicular Activity," Peters clarified. "Your trip out of doors?"

"I teleported," Eclipse explained. "That's backup, too. I teleport your ship to the ground. I skip it if we can. If I teleport, I swallow your kinetic energy, you at five miles a second. I'd rather not."

"Now, young lady," Svoboda asked, "you're saying that no matter what happens we can be on the ground in half an instant? Not moving?" She waited for Eclipse's agreement. "Are you sure?" Eclipse smiled.

"Eclipse? Could you explain?" Marge Koster asked, crossing her arms across her chest, "From the beginning? What planet you're from? Where your flying saucer is?"

~~~~~

The descent crossed Canada. Twenty miles up, over Niagara Falls, the Lemuria came to a hover. The crew deployed landing gear. Miles below, Air Force interceptors streaked toward the now motionless space plane.

Eclipse stood, one hand gripping a bulkhead, the other clenched in a tight fist. The Lemuria fell into a sea-blue waterfall, a hundred chimes sounding gloriously through empty sky. Now the Lemuria was stationary, parked near one end of a long, deserted airstrip. Banks of snow on each side testified to a desultory effort to keep the runway clear.

"Welcome home." Eclipse leaned back on the bulkhead. The shuttle had been heavier than she expected. "This is the airstrip you described, I think." Janice Svoboda nodded agreement. Her fellow astronauts peered eagerly through the windows.

"Folks," Marge Koster finally said, "we're two miles from my home, and my husband says that he and our van are on the way. It's not like twenty years ago, when we had to learn to walk again after landing. We're all good to go. The company completely debriefed us while we were up there, because of course they were positive that we were never coming down. I propose you all join me at my home, including our guest cottage, and exchange our delightful union suits for comfortable clothing, following which my two oldest darlings are, God help me, cooking dinner. We probably won't be poisoned. Honest! They're actually both very good cooks. The nice people from the local Air Force Base will have Air Police surrounding the Lemuria to secure it for the investigation."

"In fact," Janice announced, "our lords and masters have been telling me on the secure channel that they would like us out of the space plane as soon as possible, because some corporate bigwig and some of our government agency funders are busy calling each other names and they all want to be sure that we don't do anything that would hide the record of what happened. I gather it will be four or five hours before they get a plane to the local airport to fly us back to California."

"That's fly you all back to California," Marge Koster said. "My resignation from this outfit was effective as soon as we touched ground. By the way, Eclipse, you and your friends would be welcome to join us for dinner."

"Thanks, but has to be another time," Eclipse answered. It would, she thought, be seriously unsafe for you to have me there when the League Peace Police, whoever, show up.

Despite the odd scarlet color of the flashing lights, Eclipse thought, the approaching car had to be bailiffs. It was time for the three to be on their way. Eclipse disappeared to the rustle of cymbals, noticing after it was too late that she still held Koster's clipboard.

~~~~~

Wind whipped snow across a North Dakota cornfield. Aurora and Star had moved five large duffel bags twenty yards to the side of a stream bed, arranging them in a parapet to block the worst of the wind. Star had insisted that Aurora wrap herself in his sleeping bag, while he stayed warm behind his force field. "After all, Aurora, you kept Comet and Eclipse warm last night, so I should return the favor. How much longer is this taking?"

"Eclipse is on board the Space Plane," Aurora answered. "Comet and

Cloud are slowing it down. It still takes a while. Comet says the space plane is real fragile, so she can't accelerate it very fast. But they're over Buffalo now. No, Comet says they're over empty fields, because most of Buffalo isn't there. And now they're on the ground, and Eclipse is teleporting them all back here."

Eclipse appeared in midair, hovering above the field a distance from the twins. Comet and Cloud, equally in mid-air, appeared a short ways away. "Here we are," she shouted.

"We did it," Cloud said. "Thanks to you two. Now can we go to someplace warm?"

"We're over here, Eclipse," Star shouted. "By the way, I think the Tunnels did time travel again. There's no way this weather is the start of April."

"Back to where we slept last night?" Eclipse asked. Hearing no objections, she teleported the five and their luggage to Oregon.

"Oh, good," Star said. "Now we can find the dooms and smash them."

"Where do we start?" Aurora asked.

"We start by letting your sister have a nice long nap," Comet announced. "I thought I'd recovered from all that flying, but I'm completely exhausted again. That thing was heavy as all get out. I'd never have handled it without your help, Cloud." Comet smiled at the older boy, then pulled her ground tarp from her duffel bag, wrapped up in her blanket, and fell asleep.

"That's why we're a team. Aren't we, Eclipse?" Cloud answered.

"The Wizard of Mars chose us." Eclipse shrugged. "He didn't say why."

"We should be out there finding dooms," Star said. "Why are we sitting here?"

"We rescued that space plane, the way we agreed," Eclipse said. "So your big sister needs some time to recover. That thing was heavy."

"And you teleported it," Cloud pointed out. "Are you feeling OK?"

"I had to catch my breath afterward," Eclipse answered. "Just for a moment."

"I found the date," Aurora said. "Newspaper in the open at a news stand. It's February 14. That's why this weather."

"Then the Star Compass takes us to the dooms, doesn't it?" Star asked.

"We get to find that out," Eclipse said. "Meanwhile, we're sitting here. You three all have your lesson comps with you. Catch up on school work. Unless one of you can manage to tap into the new DataLink." She yawned deeply.

"Are you taking a nap, too, Eclipse?" Cloud asked.

"I'm tired," she said, "but not that tired." She reached into her duffel bag, then dissolved into blue sparks and the distant clangour of brass bells.

CHAPTER 7 WELCOME TO NOT-EARTH

First stop, Eclipse thought, is someplace entirely private, someplace where I can dress as Jim without Cloud and friends seeing whom I become. A bath first would be nice, but that's not likely to happen.

A few minutes later, her garb carefully folded, Eclipse contemplated the view from five thousand feet. There was the Columbia river, flowing as magnificently as ever to the blue ocean. Comet was right, Eclipse thought, when she said the river looked odd. To its north should have been Cosmopolis, West Columbia. There were pretty homes, what appeared to be a hotel, roads laid out in neat squares...but Cosmopolis, one of the larger cities in the American Republic, was simply not there.

And the coast? The ruined towers of ancient Leaviork were gone. The coastal highway, the remains of the Grand Processional of All Marik, wasn't there. She braced for flight in vacuum, teleported a hundred thousand miles into deep space, waited for pursuit, and teleported back to a particular valley in coastal Oregon. Her pond was its deep and tranquil self. Her barn was gone. The fields were all planted with fruit trees. There was a house in about the right place, but it surely was not her house. Four odd-looking cars were parked under a wide canopy.

Eclipse reached out mentally, searching for her pets' null links. Ponies and barn cats were nowhere to be found. She reached deeper into her levels, driving her mentalic sensitivity harder and harder. No matter where they were in the world, she should have been able to find them. Nothing. Her pets were gone. For a moment she squeezed tears from under her eyelids. Whatever had been done to her innocent pets, she could only hope it had been painless.

Lunch? Perhaps takeout from Kniaz Kang, she asked herself? That was assuming Kniaz Kang was still in business, probably another bad assumption.

Another pair of teleports brought her to North Cosmopolis, rather, to the former location of North Cosmopolis. She'd deliberately appeared a hundred feet off the ground, just in case buildings had changed a bit. The town had changed a lot. It was much smaller. She counted. This place had a few dozen houses, two churches, and a somewhat bedraggled Main Street. Where Atomic Tech had stood, there was a small elementary school, with children playing outside. Kniaz Kang's restaurant was gone. In its place were a gas station, what appeared to be a hot dog stand, and a modest supermarket.

She'd attracted attention. Three children in the playground pointed in her direction and started shouting. A widening circle of their friends stopped and pointed. Finally, two teachers strode out to mid-field to find out what had distracted their charges from an opportunity to play. Eclipse waved. Children waved back. They obviously thought the exchange was wonderful, as though they'd never before seen a persona in mid-flight. Of course, Eclipse considered, perhaps they hadn't. The teachers looked at the sky, pulled what appeared to be small books from their pockets, and held them above their heads. What were they thinking? Eclipse wondered. Were the books some sort of religious token, because the two adults thought she was a demon? Perhaps they were some strange sort of camera. They looked very vaguely like RadioBells, except the shape was wrong, the thickness was wrong, and the color was completely wrong.

She could still get lunch...wrong. If these people didn't recognize her, why would they recognize her money? She reached out mentalically, looking through the eyes of the person in the hot dog stand, the fellow manning the cash register. That was severely impolite, even though it told her nothing about his private thoughts. There were treasury notes lined up in his cash register...they were all some lurid shade of green. They didn't look like real money at all. The coins were even stranger. She withdrew her mentalic probe, noted the person at the register blinking deeply to clear his eyes, and went on her way. She had ration bars stowed in her pack, but not enough to feed all five of them for any length of time. She was more prepared than the rest of them, but not infinitely prepared. Money for food was perhaps a challenge. Aurora hadn't even packed camping gear. How could Aurora's parents possibly have expected Aurora would always have a bed to sleep in?

What were they going to do? Someplace, a quiet voice in the back of her mind reminded her about the possibility of robbing a local bank. If these people didn't have persona, they might have some problems stopping her. No, bank robbery was hardly gift-true. Cloud, for one, would be deeply shocked by the suggestion. Comet was much more practical. She might still suggest that since Eclipse was already a wanted criminal, at least in most of the world, she should be the bank robber. She could just add bank robbery to the long list of crimes she'd already allegedly committed.

Finding a persona league, someplace in America, would help. They might not know who she was, but they might well be friendly enough to exchange some of her money for local money. Great Thalers, after all, were gold and silver, which probably had some value.

~~~~

Comet awoke from a deep sleep. It hadn't been that long, she told herself, only hours, but she'd really needed it. Her two siblings were staring at lesson-comps. They'd all done trips with Dad or Mom, and had drilled into them that trips were no excuse for getting behind in school. If nothing was happening, you could pop open the comp and learn something. Then Dad or Mom would insist on your proving it by explaining it to them. Cloud appeared to be doing the same, if with less enthusiasm. Aurora obviously kept wanting to look at games instead, but she didn't, not until the comp said she'd done the day's coursework. After that, of course, only a wrecking bar could pry Aurora away from her games literature.

There was the moon, rising over the trees, not yet in first quarter. It was a friend, a friend who never talked her down. She looked at it closely. Her jaw dropped. "That's impossible!" she said.

"Oh, good afternoon, Comet," Aurora said. "Did you say something?"

"That's impossible," Comet repeated. She called her flight field. For half an instant she was a bright orange flame. She took off, climbing skyward with all the acceleration she could muster. After the first few seconds, she remembered Star's warning about invisibility and vanished from sight. She focused her will on her gifts. Her course arced skyward, faster and faster, clouds and earth falling away below her. The heavens made their swift change from sky blue through luminous grey to flat black. In a few moments she was so high that even Cloud could have seen the stars. She rolled her course south, still climbing, the curve of the earth clearly visible below her.

"Where'd she go?" Star asked. He scanned the sky, seeing the moon and a few wisps of cloud. "What was impossible? She said something was. She was in a real hurry."

"I think we have to wait for her and Eclipse to come back," Aurora answered.

"Girls," Cloud grumbled. "They know perfectly well we're depending on the two of them to find these dooms so that I can save the world by destroying them. Instead of staying around to find the dooms for me, they take off by themselves on some whackdoodle quests that they don't even bother to explain to me first, so I can give them permission to go. Aurora, I don't suppose that you can tell Comet to turn around and come back, can you?"

"No," Aurora answered. "And I'm busy with this Editing homework. I hate Editing. Yes, I know it's actually good for something, but that doesn't mean I have to like it."

Far above, Comet sped toward the lunar disk. She could clearly see Mare Crisium, the small oval dark spot in the upper right corner of the light side of the moon. But the moon was only approaching half-full! Mare Crisium should have been out of sight on the far side of the Moon, the side away from the Earth, while Mare Imbrium should have been visible on the illuminated half of the lunar disk. The dark half of the lunar disk, the moon being not yet half full, was supposed to be the never-illuminated dark side of the moon, the side of the moon that you couldn't see unless you had vision like hers.

Now that she was well above the atmosphere, she had no trouble seeing features on the entire lunar disk. It was impossible! She was looking at what should have been the light side of the moon, exactly as everyone would see it at full moon, except somehow the moon had rotated. The moon was half-full, but she was looking at the moon's full-moon face. There was Mare Imbrium, in darkest shadow on the side of the Moon away from the Sun. Did that mean that part of the dark side of the moon was now exposed to sunlight? She'd need a couple of minutes to find out, first to reach solar escape velocity, and then a faster-than-light transition farther into space.

Three minutes later, she was far above the lunar North Pole, looking down at the lunar surface. Half of the moon was illuminated, but it was the wrong half. The moon had been rotated so that half of the light side of the moon, and half of the dark side of the moon, the side that never saw sunlight, were in fact now facing the sun. She couldn't swear from memory that the craters on the dark side of the moon were exactly right, but exactly as always the dark side of the moon—the side that was supposed to be dark—was covered with craters, except not a single cyclopean stone city of the unknown builders of the Lunar Darkside was in sight.

She dropped down to hover above the Lunar surface, close to the terminator. Shadows trailed across the plain, long coal-black banners blown out from every rise. The Sun was a disk, she thought, not a point, so the shadows were very slightly fuzzy. A motion, a movement where there could be no movement, attracted her eye. What was it? There was the tip of a shadow, the stone casting it being many yards away. The shadow was changing its length, at least to her vision. Ever so slowly, much more slowly than shadows seen near sunrise on earth, the shadow relinquished its tenuous grip on an isolated shiny pebble. How was that possible? It had to be that the moon was spinning on its axis, so that as time went on a Lunarian observer would see the Sun move across the sky. That was ridiculous. The moon didn't work that way. But if the Sun was moving, what was the Earth doing? She found a pair of rocky prominences, a pair she could sight across to look at the Earth. She waited patiently. Very clearly, the Earth was not moving across the sky significantly. It hung there stationary.

She forced herself to imagine carefully what she had found. How would the moon be moving to show what she now saw? It was as though the moon were spinning on its axis, so that it always pointed more or less the same face toward the Earth, instead of always pointing the same face toward the Sun, the way the Moon was supposed to do. Finally she chose a rock, pretended it was the earth, and walked in a circle around it, always facing the Earth. First one side of her face, then her full face, then the other side of her face, and finally the back of her head were in direct sunlight. That was so strange. The Moon no longer had a light side and a dark side.

She consulted her StarCompass. It ignored the Moon, pointing her back toward the Earth. Whatever had been done to the Earth's largest satellite, it wasn't related to the oncoming dooms they were supposed to stop. Dooms weren't the pleasantest set of thoughts to remember. The five of them were supposed to stop something, and then return. Some of them would probably die. The Wizard of Mars said so. She told herself that she and Eclipse couldn't both die, because then Aurora and Star and Cloud would have no way to get home, except of course that this was home, even if a few things were a bit strange.

The Wizard of Mars had gotten her into this mess. He owed her an explanation. How did she return to reality? Where was Mars in the heavens? The moon was where it should be, in orbit around the earth. Mars should be the same. Her vision swept across the constellations. There were the planets, all in an arc, Uranus and Neptune and all the rest. A ruddy star that showed a disc and detailed features without looking carefully: that was Mars. Well, she told herself, it showed a disc if she looked, others needing a telescope. The flight field that trapped light until she was invisible enhanced her vision, revealing glories of the heavens unsuspected by the ungifted.

Invisibility fell away, her flight field flaring its gaudy tangerine orange as she reached for the depth of her gifts. A minute's effort flattened local geodesics. She had passed solar escape velocity. The stars trembled. Her speed soared as she passed from mere tens of miles per second through the speed of light. The Lords of Eternity had told her she was a little girl who should go home. She should stay home until she learned to use her gifts better. No matter! None of them, not even Starstreak, could match her speed when she set her mind to it. Mars was now minutes away.

A landing spiral brought her to the Martian northern hemisphere. She knew where she was going. The Wizard of Mars had promised: If she lived, and if she willed it, she could return in triumph. She repeated to herself the argument she was about to use on the Wizard. Returning in triumph was impossible if you couldn't return at all.

Mons Olympus rose across the horizon. The solar system's largest mountain was a volcano whose entire volume had been sculpted into the Scarlet Castle, a huge building honoring its omniscient resident. She swooped around the volcano, lining up for the polite approach that so gratified the Wizard's substantial vanity.

At the sight of the northern face of Mons Olympus, great falls of lava manifestly untouched by rational hands, she lost all control of her flight, spinning wildly through the sky into a dramatic tooth-jarring landing. She didn't often hurt herself by flying into something. The boil of sand reminded her that she was decidedly not indestructible.

For a time she walked across the sand, sneakers sending up puffs of slow-falling dust, each step bringing her infinitesimally closer to the impossibility glowering before her. The sky was its familiar pink. This was Mars, its lower gravity transforming steps into graceful leaps, its near-vacuum of an atmosphere warping the sound of sand crunching under her feet. The slopes of Mons Olympus had not been sculpted into the Temple of the Wizard, the Wizard's private residence. Where was the Wizard? Where was his home?

A hop, a skip, and she went into flight again, her destination the north face of the volcano. The bulges of rock did loosely resemble the Temple. Its vast approaches stretched for tens and tens of miles. Of course, she considered, those rocks might have been the starting point for the builders. The builders removed rock, so where there were stairs or porches in the Temple, there had to have been natural rock formations before they started sculpting. Where was the Temple now? Had she travelled back in time, back so far that the Wizard was not yet in residence? That was billions of years ago, back so far that there were no human beings, let alone American cities that were almost-copies of Buffalo. The rock looked natural. A good hard kick convinced her that the stone was as solid as it appeared.

She shook her head. It didn't make sense. It couldn't make sense. Nothing made sense. Nothing at all. This was beyond her. Mayhaps Eclipse could puzzle it out. The rest of the gang would try. She for sure couldn't herself. She squeezed eyes shut. Another bursting of the waterworks wasn't going to help. She wiped her face, stray tears boiling violently when they passed outside her body field.

CHAPTER 8 ECLIPSE AND THE KOSTER FAMILY

Late in the day, Eclipse appeared in the clearing. The sun touched hilltops to the west. Aurora sat on a log, her mind a million miles away as she studied chess positions.

"Hi, Aurora," Eclipse said. "Where is everyone?"

"Why not Bishop to d5?" Aurora mumbled to herself. "What am I missing?" She stopped and looked up. "Oh, hi, Eclipse. I've got this article, fellow claiming the Sarnath opening is solid. He's wrong, but why? Where did you come from?"

"I just got back," Eclipse said. She wondered if Aurora had actually noticed her saying hello, or if her shadow across Aurora's lessoncomp had drawn Aurora's attention to the real world. "So where is everyone?"

"Oh, I see, pull the queen back to the one rank. Nasty! That wrecks his claims. Star and Cloud talked about us," Aurora said. "It was about camping. Cloud was an American Scout. He'd gone on group camping trips. He said when they had girls along, the girls had a camp. The boys had a different camp, a distance away. No, he wasn't sure why, but it was a rule. The two of them agreed that the three of us could stay here. He talked Star into going around the pond. They set up way over there. So that's what they did. They're over there."

"I suppose," Eclipse said. She shrugged. From what she could see, the two had been careful about cleaning up the ground before they left. "But where's Comet?" she asked.

"Oh, she woke up sometime this afternoon and looked at the Moon," Aurora explained. "It looks the same as ever to me. Round and white. She got really annoyed about something. No, she looked at the moon and said it was impossible. I don't see how a moon can be impossible. She cranked her flight field all the way down, so she looked like a big gas flame, and took off lickety-split. After a moment she went invisible. I don't know where she went. I don't know why she was upset."

"Did you track her?" Eclipse asked. "Keep an eye on her, in case she got into trouble?"

"She didn't ask me to," Aurora said, "So I didn't. When she left, I was busy with Editing homework. English Editing is a real pain in the neck. It's dull, tedious, you have to get absolutely everything right, and what does it do?"

Eclipse looked at the Moon. The part she could see looked the same as ever, didn't it? She'd been doing astronomy lessons before the Wizard of Mars said he needed her. But that was about planets and asteroids and Kuiper objects, and what you found on their surfaces. Those were ruins from long ago.

She felt for her null link to Comet. The link was very weak. Comet was doing faster than light to someplace. Mentalically tracking her when she was moving so fast was not fun. Where was she? Null links were terrible locators over long distance, but Comet looked to be flying to Mars. If that's where she is, Eclipse thought, I'll leave her alone. For sure, I don't want to be getting into debt to the Wizard of Mars. I can't afford what he charges.

There was one more thing she could do. "Aurora," she asked. "Can you find where the astronauts are now? I accidentally walked off with Marge Koster's clipboard, and need to return it."

"If they haven't gone too far," Aurora answered. "And if I'm not invading anyone's privacy too much. I stop my clairvoyance outside of people's houses." The silver pyramid and lidless eye appeared above her head. "One of them is still in that stupid Space Plane, waiting for her bosses to show up. I can feel how cold she is. Four of them are a few miles away. I'm looking down from above. OK. there's a fancy car, wheeled, not flying, with three of them being driven away. The fourth and someone else just went inside. They were thinking about how cold it is. The car...it has some sort of escort, cars with those strange red lights. I think the fourth is that Koster person. I can see her hair color."

"There's a State Police car at each end of the street," Aurora continued. "Yes, State Police, like in Prussia, it says so on the side of the car. The mailbox in front has 'Koster' as the name on it. And one of the kids who lives there? She's building a snow sculpture out in back. No, she's just going inside."

Eclipse stared at the associated image. She recognized the child from their mother's memories. No time like the present, Eclipse thought, to deal with this. "Yes, that's them. Thanks for finding them, Aurora. I would have needed a week. OK, I'll be back in a bit." Eclipse's teleport brought the blue depth of an ice cave and a chord from a xylophone. A brief detour let her change back to her garb. That's how Koster had seen her before; she should wear it now to be sure to be recognized.

Eclipse appeared in the home's back yard. The snow had been three feet deep. Near the house, children's play had beaten it completely down. Where she was standing, it was much deeper. The snow squeaked under her boots as she walked. It was indeed cold; later would be even colder, no matter that clouds overhead would keep what little warmth there was near the ground. Snow flakes whirled around her in a light flurry, to skitter across the yard, driven by the frigid breeze.

If there was a door knocker, she didn't recognize it. She tapped firmly on the glass.

A voice, dimly heard, called "I'll get it, Mom." The inner door opened. Looking through the storm door's glass, she faced a boy perhaps her own age.

"Hi!" Eclipse shouted. "Is this the Koster house?"

"Yes?" the boy answered.

Eclipse recognized the boy from his mother's memories. "You're James. And this clipboard," Eclipse said, speaking through the glass, "is your mom's. I'm just returning it."

James Thomas stared at her. "Oh, sure. Wait! You're Eclipse! Aren't you?" he shouted. His three siblings had been spread across the floor, playing some sort of game that Eclipse didn't recognize. They shot to their feet and ran to join their brother.

"James Thomas, do not unlock that door to strangers!" Eclipse recognized Marge Koster's voice, shouting from up the stairs.

"She's not a stranger. She's Eclipse," James answered as he unlocked the door. "I can tell she's a superhero. And she's outside in nothing but a shirt, and the wind chill is minus twenty."

Eclipse stepped through the doorway, carefully closing the storm door behind her. No, Eclipse thought, these people are absolutely not used to meeting personas. She was still happy to step out of the snow. "James?" she said to the boy in front of her. "And you three are Peter, Rebecca, and Heather. Did I get that right?" They all nodded.

"You saved my mom's life," James said. Eclipse looked bashfully at the four children and nodded. Suddenly Heather jumped at Eclipse, hugged her, and kissed her on the cheek, to be followed by hugs from James' three siblings.

"James! Wait!" Marge Koster's voice rang clearly above the hubbub. She appeared at the top of a short flight of stairs. Eclipse waved in her direction, then held up the clipboard and pointed at it. "Eclipse? You must be freezing. You'll get frostbite. Your parents let you out like that? In this weather? Don't you even have a sweater to put on top of that blouse?"

"I greet thee, Senior Mission Specialist Koster," Eclipse responded. That was as formal as she could remember. She wondered how these people handled titles.

"Eclipse, here I'm just Doctor Koster. Or Mom. No, for you it's Marge, if you please."

"Yes, Marge. And for you all, I'm Eclipse."

"And I'm Adrian. Or Dad to these four." The tall, solidly framed man now standing next to his wife pointed at his four children. "And you're the girl," he tried to choke back tears, "the girl who saved my wife."

"Eclipse, you come up here," Marge Koster said. "If you're not in a total hurry. Aren't you cold?"

"I'm fine," Eclipse said.

"Mom," Peter explained, "she's a superhero. She's indestructible."

"I wish," Eclipse said. "But I'm quite weatherproof."

"Please join us up here," Adrian said. "If your mom and dad won't worry that you're late for dinner."

Eclipse shook her head. She'd just missed something in the conversation, but what? "I'm happy to join you," she answered. "That's not a problem." From the kitchen she could smell roast beef and still-warm apple pie, redolent with cinnamon and raisins. She started up the stairs, then paused to look at a big map taped to the wall. Around the world, national borders were completely wrong.

"I'd offer you pie," Marge said, "and ice cream, but you're from a different planet, so I might poison you."

"I'm not from another planet," Eclipse answered, "and I'd be happy to have a piece of pie with ice cream."

"You aren't?" Adrian asked. "But no one has ever heard of real superheroes..."

"Personas," Marge corrected,

"...until now," Adrian continued.

"I'm puzzled, too," Eclipse said. "We went off on a very long flight. When we came back, everything was different. The countries are all different. You've never met a persona?"

"Tell us more," Heather asked. "Please? How do I get to be a superhero, ummh, persona?"

"Where do I start?" Eclipse asked. "Comet, Aurora, and Star...you didn't meet Star...are brother and sisters. Cloud is a friend. The Wizard of Mars..."

A half hour later, Eclipse had almost finished her story, interspersed with her questions that the Kosters were all too happy to answer. "Your country," she finally asked, "this one. What is its name?" You already know the answer, she thought. You saw that map.

"America," Rebecca blurted out.

"The United States of America, founded 1776," James answered.

"Not 'The American Republic'?" Eclipse asked. "That's Fourth Republic. And just south of here isn't the Empire of the Aztecs and the Incas?"

"Never heard us called 'the American Republic'," Adrian answered. "I should know. I'm a history teacher. And Cortez wiped out the Aztecs, oh, five hundred years ago."

"Once upon a time, this man showed up in Vienna," Eclipse said. "He claimed he was the American Ambassador. But he was from 'The United

States of America', and he was looking for the Austrian Republic, like on the map downstairs, not the Austro-Hungarian Empire. You'd think he was crazy, but telepaths all agreed he was totally sane. It's just his memories were wrong. Then he disappeared, leaving behind his United States passport and some strange money. He'd traded his money for real Austro-Hungarian Thalers."

"What was his name?" Peter asked.

Eclipse ransacked her memory. "Morgenthaler. Cyrus Morgenthaler." Eclipse nodded with certainty.

"Morgenthaler. The man who vanished. Let me get the book," Peter said. He stood and dashed from the table.

"How many people are there in the world?" Eclipse asked, already dreading the answer.

"Seven billion," Rebecca said. "I studied that in school last week."

Eclipse took a deep breath. She could feel the hairs on her scalp rise. "Before we left," she said, "the Wizard of Mars said that we five had to beat the impending dooms, or eight billion people would die. That was impossible, because the whole world has only one billion people. But if you have seven billion...we succeed, or everyone from before, and everyone now, dies. And we don't know what the dooms are, let alone how to stop them." The room became very quiet.

"Here's the book," Peter said. He set it on the table in front of her. "Morgenthaler said he was in Vienna, except the Hapsburgs still ran the place, and they owned eastern Europe. It was a big scandal. He was going to be elected President in two years, but then everyone thought he was crazy, so he quit politics. That circle on the cover is the one of the coins he brought back."

Eclipse stared at the book cover. "Wait," she said. "That's a Thaler, down to the Emperor on the front." She reached into an inner pocket of her cape, pulled out her coin purse, and looked inside. "Does this look familiar?" she asked. There was a soft 'cling' as the coin dropped onto the tabletop.

"They're the same," Peter announced, "except the year is different. The guy in the middle of yours looks older."

Eclipse pointed at the two dates. "About 30 years difference. So Morgenthaler went from now to us, and we came here. That doesn't make sense. Which way was the world being changed, back then?"

"The Morgenthaler coins are worth a huge fortune," Peter said, "because they wrecked an election. They can't be faked, because they're alloyed with one-isotope silver, not natural silver. Here's a picture of one being auctioned at Southward's in London. For seven hundred thousand dollars." Eclipse stared for a moment at the text.

"Marge? Adrian?" she asked, "Do you still have DataLink?"

"Not called that," Adrian answered. "What is it?"

"All the computers in America, my America, well, not quite all, talk to each other." Let us, Eclipse thought, skip why my home's computers are totally isolated from the world. "So I can go to a library here, and read a book that's in the Rogers Tech Library, four hundred miles away. Or I have a store, so I put up a display on my computer, and people learn when I'm open."

"Internet!" All four Koster children interrupted.

"Could you find please this Southward's place on the internet for me? And when they are open? They might want to buy that." She tapped the Thaler. "I'm in a silly position. I brought plenty of money, just in case, but it's not your money." She returned the coin to her purse and pulled out a pair of paper bills. "That's money from before, and it can't be worth anything now."

"Who's Vespasian?" Heather asked, looking at the image on the bill.

"Roman Emperor," Eclipse answered. "That's him addressing Congress, meaning we had peace with Europe. Famous historical event. Wait, America here was founded in seventeen seventy-six? Only two hundred fifty years ago?"

"Yes," Adrian answered. "Yours was earlier?"

"The Fourth Republic dates to 17 A.D.," Eclipsed answered.

"So you can fly?" Heather asked. "And, I don't know. UltraGirl is bulletproof, isn't she?"

"Heather, UltraGirl is a television show. She isn't real." Marge looked firmly at her daughter. "And Eclipse might not want to say."

"But Eclipse is real. She's right here. She saved you." Heather stared at her mother.

No, Eclipse thought, Heather has no reason to think her question is impolite. "Several people who shot at me discovered that their bullets bounced. That goes double for whoever used the lithium bombs on me and the Sera Lama. But that reminds me. Marge? Your spaceship? Is that the best in the world?"

"Technical failures notwithstanding," Marge answered. "Yes."

"Can it fly to other planets?" Eclipse asked. "Fly faster than light?"

"Mercy me, no," Marge answered. "The only people who ever flew to the moon used a Saturn rocket. No one has ever gone farther. We don't even make Saturns any more. And faster than light is impossible. It's against the laws of nature."

Eclipse stared at her, a quizzical look on her face. "Morgenthaler talked about Saturns. He said Americans flew to the Moon. With a chemical rocket called 'Saturn'. No one believed him. And I can fly faster than light. That's how we got here."

"I see," Marge said. The most important atomic bomb secret, she thought, was that they go ker-blammo. And here is the most important faster-than-light secret, handed to you on a silver platter. "Special relativity says you can't do that."

"Einstein relativity? He had special relativity, and general relativity, and finally transitivity." Eclipse nodded. At least, she thought, I think I have the order right.

"You don't happen to know how this transitivity works, do you?" Marge asked hopefully.

"Sorry. No idea. Except there are a lot of derivatives in it, and I only sort of understand what a derivative is. I'm still grinding through trig proofs."

Peter returned from elsewhere in the house and handed Eclipse a sheet of paper. "You're ahead of me, then," he exclaimed. "I'm just starting trig."

"Could we go back to this doom thing?" Adrian asked politely. "You were sent off to stop it. You have no idea what it, they, are. So it's you, and Comet, who's about your age, and Aurora, who Marge says sounded younger, and some other people as old as you. More or less. Dooms? I don't mean to scare you, but what if there's violence? Then what do you do?"

"Violence?" Eclipse repeated.

"Violence. Like Gorgonzola," Rebecca said.

"Gorgonzola?" Eclipse asked.

"Fifties black and white movie. Giant komodo dragon! Ate cities," Rebecca said.

"That was another motion picture," Marge said firmly. "And, Rebecca, you should let Eclipse answer your father's question."

"Yes, mother. Sorry," a chastened Rebecca responded.

"What do we do? Smite it! The Wizard of Mars makes strange choices." Eclipse leaned back in her chair. "Once upon a time, the doom that almost came to Sarnath, he told their most powerful persona to fix things. Cashlord saved Sarnath. Besides being strong, he was a fantastic wine-taster, and that's the only thing that mattered. He identified barrels by their vintage. The Wizard could have sent me because I like cats. But he sent me, I think, because dooms get stopped by pounding on them. I'm good at pounding on things. He said anyone else would fail."

"But you could get hurt." Heather objected.

"The Wizard said some of us probably get killed. But if we stayed home, for sure, we die and everyone in the world dies, all eight billion people. So Star and Aurora's parents agreed they should go, the other choice being worse. So did Cloud's. Comet is a mercenary; she was paid. And me*? Life, lighter than atoms. Duty, heavier than worlds."

"Comet's parents agreed she should go? At her age?" Adrian asked. "We saw her picture on TV. When she was in front of the space station."

Another messy question, Eclipse thought. "She doesn't have parents. Not now." Eclipse realized Marge and her husband were taking something very oddly. They looked really bothered. "Does 'Heinlein Divorce Act' mean anything to you?" They shook their heads. "It's complicated. Short form. Comet's legally a grownup. The Speaker of the House said so. So am I. Comet agreed to come. That's all that counts. And in our League I'm Athena's Shield and Spear...if someone dies, it's probably me." Six Kosters looked baffled.

"You can't die," Heather said. "You're so wonderful. And you saved my mom!"

"The world somehow changed a lot," Eclipse said. "The Wizard only said we might die, some of us. Mayhaps I shouldn't have told you about Comet and me. But, Marge, you said your children had to go to bed early, because they had school tomorrow. And it's not very early now. Let me give you a last couple-three memories. Then I should be going."

"Please stay!" Heather asked. Eclipse shook her head.

The memories. Yes, this is telepathy. If you don't like it, just imagine you're stepping back. But that's the Clarke Spire. It's a skyhook. An elevator to space. [Image of a building reaching up through the sky off toward infinity.] And that's the surface of Pluto. [Image of near-darkness with jagged hills.] These are the Mercury ruins. No one understands them. [Image of cyclopean blocks cut in unnatural angles.] And these images are the sun. Three million miles out. [A wall of incandescence.] In the middle of a sunspot. [Walls of flame on all sides.] The starcore, temperature ten million kelvins. [Outside her force field was a uniform bright white.]

"You flew into the Sun?" Peter whispered in amazement.

Not fun. Had to do it, Eclipse answered.

"Could we get some photos?" James asked. "At least you and Mom. You saved her life."

"I'll get the camera," Peter announced. A few minutes generated a dozen photographs.

"Can't stay longer." Eclipse clasped Heather on the shoulder. "But I might come back."

"Eclipse! Wait!" Adrian said. "If everyone is gone, your parents are gone. Where are you going?"

"For me, there's no problem." Eclipse stood up and faded into cerulean haze, the tinkling of tiny bells surrounding her.

"Ady," Marge Koster said to her husband, "There was something very strange about her last answer." Adrian nodded.

"What's a lithium bomb?" James asked.

"That's how you build a hydrogen bomb," his older brother answered. "They actually use lithium, not hydrogen."

"Lithium deuteride," Marge corrected. She wonder if Eclipse had been exaggerating about her superpowers...gifts, as she called them. Why would anyone drop a hydrogen bomb on such a nice little girl? And how could anything survive flying to the center of a star?

"I have a riddle for the four of you," Adrian announced. "And then it's off to bed. For once, leave your game set up. And the riddle is: How old is Eclipse?" Four children looked at each other.

"Fifteen," Peter said. "She's my height. And studying trig."

"Older than me," Heather said. "She sounds older. So, thirteen?"

James whispered to Rebecca. "Looked like you, two years ago?" he asked. She nodded. "She's real tall. Except for that, she looks like eleven."

"Could be older if she's a jock," Rebecca added. "Just before she came in, the wind plastered her clothing—she has to have been freezing out there—against her arms and legs. Her arms weren't pipe stem thin, not at all, and she wasn't fat."

"She sounded older," Peter said. "But I take fifteen back. Way tall, but she looks your age, Heather, but, come on, eleven-year-olds don't get to study trig."

"Thanks for expert opinions," Adrian said. "Time for bed. All upstairs."

CHAPTER 9 COMET LOOKS FOR HOME

Eclipse returned to the camp site. The adjoining hills shrouded the woods in deep shadow. A stiff breeze moaned and groaned as it shook the tops of nearby trees. Aurora, perched on her tree stump, stared at a portable chessboard. "How can he possibly think this works?" she grumbled to herself. "He just assumes people make stupid choices on their moves."

"Aurora?" Eclipse said, "Still looking at chess positions?"

"Still looking at the same article, the Sarnath opening," Aurora answered. "The guy who wrote it is a complete nut. But I'm getting reminded of all the ways the opening is bad, and how to exploit them."

"Where's Comet?" Eclipse asked.

"Coming back from Mars," Aurora said. "Taking her time, going way slower than light. She's unhappy about something, wanted to be by herself. She didn't want to talk. You were gone a while."

"The Kosters were nice people. They invited me in. We talked," Eclipse said. "I think I solved our money problem, short-term. We find out day after tomorrow, early."

"Money problem?" Aurora looked up in surprise. "Didn't you bring any?"

"I brought plenty. But...everything changed? So did money." Eclipse wished Aurora would give a bit more thought to their mission. "I have a stack of Great Thalers....Austria-Hungary isn't even a country at the moment. Silver cartwheels—they don't use big metal coins. And American paper money...it's now some green color, not like real money, not at all."

"Strange." Aurora looked back at her chess board. "Wait!" she suddenly said. "If they use different money, how can I buy chess magazines?" She paused. "No! How do we even pay for food?"

"That's a bit of a problem." Eclipse looked gratefully skyward. Aurora had finally started paying a little attention to the world around her. "Is Comet getting here soon? We need to talk."

"She'll be here in an hour," Aurora said. "She wants to think. Oh, she noticed I was keeping track of her, just now, and asked me to say 'hi!' to you. She wants to talk to you. She wants that a lot. She's really unhappy about something. I didn't pry into her mind. I could hear the tone in her thoughts."

"Good," Eclipse said. "I can take a nap." She unfolded her ground tarp, rolled up in her blanket and slumped down onto the pine needles.. "I'd get out my hammock, but I'm too tired. Later."

"Eclipse," Aurora asked. "Are you sure you're recovered? You look pale."

"I need a couple weeks to recover," Eclipse said. "At least. Though, as the line goes, 'you should've seen the other guy'."

"Can I help?" a concerned Aurora asked. "Comet and I can do healing."

"It's not that sort of damage," Eclipse said. "It's very kind that you offer. I saw what that takes out of you. No, this is something where I just need sleep." She leaned back and closed her eyes.

It was almost dark when a puff of wind blew leaves across the ground. That was Comet, Aurora thought, being invisible. Comet appeared out of nowhere, a few feet off the ground, and settled gently to earth.

"Eclipse?" Aurora said quietly. "Wake up!"

"Oh, right," Eclipse mumbled groggily. She managed a deep yawn.

"Eclipse!" Comet said. "We've got to talk." She limped towards the other two girls.

"Hi, Comet. What's wrong with your foot?" Eclipse asked.

"Just an ankle sprain," Comet answered. "I landed a bit hard when I reached Mars."

"Star and I can fix that," Aurora said.

"I'm supposed to walk it off," Comet answered. "That's what my gifts tell me. Walk it off and all will be well." She sat down on a large log.

"What did you find?" Eclipse asked.

"I flew to Mars. I was going to ask the Wizard how his promise could be true," Comet said. Eclipse momentarily considered fleeing for her life, not that it was likely to do any good. She was dealing with someone who had asked the Wizard a question. She might get a due bill, no matter she hadn't asked anything herself. "He wasn't there. The Temple of the Wizard is gone. It's just this huge mound of rock, roughly the right shape."

"What!" Aurora shouted.

"Fits in with everything else," Eclipse said. "Something happened while we were away. Something odd. I think time was reset."

"Start at the beginning? You know how tiffed you get if I start in midstream, which I should really know better than to do, it being like starting a plane geometry proof in the middle? Well, I can be there, too. What's resetting time?" Comet asked.

"You're right. I should know better. I think a beginning was the astronauts. I visited Marge Koster and her family. They don't have any hint who we are," Eclipse answered.

"Hey, great! That's a problem? I mean, if they caught us without dominos, they could connect our faces to our private personas, though I suppose that's not so much trouble for you, everyone in the whole world already knowing exactly what you look like."

"You don't understand. No. My fault! I'm not clear," Eclipse apologized. "The astronauts in the space station didn't know you? Fine. They didn't know me! And I'm a bit more notorious. After all, I'm wanted by the League of Nations, the War Crimes Court, not to mention more countries than I care to count. I don't mean they don't know who you are. They don't know what you are."

"Huh?" Comet asked.

"We are not home," Eclipse announced. "Everything is different. Completely different. New countries around the world. The Aztecs are a bunch of little countries. And they're mostly friends with us. Our money is not their money...their silver certificates are bright green. The Kosters were sure. No past civilization had electricity, let alone antigravity or faster than light spaceships. There are no personae."

"This is a time reset?" Comet asked.

"There are no public personae any more. None!" Eclipse explained.

"Huh?" Comet gaped, open-mouthed.

"The Kosters have never heard of personae," Eclipse explained. "Marge Koster is a real scientist with patents and secrecy passes. There's video coverage of her stranded spaceship. It's pretty feeble. It barely gets to orbit. It's the only type they have. There's no hint you could fly and carry it down. They all agree. Personae never existed. Historians never heard of Solara or the Screaming Skull. I looked at their world map! Europe and Asia have countries missing. The borders are all squeezed together. According to her maps, east Asia is one country! Austria-Hungary is split in a dozen pieces."

"Koster is perhaps a bit scrambled? You looked at her mind. Could Aurora fix her?" Comet said. "But why would someone scrambled get to ride in a space plane?"

"I can try," Aurora said. "If I know what's wrong."

"Ummh, the problem's a little bigger than her. I looked farther away: Los Angeles, Chicago, New York. I didn't have the nerve for the Federal District. I don't want to meet FedCorps me-on-them. Not me half-dead and them seriously motivated to be sure I resisted arrest so they could kill me. Slowly. But in cities that big, you have decent numbers of people whose screens block ultravision, right? There wasn't one. No one was flying except in airplanes. We don't exist now. Public personae don't exist any more," Eclipse explained.

"We don't exist?" Comet asked.

"I read minds here and there, random people on the street. I didn't find a hint of personae. I tried my home. The foundations were gone." Eclipse looked momentarily forlorn. "Someone reached back in time and changed history, like Einstein's time-travel theory says. You go to the past and change it. When you return to the present you remember the past before you changed it. Everyone else remembers the past after you changed it."

Comet felt deeply confused. "Reached back in time? Not even Solara...well, I didn't think anyone could do that. Can they?"

"It seems someone can," Eclipse answered.

"Read minds of people on the street? No, don't say any more. You'd give my twerp brother something more to whine about, one more reason he wants me not to like you, and he's got too many wrong reasons now. But no one's heard of a persona? That's impossible!" Comet said emphatically.

"That's why you might have problems fixing things, Aurora." Eclipse slumped back against a tree. "Sure. You can heal one person's mind, if you can spot what to fix. I couldn't see anything broken. But fix a whole city, even if you try very hard? Mayhaps when you grow up. You've got a wicked lot of potential. But how do you telehypnotize a Goddess-have-mercy-on-us-all planet so it grows extra countries?"

"It's more than that," Comet added. "Someone changed the moon. A lot."

"How?" Eclipse asked. "I remember it was there when we flew in. It's different?"

"It doesn't have a light side and a dark side any more," Comet answered, "not the way it did before, yes, the sun only lights half of it at a time, but it's not always the same half. Instead, the light side of the moon, what was the light side of the moon, always faces the Earth, so sometimes that side is dark. Here, I'll show you: Pretend that rock is the Sun and this rock is the Earth; it used to be that the moon rotated around the earth but always had the same face toward the sun; the moon still goes around the sun, but it always has the same face toward the earth. Watch how I move." Comet demonstrated the two lunar orbits. "Also, there are no ruins on the dark side of the Moon, at least none that I spotted."

"Stranger and stranger," Eclipse said.

"That's not right, either," Comet remarked, pointing at the sky.

"What?" Aurora asked. "There are stars. Even I can see them."

"Only saw it because the breeze stopped," Comet said. "That way is North. The pole star should line up roughly with that big tree, so we sit here and all night the stars wheel around the pole. Cloud had those neat photos the low-light attachment on his lessoncomp took, stars as bright circles around the pole star. Except, that tree gives me rigid lines of sight, something is wrong with how the stars move."

"What's wrong?" Aurora asked.

"I can't tell. Not quickly," Comet said.

"I'll ask Cloud," Aurora interrupted, "get him to take some more of those pictures. He'll even feel appreciated, me asking him."

"You asking...good idea. Go for it," Comet nodded agreeably.

Aurora was quiet for a while. "OK," she announced, "He says he has a good picture of the stars now, and will run time exposure for a few hours to see what he can see. He's repeating that your eyes are way better than his computer camera."

"Tell him he's right. But I can't see those pretty circles. He can." Comet nodded.

"He agreed. I could tell. He's grateful he's doing something useful."

"This makes no sense." Eclipse yawned deeply. "Or I'm too sleepy to figure out what's going on. I'm so tired I can't sleep; it hurts too much. And a cross-country jaunt? Scans and reading minds? I want to sleep forever. But we're safe here. I think."

"I remember how I felt when I landed; it must be the same, mustn't it, except I didn't really hurt, I just fogged out; I've never done flight like that before, pushed so hard for so long. I had to make myself eat; I just wanted to fall over, too tired to remember to lie down. That was you, wasn't it, scooping me up and wrapping me in a blanket?" Comet asked, knowing Eclipse didn't want to confess to doing even that small a favor. "I figured. But if you feel safe, we're incredibly safe. Go lie down. I have to see what happened."

"I didn't try looking close at the Federal District," Eclipse added. "Someone might recognize me and have a reception waiting. You know, 21-gun-salutes? Just like for the Speaker of the House? Except he gets blanks, and I rate armor-piercing shells?" Eclipse managed a mordant smile.

"That's impossible. Where is everyone?" Comet looked momentarily thoughtful. "Time for a disguise." Her form shimmered. Now she was dressed in girls' blue jeans, floppy robin's egg blue sweater over long-sleeve T-shirt, and proper white sneakers. "I'll be back!" she announced. Her figure faded into a glowing veil of delicately-shaded pastel draperies. Without the least apparent effort, she did a back-flip off her log and accelerated skyward, swiftly vanishing from sight.

"Now what?" Eclipse looked at the empty sky. "Aurora, would you please help me set up my hammock? It's easier if two people set it up. My shoulder is still bothering me from the Maze. The hammock is flat inside, and big enough for two grownups, so we could share until Comet gets back."

"I don't mind sleeping on the ground, if I can borrow your blanket." Aurora smiled. "Comet needs your hammock more than I do."

"I was going to let the two of you use it. I've had practice wilderness camping."

"You're always so generous." Aurora stood. "Let's set it up. But I can't imagine what Mom and Dad thought I'd do for a bed."

~~~~~

A mile above the ground, Comet flew south along the Pacific coast. No such thing as a persona? That was crazy. It couldn't be true. A fast trip to San Francisco, the City of Good Sense, would prove that. It wasn't quite true that the city had more personas than ungifted, but there were enough personas that they were a big voting block, larger than the Szechuanese or the Tibetans. Enough people to be a big voting block should be easy to find, even if twilight was fast fading.

Humboldt Bay and coastal ranges blurred by. The great sweep of San Pablo and San Francisco Bays appeared to her left. Over the hill would be the Golden Gate with its bridge across the narrows. She could remember the first time she'd seen its snow-white columns peeking out of the fog to gleam in the morning light.

Her jaw dropped. For half a dozen seconds she lost all concentration, flight field collapsing virtually to nothing, leaving her body-planing through the air, staying airborne by trading speed for lift. The Marin Temple was gone. Where should have risen the Western Mother Temple, right on the north shore of the Golden Gate, stood instead an assortment of obviously expensive private homes, perched facing the water. And the bridge! What had been done to it? Its marble sheathing, whose detailwork made it a wonder of the modern world, had vanished. Only its steel core, now painted a hideously garish red-orange, remained.

A glance took in the sky from horizon to horizon. There were airplanes. The tightly bunched lights with jerky motion were, quaintness of quaintnesses, vernian aeronefs hanging from single horizontal airfoils. But where were the primaries and gaudy pastels, the shimmering glows marking personas in flight? There were lights on the ground and cars wheeling along freeways. Above them the sky was virtually empty.

She looped around the bridge once and again, then set foot on the upper railing. Using one hand for balance, she could lean over and feel the steel, removing all doubt that it was indeed steel, not marble plates in disguise. Impossible. Impossible! What had been done to San Francisco?

She closed her eyes, trying to push back very real tears. She'd flown them all home, brother and sister and Cloud and Eclipse. She knew she had. She'd flown farther and faster than ever before in her life. This had to be home! The StarCompass said so. What could possible be wrong? It was too much to bear. Comet threw herself off the railing at the waves far below.

The wind set her hair flying. Ocean-chilled air fanned her arms and legs. The surf loomed below, closer and closer. Now she could hear the beat of waves over distant traffic noises, taste the salt spray in the air. So soon, she would hit the water. So very soon.

She called her flight field. Swathed in light, she executed a hairpin turn away from the water and turned east, climbing faster and faster, leaving behind an unsolved mystery. It didn't matter. Soon she would be home. Well, the place that had been her home. So soon. So very soon. There was only a small continent to be crossed, a step needing but minutes to complete. It wasn't her home any more, but Professor Lafayette would explain everything to her.

Boston Harbor. Almost home. Dipping below the clouds, she could see the coastal islands. A soaring of towers marked Republic Square. She zoomed along the Carolus Fluvius, a thousand feet above its broad still waters, her eyes focused on the floodlit limestone walls of Rogers Technological Institution. Almost there. Almost home.

Sleep-fogged thoughts at first refused to recognize the anomaly. Right between the old dorms and the new chemistry buildings, there rose two dozen stories of tesdrome topped skyscraper. Impossible. She'd played tossdisc there with her dad's grad students last summer. Now half the playing field was filled by this hulking, green-shaded, old-looking slab of a windowless—well, side face windowless—building. She soared the height of the building, saw the windows on its front face, dropped to half its height off the ground, then killed speed, floating to touch its concrete and peer through a lighted window.

Within, a bearded figure in shaggy wool sweater, sipping from a cup of coffee, glanced up from a terminal. Two pairs of eyes met, separated by an inch of glass set firmly in poured concrete. The figure dashed to the window, hands pressing against the glass. Comet instinctively flinched, drifting a few feet back from the building. The figure took in her location, her apparent lack of support, and her age. Coffee cup dropped onto a radiator. Fingers tapped on a Bell extension. Unwilling to wait, Comet fluttered west across the campus, dodging chimney stacks and library dome, pausing once and again to sample the view, in the end coming to a hover at the main entrance.

What was wrong? What had happened? Except for the skyscraper where none should have been, everything was familiar. This was almost home. No, not quite. Above the main entrance, in letters nearly her own height, was the school's name. The letters, to judge from weathering, accumulation of grime, and pigeons nesting in one cornice, had been standing for decades over graceful Ionian columns. Letters that last week proudly identified her father's employer as Rogers' Technological Institution Founded 1862 now referred to

MASSACHVSETTS INSTITVTE OF TECHNOLOGY
WILLIAM BARTON ROGERS FOVNDER.

Too stunned to speak, Comet pushed off from the columns and drifted slowly across the street.

"Hey!" voices called up from the ground. "Incredibly neat hack! How do you do it?" "I want it. I want it for my next Assassin game." She glanced streetward. A few moments had attracted a small crowd of goggle-eyed students. Hands waved. A minicam hummed. She put hands to face, confirming she had remembered to wear her domino.

Baffled by the words, Comet waved back. Nothing made sense. She couldn't wait any longer. She was almost home. Soon it would be over, at least for her. Soon it would be over, even if she could only look in from the dark at her parents before fetching the rest of the gang. Soon it would be over, her three friends returned safely home, if not four minutes later as the Wizard had promised. What happened to her afterward was less important. She was responsible for bringing Star and Aurora home, so she would. Comet accelerated diagonally upward, north along Massachusetts Avenue, supersonic before she reached the Piazza Leprecano, flight field damped to stealth mode black as she bent gently west to Arlington and home.

Behind her, an irate geophysicist, three Campus Policemen, and an Assistant Dean confronted the President of the Tech Hackers Association. "Can you explain why someone roped a child off the top of the building?" the geophysicist asked. "It's not funny, the way it was funny when my classmates floodlit the Great Dome bright orange, back when HoJo became President."

"That is precisely my point," the Dean continued. "It's not amusing, and your friends risked someone's life to do it."

"Hey, we didn't do this," the student countered. "No way. Did your office get a notice? No! Did the Campus Police get the schedule in advance, like they do for tuition riots? No! Did the TV station get notified to cover it? No! This wasn't us, it was someone else, someone less than marginally clueless. What if the turkeys on the roof had tried to lower the kid to the ground, and found their hoist was gronked? I mean, back in '65 when someone rappelled down a dorm wall, there was a good reason. She had a reaction going in organic lab, and the only panty raid of all time was in her way. But she was a mountaineer, and knew what she was doing. This hack was just dumb."

The Campus Policemen looked at each other, eyebrows rising. One of them tilted his head, listening to a helmet radio. "We have another sighting. Outside the Building 7 Entrance. Airborne. Next to the Lesser Dome. Keep in touch?" He pointed at the student. Campus Police and Assistant Dean headed out the door.

"I told you it wasn't us." The student looked at the Professor. "I've got an exam Monday, and need to do some serious tooling. Wait. Did she look like one of the kids who rescued the Space Plane?"

"It was a well executed hack, ignoring that the concept was totally wedged beyond belief. Even up against the glass, even with all the lights she was wearing, I couldn't see the wires. It really looked like she was flying. But she wasn't wearing superhero spandex and a cape, so, no, she looked different." The Professor returned to his terminal.

~~~~~

Arlington. So close to home. So close to certainty. Comet dipped over side streets, dodging misremembered tall trees. There was the gentle triple bend of her street, a six-point intersection anchoring its northern end. There was home. Well, she thought, there was the right house. Assuming it had been repainted in the last three days. Assuming the house next door had grown a twenty-foot-deep extension overnight. But her treehouse was gone. The cars in the driveway were wrong. Someone was coming in her front door, a strange man in a strange suit, blue and two-piece, someone who turned to kiss a very young woman and hug a pair of three-year-old children.

So close to home. Comet folded her flight field around her, tighter and tighter. Against the night sky she was not so much as hazy black crepe. So close to home. Slowly, silently, she floated from the street, finally drifting down to look in through the windows of her rooms. So very close to home.

An instant of horrified emptiness. Her bed was gone. Her desk was gone. Furniture, toys, posters, her half-read carefully annotated Fundamentals of Trigonometry...all gone. All replaced. The tower was a sewing room, clothes matching the two little ones she had seen below with their parents.

Float to sister's game room. Look for well-known furniture, stacks of old magazines, playing boards, postal chess and stones games frozen in mid-play—first tournament prize framed on wall. Not there. See stacks of books, magazines, work in neat piles on desk. Books on—Theory of Torts? Principles of Constitutional Construction? Pictures on walls. Class photos, diplomas. The woman she'd seen downstairs, a name she'd never heard before—this room was the woman's law library.

Comet shuddered. This was her house, but her former home was not to be found.

Burst skywards, throat stifling a scream from the deepest heart. Roll over to west and south, masking path of departure. Accelerate southward hard, flight field bursting to bright flame, finally able to voice shrieks of denial.

~~~~~

Above every cloud, higher than the sky itself, the night was brilliantly clear, stars flaring like magnesium torches. North of Baltimore, Comet dropped out of the ionosphere, her flight field glowing brilliantly, trailing the fluorescent wake from which she took her name. Enhanced vision, her flight field trapping incident photons and passing them to her eyes, gave her a view as clear as full daylight. She banked eastward, her path taking her over Annapolis and down the Chesapeake. A tighter turn sent her northwest to follow the river she recognized as the Aquea Potomaciea, with the Federal District close beyond.

As she closed on Washington, she began to worry. FedCorps—the Federal Volunteer Persona Corps—was sensitive about unidentified personas flying near the Capital. She knew the drill. There was a specified approach, a specified range of very low altitudes and slow speeds which let one or another Corpsman mindtouch anyone entering the district, so FedCorps had plenty of time to react or to confirm visitors as friendly. Soon everything would be all right. FedCorps knew who she was, at least in persona, however uncomfortable they might be about someone her age doing a public persona. Soon she would be safe with them. They'd tell her what happened. Just be careful, she reminded herself, not to tell them you're with Eclipse. They might not take that too kindly, given how many Corpsmen had died over the millennia, trying to thread the Maze.

Half a continent away, under miles of granite, the headquarters of American air defenses tracked the unknown. Whatever it was, it had appeared forty miles above central New England, speeding southwest along the coast at more than four thousand knots. Multiple types of radar confirmed position, altitude, and speed. The target was electromagnetically quiet, with no hint of radar or radio emissions. A transport aircraft contacted by ground reported being passed by a faint tailed star. "Looks to be a meteor, but just keeps on going, no sign of burning out..."

Coded warnings were dispatched from higher headquarters. Missile tracking centers reported no other targets, no missile launches by unfriendly nations. Operational orders prescribed precautionary alerts along the Eastern seaboard. In New Jersey and Maryland, interceptor aircraft were hastily scrambled. At Baltimore the target began a descent, simultaneously swinging out to sea. Satellite communications, after several decades fully integrated with reports of unit status and disposition, retrieved radar data from warships in Chesapeake Bay. Computer searches confirmed what specialists and non-commissioned officers with thirty years experience had already stated: The target's flight, radar, and infrared characteristics bore no semblance to any known aircraft. The target, now down to thirty miles altitude and 2500 knots, was heading slightly east of south, away from sensitive military and political targets in the District of Columbia.

At the mouth of the Potomac, the unknown executed a sharp turn, almost reversing direction to head west of north, moving along the Potomac basin directly at the nation's capital. Its acceleration exceeded 1100 meters per second per second: one hundred ten gravities, far sharper than possible even to an unmanned missile. Simultaneously, the target showed a drastic loss of altitude and speed. Trajectory computations suddenly predicted that the unknown would come to earth near Washington. Aircraft at full afterburner screamed to intercept. Across the Capitol, men and women struggled to ready the city's minimal point air defenses, historically optimized to protect buildings from terrorists flying low, slow private planes.

The target dropped lower and lower, slowed to subsonic, then disappeared into ground clutter many miles short of Washington, out of sight of the city's recently-deployed Patriot-X surface-to-air missile batteries. For minutes, nothing more was reported. Then the target reappeared. Airliners approaching Reagan National Airport reported being passed by a glowing salmon-orange sphere with glittering tail.

Comet flew south of the Potomac, puzzled by the silence in her mind. She had done this flight before, more than once, the first time with considerable trepidation, other times with more self-confidence. Where was the voice without a sound, the gentle greeting that marked recognition by the Federals? Where were the Washington defenses? Even if it wasn't energized, she should have been able to see the force dome over the City of Washington.

She crossed the last stretch of water, the Washington Monument looming before her. Was everything going to be strange again? It couldn't. Not here. She'd pass the Solara Monument, overfly the Capitol Building, and there would be her friends at the FedCorps Headquarters.

On the ground, consternation reigned. An unknown object, ignoring all radio warnings, was approaching the Washington Air Forbidden Zones. Secret Service detachments armed with Smiter-Z antiaircraft missiles moved to open ground. Marines manned certain inconspicuous rooftop structures. In a secret underground facility adjoining Union Station, technicians scrambled to top off condenser banks and enable launch controllers. To those on the ground, the unknown target was closing on the White House. On rooftop after rooftop, firing crews struggled to persuade infra-red homing weapons to lock on a plainly visible target.

Comet, barely at treetop height, stopped in astonishment. Her reflexes were still hypered, tied to her flight speed; to her senses, seconds passed like minutes. Pedestrians appeared frozen in mid-stride. What seemed to those on the ground to be the slightest hesitation allowed her minutes of thought. There was the Ellipse, but where was the Solara Monument? Where was the eternal flame burning over golden sun-disc in a tribute now fifteen centuries old? On its site was a white stone building, fenced and gardened, in a style that could have escaped from the Crittenden War. What was it? Where was the Monument? No one would tamper with that! Well, Eclipse might; she seemed willing to dare almost anything.

In the Pentagon, the Ready Officer noted in his log that at 0031 hours an unknown object had entered the White House Air Forbidden Zone and been engaged by defensive fire. As he wrote, jets of flame marked antiaircraft rockets beginning uncertain climbs toward their prey. Point defense antiaircraft guns, some radar aimed, others hand sighted by their crews, opened up in a deadly hail of explosive and armor-piercing rounds. Breakaway plastic plates, painted as ventilator shafts, crashed to nothingness under the impact of emerging 20mm shells.

To Comet's eyes, missiles floated slowly from launch tubes. Anti-aircraft shells, glowing brilliantly in the infrared, drifted from weapons mounts. For critical moments she froze in surprise, not understanding what she faced. All these weapons, she finally recognized, are targeted at me. What did I do? What did I do? Why are they all trying to kill me? Even with enhanced reflexes, her mind moving at near-computer speed, the first rounds were almost to her before her flight field engaged. She sideslipped, swift glances taking in each shell's position. For most, she had enough time to dodge. A few were impossible to avoid. A side-palm swat, her flight field a web between her and the hot metal, deflected those the needed inches to safety, sending sparks of incandescent lead plasma scattering in all directions. Infrared homing missiles, initially baffled by the lack of a target, locked on a cloud of plasmized lead.

The Magnetically Augmented Vehicle Interceptor, Sabot-Based (MAVIS-B) represented one of several possible compromises between conventional and rail-gun technologies. Its munition was the hittile, a non-explosive smart munition descended from SDIO technology. A short-barreled 120mm cannon fired discarding-sabot hittiles in the general direction of its target, digitally-controlled electromagnetic drivers providing boost and guidance. The nose of the hittile was transparent sapphire, behind which lurked optical imagers and a neural network targeting system. Once beyond the rail gun, fin stabilizers deployed; piezoelectrically-driven tab drag points provided terminal guidance. With an effective muzzle velocity of more than 4000 meters per second, MAVIS-B's depleted uranium hittiles could strike and penetrate any known airborne target, including aircraft too maneuverable or armored to damage with conventional projectile munitions. A crump of burning propellant and whine of discharging condenser banks signaled the dispatch of a half-dozen hypervelocity projectiles at Comet's unprotected stomach and back.

Almost too late, Comet noticed glowing cylinders of white-hot metal sliding rapidly through the air. Accustomed to a world in which bullets and missiles crawled, she suddenly had to pivot, turn, and dodge objects as fast as she. She almost succeeded. A single hittile crashed against her flight field and ripped across her back. There was a crunch of breaking bone. Vaporized metal sprayed across the sky, the recoil driving her into a sudden uncontrolled spin.

Her trajectory dipped groundward. She struggled to regain control of her flight and stay above the line of fire of the anti-aircraft cannon. The crews could repoint their weapons, but that would take time, time that they had not yet had. She pulled out and up, a half-dozen Smiter missiles closing rapidly on her. She had not been a good target, but the glow of volatilized uranium gave a sharp infrared source. Terrified, Comet's flight became a wobbling erratic climb. The missiles surged closer, then fell away, unable to match her panic-driven skybound thrust.

Several thousand feet in the air, her presence of mind returned. Her flight field infolded. She faded into invisibility. To ground-based observers she simply vanished, denying hastily-readied Patriot-X batteries a parting shot at a fleeing target.

Pain caught her. The shell's impact had been almost parallel with her skin, skimming along the surface of her flight field. The field was not a true defense; it wouldn't stop even a low-caliber bullet that hit square on. Her last-microsecond pivot had prevented fatal damage, but the shell's brush across her back had been enough to flay her back and crack a shoulder blade. Her thoughts collapsed on themselves, leaving her with an awareness of excruciating agony.

Moments ticked away. Across a continent, Aurora gasped to full awareness, flung by dreams from a sound sleep. "Comet?" she called softly, knowing something was terribly wrong with her sister. More loudly: "Comet?" There was no answer.

CHAPTER 10 ECLIPSE TO THE RESCUE

Aurora rolled out of the hammock. Eclipse stirred slightly, then drifted back into her dreams. Where was she? Aurora asked herself, memories not yet coming to the surface. No time for that! Where was Comet now? There was Comet's garb, neatly folded on top of her duffel bag. A spiraling shadow fogged the air around Aurora's head. She had heard the cry for help, but where was Comet? Where? She always knew, deep inside, where her siblings were. Where? There! There was Comet, across the continent, soaring skywards.

Comet? What's wrong? The telepathic call found its familiar match. Aurora's thoughts interwove lovingly with her sister's.

They're crazy. All crazy. All the world. Hurts. I hurt. Comet's thoughts fluttered to the edge of unconsciousness. *Have to keep...going. Want darkness.*

 Comet!* Aurora's thoughts were a paroxysm of terror. * Comet!*

Rising from dreams laced with wheat stalks and rolling fields of blooming blanket flowers, Eclipse dragged herself awake. "What?" she whispered. She forced herself to think. Had someone shouted someplace? No, she didn't have a ghost of a memory of hearing something. Aurora? Was it Aurora? *?* a mental probe, slightly stronger, drifted across the field.

Comet! What HAPPENED to you? Aurora was at the edge of panic. *WHO'S crazy? WHAT HAPPENED TO YOU?...Who's there?*

Aurora? Eclipse. Why are you shouting? The older girl's thoughts were completely tranquil.

It's Comet. She's hurt, and flying, and passing out. And she's THERE! [Images of Washington. Comet, one arm hanging limply, streaking higher and higher.] *We can't help her. She's too far. You can't fly there IN TIME. We can't do ANYTHING. I DON'T WANT HER TO DIE. WE CAN'T do anything!*

Aurora? Calm down. Eclipse cringed at the thought of another rescue. If she had been alone, she could have slept off her exhaustion, exhaustion so total she hadn't felt Comet's null link triggering. Linking with Aurora and friends meant that she had to perform at their call. What had Comet done? Joining the company of Aurora and siblings seemed to have made her perpetually responsible for saving them. Eclipse told herself she was being unfair. If she had been by herself at the Tunnels, she would have had to do the same things. Duty, heavier than worlds, weighted on her. However much she craved sleep, she had to come to Comet's aid. She gently chided herself for considering the words she had

not quite used to describe the situation. Aurora was touching the fringes
of her mind, and Aurora really did not need her vocabulary broadened,
not in those directions.

We CAN'T do ANYTHING. And she's DYING! Aurora screamed.

Please! Calm yourself! Eclipse ordered. Aurora ignored Eclipse's
rational inner voice. *Put your body field up!* Eclipse felt a tension in
the air as Aurora's gifts locked breathable air around her.

A shimmer of blue-violet light, the delicate ring of distant wind-
chimes. Eclipse, dressed in her frilly, long-sleeved, close-necked
nightgown, now stood at Aurora's side. "Calm down," Eclipse
demanded. "Calm down! I'll save Comet. You've got to help. Where is
she?"

Eclipse let Aurora pass images to her, images showing places a
continent away. Comet was above the atmosphere, madly climbing away
from the city Eclipse dreaded. Eclipse tried to target Comet's geodesic,
found it bending away faster than she could adjust her aim. Goddess-be-
praised, thought Eclipse, Comet's pulling a hundred fifty gees, not
counting the jinks. I'm supposed to target that? "Can she hear you?
Aurora, listen to me! Can Comet hear you?"

*Eclipse, where'd you come from? Comet? Of course she hears me.
We're sisters,* the younger girl answered.

Eclipse swallowed slightly. Aurora was so completely panicked that
she hadn't noticed the flare of a teleport, even when Eclipse appeared
half an arm's length away. "Tell Comet to coast. Relax and coast. I need
to lock on her. I can't if she keeps boosting." If Comet doesn't listen,
Eclipse thought, mayhaps I can push something firmer through Aurora;
that sure doesn't leave me much reserve for a rescue. Not to mention
what I'll do to Aurora. To Eclipse's delight, Comet eased away from
headlong flight.

A moment's calculation. An infalling violet glow lit the surrounding
trees. A cascade of calling bells rang unheard. Two figures vanished
from the campground, reappearing far above Maryland, tens of yards
from Comet, velocities matched. Stars swam before Eclipse's eyes. She
shook her head, clearing a dazed gloss from her vision.

Comet! shouted Aurora.

Aurora? Comet answered, letting foggy thoughts be intercepted.

I'm here, sister. Three bodies touched. Comet swayed out of
consciousness. Eclipse clutched the sisters' waists, holding the three of
them together, her body field shielding them from the vacuum of outer
space.

Too high to speak. Too little air for sound. *Aurora?* Eclipse joined
the sisters' mind-to-mind link. *Is Comet out cold? I'll get us back. But

she mustn't start flying again. *

**She's asleep... No, I CAN'T HEAR HER. Her DREAMING mind
SHUT OFF! I think SHE'S DYING! She ISN'T even DREAMING! ShE
IsN't ThInKiNg AbOuT BrEaThInG! WhErE ArE wE?** Aurora's terror
interlaced her thoughts *Where's my hammock? Your hammock? How'd
we get here?* the twelve-year-old demanded.

I, oh, I teleported us. Eclipse responded. Aurora, she thought, was
so panicked she hadn't noticed anything around her. Eclipse took another
moment of calculation, this time targeting a deliberately memorized
point in the clearing. A violet flare folded in on itself, chimes echoing
triumphantly into the starry void. Three figures materialized two feet
above the ground and fluttered to earth.

She's dying. SHE'S DYING! We've GOT to DO SOMEtHiNg! *
Aurora screamed into Eclipse's mind.

"Aurora? Aurora! Stop being a baby!" Do I have to do everything?
Eclipse asked herself. "You three heal each other! Don't just stand there
squawking, heal her!" To Eclipse's eye, Comet was seriously injured,
arm broken, third degree burns and blisters across her back, but dying?
Not likely. Not unless there was a lot wrong internally. Eclipse reached
out with her healing gift. Medico's glyphs flashed blue-green. Comet
was hurt, but nothing was critically wrong. The Wells children did a far
better job of healing each other than she could, so they should take care
of each other.

*I can't! I can't by myself. It has to be two of us. I need a power base.
Star's asleep across the pond. It's TOO LATE.* Aurora squeezed back
tears.

"Aurora. Aurora!" Eclipse, a semi-conscious Comet draped over her
left shoulder, grabbed the younger girl by her T-shirt, hoisting her one-
handed almost off her feet. "Cut that out!" Eclipse shouted. Then she
blinked, hard, lines of trees swimming around her. "I did this before. I
did it with Comet. We healed you. Remember? After you stopped the
Emperor Roxbury? We healed you. Use me as base. Just heal her. Do it
now!" Do it, thought Eclipse, before I fall flat on my face.

But I could hurt you. If I draw too deep, I could... a frightened
Aurora protested.

"You? Draw too deep from me? Don't be silly. I worry about myself,
you don't! OK? I'll just get dizzy." Inwardly, Eclipse recited the steps of
mastery, the link to the infinite deeps. She felt lines etch along her bones.
Someplace not reached by normal vision, she saw a golden eye masked
under black veils, the physical realization of Aurora's seal. Comet's
burns disappeared, flesh returning to a healthy tan. Her shoulder lost its
odd bend. Comet flashed back to energetic awareness.

"Comet?" Aurora whispered.

"Aurora? Sister? What happened?" They hugged each other gleefully, their joy shared through Aurora's mind-link. Eclipse sagged bonelessly to the ground, her last threads of consciousness contemplating the stars above, while the sharp smell of fresh-crushed pine needles came pungently to her nostrils. After what seemed to her like minutes, two small pairs of hands rolled her entirely onto her back. She stared blearily into the starry void, wishing she could close her eyes and sleep, though reason said she had responsibilities to perform.

"What happened?" Comet's voice came. "What did she do?" Comet peered around the clearing. "How did we get here?"

Comet? Don't you remember? Eclipse came for you "Eclipse? Are you all right?" Aurora asked.

"Me?" Eclipse answered wanly. "Sure. Just looking at the sky." She paused. "I did things a little fast. Wore me down. A trifle. Dragging you both here was a bit much. What did you do, Comet? You were completely wrecked up."

"They shot me," Comet answered. "They shot at me, and I couldn't dodge them all, and there was something so fast I couldn't get out of its way, not when I'd never seen one before, and now I'm okay, and you fell over and lay there, well, your eyes were still open, but you looked as limp as an overcooked asparagus."

"A little more slowly. Please? Where did you go? Someplace that has guards?" Eclipse was now very confused.

"F. D. Washington, F. D. Maryland. Oh, right." Comet turned to Eclipse. "I need something decent to wear; this top is a total wreck. and my other clothing is way at the bottom of my bag."

"I've got another nightgown," Eclipse answered. "It's the way-too-large one I was sent by mistake. We'll have to pin it at the neck. Where did you go?"

"I went to San Francisco," Comet said, "and someone stripped the marble off the Golden Gate Bridge and painted it icky orange, and I went to Boston and someone renamed the Rogers Institution, and I," she failed to force back tears, "I went home and it wasn't there."

Aurora went almost white. "No Rogers Institution?" Her interruption let her miss the reference to home.

"It got renamed, since three days ago," Comet continued. "And I went to Washington and the force dome was gone and the Solara Monument was gone and the FedCorps Tower was gone and they all started shooting at me—they didn't ask questions, they just started shooting with guns and rockets and weird things so fast you could hardly see them fly, and then it hurt, so I ran away. It hurt." Now crying helplessly, she leaned against Aurora. "It hurt. They wanted to kill me." Eclipse climbed shakily to her feet and held them both. They pressed heads together, falls of black, copper-red, and frost-white hair almost entangled.

"They shot you?" Aurora repeated.

"They shot at me," Comet gasped. "They shot me. No warning. No one touched my mind. No one asked who I was. There were just guns and rockets."

"Absolutely everything has changed," Eclipse said. "They had no idea who you were. They know who Comet is, but only from her garb, which you weren't wearing. Just as well. It would have been as wrecked up as your sweater. For some reason, you scared them. Scared people do dumb things."

"Eclipse, I should've taken you with me," Comet said. "Then I'd've been safe. But I brought an extra set of garb. And that was my old outdoor chore sweater, not something precious."

"You're safe," Eclipse said. "Thanks to Aurora. Yes, I helped a bit. And tomorrow, no, not tomorrow, that's Saturday, we have to wait until Monday, the two of us go to London, and turn my money into real money."

"Money is different?" Comet asked.

Eclipse nodded. "Talk in the morning? I'm real sleepy. And you're about to be sleepy. All that healing does that to you."

"I feel fine," Comet countered. Her eyes fluttered. Aurora and Eclipse grabbed her as she folded toward the ground.

"Aurora," Eclipse said, "I caught her in my flight field. Can you line up the lower blanket in the hammock?" Eclipse picked up the older but now weightless girl. "OK, and take her shoes off? In we go. You're next. Yes, she'll feel much safer if it's you next to her." Aurora shook her head, then shrugged and did as she was asked.

"Eclipse," Aurora said, "your hammock is big enough for two big grownups. That's three of us, and you're about to have chills again. Just shake the pine needles out of your nightgown and join us." Eclipse did as she was told.

~~~~~

It was the still of the night. An onshore breeze had brought clouds and cold air damp with the promise of rain.

? A wordless interrogatory stroked Eclipse's consciousness.

Ummh? she answered.

You're awake? My ? wasn't loud enough to wake you up? Was it? Aurora, having intruded, suddenly turned shy.

Me? Eclipse responded. *I was awake. Be a while before I sleep. Your probe was very well done. Wouldn't wake someone. Just be heard if I were awake. Mayhaps trigger good wards.* The compliment came with the feel of muscles tensing: a warm, approving smile. Behind the smile lurked the source of Eclipse's insomnia: dull aches in arms and legs, sharp pains that came and went without pattern, a splitting headache, overwhelming exhaustion.

Eclipse? Are you OK? Aurora pulled, not gently, at Eclipse's self-perception, sampling what the older girl felt. *You're not. You're as bad off as Comet was. Worse, even. She hurt her back. You hurt all over. Why didn't you say?*

Me? Say something? About what? A grey shadow cloaked Eclipse's mind, shielding Aurora from what passed there.

But you feel awful. You were hurt in the Tunnels, weren't you? And again when you saved Comet. I know what you did. Aurora's tone was the well-brought-up little girl who suddenly notices that a friend is seriously ill.

This? Promise not to tell? Eclipse caught a kinesthetic message, Aurora nodding agreement. *I get this way when I call gifts deeply. This came from grabbing Comet at, Goddess help me, must have been a hundred miles a second she was doing, and five thousand miles up. And bringing us all back here. At dead stop. In one jump. And me barely awake.*

You did that? For Comet? When you knew how you'd feel after? Aurora's words came with a feeling of very deep yet puzzled gratitude.

The way I feel? It doesn't signify. It's not like I truly hurt myself. Not permanently. I'll be OK tomorrow, Eclipse answered, grateful she'd never had to be honest while talking mind-to-mind. 'Next week' was more likely than 'tomorrow.' *And I still have to do for Comet what I did last time. So she doesn't get nightmares.* If I'd stayed by myself, Eclipse thought, I'd've been far more cautious about calling my gifts. Promising to join this expedition keeps requiring me to push painfully deep. *I couldn't let Comet die. She wasn't that badly wrecked up. Hurting, scared, more than dying. Don't worry. This isn't killing me. It only spoils my sleep. This isn't bad like the Maze! And I walked out of that. Smiling.*

Eclipse, resigned to the price for tapping her limits, pulled her blanket over her head. *Aurora, dear, it's very, very late? Why don't you sleep? You don't have to stay awake, just because I am. Whatever got Comet so upset, it'll be easier in the morning. Now follow the dream clouds...* Eclipse morphed her voice to images of sunlit grain fields, dust-yellow frozen waves whose fragments were marigolds bobbing in a gentle breeze.

Late. And I'm Aurora's thoughts cut sharply off as she followed Eclipse's lure into deep sleep.

Comet dreamed of deep space, the sky in every direction spangled with stars. Here it was so quiet, so safe. Now Eclipse was at her side. She'd always been there, hadn't she? *Comet?* Eclipse was inside her dream, but they were talking, as if they were awake. *Do you remember what I did for you, when the Aztecs jumped the three of you? And later that fellow slugged you?*

How can I forget? I still remember everything, but I don't get upset about it. But I keep remembering how terrible it was just now.

May I do it for you again? Please? Eclipse asked. *Divorce? Getting shot? You don't need that on your shoulders, not when we're trying to save the world.*

Yes. Will I forget things? Comet asked.

You don't lose memories. If I do that to someone, their mind falls apart. Eclipse tried to sound confident. The rules engine for this was very clear on how to help Comet. *But you won't keep thinking about them. And you won't be angry or afraid, so you can rest.*

Please?

OK. Think of falling into darkness, falling sound asleep. I'll do the rest, Eclipse promised. Comet drifted into darkness. Eclipse finished her task and followed Comet into deep sleep.

CHAPTER 11 USING THE STAR COMPASS

The morning sky was bright. "Cloud," Star said, "we're lucky you brought real camping equipment." The younger boy stared at Cloud's cookpot, now hanging from a tree branch, and concentrated. The gentlest use of his plasma attack kept the soup close to a boil. To his eye, the manestra was plumping nicely, the freeze-dried vegetables were almost recovered, and the fish was poaching properly.

"I used to go camping all the time," Cloud said. "I was an America Scout. I'm glad you're here, so I don't have to try to build a fire and worry about burning down this forest. And it was really great, Eclipse, that you teleported to Greenland and recovered that glacier ice. No need for us to worry if the water is safe to drink. It was nice to be clean, too, once you melted enough ice for decent baths."

"We're supposed to be working together," she said. "Cheers also to Comet and Aurora for catching the fish. I'm lucky, Cloud, you could hold the bath water in midair for you and Star. To TK-levitate that much water, I sort of have to be looking at it, which you might have found inconvenient."

Cloud hesitated, then smiled. "Just a bit," he said agreeably.

"We cheated," Aurora said. "Fish have minds, sort of, so I found some nice big ones. They dropped dead on command, and Comet grabbed them. Grandma insisted we all learn how to clean the fish we caught, so we did, thanks to Eclipse's really sharp knife."

"I'm just glad you're all better, Comet," Star said. "The Federal District was terrible."

"I should have realized," Cloud said. "Everything different means going places can be dangerous. Then you'd have been safe, Comet."

"It was mostly safe," Comet answered. "And it ended OK. I should've stayed invisible."

"FedCorps shooting at you, Comet, was just crazy," Star said. "No way to expect that. So don't blame yourself, Cloud." The older boy nodded in agreement.

"Thanks to Eclipse for pan-frying—is it frying if there's no oil?— some of the fish, and Star thinking of putting the rest into the soup," Comet responded.

"And cheers to Cloud and Comet for bringing along extra eating utensils," Aurora said.

"I just asked myself what you guys were not packing," Comet said. "OK, it was really really dumb of me not to notice that Aurora didn't have a blanket."

"Mom said I wouldn't need one." She said so, Aurora thought, so it had to be correct. "And Dad said not to bother taking any food along, so I didn't."

"You made up for it," Cloud said, not quite reluctantly. "These fish are great."

"I think the soup is ready," Star announced. "Who's the guinea pig?"

"You two did the work," Comet said. "It smells really good. You get the first taste."

"I'm the guinea pig?" Star asked.

"It really does smell good," Comet said. "OK, I'll taste." She dipped a spoon into the pot, caught a bit of fish and a few plump rice-grains of manestra, tasted, and nodded vigorously.

"We need a ladle," Star said.

"Telekinesis," Aurora responded. "Cloud, please, your flight field below in case I drop something? I can't do the weight Eclipse or you handle, but this needs a more delicate touch." The older boy gestured, a pale white haze appearing below the cook pot.

Soon enough the five were enjoying an unusual if slightly late breakfast. "This is almost as good as your fish, Eclipse," Cloud said politely.

"Thank you," Eclipse answered. "Your...I think the word is 'stone soup' if you know the story...is better."

Cloud nodded, then felt puzzled. That was a very old Army story. How could a girl know it?

"There's a reason we're here," Eclipse said. "Well, the four of us; I'm not sure what Morgan had in mind for you, Cloud, but I know you're gift-true." Cloud smiled.

"We use the StarCompass and find exactly where it points," Comet said. "Me invisible. Aurora follows me mentally."

"I'd like to be with you," Star said, "but my forcefield shines through your invisibility." Comet grimaced. "You've been doing invisible for how long?" Star asked. "A couple weeks? And you're getting better already."

"There are plenty of clouds," Comet said. "You and Cloud can stay close, right above me, if Aurora can tell you where I am when no one can see me."

"We practice that first," Aurora said. Cloud began to look doubtful. "Please? I mean, Cloud, if we were a soccer team, we'd practice new plays before we got into a real game, wouldn't we?" Cloud nodded enthusiastically.

"And I stay with Comet," Eclipse said. "My force field down, and presets up?"

"Are they fast enough," Star asked, "so your force field comes up before Comet gets hurt?" Comet, he thought, had been badly hurt once. He didn't want it to happen to her again.

"Remember someone teleported the lithium bombs onto me and the Sera Lama?" Eclipse answered. "The bombs were exploding before they were teleported. That's a speed of light attack, but my presets are faster. Yours will be, too, Star, soon as you practice a bit more." The younger boy nodded his approval.

"OK, we follow the Starcompass," Aurora announced. "By the way, Comet, exactly where is it pointing?"

"I need to find out," Comet said. "First I dress in something less conspicuous, in case I run out of steam and turn visible." She disappeared into the brush, reappearing in a few seconds in long-sleeved blouse patterned in polychrome butterflies and loose blue jeans. "Whatever changed all the satellites changed clothing styles, too. Last night I did an overflight of San Francisco. This is close as I can get to what I saw people wearing."

"Looks pretty," Cloud said. "Won't people wonder you're not cold?"

Comet grinned at him. "Good thought. Except while we were landing the Space Plane I flew over towns with snow on the ground. There were guys in shorts and T-shirts walking through slush from stores to their cars." Cloud shuddered at her description. "They couldn't all be personas. Not when no one has ever heard of personas."

"Weird," Aurora said.

"Now what?" Star asked politely.

"I go where the StarCompass takes me," Comet answered. "I have no idea how long that takes but I need to hold invisible while I'm looking. That's invisible me and Eclipse, and mayhaps I need a break in the middle."

"Invisible?" Star asked. "Break?"

"Like this." Suddenly Comet was not there. "But I've never tried holding it for hours and hours."

Eclipse looked carefully. I knew she had invisibility, she thought. I've been inside her invisibility field. I've seen pretty decent invisibility. Comet is really good. I know she's there because I can still hear the faintest of tunes, her mind thinking, but I can't see her at all, even cheating and looking way outside the visible.

"Call it an hour?" Eclipse asked. "Everyone else is ready?"

"So soon as we wash the dishes," Cloud reminded. Heads nodded agreement. "Oh, wait, I did that astronomy thing last night. For you, Comet. Let's take a look at it." He opened his lessoncomp. "There's a picture of the stars, and here they are rotating around the pole."

"Cloud," Comet asked, "Please put your finger right below the pole, and flip back to the star picture?"

"Done," he said. "See? Wait, that's wrong. What did I do?"

"What's wrong?" Star asked.

"I'm not pointing at the pole star," Cloud answered. "That's not Thuban. It's the tip of the horn of the Baby Unicorn." He typed a few commands. "Phoenice, it's called. Never heard the name before. I have this neat image program; I need a few moments to get something to work." The star field became bright red dots on a white field. He superposed it on the time-lapse image. "That's crazy. I thought I'd managed to bump the lesson comp after starting the time lapse. But I didn't. All those red dots match where the circular trails start. The pole star really is Phoenice now, not Thuban. Super work spotting it, Comet!"

"It makes absolutely no sense," Aurora said. "How can you change the pole star?"

"Happens automatically," Cloud answered. "The pole rotates. We covered it in science class last year. I need to look something up." He typed a few more words. "That's weird," he said. According to this, in five thousand years Phoenice becomes the pole star."

"We're in the future!" a disbelieving Star said.

"Or way in the past," Comet said. "It's a cycle, isn't it, Cloud?"

"Every, like, 26,000 years. So we could be in 19,000 B.C.," he answered.

"Or 71,000 B.C.," Eclipse said. "I prefer 'in the future'. Time travel backward is seriously dangerous."

"So we do this search. Then back to lessoncomps?" Star asked. "Didn't you bring yours, Eclipse?"

"I have real books," she answered. That was true, she thought. No sense having anyone learn her real lessoncomp was an underdesk nonportable. "I expected continuous combat, not 'where are the dooms?', so that's what I packed for. "

"So this afternoon it's back to Editing English," Aurora said. She frowned. "My least favorite course, even if the teacher is real good." She decided to ignore Comet rolling her eyes.

~~~~~

Comet and Eclipse, fifty feet off the ground, glided down the main highway into town. "Table Rock," Comet said, pointing at a sign. "Home of the Great Indian Solar Calendar." The sign featured an image of a large spiral filled with strange writing. "Do you recognize the language?"

"No," Eclipse answered. "There are lots of old languages, writing all different ways, but 'spiral' doesn't ring a bell. Those cars look really strange. Huge. Massive trunks, I think. Oh, come on! That one has a video screen for the kids in the back seat. That's ridiculous. But I don't see anyone pointing at us."

"Starcompass wants a left turn," Comet said.

"On it," Eclipse answered. "Does it let you point? Give a distance to target?"

"No. And we seem to be headed out of town. Perhaps climb a bit?" Comet said. "OK, there's a lake. Do you see that house?" The house in question was a Neovictorian Gothic gingerbread structure plastered with turrets, multi-floor walls of glass, and a two-deck widow's walk corseted with ornately railed balconies.

"Incredible! Can I take it home with me? No, I guess not." Eclipse shook her head.

"We're targeting that garden in back. Do you see anyone?" Comet asked.

"No. And mindscan says no one is home."

"There's a mailbox," Comet said. "It reads 'Doctor Professor von Pickering'. I don't remember that name from before."

"Me, neither," Eclipse agreed. "No closer!" Eclipse reversed course.

"Something wrong?" Comet asked.

"Presets triggering. I need to land to look. There's a spot." Eclipse set down in the woods. "Give me a moment?" She closed eyes and pressed her fingers together. "OK," she finally said. "Perfectly safe. Someone did a big fourth order working in that garden, but it's not there any more. I just felt a few traces left behind."

"Trap?" Comet asked.

"I don't think so. At least, the traces look like the after-its-over traces I was shown, the other time," Eclipse answered. "But I'm not real sure. I can't do fourth order stuff. I only barely see it. Sometimes I can't. Where's the StarCompass pointing now?"

"When you turned around, it started pointing back into town," Comet answered.

"Now what?" Eclipse asked.

"I think swing around the house, then back into town," Comet answered. "Unless you think it's not safe."

"Let's do it," Eclipse agreed. "Invisibility up?" Comet nodded. They took off again.

"It was a pretty house," Comet said. "We need to visit it when someone's home. Meanwhile, somewhat left again?" She pointed. They flew over block after block of attractive, well-maintained frame homes.

"Nice park," Eclipse said. "Pretty pond. Old wall." She stopped. "Comet, did you ever spot any old ruins? Something from Sarnath or

Atlanticea?"

"I wasn't really looking, but, no. You were right. Someone really messed with the past...except this is almost America." She shook her head. "StarCompass is pointing at the end of the wall. There's a girl sitting there reading."

"Shh," Eclipse said. "Don't want her to hear us." Eclipse made a circle around the girl, who continued to read. To Eclipse's eye, she looked to be fourteen or fifteen.

Name? Home? Eclipse tried gentle telepathy in the girl's direction.

"Victoria Wils..." The girl's head snapped around. "Who said that?" No one was there. She sprang to her feet.

Eclipse dropped behind treetops and accelerated away from the scene.

"No different than talking to her," Comet said. "But you took off."

"There was something really strange near her. I didn't recognize it. It appeared when she got up. The air, it curdled." Eclipse shrugged. "I saw a memory of her bedroom, just for a moment. I'll know it if I see it again."

"Now the Starcompass is pointing another direction," Comet reported. She pointed.

"Comet?" Eclipse asked, "Do you want to take a rest? You've been invisible a long time."

"I'm good for a while yet," the older girl answered. "Wouldn't like to do this all day, though. The starcompass is pointing at that house. Eclipse, please look through my eyes. See if we can spot her bedroom."

Eclipse flitted from window to window. "There. And homework with her name on it. I'll flip upside down so you can read it."

"Victoria B. Wilson," Comet said. "But why is a fourteen-year-old just starting plane geometry? Perhaps they do that late, not early?"

"Is there another StarCompass destination?"

"Doesn't seem to be." Comet shrugged.

"Back to base, then," Eclipse said.

~~~~~

Cloud and Star soon joined Comet and Eclipse at their campsite.

"No one saw you," Cloud said. "No one looked suspicious. We couldn't see you. What did you find?"

"The StarCompass pointed at three places," Comet announced. "I snuck up on them. It pointed at this fantastic house with no one home. Then it pointed at this girl who's a couple years older than us and what had to be her bedroom. OK, she's my age or older."

Comet, Eclipse thought, is a month younger than Cloud. She's barely thirteen, and has nearly a year on Star and Aurora, who just turned twelve. Every so often, she won't let them forget it. Usually she's better than that, but sometimes she pulls the 'I only play with people my own age' line. That gets serious annoying very quickly.

"Who do we talk to?" Star asked.

"I found the girl's full name," Comet said. "On her homework. Stacked by her desk—the window was wide open, so I could look in. 'Victoria.' 'Victoria B. Wilson'. And he is Professor Doctor von Pickering. It says so on his mailbox. She's sitting on a stone wall, right above the town park pond, reading something. She's all by herself. There's no sign of him. His house is empty." Aurora shared a mentalic image of Victoria and the town pond.

"She's the better choice," Comet said. "She's close to the same age as the five of us." Eclipse told herself not to point out that Comet was always mentioning her age and everyone else's lesser ages, and now suddenly everyone was the same age.

"I peeked at local newspapers," Aurora said. "Eclipse, you're on every front page. Actually, your face is the whole front page on some of them. They think you saved the space plane. They mostly saw you, not Comet and Cloud doing the real work. They think they owe you a big huge favor. Oh, and no one has any idea who you are." The line 'they owe you', Eclipse thought, had alarming implications as to what Aurora might be about to ask. "Why don't you simply ask these two people for help? See what they say?"

"Garb or formal dress?" Eclipse asked. That's a lot better than what Aurora could have wanted, Eclipse thought. Sometimes Aurora's tactical ideas were a bit demanding. Well, they would be demanding, she thought, if I weren't me. The problem with being a Highly Esteemed is that if 'Over the Top with Gauss Rifles' is a valid tactic in some game, you tend to think Over the Top with Gauss Rifles is a good real-world idea.

"Formal." Star, Eclipse thought, had a boy's reaction: Important events want important clothes.

"Garb...Will they recognize you if you aren't in garb? All your photos are garb." Aurora tried to sound unsure.

"If you show up, an inch off the ground? With flight field glowing?" Cloud asked. He shook his head. "No, I guess I agree with Aurora."

"Fair enough," Star said.

"Garb," Comet said. "Protect our private personas." Star nodded vigorously.

"Cloud is right," Eclipse answered. Except, she thought, for one detail. That glow is a layer of screens, not my flight field. It's a bit ostentatious, but unlike most people I do actually get to worry about someone trying starcore weapons on me. Again. You'd think they'd have a clue starcore weapons already failed once, incidentally wrecking up local real estate, but some people just keep trying the same old approach.

Cloud smiled. "Let's do it," he said.

"Wait," Eclipse said. "Aurora, could you please put a solid mind screen around the four of you?"

"Sure," she said. "Done. Why?"

"Something's bothering some of my presets, and I can't tell what. I'm going to try listening hard." Eclipse touched one finger to her lips. "Okay," she finally said. "It's like I'm not hearing something that I always hear all the time. Now I don't hear it. But I'm not hearing something, not with my mind, and I can't find anything I'm missing."

~~~~~

Comet and Eclipse, now in their persona garb, fell into a giant morning glory, bells ringing in the distance. They appeared, hovering an inch off the grass, a few feet behind their target.

"Pardon us," Eclipse said.

"Don't be startled. We'd like to talk. Please?" Comet added. Victoria started. Eclipse tensed, then relaxed. If Victoria actually fell off the wall toward the water, Comet would grab her before she'd fallen more than a few inches.

"Oh, hi. I didn't hear you," Victoria looked over her shoulder, "coming up be...hind mm, me." She managed to get her legs under herself and stood, her mouth an oh of wonderment. "Are you friends of Adara's?" she asked. Having said the question, to Comet's eyes she now looked as if she regretted asking it. "You're the people who rescued the space shuttle, aren't you, the, ummh, personays?"

Eclipse let Comet do the talking. "That's us. I'm Comet. This is Eclipse."

"And I'm Victoria Wilson, the definitely-not-persona. I'm just a person." Her eyes were wide, taking in Comet and Eclipse as though they were dragon slayers freshly stepped from a storybook. Of course, Eclipse thought, from her perspective we are escapees from a 'comic book'—and I forgot to remind Aurora to find out what the spaceship crews thought comic books are.

"We helped you. Your people. So we were hoping you could help us," Comet said. "Please?" Eclipse bit her tongue. She was sure. Comet had more practice with this girl-to-girl thing than she did.

"You want my help? Why me? What's the deal? I mean, I'm

incredibly grateful you saved all those people from dying. Is there maybe something I can do to help you?" Victoria sat back down. Eclipse listened carefully. Victoria Wilson was really not speaking Modern English. Her accent was odd. Also 'deal'? 'Maybe'? Eclipse chided herself. She hadn't thought about it until now, but when these people talked some of the words were wrong. That was very odd. She was sure: Ancient civilizations that spoke English all spoke Historic English or Modern English, one or the other. She told herself she spoke them both, flawlessly, thanks to Mum being completely insistent that she learn them. Now Victoria was speaking something else, something Eclipse couldn't name.

"That's our problem. We don't know what we want. We just know you have the answer." Comet realized that didn't make a whole lot of sense. "We went on a long space flight, and when we came back, everything was completely different. For starters, America isn't at war with the Aztecan Empire, in fact there aren't even any Aztecs any more."

"Like on the old Dawn Area shows," Victoria said. "Oh, wait, have you ever heard of Dawn Area?" Comet shook her head. "TV SF show. Go on."

"Tivi?" Eclipse mumbled. "Never mind." Some island in the Pacific? she wondered.

"The Wizard of Mars, he's not there any more, he's lived forever and knows everything, said the world was doomed twice," Comet explained, "so Eclipse and Cloud and me had to fly here and beat the dooms or everyone would die, except he didn't even tell us what the dooms are or how to beat them." To Eclipse's great happy surprise, Comet remembered not to mention that her twin siblings had come along.

"It's the end of the world, and he sent you guys?" Victoria voiced her disbelief. "Aren't there, like, any grownup superheroes, err, personays? You're how old? Barely eleven?"

"The Wizard of Mars is almost never wrong," Eclipse said. "He was real certain it had to be us. And I get to be Athena's Spear and Shield. Except I'm twelve."

"I'm thirteen," Comet added. "That's three days ago, Eclipse, and, no, you didn't hear about the party because there was no party. Dad forbade it." Victoria stared at Comet.

"When you have strong gifts," Eclipse explained, "flying is a gift, you grow up when you're older than other people. So I look younger than you expect. My mother thought this was a big deal for some reason. But why are we right here?" She pointed at the ground. "Because the Wizard gave Comet a StarCompass; it takes us to the places that let us find the dooms."

"You're one of them," Comet said. She produced the Starcompass from a cape pocket. It pointed, vigorously, at Victoria. "It says you find the dooms for us. The other is this empty house at the edge of town, at least, this Professor von Pickering whose name was on the mail box wasn't there."

"I'm going to destroy the world?" Victoria asked. "That's silly. What's Athena's Shield?"

"No, no," Comet answered. "You're somehow where the clue is located."

"Athena's Shield?" Eclipse said. "The Wizard said some of us likely die to save the world. I'm the Shield and Spear. I likely get to do the dying." Victoria stared, speechless.

"May I start from the beginning? Please?" Comet asked. "Let Eclipse show you images using telepathy?" Victoria nodded her agreement.

Comet repeated her story. Eclipse's telepathy showed images of the sky jellyfish, the Wizard of Mars and his Mons Olympus Palace, great cities of the American Republic, ruined Leaviorkianu towers off the Oregon coast, an Aztec Army invading, and more. She caught a memory from Victoria. Here Mons Olympus was a giant volcano, not a palace a hundred miles across.

"The jellyfish," Victoria finally announced, "is a hrordrin. I recognize it. They're frightful creatures. They don't exist on Earth. Adara knew about them, but she's gone. And you're here to save the world, but don't know from what? I'd love to help you, but how? Professor Pickering, I know him, you found his house, can maybe tell you more about hrordrin."

"Perhaps you know something that's the clue?" Comet asked. "And we have to follow a clue trail until the doom shows up? Has anything, I don't know, doomish, happened in your town recently?"

"There were the escaped prisoners last Summer," Victoria said. "They got caught, the ones who weren't killed by...but that's last Summer. The morning paper today said the town constables caught a drug dealer. He's in the town lockup."

Eclipse and Comet looked quizzically at each other . "Mayhaps I asked the wrong question," Comet said. "That somehow doesn't sound like an end-of-the-world doom. Wait. What's a 'drug dealer'?"

Victoria stared suspiciously at Comet. How could she not know? "Someone who sells drugs. Illegal drugs."

"Medicine is illegal?" Comet started to feel strange again. This conversation was like Washington, except Victoria seemed unlikely to start shooting at her. "Before we left, the American Republic had the best doctors in the world, and the best medicines. Why are they illegal?"

"Umm, err, wait. When I said 'drug', you were thinking medicine drugs like aspirin. Weren't you?" Victoria asked.

"Medical drugs," Eclipse said. "Aspirin. Penicillin. Eternalife."

"Oh. How do I explain this?" Victoria said. "I meant illegal drugs. Heroin. Cocaine. Extasy. Borgiabizin. They make you feel strange. People want to keep feeling strange, so they pay tons of money for the drugs, and sit there feeling strange rather than doing anything. So the drugs are illegal."

"Huh?" Comet managed.

"Chocolate!" Eclipse had a flash of recognition. "Like chocolate during Rectification. Chocolate makes grown-ups do stupid things, so they made it illegal. Did you have Rectification, making chocolate illegal?"

"Make chocolate illegal? Why?" Victoria managed. "That's, like, totally crazy."

"It's legal now," Comet said. "I can eat it safely; I'm a persona. But if grownups saw me walking down the street, eating a chocolate bar, they'd try to stop me. At least they would, before everything changed."

"I don't see a doom here," Eclipse said. "But this fellow did something illegal, got caught, and is in jail. Do you know where the jail is?"

"Yes. Can you see it in my mind?" Victoria asked. Eclipse looked, carefully. Victoria had a clear mental image, the town's main streets and its police station. "They want to question this fellow, because he knows where he got his drugs. But he doesn't want to talk. The paper said so."

"The police telepath can't just get a court order to read his mind?" Comet asked.

"There are no telepaths," Victoria answered. "Well, except you, Eclipse. That history you just gave me was incredible, but if someone heard a voice inside their mind, speaking to them, not knowing it was you, they'd be sure they were crazy."

"How can criminals be convicted, if there are no telepaths?" Comet asked.

"Way different set of rules," Eclipse said. "I guess it was supposed to be obvious, once we found out they don't have personas any more."

"If you can read people's minds, why have trials?" Victoria asked. "This 'the world changed' is just so strange."

"Do folks selling illegal drugs have any money?" Eclipse asked.

"Big crime bosses have tons of money," Victoria answered. "It says so on television." She looked at her watch. "But I've got to be home in ten minutes. Now I'm late. And it's way across town." Eclipse considered Victoria's tone of voice. That *got to be* was very strong parental expectation, the same as what she had once had from Mum. And she'd done what Mum expected. Well, mostly. She'd not told Mum she'd teleported into a theater to watch King Lear, a play so perverted that no one her age was allowed to see it. She told herself King Lear was horribly sad, not twisted, and in any event that wasn't why Mum threw her out of the house. At least, she didn't think it was. She wasn't sure, but she didn't think so.

"What if we teleport?" Eclipse asked. Eliminating all travel time, she thought, should solve her problem. "We know where you live. We can leave you in your back yard where no one will see you arrive."

"How did you know? I never told anyone!" Victoria didn't quite shout. Comet managed a 'huh?'

Eclipse looked at Victoria very carefully, not with her eyes, realizing what Victoria meant. Except Victoria's teleport gift was not any gift she'd ever seen. It looked alarmingly like a fourth-order schema. "If I teleport us, I mean," Eclipse added hastily. "You don't have personae who teleport." My shields, Eclipse told herself, can handle second-order attacks. Actually, they are supposed to survive third-order attacks, long enough for me to run. The emphasis is very much on the 'supposed to', because they've never been tested that way. Fourth order? Better not to find out. "We can talk about, whatever it is, later, but we're very good at keeping secrets. Don't worry." She took Victoria's hands, reinforcing the touch with gentle mind-to-mind thoughts of solidarity.

"OK," Victoria agreed. "I'd love to talk more, but I can't, not right now," she added. "If I'm not there on time my parents will kill me. I have work tomorrow morning, but I should be free tomorrow afternoon. I'll be here waiting if I am."

"It's simplest," Comet said, "if we have a bit of altitude." A flicker of orange sparks surround the three girls and Victoria's bike. They drifted up. Victoria's hand clamped down hard on Eclipse's wrist, then relaxed when she realized nothing dangerous seemed to be happening. A blue fog enveloped the girls. They found themselves hovering two feet above the back yard of Victoria's house. Victoria let go of Eclipse and took the drop to ground as though she did it all the time.

"Tomorrow?" Victoria asked.

"Tomorrow it is," Eclipse answered.

~~~~~~

"I'm home!" Victoria called as she closed the back door.

"And early, too," her mother answered.

"I was in the Park reading. And then...if I told you, you wouldn't believe me," she added. For a change, she thought, be honest with Mom and Dad.

"Of course we would," her mother answered.

"No, Clarissa, you wouldn't." Victoria's father James intruded. He almost never disagreed with his wife.

"Of course I would," Clarissa answered.

"And I wouldn't either, except I saw the three of you materialize, whatever it is, in the back yard," James added. "That was the two kids who rescued the space plane, wasn't it?"

"Two of the three," Victoria answered. "It's called 'teleportation'. The Park to here in no time at all. Eclipse...she was in white, does that. Comet, she was in the green body suit, flies."

"You're both trying to fool me," Clarissa said. "Two of these superheroes in my back yard? That's absurd."

"I was on the phone," James said. "I snapped a shot. Should I put it up on HeadScroll?"

"No! No!" Victoria screamed.

James stopped. Victoria was terrified. "OK, I'll erase so soon as Clarissa sees it. But what's wrong, honey? Nothing ever upsets you. Here, Clarissa, look."

"It's them. And you're all flying!" Clarissa shouted. "That's impossible."

"Comet's flying. And carrying me," Victoria said. "But, Dad, it's not nothing. It's the end of the world, absolutely everyone dies, unless Comet and Eclipse can stop it. And Eclipse thinks she dies, win or lose, to save us. She showed me with telepathy. You see..."

~~~~

Comet and Eclipse returned to their camp site. Across the pond, Star was hard at work with his small hand saw, trimming branches for what promised to be a large lean-to. Comet listened carefully to Cloud, who was explaining to Aurora how some nouns, ships and airplanes for example, took feminine pronouns. It was remarkable, she thought: Aurora was listening to a boy her own age, as though he could teach her something. Miracles would never cease! And the trip, the importance of what they were doing, seemed to have shifted her own thinking, so that she wasn't offended by the sight of Aurora being taught by a boy.

"Folks!" Eclipse called. "We went, met Victoria Wilson, and have returned, perhaps even with some clues." She waited for everyone to gather around. "Comet, you did the talking. Tell us."

"So the StarCompass led us to Victoria Wilson," Comet began. "She was by herself, so we could talk. She's about our age, except she looks more like fourteen or fifteen. She perhaps had the front end of a clue trail, a prisoner in the local jail. The trail leads to criminals with money we can salvage after we arrest them. And she'd seen an image of a sky octopus, except she had a name for them. *Hrordrin*, a word I've never heard before. This Pickering fellow we found? She thinks he knows about them." Comet continued her description of the conversation. Cloud tapped keys on his computer.

"So this Pickering person is the next step?" Aurora asked.

"The medicine smuggler," Star responded.

"Why?" Aurora countered. "We have two trails to him, and only one to this, this medicine smuggler."

"Money," Star answered. "We're running out of food, building even a lean-to takes forever, and soon we need at least a washing machine and drier. These people are criminals, so we can arrest them and salvage their loot."

"Do their laws say we can do that?" Cloud asked.

"We're inside the American Republic," Comet said, "even if these people are a bit confused at the moment. American laws trump local law, so we can perform an action. If we can find the fellow with the money."

"Step one is this fellow in jail," Cloud said. "Except we can't get the court order, there being no courts here that know about telepaths."

"Then we're like the founder wagon train, headed east through the Dakotas when it was trapped by a surprise snowstorm," Aurora said. "That was 2500 years ago, but Professor Lafayette said the rule applied. I can read his mind if it's good faith, for a good purpose. Besides, if I discover he's innocent, I can make sure he's set free. So Cloud and me get someplace close to this jail, so I can find the guy and read his mind, and Cloud checks I did things right."

"Then the five of us do an action against this crime boss?" Star asked.

Eclipse leaned back against her tree trunk. "Surely four of you is enough? There aren't any personas. Their spaceships are unarmed."

"And what will you do?" Star asked. "Not that you haven't saved Comet and us twice, already."

Something, Eclipse thought, was odd about Star's question. He hadn't immediately dumped on her for being a girl. "I'm going to visit Pickering," she announced. "I'll see what he has to say. At a guess, I stake out his house until he comes home. If something goes way wrong with you guys, Aurora shouts for help, and I come to your rescue, not that you'll need it."

"OK," Star said. "I need to work on my lean-to. It's taking forever."

"I'll help," Comet said, "if you trust me with your saw." Star smiled and nodded. "But no superspeed for a bit. All that invisibility was tiring."

"That's the search," a distracted Cloud interrupted. "No such word." The other four looked at him. "My lesson comp has the universal translator in it. It chews up tons of memory. But every word in every known language is in there. And *hrordrin* isn't close to anything that makes sense. So when Victoria said its name, she made it up, or there's a new language along with new everything else. OK, Aurora, I'm ready to visit this bailiffwick, whenever you are."

"New language?" Comet wondered. "Wait! That might be its name, what its minders, those weird people Eclipse fought, call it." Cloud gave Comet a thumb's up. Eclipse's eyebrows rose slightly. Suddenly boys and girls were being nice, not just polite, to each other.

"I'm on my way to Pickering's house," Eclipse said, "as soon as I dress. This time, 'formal' is the answer." Formal, Eclipse thought? Silver-gray trousers, white silk blouse and gray quilted vest fringed in silver, broad silver-lace belt, blue-green-grey patterned scarf shot with silver threads, coordinated earrings, and pendant necklace. Pendant, earrings, blouse, and trouser pockets all featured the same device—my sigil, a sun in glory passing behind the new moon. The black shoes were eminently practical in their soles. Handbag. Actually, a fairly heavy handbag. Even with carbon composites, a Ruggels 0.70 semiauto pistol added a considerable mass. "I'm back in a little while," Eclipse promised. "The trick with water-wet synthasilk and outer-space vacuum, to get wrinkles out, is pretty fast, but it takes a bit."

CHAPTER 12 THE MISCREANTS AT BAY

The Table Rock police station held a four-cell lockup, designed primarily to accommodate the occasional drunk or burglar awaiting transport to the county seat. The presence of Table Rock's sole reputed drug dealer had provoked a burst of security precautions, motivated partly by the fear that the prisoner might escape and partly by a desire to impress the town newspaper with the professional competency of the town constables. Aurora's unseen reconnaissance revealed a pair of patrolmen and a dispatcher on duty inside the station, and another plainclothesman covering the jail from a tall roof opposite the building. She decided that getting close enough to the jail to be sure of reading the right mind looked tricky. Worse, the cells were windowless. Reaching unfamiliar minds, when she didn't have a path that light could take to them, was close to impossible.

With Cloud disguising them as a patch of grey haze against a grey sky, the two descended swiftly into a church tower, then waited tensely. No one came bounding up the stairs. No one had seen them. Aurora summoned her gifts. She told herself she was doing something perfectly safe, because there were no telepaths any more to catch her. It was even legal, there being no local laws regulating telepathy. Still, reading the mind of a chance-met soul on the streets was wrong. Only the prisoner, who had forfeited his civil rights by rejecting society, was her legitimate target. A worry returned: If there were no telepaths now, the bailiffs had no way to know that the prisoner was guilty. He might be innocent, in which case she was reading the mind of an innocent man. That was wrong. She told herself that if he were innocent she'd free him; that made it OK. Her perception passed through a police station window, by the waiting guards and into the lockup. Only one man was being detained.

A few seconds in the thickets of the prisoner's consciousness relieved her of her final worry. He was a medicine smuggler and habitual thief, a man who routinely assaulted others, and at least once had left someone for dead, making him an unsuccessful murderer. To Aurora's prim image of the world, he was grossly dysfunctional. Not insane: She had read the minds of people with diseases of the mind. He was not diseased. He just had no sense of his community, of his future, of anything except himself, his present, and his chances for stealing wealth others had created. She wondered how long it would take Victoria's people to deal with him in a civilized manner. The smuggler seemed to have no fear of the gallows he obviously would soon be facing.

She sorted through his memories. Here were his suppliers, the men who sold him the illicit medicines that his customers craved. Here was a list of places the suppliers could be found. There was really only one place, a decrepit motel that went by the name *The Magpie's Roost*. She noted his customers. If she couldn't find his wholesaler, his customers knew a competing retailer who might lead them to the right place. Finally, disgusted, she withdrew from his thoughts, wishing she could forget his sordid criminality. Emperor Roxbury had had grandiose schemes for exalting his image of the virtuous life, schemes that incidentally would have decimated the world's population. This liquor-sodden wreck of a criminal mind was lucky he could remember where he lived.

~~~~~~

The Magpie's Roost was an ill-patronized roadhouse located a few miles north of Table Rock. A confluence of roads gave the tavern a variety of approaches. Ill-tended evergreens and a battered, sinking wooden fence obscured the view from its parking lot, so that no one outside the property could easily learn who frequented the place. The second floor with its private entrances had once been a respectable inn, declining with passing years to the status of a sleepeasy, and was now the place of work of Marcus Salvadore, distinguished leader of Center County's criminal community. An abbreviated stay in one of America's premier universities had affected his speech, though not his morals. To his confidants he was not a pusher but an illicit purveyor of controlled narcotic substances. Extreme discretion, coupled with reservation of several well-decorated, clean back rooms for certain officials and their very close friends, had rendered his place of work virtually invisible to the constabulary.

Four personas watched the Roost from nearby trees. The four were fully garbed, dominos in place, gloves covering freshly washed hands. They'd let Eclipse find Pickering. The roadhouse's owners had thoughtfully provided a great deal of privacy for their clientele, but those provisions had not allowed for visitors who flew, let alone visitors who could read the minds of the Magpie's clients. Fencing and evergreens did not obstruct the view of someone in a tree forty feet off the ground.

"How are we doing?" Star whispered. They knew who they were looking for. All they had to do was to trap him at his work. Star wondered about the why of the laws he was enforcing. They didn't make sense, though he was more puzzled about why people wanted to break the laws in question than why the acts were illegal. He hoped that the locals would approve of personas enforcing their strange code of justice. Still, smuggled medicine was illegal. Even though the laws were obviously dumber than the Rectification that personae had died enforcing, it was his duty to enforce them.

"Not yet," Aurora grumbled. He'd asked the same question five times in ten minutes. She was waiting for someone to open a door, raise a window shade, or come outside. The outer walls of the building were mentally inert. She could follow line-of-light through an open window or unstopped chimney, reading the minds of people she encountered on the way, but the drapes and blinds for key rooms were pulled tight. For all that she could locate a familiar mind in the dark from across the continent, searching for a stranger's mind through obstacles was close to impossible for her.

Comet saw thermal handprints on the back door. Someone had recently entered. Aurora needed someone to come outside, or someone inside to make a mistake, so that she could scan within. Making an arrest would be very obvious. If they went into the building and their target wasn't there, the target would learn that a persona league was hunting him, and would go into hiding.

Minutes dragged into an hour. Star and Comet set up a chess board and played quietly. Cloud worked his lesson comp. Aurora tried to ignore them. At least Star hadn't decided that he was hungry. She'd looked for snack food in the local store, even if she couldn't pay for it. She couldn't believe how much chocolate the locals laced into their foods, down to store-chocolated milk for breakfast. The trail bars Star had packed were fine. She'd neglected to tell the gang that the grocery store stocked bars of solid milkfat chocolate that you were supposed to eat all in a piece. She'd even seen someone eating one. In public! Unbelievable!

Cloud nudged her. She'd looked away for an instant, and now the door was shutting. Her gifts lanced through the shadows, past the closing door, locking on the minds inside. One, two, three,...she'd lost her chance on the rest. She tagged the minds she'd found, then switched to the outside, sweeping through the thoughts of the person leaving the building. The target was thinking only about the package she was carrying, a tenth of a kilogram of white powder. Her memory of the seller was the person the quartet sought. Aurora switched back to the closed building, surveying the minds of the people she'd found. Two were non-entities, men of minimal intelligence hired as bodyguards. She whispered a weapons list to Cloud. The guards watched the property's perimeter, but were forbidden line-of-sight on the entrance. They saw approaching cars, never approaching faces.

The third person was their target's banker, a man who kept seas of numbers in his head and tightly coded files. The banker knew numbers, but not people. Thirty Nine might owe the boss sixty thousand dollars, but the banker did not know who Thirty Nine was. The boss, however, was now seated eight feet in front of his banker, running down a new list of transactions.

"Got him," Aurora announced tonelessly. The transfer to the boss's mind was difficult, but accomplished. The mind she searched was indeed the wholesaler named by the first smuggler, someone who smuggled strange medicines in large lots. Aurora uploaded his mental map of the inn and passed it to her friends. A line of attack was now apparent.

Comet's flight field wrapped them in invisibility. She dropped Aurora in the woods a quarter mile away, safely out of lines of fire. The others landed in the parking lot. Cloud's kick slammed into the rear door. It crashed from its hinges to bang flat on a vestibule carpet.

The three advanced at a near-run. Guards called back and forth. They had heard a noise. What was it? Carpeting on the stairs was new. Walls were freshly plastered and painted bone-white. The quiet cleanness of this place contrasted vividly with the unwashed windows and aging window shades seen from outside. Aurora's mental images pointed the way. Star padded up the stairs, his companions hovering above the treads.

At the top of the stairs another locked door waited. Cloud punched through the latch and shoved the panel open. The three crowded through the doorway. Two men inside stared in shock.

"You're both under arrest," Cloud announced.

"I'm what?" Salvadore snapped, his walrus-spread of mustache quivering. "Arrest? You're too late for Halloween. Is this a practical joke?" Salvadore told himself this had to be a really tasteless stunt by some of his customers, that a trio of ten-year-olds had not just blasted the locked door of his office and threatened to take him into custody. The clothing said 'jape'. The fellow doing the talking was merely colorful, but his sidekick wore a private light show, while the third was buried in enough diaphanous-green veils to stock a sultan's harem.

"I said, you're under arrest," Cloud repeated. "Raise your hands and come quietly."

Salvadore's banker tried sneaking around the three and out the door. If this was some sort of a joke, it had to be on the boss. If it wasn't a joke, the boss would handle it. He had not expected Cloud to grab him, casually plant one fist in his stomach, and toss him retching onto a settee.

"Holy Mother of God!" Salvadore exclaimed. "I don't care who you are, you don't punch out an old man. Benito! Guido! Take these three outside. Give them the thrashing of their life! Then bury them in the old manure pile."

Benito and Guido were the codes for Salvadore's two squads of enforcers. None of them had ever come closer to Italy than the local pizzeria. Their jobs were conditioned on satisfying the boss's eccentric whims, almost all of which were boringly legal. When the boss's call came, a few had been inspecting the remnants of the back door, whose steel frame and core were supposed to prevent rapid entry. The rest were scattered around the building, idling away their time, confident that their services would not be needed.

The stairway resounded to the beat of running feet. Cloud turned to face the guards, trusting Star and Comet to cover his back. The first villain reached the head of the stairs to be met with one of Cloud's kicks. The guard sailed backward, a flurry of bumps and thuds marking a half-dozen men falling down a half-flight of stairs to pile in a heap at the bottom. Cloud winced at the language the men were using. They shouldn't use words like that, he thought. If nothing else, there was a woman—well, a girl, Comet being thirteen—in earshot.

"Move it!" Salvadore screamed. "Get up here! This instant!" He could hear shouts as his men untangled themselves, put themselves shoulder to shoulder, and pounded up the stairs again.

Two men reached the landing, one spreading out to each side to make way for the pair of men behind them. "Now!" shouted a fifth, the four throwing themselves across the landing at Cloud. To their surprise, the boy neither flinched nor ran. Instead, he lunged forward, grabbed the nearest guard by his lapels, and tossed him head over heels at his compatriots.

Salvadore winced as two guards collided, rolled over the banister, and dropped out of sight. A loud crunch marked the other guards slamming into Cloud and, impossibly, failing to knock the boy off his feet. Instead, when he lifted, they went up, so neither guard touched the ground. Cloud's firm heave sent the two guards up at the ceiling. They ricocheted across the landing, bounced off the farther wall, and slid down the risers toward the ground floor.

Salvadore decided that the situation was totally out of hand. What was wrong with his guards, whom he had salaried and fed and clothed? By now they should have had these three bound, gagged, and flayed alive. Instead the fellow in blue was thumbing his nose, daring them to try the stairs.

Salvadore pulled a pistol from his desk drawer. He knew his customers, knew the faces of their children. It was an excellent insurance policy. These three weren't children of anyone he knew. They didn't dress like children of anyone he knew. Worse, they apparently had learned martial arts from late-night ninja flicks. One of those skills, though, was surely not 'bulletproof'. The staccato bark of his heavy-duty handgun drowned out all other noise. Four rounds were for the back of the kid with the mouth, four were for his friend with the light-show, and four were for the green one.

To Salvadore's intense surprise, nothing happened. He didn't practice as much as he said he did, but he was not twenty feet from his targets. The first rounds might as well have been blanks. The second cluster of shots created sparks and puffs of smoke at their target. The third cluster knocked the green figure back a few feet.

He fumbled for another magazine. A clumph and clatter was his guards, again reaching the landing and again being thrown bodily down the stairs. The green blur solidified into a masked girl, copper-blonde hair combed in neat falls, who set four bullets down on his desk. "You dropped these," she said. "You should be more polite. The noise could annoy your neighbors." Salvadore told himself that she couldn't possible catch bullets in midair, that the bullets now on his desk had to have been in her pockets all along. He played for time.

"Okay, what will it take?" he asked. "Money? A cut of the business? You want some B-powder? Real hot stuff? The best there is, guaranteed." Salvadore had no intent of honoring his offers. In only a few moments, the fools downstairs would get themselves organized, break out the iron, and retire with extreme prejudice three underage perps.

"Cloud already told you," Comet explained politely. "He's here to arrest you. That's all."

"All?!" Salvadore moaned, slamming another magazine into his pistol. He leaned back and brought up his weapon. His target faded to a green blur. Holes appeared in the wall opposite. At a range of four feet, every shot had missed.

From downstairs came a fusillade from pistols, shotguns, and a pair of illegally-converted automatic rifles. Cloud stood in the doorway, not flinching or ducking. Bright lightning flashes filled the stairway. There were screams of pain. All became quiet. Salvadore's remote monitor, finally warmed up, relayed a picture from a hidden camera. His men lay in the vestibule, bodies unmoving, their weapons scattered across the floor.

Salvadore reached slowly into his desk drawer, cautiously withdrawing a plastic sack the size of a box of sugar. A razor cut surreptitiously slit the seals. "Little girl?" he asked, "I have a present for you. A peace offering." Comet paused, a questioning look on her face.

"Here." Holding his breath, Salvadore tossed a quarter-kilo of uncut borgiabizin powder at her.

Star saw a shower of white dust engulf his momentarily hesitating sister. She gasped a half-word question and collapsed motionless to the carpet. Her mind dropped out of Aurora's network. Star's body fields soared to maximum intensity, so that he burned like a miniature sun, his light illuminating every shadow. Only Aurora's mentalic shriek stopped him from reducing Salvadore and his entire headquarters to ash.

Salvadore hesitated. The fellow in the light show costume stood in the middle of a cloud of borgiabizin, seemingly unaffected by the narcotic. The costume included a laser display, Salvadore noted, directed by the fingers. A crash and sudden burst of sunlight marked the outer wall of the building falling to earth behind him, risers and joiners slashed by Star's attack.

Fierce gusts of wind scoured the room, sending papers flying in every direction, half lifting Comet's inert body from the carpet, blowing a fortune in illicit narcotics into the open air. The two boys knelt intently over the girl. He aimed his pistol. He still had a few rounds left. Now he had them. They weren't looking up, weren't moving. He couldn't possibly miss. Now they would surely die.

No. The voice had no direction, no apparent source. *No. They're not yours. You're mine. No one does that to my sister!* The voice echoed through Salvadore's mind, cold and inexorable as glacial ice. Salvadore saw a gleaming pyramid within which waited a lidless, merciless, all-knowing eye. He tried to mouth another curse, denying the impossibility that the fates had prepared for him, but found himself mute. He could see what the eye revealed to him. It was too late to tell his visitors to go to Hell. He was already there. His sanity flickered, a guttering candle in a storm.

Minutes later, Salvadore and his banker lay unconscious on the floor. A shaky Comet, her garb sweat stained, leaned back against Salvadore's desk. Cloud, one arm propping her shoulders, helped her drink. To her the simple glass of water was overwhelmingly refreshing. Star slumped on the couch. Killing the villains, he thought, had been easy. Healing his sister, with Aurora a long block away, had been much more draining. A patter of feet was Aurora, not quite out of breath, running up the stairs.

I found what we wanted, Aurora announced. *None of them remember us clearly any more. They only remember shadows. And ghosts.* She showed the mesh of Salvadore's memories: friends, contacts, sources, cash flows. *Cloud, try to stop being pigheaded. I can't talk so fast when I have to shout at you. You guys want more facts?* Aurora paused. She'd pushed herself so hard the space behind

129

her ears hurt. Eclipse, she decided, made everything look so easy. For Aurora, finding the right memories, not a hundred others, had been a struggle.

"So I hand these two to bailiffs?" Cloud asked. "It's their laws, but your proof." Comet nodded politely. Her hands were still shaking. She knew she should have kept her guard up, but even after a year of doing a public persona talking, breathing, and being polite to criminals were still completely natural. She hoped the last behavior stayed that way.

"Guys," Star said. "They don't have mindreading here? Right? So Aurora walks into the courtroom. No one knows her. No one believes her. They just see a ten-year-old..."

TWELVE! TWELVE! Aurora reminded.

"GIRL. They won't believe her," Star continued.

At least I'm not a BOY! Never anyone'd believe you! Aurora riposted.

"So no telepathy in Court? What do we do?" Comet asked. They couldn't just let Salvadore escape. Could they? They were in a quandary. Before the change, there were people who'd said Star and Aurora should go home and wait until they were older, before they did public personas, but they'd never had anyone refuse to believe Aurora's mentalic evidence. Now they faced bailiffs and justices who'd never heard of telepathy.

"I know!" Star said. "I've got it! Owning this medicine stuff—poison, more like, what it did to you, Comet—is a crime. Let's tie them all up, take a pile of their medicine, a little of the money, and all those papers. Leave them on top of the bailiffwick. Call the bailiffs, tell them look on their own roof." The others looked for a hole in Star's plan. Salvadore couldn't remember them, not after Aurora had finished scrambling his mind. There'd be no inconvenient questions from people who didn't have the persona concept and couldn't understand that the four had done their legal duty. Salvadore would face the bailiffs, and they'd be on their way.

"The guys downstairs should all be unconscious," Cloud said. "I don't think I killed any of them. Leave them, tied up, and their guns, too, on the bailiffwick roof? It's flat. They won't fall off."

CHAPTER 13 ECLIPSE AND PICKERING

The doorbell rang. Alexander Pickering looked up from his calculation, his latest unsuccessful attack on a seemingly simple problem. It was almost time for lunch. How could the doorbell be ringing? Dragon House had the best security systems in the state. It should have been totally impossible for anyone to reach his front door without his being forewarned of their arrival.

"Guten Morgen, Telzey," he whispered. The code phrase drew the attention of the house's AI system.

"Good morning, sir," was the programmed response.

"Is there someone at the front door?" he asked.

"Yes, sir."

"Front door camera on screen three," Pickering ordered. The picture showed a young girl, very well dressed, peering earnestly toward the camera.

"Telzey, camera record, front door camera, the five seconds before the door bell rang. Screen three." To Pickering's astonishment, the girl appeared out of noplace, took two steps to the door, and rang the bell.

"Telzey, condition yellow-two, and off-site store all records. Front door intercom, my mike."

"At once, sir, condition gelb-zwei, off-site store, intercom," the AI answered.

Pickering spoke into his microphone. "Hello at the door. I'll be down in a few moments, but I'm on the top floor."

"Happy to wait," the girl answered. Her voice was a brilliantly clear soprano, every consonant sharp. Too sharp, Pickering thought; she had an unfamiliar accent.

Eclipse took the moments to admire the house. The house front was wrapped with a deep sitting porch. Near the front door, the roof rose to a shallow dome, the underside being painted in deep blue, sprinkled with coppery stars and polychrome circles that perhaps marked planets. She heard an inner door open and close. Then the front door opened.

"You rang?" Pickering asked. He smiled at the girl, then took in what she was wearing. He stared for an instant at her matching bracelets, inch-wide bands of glittering silver wire and sea-blue stones. Those aren't real sapphires, he thought, or the kid's wearing a fortune on her wrists. And in ten years time I'll feel very sorry for the young men on whom she turns her charm.

"Professor Pickering?" she asked. "I'm Eclipse, the girl who helped save the space plane. I'm sorry for disturbing you, but we really need to talk. I'm told you know what a *hrordrin* is." At the word *hrordrin,* Pickering flinched.

"I," he announced, "am indeed Alexander Humboldt von Pickering. Perhaps you need to tell me more. Won't you please come in? How may I establish your bona fides? You claimed you are the real Eclipse?"

"The world now has more-or-less no personae," Eclipse said. "No one who can see through walls, shoot lightning bolts from their fingertips, watch bullets bounce from their chest,...I also fly."

"You can fly?" Pickering asked. "Really?" A ghostly touch passed across his mind.

"Alex, you really don't believe people can fly. Do you?" Eclipse responded. Long fingers brushed silver-white falls of hair back from her ears.

"Of course not, however much I love reading fairy tales. Are you offering to show me?" His jovial grin was a challenge. The events on the space shuttle, he told himself, were some trick with metallic aerosols and optical back projection, the shuttle having never actually been in any danger. However, flying inside his home would require props she couldn't possibly have hidden in advance. How would she dodge his challenge?

Eclipse hesitated. "Why not? I'm not uncloaking my public persona. You saw my garb, know who I am. The one true Eclipse. The ceiling here is a bit low. It's bad manners to leave footprints on a ceiling."

"I suppose it would be," he answered gravely. "You may use my library." He pivoted, one finger beckoning.

~~~~~

The library rose cathedral-like from ground floor through two mezzanines to a great arching roof. Pickering marched nonchalantly to the room's center. Eclipse stopped at the entrance, lips moving from gap to slight purse to enchanted smile.

"One observes," Pickering opened, pointing as he spoke, "that the central roof beam meets diagonal risers at the window surface, say thirty-five feet in the air. Perhaps three feet below is a horizontal joiner." Eclipse nodded. "And there, at the right end of the joiner, sticking out where every single guest sees it, is a pencil, abandoned by window cleaners. I'm not paying a day fee to remove one pencil. Its presence yet offends. For someone who flies, it would be a trivial matter to fetch it, but..." He shrugged.

"I'll get it for you." She was standing behind Pickering. He realized that the position of her voice was rising, from significantly below his own ears to well above. A glance over his shoulder revealed Eclipse, already seven feet in the air, toes dangling slightly. A faint glow flickered near her shoulders.

Pickering swallowed. "Young lady, the New Yorker cartoon runs 'That's impossible. Stop it right now.' The instruction is not literal. I'd rather you land first. You'd find it a bit of a drop elsewise." Eclipse, having reached the pencil, obliging headed groundward, not quite pausing in her descent to perform a graceful triple-and-a-half somersault, at last coming eye-to-eye with Pickering. He, however, stood firmly on oak parquetry, while she hovered upside-down, hair streaming toward the carpet, her toes a good ten feet removed from the nearest solid surface. Gravely, an impish smile not quite suppressed, she handed Pickering his pencil. He accepted, then impulsively tugged on her hand. She resisted; Pickering recognized a gymnast's strength in her fingers. If she had stood on a solid surface, she could have held her position no more firmly. He released. Her landing was a reverse pike half-somersault with half twist, ending on the floor facing him.

"You were flying," Pickering observed. "You really were. Remarkable. And not on wires; you didn't sway when I pulled."

"I said I'd show flying. I flew. Right?" She stared in fascination at his collection of globes, maps of the world covering the last half millennium.

"Can I complain of a guest who grants my wishes?" he asked.

"Now do you believe in flying?" she responded.

"It appears impossible to avoid the observation that you can fly," Pickering answered gravely. "And that you are the real Eclipse." A bell chimed in the distance. "Have you had lunch yet?" Eclipse shook her head. "Then please join me."

"I'd be delighted to," she answered. "May we talk as we eat?"

"But of course, though you get to do most of the talking. I would appreciate a little help setting the table." Eclipse nodded in happy agreement.

Pickering's breakfast room was an irregular octagon with glass on seven sides. A picture window framed a view down to his lake, bright with diamond sparkles where wavelets caught the sunny sky above. Pickering noted approvingly that Eclipse had no difficulty putting out the salads and setting a place for herself. At first she'd set out knives and forks not where he expected; she then rearranged her place setting to match his. She watched as he carved the chicken and put out the potatoes and carrots.

"Would your parents complain if I offered you tea?" he asked. "Captain Hawley's Smuggler's Blood?"

"I'm, oh, you'd have no way of knowing. I'm legally an adult, and I'd be delighted to try your tea." She allowed that the tea might be Captain Hawley's Smuggler's Blood, but perhaps had not actually been smuggled from exotic England. "However, everything has changed, so I apologize if my table manners aren't yours."

Pickering, Eclipse thought, was a more than adequate cook. The chicken had been seasoned with savory and thyme. The carrots benefitted from cinnamon, and the sliced potatoes while roasting with the chicken seemed to have been dusted with curry power. The salad dressing was Roman, now called *Italian*. The meal having fairly begun, she launched into a description of the Wizard's warning and their flight across the universe to save the world, only to find that the world was now completely different.

"If history was reset, what happened to your parents? Your homes?" Pickering asked. "If it's not a secret, where are you and your friends staying?"

"Their parents are gone. My base vanished." She frowned deeply. "Some of us packed for camping. Someplace in the world, not telling where, we have a camp site. I brought lots of money, but it's not your money. I have a legal solution, come Monday. Until then, I'm broke, not even money for food. I packed rations. The rest of us are worse off."

"I see," Pickering answered. Now, he wondered, is this some elaborate scheme to separate me from money? Or at least to cadge a free meal? Surely there are simpler paths to scamming an old man?

"But I want to hear about the hrordrin," Eclipse said. "Preferably about its weaknesses, before I have to fight another one."

"The hrordrin is part of a long and complicated story, of which I only know a part, except that it actually begins with Adara and Table Rock Park. That part I need a friend to tell, and she'll be here tomorrow, I expect." Pickering nodded firmly. "I gather that they are unpleasant creatures, dangerous to those around them."

"To put it mildly. I fought one. And its keepers." Eclipse frowned. "The hrordrin seems to be indestructible. Its keepers are almost as bad. Between them, they've wiped out a series of small towns."

"Before the change, before you left, didn't America have an Army or Air Force? Why did they leave it to you to fight this thing?" Pickering asked in puzzlement.

"We do. But for really high-power attacks, America has people like me. Actually, at the top end, it has me," Eclipse said. "And Morgan Le Fay. But we were sent here to stop the dooms, not the hrordrin. Unless the hrordrin is a doom. The Wizard of Mars wouldn't tell us what the dooms are. The hrordrin might just be a side show." She shuddered at the latter thought. "OK, the Wizard said I probably get to die stopping the dooms. So probably the dooms are even nastier, whatever they are, than a hrordrin."

"This is a difficult situation," Pickering said. Which, he thought, you seem to be handling absurdly calmly, even better than my own children would have done at your age. "America now is under attack, by unknown forces, but they don't appear to be up to killing all seven billion people in the world."

"The StarCompass led us to this house. Somehow you lead us to the dooms. 'America under attack' is the best clue I've heard. Unless the doom is the time pirates, whoever reset history. Mayhaps someplace in your history there's a clue about them. Resetting history sounds complicated. It's be easy to miss some detail. Some maiasauric statue would get the wrong number of fingers, whatever."

Pickering held up one hand. "In our history, maiasaurs were a species of dinosaur, millions of years ago. What do you mean, maiasauric?"

"Maiasaurs, they're dinosaurs, well, they evolved a lot, were earth's first civilization," Eclipse said. "Not that anyone knows much about them."

"Assuredly," Pickering said, "there is no credible evidence for a dinosauric civilization. Not at all. Dinosaur brains were very small." The look on his face suddenly changed. "Wait," he asked. "You flew across the universe? You're saying you can fly faster than light? Or you and Comet? Modern science—Einstein's Special Relativity—says that's impossible."

"Einstein? Albert Einstein?" Eclipse said. "A hundred years ago, 1922, Solara appeared to Einstein. She took him in the space of hours to the AutumnLost Galaxy. When you travel very fast, things look very different. Einstein saw it and replaced Special Relativity with Transitivity. Relativity is the low-speed limit of Transitivity. Transitivity explains faster-than-light travel. It also tells you how to do time travel. There aren't paradoxes because he replaced time with three time dimensions t, u, and v. Transitivity lets you go faster than light, and also go to the past, change the past, and return to the present, a present not like the one you left."

"You don't happen to remember details on Transitivity, do you?" Pickering asked.

Eclipse thought carefully for a few moments. A photographic memory was wonderful, she thought, but you had to search through all the photographs to find anything. "No. It uses derivatives, and things made from derivatives, and infinitesimal geometry, and Lie algebras whatever they are, of which I sort of understand what a derivative is. I think. Mayhaps. If someone else actually takes it for me. Sorry, but it's serious hard math, and I'm only working on trig yet."

Pickering sighed. "Ah, well. But you want to know about hrordrin. And I'd be interested, if you can do it, in going on some faster than light trips, so I can at least see whatever Einstein saw. Does that sound to be a fair trade?"

"I can take you faster than light," Eclipse answered confidently. "And breathe for you, since we'll be well outside of the earth's atmosphere. If you tell us about hrordrin."

"There are two long stories here," Pickering answered, "but perhaps less detail than you need."

"Someone reset time a lot. I need some clues," Eclipse said. "You said America is under attack. Do you have newspapers or datalink—no, internet—anything on the attacks?"

Pickering nodded. "Are the rest of you as well-mannered as you are?" Pickering asked.

"Yes," Eclipse answered. "Well, boys and girls do snip and snarl at each other. It's stupid, but it's the way things are." She hesitated. "I'm less sure about Cloud. But Comet and siblings were very well brought up. Why do you ask?"

"I'd like to meet all of you," Pickering said. "Perhaps a late dinner. You want to hear about the hrordrin. I want to see faster than light. You want clues about these dooms. There might be options here."

"Options?" Eclipse asked.

"My wife died, many years ago," Pickering said. "My three daughters are out in the world with their own families. But they and husbands and children visit on occasion, so Dragon House is not short of bedrooms. You could all stay here while you are looking for these dooms. After all, if the world faces doom, I face doom too, so helping you all is just good sense. I do worry about strange people using the house, but if you were here, it would be easier to answer your questions."

"Alex," Eclipse said, "May I please read your mind? Just a bit? Enough to see what you mean by 'worry about'? Your secrets remain your secrets."

"Go ahead," he answered. Not, he thought, that I could stop you if you chose to do so.

Pickering felt a ghostly touch in his thoughts. *This is telepathy. Asking is good manners,* Eclipse answered. *Not asking is extremely bad manners. Unless you're a dangerous villain, which you aren't.* Eclipse found what Pickering meant by 'worry' and recoiled in shock. "Children, not your daughters or grandchildren, but children out there. They must have incredibly bad manners. No, you've got nothing to worry about. And if you tell us to leave, we'll be out of here, lickety-split."

"So we need to schedule. When can the three of you...or is it four...show up?" he asked. "Would, say, 9 P.M. our time work?"

"It's five of us," Eclipse answered. "But if we stayed here we'd do housework and things. Do our own laundry. Be good guests. Oh, wait, please don't ask Comet to do things. She just divorced her parents, and is still way upset about it. She'll do things, but don't ask her. Please?"

"Divorced her parents? How?" a bemused Pickering responded. "However, I shall try to remember not to ask her. For the grandchildren I have a mud room entrance and second heavy-duty washer-drier arrangement. If you've been camping, that might be advisable." Not he thought, that I am worried about trivia like the house being leveled, not with the secret of faster-than-light travel perhaps within reach.

"You don't have a Heinlein Divorce Act." Eclipse said. "It's unpleasant for her and I can't tell you most of it. But Comet's really a very nice person."

"Good. And tonight?"

"Let me check with them," Eclipse said. For a moment she appeared lost in thought. "OK. They're chasing a clue. They're all waiting for something. They say 9 PM—that's after dark—should be fine. Meanwhile, may I please use your library? Read what's happening to America? After I clear the dishes?"

"Of course. You're my guest. There's a stack of newspapers," he answered.

Pickering led Eclipse back to the library, then took the spiral staircase to his second-floor study. He watched the girl from the corner of his eyes. When she thought he was watching, she carried herself erect, moving briskly from one shelf to the next. When she thought he was focused on his own reading, she sagged into herself. To Pickering, her pose showed exhaustion laced with twinges of pain.

In late afternoon, Pickering heard the distant sound of wind chimes followed by a flare of violet light. Eclipse had vanished. A half-hour later, she returned, appearing out of nowhere a few feet above the library floor.

"Apologies for the sudden departure," she said. "Comet was doing what good personae should, and didn't expect one of your criminals would use poison gas on her. Yes, many personae are more or less immune to poisons, but some of us have to be careful to invoke those gifts before we are completely safe. She's recovering. She'll be fine. Getting the poison out of her garb was trickier."

"Which poison gas?" Pickering asked.

"Borgiabizin, whatever that is. She inhaled a good bit of it."

Pickering turned to his computer. "Something I've not heard of. Soap and water," he finally announced. "Highly water-soluble. Isn't she your age?"

"Close enough," Eclipse said.

"There are a series of medical warnings," he said. "In people your age, people from here maybe not you, borgiabizin generally causes cardiac arrest. If the victim lives, it's very rapidly metabolized and becomes harmless."

"It did," Eclipse said. "They brought her back to life. Just a second. I'm telling them about soap and water for their garb."

"Do I want to know what they got into?" Pickering asked.

"They arrested some criminals," Eclipse explained. "The criminals fought back, but are now unconscious and being tied up. They and their poisons and all their guns are being put someplace where they get arrested by your bailiffs."

"This is a doom?" Pickering asked.

"It seems pretty feeble to be a doom. We have several places to look for dooms," Eclipse said. "Or clues. One of them pointed to a trail, a strange trail that led to these criminals. These people doing bad things. They were the first step on the trail. We don't know where it leads. Yet."

"Oh." Pickering wondered what was actually going on.

"Now they're afraid to meet you," she said. "They might have this poison in their hair or something."

"Soap and water," Pickering said. "There are extra bars under the kitchen sink; please take two." Eclipse disappeared, leaving behind a carillon's chimes.

CHAPTER 14 THE FIVE MEET PICKERING

Not quite at nine in the evening, there came a knock at Pickering's back door. Waiting outside, he found Eclipse and four companions. It was already a cold and dank night. He could see the transient cloud where his breath condensed. He surveyed them carefully. Eclipse now wore a simple gray jogging suit and long hooded cloak. On the other four? Surely he had never seen so much lycra all in one place before. All of it was brightly colored, no two costumes the same, with obvious pockets, fine embroidery, and piping on collars and cuffs. To Pickering's eyes someone had put taste into the colors and trim, not like the usual run of modern children's clothing. Modern clothing was sometimes obscure; still, two boys, three girls. Hair color ranged from platinum white— Eclipse—through black with a patch of white at the forelock—the girl in black. Each carried a very large duffel bag.

"Alex, this is Cloud." Eclipse introduced the older boy. For someone Cloud's age, the handshake was remarkably firm. Cloud's jumpsuit and cape were sky blue. An oversize feather draped over a bright-blue beret. Given the name, Pickering realized that the white trim on arms, legs, and cuffs could be cirrus, while the chest emblem was a well-delineated cumulonimbus. Pickering tugged at his memories, not finding a manufacturer's logo to match the foot-tall thunderhead. His lack of recognition proved little. He had spent the past decade trying to deduce the nature of one product, heavily advertised without being explicitly identified, never progressing beyond the conclusion that WorldView would not countenance the illicit purveyance of underdressed young persons of indeterminate gender.

"And this is Comet." Eclipse gestured at the girl in green. Comet cleared copper-blonde curls from hazel-green eyes. The front of her tight-fitting body suit was covered by the gold-embroidered comet of her asserted name. The comet's head rose almost to her neckline, while its twin tails swept down across her ribcage and waist to wrap around her legs.

"Charmed, I'm sure." Pickering beamed at the older girl. Comet might or might not be the oldest of the lot, he thought; she was certainly the shyest. Only after a pause did a smile cross her lips to wrinkle her eyes.

"Pleased to meet you," Comet managed. She offered her hand. Her grip, Pickering found, was as firm as Cloud's. She yawned. "Apologies. This is way beyond my usual bedtime, not to mention I'm recovering from this afternoon."

"The poison? Borgiabizin is nasty stuff," Pickering observed. She nodded vigorously. He wondered which parts of Eclipse's tale were true.

"Aurora and Star are twins," Eclipse explained. Aurora was indeed of a height with her brother Star. They shared high cheekbones, a long, narrow face, and wiry build. Their garb featured identically-cut loose-fitting trousers and pullovers, open-face jackets, and waist-length capes. Star wore orange and yellow, while the girl wore darkest black, both with silver trim and embroidery. Centered on the boy's pullover was a silvery eight-rayed star. Aurora's clothing was intricately laced with silver thread. Pickering recognized the pattern running from her neck to her waist: it was a slight modification of the dollar's pyramid, eye, and radiants.

"Please," Pickering said, "come in. At least to warm up. No one else knows you're here. You might all find hot chocolate to the point, though I have prepared dinner."

"Hot chocolate?" a surprised Aurora asked. "Hot real chocolate? For us?"

"And something more solid to eat?" Pickering asked. "Say, fresh-made bread and Senate bean soup and cold chicken? And a proper Russian salad?"

Aurora stared intently at Pickering. The hairs on his neck prickled. "It's OK," she announced. "He's really a chill guy. I can tell. Let's go! I'm starving!"

"Yes!" The chorus was unanimous. The children surged toward the door.

~~~~~

To Pickering's modest surprise, his guests had impeccable manners, so long as he ignored how they set the silverware. Duffel bags were properly stacked in the vestibule. Without being asked, Comet had collected laundry bags and started the mud room washer. Dinner was as successful as Pickering had hoped. In his experience, hungry children were the biological equivalent of black holes, able to make arbitrary quantities of food disappear. His guests were more polite than most children, but also far more hungry. Their conversation was confusing. They kept referring to countries that did not exist, at least not in this century.

Having eaten, Comet fell into a doze. Comet's siblings soon followed Comet's example, their eyes becoming heavier and heavier. Pickering maneuvered them to window seats, covered each with quilt or afghan, and let them drift into deep sleep.

"Apologies," Cloud finally said. "We're hours and hours after our bedtimes, and Comet had a rough day." Cloud and Eclipse, Pickering noted, had had a few heated words, culminating in Eclipse decreeing 'Tomorrow! Not here!', a demand to which Cloud acceded. Soon Cloud followed his three companions into sleep.

Pickering and Eclipse remained awake. To his eyes, she looked haggard, straining to stay conscious when she would rather set sail to slumberland. "There's another window seat if you'd prefer to drowse away yourself," Pickering noted.

"Don't tempt me. Please? It's been a long day. I promised I'd watch them. So I have to stay awake for a while. I know I don't need to, not with you," she smiled, more knowingly than Pickering thought reasonable, "but I always try to keep promises."

"If you'd like TV, there's a headset. It's local news." He gestured at a wall screen, then powered up the system. Pickering stared in surprise as the reporter described the two dozen drug criminals who had been found, unconscious and hog-tied, on the roof of the local police station. The reporter blandly ran down a list, describing how many pounds of each narcotic had also been found on the roof, and how many weapons the criminals had been carrying.

"These were the people those four arrested," Eclipse remarked, "first the group they caught locally, and then some people farther away. The one with the weird beard is the fellow who sprayed Comet with the borgia-whatever-it-is."

"Borgiabizin. Before this change," Pickering asked, "did your four friends usually spend their spare time arresting criminals? What if those fellows on the roof had shot at your friends?"

"Cloud is bulletproof," Eclipse said. "Star is better than that. Comet catches bullets in her hands and gives them back to the criminals. She just wasn't ready for gas. The only time those four ever arrested anyone—that I know about—is when the Emperor Roxbury and his giant robots attacked their school. I've done more, but it was part of my training. Well, there was the time I rescued Comet and Aurora. That was an accident. They were lucky I was there. Otherwise they would have died. They were way younger then. If those characters tried kidnapping Aurora now, they'd be dead in half an instant."

"I see," Pickering said.

"You asked something else," Eclipse said. "When the world is full of personas, you don't have much crime. Criminals get stopped—OK, criminals who are personas sometimes get away with committing crimes. For a little while."

Pickering began loading the dishwasher. "I'd've done that," Eclipse said. "I should have done it earlier." She stared at the machine. "Except I have no idea how that thing works. Or how it is supposed to be filled."

"No matter," Pickering answered. "You've done lots of work tonight. More than your share. And they," he gestured at her four companions, all sound asleep, "are far too tired to help. Now, I have guest bedrooms, rarely used these days. Your friends—so to speak—will be better for sleeping in real beds. So will you. I could carry Star or Aurora, but Cloud and Comet look to be a mite too heavy for me. I used to go for a walk, late at night, but the world is now more dangerous."

"Dangerous?" Eclipse said.

"The property is safe," Pickering explained. "Security systems would warn of trespassers. It's safe, if I don't go too far. If I were going into town, I'd take precautions." Not enough precautions, he thought; it's safer here. Table Rock is a very pleasant, well-to-do place, with hardly any crime, but what's happening elsewhere is unbelievable. Worse than the antiwar terrorists back in the sixties, except there is no cause now, no explanation for the violence.

"I'll carry Cloud upstairs," she announced. "Once I see where we're going, teleport is faster. Oh, no personae? Have you ever been teleported? I can give you that experience, if you want. And I promise not to drop Cloud on his head. Not there's something in it to damage."

"For a group of travelers, you don't like each other much," he observed.

"Cloud got Comet injured, by not thinking. Cloud half-hates me. We disagreed about something. Something important." Something, she added to herself, something you and the Kosters couldn't possibly not know about, if you were before the change. And you don't, because the world got changed. "It was a moral question. I won't take back what I did. He's bitter tiffed about it. You're right. He should be home with his mom and dad." If you can find his home, she added to herself. It has to be here someplace, doesn't it? Your navigation checked with Comet's; this must be Earth.

"Sometimes, if you really want to apologize, pride can be overcome." Pickering nodded sagely, not sure what Eclipse meant.

"Not something I said. Something I did. Something I can't undo. I had to," Eclipse said emphatically. "No matter how many people got tiffed at me. Oh, wait until Cloud wakes up. He'll tell you all about it. Probably several times." Do I dare, she wondered, sleep under the same roof with Cloud and Star? She put her carry-all across her back, squared her stance, and carefully lifted Cloud. Her knees protested silently. Pickering estimated the load. Eclipse might outweigh Cloud, but not by much. From its heft when he'd moved it, her carryall held considerably more than a change of clothing.

Cloud stirred groggily to awareness. "Comet?" he asked, not recognizing that it was Eclipse who held him in her arms. Cloud, his eyes closed, blissfully unaware of who was carrying him, lapsed into profound sleep.

"I would guess," Pickering said, "I can give Cloud and Star the one bedroom, Aurora and Comet the other, and night lights so they don't trip in the dark. Or should I know something else about sleeping arrangements?" Eclipse shook her head. "There's a bedroom on the third floor. I could move a cot to the second floor for you. Perhaps you'd rather be more isolated from the others?" Her smile was swift and brilliant. "In that case you have the tower suite."

She dropped Cloud in one of the bedrooms. A final rise of stairs brought the two of them to an octagonal bedroom, five walls being extensively glassed, while sixth and seventh hid bath and walk-in closet. An eighth framed the entrance. The room was decorated in shades of yellow: auburn curtains with patterned wheat sheaves, wall paper in cream with gold and sun-orange marigolds, flame-yellow circular pillows on a vanilla-white solar-disc pattern bedspread, and a giant sunburst dominating a flat-white circular throw rug. Eclipse gave a gentle gasp of surprise. "It's lovely! For me? Tonight? It's wonderful. Thank you! Is that a porch?" She stepped to the farther wall, looking to the north along the lake. "This is beautiful! I don't deserve this. I'll teleport the sleeping beauties upstairs."

"And then you go to sleep," he ordered. Eclipse gratefully nodded and closed the door gently behind him.

~~~~~

Pickering finally returned to his library. The drier was emptied, clothes folded and stacked on appropriate dressers. Eclipse, now in a long-sleeved nightgown, hair slightly moist from bathing, had gratefully accepted her clothing. His careful search of pockets and labels uncovered no evidence as to the children's identities. Fancy clothing bore hand-sewn maker's signatures. Underclothes came from unfamiliar manufacturers, but were free of laundry marks. Pickering decided that it couldn't be every child who went off to summer camp and had parents insert name tags. Cloud's T-shirt might say Marcus Garvey Linguistic Middle School, City of Roxbury, but Telzey's search confirmed that no school or city of that name existed.

Star and Cloud had both left pocket change in their garb: pennies, dimes, quarters. The coins claimed to be from the American Republic. The patterns were wrong. The Roman fasces had been removed from the dime eighty years ago, yet Cloud carried a 2020 dime on the pre-Roosevelt pattern. The 1784-2009 quarter showed a Revolutionary War musician—except the coin said 'King George's War'—playing bagpipes.

~~~~~

Awake! Gasping for breath, heart hammering against her rib cage, Eclipse shuddered into consciousness. For minutes she stared at her pillow, trying to descend from the heights of total panic. "You won," she whispered to herself. "You won. That's not what happened. You won. That was a dream." Memories tore through churning remnants of dreams, setting down the night terror. Gradually her breathing slowed, her pulse beating less and less insistently against her skull.

? A thought tinged with Aurora's mindset touched Eclipse. *Eclipse? What's wrong?*

"I," *I, don't worry. Only a dream,* Eclipse answered, choking down a gasp for air, still more focused on her fear than on Aurora's voice.

What happened? That was only a dream? I woke up, said Aurora.

Lesser Maze. For an instant Eclipse had been back in the Maze, locked in hand-to-hand combat with one of its guardians. The trap was power and its undisciplined use. Any gift she invoked would be available at tripled level to the Guardian. The choice of contests belonged to the Maze. The requirement was to win by drawing on natural strengths and skills. Two centuries back, an American Master of Games, cheated of his opportunity to play for the world chess championship, had come to the Maze, knowing his life was the forfeit for defeat. He crushed the Maze's defender over the chessboard, and taunted the World Champion to try the same.

Hand-to-hand against a man taller and heavier sounded impossible to third parties. No, she told them, say 'interesting' or 'challenging'. In the real Maze, she drew on skills with Sarnathi hand-fighting. A Sarnathi trader had always to appear unarmed, but never be without weapons. He had pinned her against a wall. In reality, a desperate twist let her reach a boot and withdraw its steel shank, edges polished to razor sharpness. The rules gave them both the same garb—but that only helped if you knew the garb's uses. He—it?—made a grab for his own feet, then shuddered in death as she drove the steel up under his ribcage, piercing his heart. In the dream, her move failed, boots staying perpetually just out of reach, leaving her to be battered through unconsciousness into death.

That was the Maze? Aurora asked. *You did that?*

That was a piece, Eclipse said. *A small piece. Messy, not the worst. I have dreams. Oh, drat! I woke you up. Was I broadcasting,*

Aurora? All I need, half the world chasing me, is to set 'come hither' beacons when I dream.

Broadcast? Mentalic? No, not at all. We shook hands to be a League, remember? Right before the Eye? I can tell if Star or Comet or Cloud are in trouble, no matter what. It works for you, too. If you're close and not hiding. It's not telepathy, it's a tap. I don't know where they are. With you I only know something's wrong. Your screens are polished steel.

Oh, right. You told me. I didn't understand. My fault, Eclipse apologized.

You want me to stop? Mayhaps I should've stopped already? Her tone carried the apology she dared not speak.

Don't apologize. Aurora? Eclipse's thoughts swirled around her, warm and comforting as a mother's hug. *You're fine. You're great. Keep it until we get home.* An introspective pause. *Well, jettison the tap if something serious is chasing me? Mayhaps you can't track me through a tap, but [meaningful shrug].*

Are you OK now? For sure? I get bad dreams, too, Aurora said. She pulled her blankets around her shoulders. *After I saw the sky octopus videos, in my dreams I saw sky octopuses every night. Reaching for me. I woke up. I had to keep quiet or I'd wake other people up.*

Oh, Aurora! That's terrible. You were very brave to lie there quiet, Eclipse responded, her thoughts warmly sympathetic.

I hid under blankets. So nothing could see me. I guess that doesn't work, does it? I hid anyway. Once I was too frightened. I woke up Comet, Aurora added guiltily.

Quiet's OK. Once I woke up screaming, Eclipse said. *Top of my lungs. I dreamed about the solid shadows. I scared Gwen—one of my cats—I spent half an hour cuddling her so she could sleep. But I'm OK. Now.* It was even true. Aurora had distracted her from her own horror, letting breath and pulse slow. Her memories—the triumphant instant when her blade sank its own length into the Guardian's chest   had supplanted nightmares. *Thanks a lot. Sleep well.*

You, too. Sleep tight. Good night. Aurora was immediately sound asleep. Eclipse rolled over on her stomach, searching for a position that triggered a few less aches and pains. A week here, never calling a gift, would be fine by her.

CHAPTER 15 SUNDAY

Aurora awoke to the first rays of the sun. Her nose was pressed to the pillow, one eye in darkness. The sun had poked into her other eye, bringing her to awareness. It took a few seconds to realize that this was not her bed. She froze, listening with ears and other senses. Comet was seven feet away, still in the deepest of deep sleeps. Her brother and Cloud were in another room, sound asleep, though it was past sun-up.

Still drowsy, she peered about. This was a bedroom, with pale blue paint, deeper blue drapes and half-open cerulean-tinted Venetian blinds, two single beds, dressers, and writing desks with cut-glass indirect reflector lamps. Each desk had its crystal-blue carafe of fresh-cut pencils, a stack of paper tablets, and a large gum eraser. Her sheets and blankets matched the color scheme for the room. The bedspread draped across her footboard bore a medieval map, an embroidered sea serpent and compass rose on exotic two-axis pattern being plainly visible. She realized she was wearing her garb. That sight brought her sharply awake. Someone had put her into bed, not undressing her the way mom would have.

Memories flooded back. The Wizard of Mars. The Tunnels of Time. Comet and the Guardian. Eclipse and the Lords of Eternity. Now they were almost home, except they couldn't go home. Eclipse? Here? Yes, once Aurora focused her perception on it, there was the faintest trace of Eclipse's mind, Eclipse being asleep a floor up. The trace was really faint. Eclipse's shields, even when she was asleep, were locked tight. Without a recollection of where Eclipse had gone to bed, she'd have been unfindable. Eclipse being here was too strange.

How had she gotten here, Aurora asked herself? They were on the West Coast, in someone's house. Someone had carried her to bed, in the company of a someone whose mind felt almost like daddy's to her not-quite-asleep memories. Comet? Comet had almost been killed. Twice. She probed the deeps of her sister's mind. Comet was all healed, but out cold. She'd used superspeed sleep on herself, so she'd slept much longer than the clock said, but she was still very tired.

Fine. Let Comet sleep. Let Cloud and Star sleep. Eclipse always took care of herself—and everyone else, too. Meanwhile, she had peace. She had quiet. They weren't going anywhere until Comet woke up; well, mayhaps not. She could always ask Eclipse. Memories of how Eclipse had felt the night before, after rescuing Comet in outer space, ruled out waking Eclipse. Eclipse would wake up if asked, but it would be perfectly beastly not to let her sleep. Eclipse had half-way died, several days in a row. Let her sleep.

There was finally time, Aurora thought, to catch up with her diary. She slid out of bed and opened a sealed pouch in her duffel bag. withdrawing a few sheets of folded paper. She tiptoed to the writing desk and began to write.

"Dear Diary,

"We flew across the universe twice, the StarCompass still pointing. It should have been pointing home, since it took us away from the Tunnels. Except we're not home. This is almost like home, but it isn't. Did we beat the dooms? Mayhaps Star beat them, and isn't telling, so he can brag himself up more. He'll like that. Boys! Mayhaps you can't figure out that you beat them. Mayhaps we found how to beat the dooms, beat them, and didn't notice, like the pearl-loined letter.

"Eclipse said she'd help fly us. But Comet and I could tell. Eclipse was hurt bad in her fight at the Tunnels. Not bleeding, but hurt inside. Star and Cloud didn't care. And when she said before, she was OK from the Maze, so it was OK for her to come along, she was fibbing then too. Polite, but fibbing. I can tell. You don't get well from the Lesser Maze, not in a couple months, not with how bad she got hurt there, broken ribs and bone bruises and things inside bleeding.

"Then we found we weren't home. It looked like America, but it wasn't. We rescued a space plane. The people inside didn't know what a persona is. There are no personas. Later Eclipse visited one astronaut, met her family, returned her clipboard, and learned our money is worthless here but our coins might be worth something.

"Comet tried going to Washington, to find out where home is, except they almost killed her. Eclipse rescued her. The next day, we used the StarCompass. It led us to Victoria Wilson, who had no idea where there are dooms, and led us to a criminal. At least, he was supposed to be a criminal. So we staged an action against him, the four of us, Eclipse being with Pickering. When we arrested him, his minions tried shooting Star and Cloud. Then they used poison gas on Comet. Poor Trisha, no, Comet, almost died. Again. Star and Cloud saved her.

"The StarCompass also led us to this real chill guy with a very frigid house. Eclipse talked to him. He had us for dinner. All five of us. He even gave us real cocoa, not caring we're not grownups. That's a stupid rule. Why should grownups keep chocolate for themselves? No one dies of chocolate poisoning. It's always 'kids don't need it'. Anyway, he doesn't know who Eclipse is! Strange!

"He's nice inside. Almost as nice as daddy or mommy. He's terribly sad about something. I didn't look to see what he's sad about. Not polite! I wish I could help him. Then I fell asleep at dinner. Rude! That's what Daddy does when Uncle Jim shows slides.

"I woke up once. Eclipse had a nightmare, worse than Comet or Star or I ever get. Lots worse. She dreamed she was back in the Maze. She dreamed she lost this fight and a guy beat her to death. Slowly. She woke up and we talked mind to mind and then she was all right. I think. If she's ever all right, all alone inside her head, when she knows most of the world except me and Comet wants to kill her.

"It's next morning. Comet and Star and Cloud and Eclipse are asleep. Alex Pickering..."

She strained, looking mentally. He was hard to find, but he was reading in his library. "...is wide awake. Mayhaps I can have breakfast, even if I should be polite and wait for the sleepyheads to get up. (No, that's not fair to Comet or Eclipse. They're both very tired.) Bye. Janie."

~~~~~

The same sunlight, brighter now, awakened Comet. She felt the bed besides her for Harold. Nothing. Her favorite stuffed frog was not where she expected it to be. Her eyes popped open, noticing in half an instant an unfamiliar bedroom with a second slept-in bed. Some of her clothing sat neatly folded on a dresser. She was still wearing her garb, but someone had taken off her boots.

She stared at her pillow. The fabric was cotton, a mix of narrow brilliant green and blue and yellow pinstripes on a white background. It was a lovely fabric, a pattern like nothing she'd ever seen in her life. She absolutely had to remember it. The pattern would be great for a blouse.

"Janie?" she whispered. No, she thought, I'm still wearing garb; we must be in persona. "Star? Cloud?" Silence answered her. She remembered Mars, sky pink as cotton candy, clouds like streaks of marshmallow, the Temple of the Wizard a vast pile of stairs and porches and pillars covering all of Mons Olympus. After the Wizard, she'd flown them to the Tunnels. For all that she'd done interstellar before, only intergalactic flight matched Tennyson's immortal line. They were here now, wherever here was.

This isn't home, she thought to herself. This whole world isn't home. I brought Star and Aurora and Cloud and even Eclipse back home, and I blew it. Completely. I went to the Wizard. I asked the questions, instead of letting Eclipse do the talking. She's way cleverer at that sort of bargaining. The Wizard gave me a real StarCompass, and they're foolproof. I flew us to the Tunnels, and then brought us home. Except it's not home. I don't know where we are, but it's not home. The StarCompass is foolproof, but not Cometproof, so it's all my fault.

Now Star will say you can never trust a girl to do anything right, not even talking. Janie trusted me, her big sister, and won't say a word that sounds like complaining, no matter how much she'll cry when she knows I'm not watching her. Eclipse won't lose her frigidkeit, but she never forgives herself her own mistakes. She won't say she blames me, but she won't forgive me. After all, she never forgives herself. Comet pressed her face to the pillow.

Her eyes stayed dry. She couldn't find tears. She had to face brother and sister and Cloud and Eclipse. She had to confess. She'd made the mistake, so she had to undo it, no matter what it cost her.

She stood, muscles protesting. She felt worse than she had after her hike with Uncle Jim, the hike to the top of Mount Washington. Being a persona helped a bit, but being a persona really only helped much on things related to your gifts. When she exercised hard, she felt it the next morning. This was worse; it was being poisoned yesterday. Every single one of her muscles had spasmed, all at once. Her mind had gone crazy. Star said her heart stopped; she couldn't remember that. Star saved her.

A shower, change to fresh clothing, and carefully making both beds improved her mood.

Downstairs? No, she had something to do first, even if her stomach did keep telling her how hungry she was, even if she wanted to talk to Aurora and Eclipse until she was no longer completely zeroed out. At corridor's end was a small second-floor porch. The view was north, looking downhill across a formal garden into banks of bare-branched trees. Beyond were woods rising into low mountains; her vision picked out the rising column of hot air that suggested a small village. She stepped outside, the door closing firmly behind her. Earlier she'd been disconsolate. Now, refreshed, she could put back her shoulders, square her jaw, and tell herself she had a task that matched her gifts, and hers alone.

Flight field cut on. She pivoted over the railing. Her flight field tightened to light-folding dark, then through a mirror finish to nothingness. Invisible to all but the most careful of observers, she soared skyward. An overflight of the village found nothing out of the ordinary. To all appearances, she was above a small American town. Except this was a small town where no one was a persona, no one had ever heard of personas, no one thought there could be personas. A huge slice of American life was missing. There had been no hidden Goetica Arcana, no shining Marik whose parades shook the earth, no colonists setting sail to AutumnLost. Eclipse had asked an astronaut, and she was sure. There were no ancient technical civilizations.

She could bring Pickering a present. He'd been so nice to them all. His library had a stock of rock paperweights, souvenirs of his various trips and expeditions. He certainly couldn't have any Mars rocks. She hoped he liked her choices.

~~~~~

"Guten Morgen, Telzey," Pickering said. It was indeed a beautiful morning, and with some luck he was a step closer to finding the secrets of faster than light and time travel.

"Good morning, Herr Doctor Professor von Pickering." The voice remained sourceless. A computer monitor showed the face of a gold-blonde, blue-eyed young lady, whom Pickering had happily described as the most beautiful woman he could possibly meet in his life.

"Telzey, I believe three of our guests are in their bedrooms and one is in the meditation room. Am I correct? Where is the fifth?" he asked.

"I confirm motion and infrared detectors showing four guests in bedrooms three, four, and tower and the meditation room. The fifth of our guests ceased to be present on the property at 0812 hours local time."

"Telzey, in which direction did the last visitor leave the property?" asked Pickering.

" I have no data on that question."

Pickering hesitated. Despite her conversational mode, Telzey was not a rational being, merely a well-supported AI program. Her conversation was reasonably coherent within limited scripts, but her understanding of the world was different from a human's.

"Telzey, the last—the fifth—visitor: generate a time series: her locations while on the property over the last six hours," he directed.

"Displaying." Telzey's monitor showed a schematic of the house, a scarlet line winding from Comet's bedroom to the rear upper porch.

"Telzey, where was the visitor at 0611 hours?" The monitor put crosshairs on the porch. Pickering increased the magnification. Comet's trail simply came to an end at the porch at 0612 hours.

"Telzey, external visual for the West wall. Commence at 0600 hours." The monitor showed Comet step onto the rear porch. At 0612 she flared into brilliant pastels. "Telzey, step back in time slowly. Stop. Screen contrast to high. Slow forward." Pickering watched as Comet burst into light, did a humanly-impossible acrobatic maneuver over the railing, accelerated upward, and vanished.

"Telzey, consult proximity radar tracking data. Search for a target starting near the West Porch at approximately 0612, and accelerating upwards. Correlate with external visual for West Porch." The screen split. The radar track showed an object leave the house, head west, and vanish. The visual track gained a superposed line with error ellipsoids.

The radar/visual line began where the Comet line stopped. Pickering scratched his head. Why didn't Telzey identify the radar track with Comet? Oh, right! One of the inferential rules was that people could not fly. A brief search of Telzey's memory confirmed that Telzey had applied the rule, inferring that the radar and visual tracks of the flying object were not Comet, who was presumed to have left the property without crossing a boundary. Oh, wonderful! he thought. I think there are people who fly, and my computer accepts that people teleport! The computer is, however, correct; I watched Eclipse do it. Radar track numericals supplied velocity and acceleration for the take-off. One hundred gees? wondered Pickering. That was unreasonable, even allowing that she was female and a child.

"Telzey, did you recover the PUBnet files I requested earlier last night?"

"Yes, Alex."

"Is the facial recognition search complete?" Pickering asked. Telzey had looked carefully at runaways, escaped criminals, lunatics, and missing residents of juvenile homes.

"Yes, sir."

"Were there matches?" Pickering asked.

"None, sir."

Pickering leaned back, pulled a soda from the refrigerator hidden under his desk, and thought more deeply. His guests did not appear to be missing, not from this earth. The powers they had used to rescue the space plane were unearthly. The coins were a mystery. According to his highly reliable confidential source, parallel worlds were very different from this one; a parallel-world origin could be excluded. Telzey stored his study of missing-person files. He had certainly made a diligent search. Given the flight demonstrations, which Telzey carefully recorded in multiple places, he could claim to future interrogators that the children were provably an elaborate practical joke. He had simply played along. After all, everyone knew that people cannot fly, so an event involving flying comic strip characters had to be a practical joke. The hologram projectors on the space plane, giving the illusion of Eclipse teleporting, were a technical tour de force.

~~~~~

Comet, returned to earth, found Cloud and Eclipse in Pickering's library, staring at a world map. At some world's map, she told herself, certainly not hers. Manjukuo, Tibet, and half of Mongolia had vanished into the Celestial Republic—China, they now called it. From the presence of city names the Sea of Glass now hosted a country. Details were wrong everywhere else, with way too many nations in Eastern Europe, too few in Asia. Pickering leaned back in a winged arm chair, legs propped on a hassock, letting his guests talk.

Distant voices were Star and Aurora, someplace else in the house, undoubtedly locked in combat over the chess board. Comet used the barest trace of lift to lighten her steps, tiptoeing so gently that her feet barely pressed against the parquet flooring. Pickering still anticipated her entrance, so that he faced the doorway when she entered the room.

"Comet! You're awake!" Eclipse's enthusiastic greeting cut through the conversation. From the sun-angle, it must be breakfast time. Comet smiled bashfully.

"And in better health than last night, I trust?" Pickering added warmly. Comet's answer was cut off by a flurry of greetings and hugs, a newly-arrived Aurora and Star pressing close around her. "Is brunch finally in order?" Pickering asked. He led an enthusiastic group of children through the Great Hall to his kitchen. Comet, too numb to reply, allowed herself to be dragged along.

She found herself seated firmly at one end of the breakfast room table, denied the chance to apologize for her mistakes while successive mugs of orange juice, milk, and hot chocolate were placed in her hands. A few shuffles left Pickering in command of the kitchen, Eclipse deftly relieving him of most real work.

The others told their tales. Aurora had been awake since dawn, to be joined first by the boys and then by Eclipse. As Comet juggled a piece of toast, she recognized that Alex had not eaten yet. He had accepted Eclipse's insistence that she would wait for Comet before eating.

"It really wouldn't be polite to the cook," Eclipse explained to Comet, "People having breakfast at five different times. So I waited." She continued to cook, not yet having had a bite to eat herself. A smooth gesture and rapid-fire tracery of cerise lines reduced a half-dozen cleaned onions and potatoes and two pounds of roast beef to neatly minced eighth-inch cubes. The gentlest shimmer of light raised the saucepan from dead-cold to onion-browning temperature, olive oil sizzling as microdrops of water came to a sudden boil.

Cloud and Star looked guiltily at each other, then stared at Aurora. Why should Eclipse do all the work? Comet nodded her agreement at their unspoken thoughts. Not saying a word, the two boys rose, marched over to Eclipse, and pointed meaningfully, first at her and then at the orange juice and cocoa already on the table. Eclipse protested feebly, but let the boys assume her role as chef.

Star took the cook's role, Cloud passing him ingredients. The window over the stove was open. Pickering noted that the rising steam from the oil made an unnatural beeline for the window, a beeline only interrupted while Cloud was moving foodstuffs to the pan.

A sizzle and whistle bespoke the bottommost bits of roast beef touching the hot oil. No sooner were they browned than shredded onions, floating half-an-inch under Cloud's open palm, made their way to the oversize pan. Pickering took a half-a-step closer to the stove to raise the gas, then realized that the stove remained unlit. Star's hand was sheathed in a golden mesh of light; hand passes over the pan bringing a crackling sound and the familiar scent of rapidly browning onions. He paused once and again to stir.

"Usually I do this Saturdays," Star explained. "Dad and Mom go to his lab early and I make breakfast for when they come back. Of course, I can't tell Mom why I cook so much better when she's not watching. Dad likes the hash, so he says not to look." The children burst into laughter at a joke they'd heard many times before. Salt, pepper, and a dash of Worcestershire sauce followed; sage and oregano were carefully palmed. "Besides, Dad knows he taught me how to cook."

Pickering had meanwhile been preparing the cream sauce, stirring beef gravy into heavy cream with just a touch of cornstarch, adding crushed garlic, and heating, pausing once and again to check the oven, where two loaves of fresh bread were rapidly approaching readiness. His guests were very well behaved; someone had done a magnificent job of parenting. He could remember cooking when he was Star's age, though to his recollection never a beef hash. Expecting small children to do a proper job of folding a powder into gravy without lumping it remained a bit much.

~~~~~

Breakfast had been excellent, at least from Pickering's point of view. His guests had relaxed, talking quietly with each other. The boys argued baseball, which they called base ball nines, and the forthcoming season. Pickering hadn't had the heart to note that Boston had not recently fielded two major-league teams, and assuredly neither team had ever been the Brahmins. The girls gossiped about friends and courses at school, Aurora doing most of the talking. Comet seemed withdrawn. Eclipse talked happily about studies, but said nothing about any school friends.

Aurora cleared the dishes, just as though she were back at home. Pickering broke out a box of molasses raisin cookies, whose long wait in his pantry had now come to an end.

"I think I'd better start this," Comet announced. She looked out the window, at the ceiling, anywhere except her friends and siblings. "Alex? I brought back some presents for you, for being so good to all of us." She fumbled through her pockets, finally depositing a collection of stones on a trivet. "I picked up these on the Moon. And the red-pink ones, they're from Mars."

Pickering reached for the first, then snatched back his hand. A curl of fog off the sides of the lunar stones suggested a somewhat lower temperature than his skin would tolerate. Gingerly, he grasped one in the sugar tongs. "Fascinating," he said. "Absolutely fascinating. The Martian rocks are absolutely lovely. That ruddy orange is wonderful. You must have worked very hard to find ones so colorful."

Comet blushed. "Mars is like that."

"They're all lovely, and merit a special place on my desk," he answered. "Though my desk lacks your pockets' insulation."

"Pockets?" Comet asked. "Oh, my body field, that's all."

"You went to Mars again?" Star asked. "Neat! You could've asked us along."

Comet stared at her hands. She could tell; this was going to be absolutely horrible. They didn't understand and weren't going to let her tell them. They were going to keep talking. The longer they talked, the worse her truths would sound. She stared helplessly at Eclipse, who'd saved her life and never thought there was any debt to be repaid.

"Guys," intruded Eclipse. "Mayhaps you could let Comet talk? I think it's...important." Cloud stared at Eclipse and received a firm nod. He shrugged affably. Eclipse backing Comet had to be one girl backing another because they were both girls. It still wasn't worth picking an argument. Not yet.

"I, oh, I don't even know where to start," Comet began. "It's all such a tangle, and it's all my fault."

"Don't worry, Comet," Aurora whispered, "We're with you. Tell us."

"We're lost," Comet answered. "Completely lost, and it's all my fault, and I don't even know what I did wrong, except it had to be me, because I carried the StarCompass. And now the StarCompass doesn't even work; I keep looking for it to point home and half the time it points right here to this house, when home isn't here at all, and half the time it points someplace else, a different place each time I look." Comet's confessional came so quickly that no one dared interrupt her.

Comet? Eclipse's words, warmly supportive, were heard only by their intended recipient. *I'd've gone with you. Even if it was only you and me. Even if it was for sure the one-way trip.*

"We went to save the world," Eclipse said. "To see the universe. To sail the silver sea of suns. Not to destroy everything."

"Yeah," Cloud answered.

"This is silly," Star objected. "We didn't do anything. Not a thing. Except fly in a big circle. No. Not a circle. The same line, back and forth. How could we change everything? We did nothing! Well, you had a little fight, Eclipse."

"My opponent didn't get hurt. Well, not enough." I didn't kill her, she thought. "I didn't get hurt, hardly. So where's the world?" Eclipse said.

"Personas? How can't there be personas?" Aurora said. "Even if someone changed the world completely, like when The Supreme Illusionist changed Harvard Square into the Piazza Leprecano, there was still a world. People still have houses, nice ones." She smiled at Pickering. "They still have books and computers and videos and airplanes, 'cause I saw one this morning. So why can't they fly?" She was answered with silence.

"Eclipse," Cloud asked, "are you like absolutely sure no one's heard of personas? Could they just have a different name?"

"I looked, Cloud," the girl answered serenely. "I looked with telepathy. Hard enough I could hear people's minds remembering how to breathe. But people flying, except airplanes and aeronefs and fixed ornithopters and, well, one guy had seen a really lousy rocket belt?" Eclipse shook her head. "I never saw anyone fly."

"Assuredly," Pickering remarked, "you are the only people I know who fly under their own power."

"I know how you change it all overnight," Eclipse said. "Time travel."

"Like the chron, chronulator, chronuplicator? Except one that works?" Star interjected.

Eclipse explained. "Someone changed the past. Someone changed things so history is different. When we came back, history was changed. No one knows us. No one remembers personae because no personae were ever born."

"Who?" Star asked.

"Why?" Comet asked. "How'd they make the Wizard disappear? And the sky octopuses?"

"If there were no personas," Cloud said, "the League of Terran Justice could conquer the world. Mayhaps it did. That explains it. Someone prevented personas from ever happening, so they could conquer the world. But look at the world map. The world doesn't look conquered."

"Mayhaps they're hiding," Aurora said. "If no one knows they're conquered, they don't know they're supposed to start a revulsion, ummh, revolution. They just sit there controlled by their secret rulers."

"Secret masters," Pickering grumbled. "Illuminati. Trilateralists. Communists. The Insider Conspiracy. The Sun Cross. If you think someone secretly runs the world, there are lots of candidates." Most of whom, he added to himself, would be hard-pressed not to botch registration at a modest science fiction convention.

"If I'd never been born," Eclipse said, "if I didn't exist, I couldn't've grabbed the Namestone. So it'd still be safe in the Maze." *Aurora? Star? Ask me afterwards about the Namestone? Frigid?* There was nodded agreement.

"Even safer than before," Pickering said. "We've never heard of the Maze, let alone this Namestone widget."

"So where is the Namestone now?" Eclipse asked. "Buried in Atlantis?"

"It can't be," said Cloud. "They've never heard of Atlantis. Unless it's under water, and they forgot."

"But I dreamed about Atlantis, last night," Comet said. "A huge marble building, burning, me standing inside."

Eclipse cut her off. "Guys? Concentrate on our here and now problem?" *Comet! Ask me about your dream! Privately? Please!* Comet shrugged.

"Catch the guys who did it! Make them put the world back," Aurora said.

"Wait a minute," Star said. "That chronuplicator gadget is just a fancy video projector. Isn't it? I mean, you can't travel through time, right? No one can change the past."

Eclipse looked deeply thoughtful. "Are you sure you have to go to the past? To change it, I mean? Wouldn't telepathy be good enough?"

"Telepathy to the past? Telep to someone a hundred years ago? How?" Aurora challenged. "If someone could do it, wouldn't we know?"

"Now, wait here," Pickering intruded. "Time travel sounds like, say, space travel. So it sounds reasonable. But it's not. After all, if you had a time machine, you could go back in time, and kill your grandparents before your parents were born. Then where would you be? You'd never have been born, so you couldn't have killed your grandparents, so they would have lived, so you would have been born after all. And now it's a paradox. Isn't it?"

The children looked at each other. "No, it isn't," Cloud answered. "You were born before you killed your grandparents. They died after you were born. I read it in a book. Einstein explained it. When he fixed his relationship theory. After Solara took him to AutumnLost."

"Einstein? He had a theory of time travel?" Pickering hoped his guests would remember more about Einstein's theory.

"Einstein," Cloud said. "E equals m c squared Einstein? His old theory said you couldn't go faster than sound, no, light. Or something silly like that. Solara showed him he was wrong. She took him to AutumnLost. It's a country. Like France and Lemuria. It's in another galaxy, awake a couple days each decade. When Einstein came back, he replaced 'Relativism' with 'Transitivity' "

"I see," Pickering said. "Transitivity says there's faster than light? And time travel?" Nods from Cloud. "And if you go back, you can change history?" Pickering was fiercely attentive. Hopefully, Pickering thought, Cloud remembers more about Transitivity than Eclipse did.

"The book said so," Cloud answered. "No one's done it. I think. Or no one noticed. After all, if you murder your grandparents, everyone would remember they got killed. And when you got back to the present, no one would know you, because no one remembers before the change."

"That's us!" A flash of recognition touched Aurora. "No one remembers us. Not at all. Someone changed time. And missed us. We're trapped. No. We have to find him. Find whoever did it. Make him change it back."

Eclipse pushed on the table, one fist clenched. "Timeward is a direction, the way up or left is a direction. I should be able to teleport there," she said half to herself.

"It's a direction?" a disbelieving Cloud asked. "You can't point your finger from now to then. How can it be a direction?"

"Not a pointing direction," Eclipse answered firmly. "A teleport direction. They're not the same. To go to Boston, the teleport direction isn't which way I'd point my hand, to point toward Boston. But I know which teleport direction Boston is. Just like I know which way to point, to say where Boston is if you want to walk there. And I can see which teleport direction timeward is."

"Get off it, Eclipse," Star countered. "Now you're saying you do time travel? Was that how you cheated the Maze?"

Eclipse held her breath momentarily. "I said I know which way timeward is." A faint violet tracery cut the air around her. Eclipse estimated the depth required. She shuddered. "If it were real important. If it were real, real important? Say, saving the universe? I think I could teleport timeward. Once. You'd have to give me an awful good reason to do it. You'd be on your own when you got there."

"As usual, not gonna do anything herself. You might work up a sweat, and want to take a bath," Star sneered. Cloud nodded knowingly at the younger boy's perceptive comments.

"I'm sorry, Star," Eclipse apologized. "I'm pretty sure my gifts won't work after I die. That's why my time travel is once only. I'd burn doing it."

"Die!" Comet squeaked. "You don't mean that, do you? Don't hurt yourself, Eclipse."

"I said I'd need a very good reason before I tried," Eclipse answered. "I'm not for sure positive it would kill me. Not absolutely positive. I could mayhaps do it with lots of time to rest first."

"Let me get one thing right?" Pickering intruded. "Einstein, your Einstein? He explained flying faster than light? He said you could reset time? You can go back and change the present? You don't remember his theory, do you, Cloud?"

"Yeah," Cloud answered. "He said that. I read it in a book. You can change the past. And when you come back to the present you remember both histories, and everyone else remembers the new one. It was a math theory. With equations. And three time directions. One that clocks use. One that time travellers use. One that tells you what caused what. And they're all different. That's how he explained it. With equations. And six clocks." Pickering nodded, forcing himself not to ask if Cloud thought there were other sorts of theories, ones without equations. However, Pickering told himself, if Einstein could work out such a theory, so can I. And then, if history may truly be changed, then that which was not to be will be made to have been, for I, the great von Pickering, will countenance no alternative. Not when her soul is the stake.

A clamor of voices, all trying to be heard at one, intruded on his reverie. "Mayhaps we should each try thinking," Cloud said, "by ourselves. So we each get a plan. Then we do a mindblitz. I need a plan. A good plan. I need to find who did this. Then we make him put the world back, the way it belongs. Until then, I think we promised to do lawn raking...not you, Comet, you weren't here."

"For Alex?" Comet asked. "Sure. I'll be dressed in an instant."

CHAPTER 16 VICTORIA AND THE PERI

Pickering stood in his back yard. His guests stood facing him, garden rakes over shoulders like a squad of infantry lined up for inspection. Pickering spent a moment silently congratulating himself on his genius. He'd persuaded his five guests that a morning of raking thatch from the lawn would pay for their keep. After all, raking lawns was a level of duty all American parents routinely expected of their children. The final statement, he noted, was even true, so long as you excluded the incompetent eighty-five per cent of all parents from consideration. Emphasizing the routine-duty issue was critical; his guests were being given a chance to perform normal deeds for a normal reward, so that they could not say that they were employing their gifts for their personal profit.

"This is an isolated area," Pickering remarked. "The gates are locked. The boundaries are posted. I've spent several years having the perimeter planted with giant long-thorn rosebushes, raspberry and tayberry canes, hawthorn and yew and sea rose and poison ivy and oak, so in most places entering the property is, let us say, entertaining. You can however trust your helper when she gets here."

The children looked uneasily at each other. They could all tell; Pickering had a reason for inviting this extra person to help rake. It wasn't that she had a gift for leaf removal. Pickering just hadn't said what the reason was. "We need help?" Star inquired.

"It is a large lawn," Pickering emphasized. "I expect the ivy and pachysandra and hosta beds to be thoroughly raked, without destroying them in the process. Your assistant did it last year. By herself. Several weeks ago I promised her a share of the work. Surely you cannot expect me not to honor my word? Indeed, Telzey tells me that she is at the front gate, so I will return with her shortly." He turned and headed down the driveway.

Only when the voices grew very close did the five discover who the sixth helper was. "In any event, Victoria," Pickering was saying to the newcomer, "it's not that I'm so short of lawn that only one person can work at a time. Besides, your helpers are interesting people."

Comet looked in surprise at the girl with Pickering. Pickering had said the newcomer would be her age, but the girl with Pickering had to be fourteen or fifteen. Then she recognized who the girl was, now dressed in working clothes rather than her school uniform.

Eclipse waved at the newcomer, who looked carefully and waved back. "Professor Pickering," the newcomer said, "this is impossible! Isn't

159

it?"

"I'm sorry, Victoria. Is what impossible?" Pickering said.

Victoria looked over the rest of Pickering's visitors, her gaze settling on Eclipse and Comet. "This?"

"As a general rule, that which happens cannot be considered to be impossible," Pickering answered.

She looked at the fivesome, still disbelieving. "I guess. But how did I find the rest of you?"

"This is something to do with the StarCompass," Comet answered.

"Perhaps introductions are in order?" Pickering named names in a round, five children named by their public personas and one Victoria Wilson. To his surprise, Pickering found that all six were entirely willing to rake, so long as they could all talk at the same time.

Victoria listened in fascination to the five's stories of their past, occasionally surprised by the sharpness of the exchanges between the boys and the girls. Sure, Victoria thought, boys and girls aren't quite the same. She knew that because she had brothers and sisters of her own. But these five took that attitude to an impossible extreme. Star and Aurora, fraternal twins, sounded scarcely willing to believe that other had learned how to count to three. To Victoria's surprise, she was included in the exchanges, as though every girl in the world was expected to know that every boy was a half-wit, and vice versa.

Victoria listened politely, tolerating needling that was so sharp it was almost funny, until Star blandly suggested that people here were never heroic, because there weren't any personas here and now. Suddenly Victoria realized why Pickering had been so insistent about bringing her here today, when the five were perfectly able to rake the lawn by themselves, probably in three seconds if they weren't politely keeping pace with her.

"I had an adventure once," Victoria announced. "A real one. Maybe I didn't go to outer space. I'm not going to boast. Some people would have found it frightening, at least a little bit. Professor Pickering knows the story. But you had to be there. I was terrified. And if my Mom and Dad find out, I'll be grounded for life!" she warned.

"Been there," Comet said.

"We won't tell," Star answered. "We've all got parents. They didn't want us to have adventures. Mayhaps except yours, Eclipse. Do yours even know?" Eclipse shrugged noncommittally.

"If your parents don't want you having adventures, aren't they upset that you're here?" Victoria asked.

"The Wizard of Mars said we should go, so Dad and Mom said to go," Star said.

"Me also," Cloud added.

"He said the other choices were worse," Aurora said.

"I volunteered," Eclipse shook her head. "Duty, heavier than worlds."

"I'm a mercenary," Comet said. "I named my price, and Speaker of the House paid it in full." Victoria looked quizzically at Comet.

"Later?" Comet asked.

"If being there counts, I can fix that. Sort of," Aurora inserted. "At least, we'd see what you saw." Victoria looked puzzled.

"Telepathy?" Victoria asked. "You mean, talking without sound? Like what we did yesterday? Or UltraGirl? Read minds?"

Read minds. Aurora shifted from voice to thought, simultaneously linking the seven into a shallow unit, so each saw out of all seven sets of eyes. *Share minds, so we hear what you want to let us hear.*

Victoria gasped and dropped her rake, her heart suddenly pounding. What was happening to her? Why was she here and there and...? The sensations faded.

"Sorry," Aurora said. "I was going to let us see your story. From your eyes. So we'd understand why you had to be there."

"Aurora, dearest," Comet inserted. "No telepaths means she's never done group telepathy before, right? It is frightening, the first time, isn't it, especially when you don't know in advance?" Comet focused her attention on Victoria.

"That was group mind-reading?" Victoria whispered. "When I got all spread out?

"Sorry," Aurora said. "I'm very, very sorry. I forgot. You never did this. Don't worry. I didn't let them see your elephant. And I didn't peek."

"Elephant?" a baffled Victoria asked.

"Your elephant. I'd never let anyone else see it." Aurora apologized.

"I don't own an elephant," Victoria said. Meeting five superheroes might be an incredible adventure, but it was becoming stranger and stranger. People who could fly were incredible, but a pet elephant?

"She won't know that, either," Comet reminded.

"It's slang," Cloud said to Victoria. "If you tell someone 'don't think about elephants' they think of one." Victoria nodded. "The telepathy elephant is the same. It's what you don't want to think about. Most people keep secrets. Things they don't want other people to know. Names of private personae. What they really think of their mom. Smart people have stray bits of imagination. The bits make up wicked things, to embarrass you by showing things you never think about. That's the elephant. The naughty bits and pieces. Aurora will show us what you want us to see. Without the elephant."

"I suppose," Victoria answered. She hesitated again. She had been sitting on her story for so long, with no one except Professor Pickering to tell. Now she'd found people who might believe her. They might even understand what being brave was really like. For all that Pickering had never really grown up, not really, he was still an adult, not someone you could talk to. "Do you promise not to tell my parents?" The fivesome nodded assent.

Victoria? She heard the softest of whispers, a voice not heard in Victoria's ears. *Eclipse here. I'm not looking at what you're thinking. If you want I'll show you what I'm thinking.*

Hi? Victoria? It's me. Aurora. We're talking. Like on the bell—the telephone. Only more private. Is that you, Eclipse? Victoria compared the two voices. Eclipse's thoughts were utterly precise, the transparent background to each word showing less about her mind than your stationery said about your thank-you note. Aurora bubbled with enthusiasm, each word bringing images, implications, traces of yesterday's memories not yet faded into darkness.

"So this, ummh, do I have to talk out loud?" *Or can I just think things?* Victoria asked.

"Are you guys cutting us out again?" Star asked. Eclipse emphatically raised one hand. Behind the gesture Victoria felt Eclipse's logic, focused entirely on Eclipse's concern for her, she who had done telepathy once, yesterday, and didn't need to be overwhelmed by a half-dozen minds at once.

Patience, Star? Aurora asked. **When we did this first time, it was scary. We were frightened. And I'm your twin sister. Even if I am a girl. We're total strangers to Vicky. You knew what telepathy is; she doesn't.**

Okay. I forgot. Weird there's no personas now, he answered.

This is what I'm seeing, Eclipse continued. Victoria saw the lawn through another pair of eyes, an image saturated with Eclipse's total inner calm, a tranquility so pervasive as to be contagious. The picture sharpened, gained meanings, names for trees and flowers, memories of the path a half-seen sparrow had taken as it flitted from branch to branch. *If I hunt around there's some elephant.* A silvery wall put a bubble around thoughts, Victoria realizing that she was inside the bubble and Aurora was outside. There was the Tower room, the bedroom Pickering had granted Eclipse, suddenly vandalized, with paint-stained carpets, holes in the wall, and shredded bedspread and curtains. *It's very small child mischief,* Eclipse explained, pained by what her own mind generated. *I suppose it's not very wicked, but it would hurt Alex. That's the elephant, thinking things I wouldn't do.*

It takes getting used to, Victoria said. *Like Adara and gating.*

With Adara's name came memories of a girl Eclipse's height, perhaps with even more muscle in arms and shoulders, red-haired, wielding a silvery fancy-hilted sword in one hand. With gating came memories of kneeling on a hilltop in the darkness, Adara's head cradled in Victoria's hands, and suddenly being elsewhere, someplace where plants were purple and smelled of lemon and nutmeg. *I got used to one; I'll get used to the other.* Eclipse was suddenly absolutely still. At the sight of elsewhere she had frozen, listening with the intensity of a starving cat stalking a squirrel to any words Victoria might offer.

Mayhaps I let you meet the gang now? Aurora interjected. Feeling the gentlest of nods, she extended a mental net. Comet brought a sunglow warmth. To Victoria, Comet was a girl her own age, not-quite-shared memories speaking of friends. There was the briefest hesitation, Comet stumbling on the discovery that she was as old as Victoria.

Cloud was a bit harsher, friendly in a slightly clumsy way, the not-quite-little-boy who wanted to be president of a club even if he had to start it himself to be sure he was President. He wanted to be the inspired leader whose decisions were always wise. He wasn't quite sure what wisdom was, but knew he must have a lot of it. After all, he was the leader. He had to be, of course, because he was the oldest and a boy. Except if you looked closer, Victoria noticed, he really wasn't at all sure of himself. She smiled and felt him smile back.

Star was an attitude, bored by girls playing girl games, wishing he could show off what he did. He recalled standing in a baseball diamond, firing bolts of energy into a flying robot: Star in Boston going one-on-one against Emperor Roxbury. Victoria stared, at first puzzled by the utter clarity of a wishful daydream, finally recognizing that she saw real memories. Star came from a place—it had to be someplace else, no matter that Star was sure it was right here in America, not three months ago—where people with strange powers, people like Star, protected the world.

Be calm, Victoria told herself. Fighting a flying creature is no stranger than Adara and you and the things. Except you were scared to tears, half out of your wits, and he was...

"I was scared, too," Star said. "I won. That made me feel better."

Scared's just being sensible. Victoria matched. *I didn't know what I was getting into. Not until I got there. You knew in advance, and went there anyway. You were a lot braver than me.* She felt Star shy away, ever so slightly, from someone bragging him up. Where had that line come from, Victoria asked herself? Star? 'Bragging up' wasn't a phrase she'd ever used.

Aurora bubbled, the slightly younger girl who was delighted to be accepted by older playmates. Not that much younger, Victoria thought. *You sound my age; are you really younger?* she asked.

Aurora smiled brightly. *I'm twelve!* she answered. *OK, barely twelve?* The three girls' thoughts were a constellation of friendship, into which Star and Cloud were swiftly dragged.

There was one more, remembered Victoria. Eclipse was a quiet shadow, unseen if you didn't look right at her. Eclipse linked her mind more closely with Victoria's, letting Victoria see a shadow of inner self that the four never knew: aching fatigue, never-mentioned pain from gifts invoked more deeply than was safe, adult burdens born without complaint no matter how much she would rather curl up with a book or ride her ponies across acres of rolling fields. **I thought you were my age,** Victoria said to Eclipse, **you're much older, aren't you?**

You're older than I. *What month were you born?* Eclipse asked.

September, Victoria answered.

I'm December. Sometimes I sound older. Eclipse's crystal letters clouded with shadowed recollections of violence, of stalking, lurking terrors. *How old's Adara?*

Older than even Professor Pickering. Hundreds and hundreds of years, for all she looks like you. Images of the red-haired girl came to mind.

Mention of near immortals sent a flurry of thoughts spinning around Victoria. She caught 'Corinne', 'the Silver General', a string of names so well-known that no explanatory references seemed necessary to the fivesome. Except, noted Victoria, that Eclipse's reaction to the names was totally different from anyone else's.

Victoria felt each of them as close to her as if they were holding hands. Star and Aurora and Comet were brother and sisters, back to back against the world, for all that Star complained that his sisters would be better if they were boys. Cloud was someone they knew, someone they liked and played base ball nines and soccer with, even though a tight knot of resentment ate at his heart, resentment that he wasn't as good a leader as he wanted to be, no matter how hard he tried. Eclipse? She was very definitely not part of their group. She was someone whom Star and Cloud distrusted, someone who was delighted to be warm and open and close, but not afraid—only sad—whenever the circle of friends excluded her.

Pickering finally joined them. If the five's minds were the constellations seen from a city park, his were the stars of the darkest wilderness firmament, brilliant fields so densely packed that the constellations disappeared. Each of his thoughts trailed clouds of memories leading to memories leading to memories in a seemingly infinite branching regress. Like a starburst dendrimer, supplied Alex, but not limited by excluded volume.

While Pickering was providing the words, Victoria knew sharply what each of them meant. When his thoughts drifted, she realized she still remembered his thoughts about dendrimers, molecules shaped like spherical trees, and excluded volume, a thing getting in its own way. Alex, realized Victoria, brought his own orchestra, so each word had its own chord, each sentence came with a complete tune. He listened utterly patiently to the thoughts linking the six of them. He's a grownup, Victoria thought, with grownup depth, but he takes to new experiences like little boys to new toys.

The alternative, dear, came his observation, *is to be a mental fossil, frozen in time like an insect in amber. [Image of wasp trapped in honey-gold solid, seen in a distant museum.] Or is it telepathic etiquette to be less forward?*

You're fine, Aurora answered. Why did she sense some awful tragedy behind Pickering, something that permeated every fragment of his being?

Victoria looked back at the fivesome, her questioning *but who are you all?* being greeted with mental images of public personas, garb, seals, gifts, and clever deeds. Comet alone had bitter memories of the past, memories she did not invite Victoria to inspect. "People in costume," Victoria said. *Secret identities and flying and costumes? Like in comic books?* She felt Cloud connect her words and images with his.

Costumes and secret identities? Star answered. *I'd say garb and private personas. Except now personas only exist in* [image of a comic book, surreptitiously inspected in a local store] *American manga.* A manga, Victoria realized from their shared memories, was a comic book. Northeast Asian. Violent. Pictorial. Lovingly drawn guns and swords. People somewhat short of clothing.

We also have manga, under that name, said Pickering, supplying a memory of a very crowded subway car, businessmen reading telephone-book thick comic books, subway schedules being in Japanese. He drew back, expanding his memories to give a dozen scenes of Tokyo, Mount Fuji, and a flight over the Pacific to Taipei. Cloud, Comet, and Eclipse, baffled, compared mental maps.

Formosa? That's the Sea of Glass, Comet thought. Cloud and Eclipse superposed images of waves of black and red-brown obsidian stretching for tens and tens of miles. *Manga are from Manjukuo and Nippon.* A shimmery mental map set these countries in Pickering's northern China and Japan, with territories extending up to the Arctic Sea.

165

Cloud? Eclipse whispered across the room, her thoughts tight-focused on his. ****This Adara, the girl Victoria keeps mentioning. That sword is octopus-keeper style. The place with purple plants, where Adara took Victoria. That's the place I found in their memories, the place I couldn't figure out how to teleport to. Try to get Victoria back to her tale, can you? If I suggest, she'll see why. She sees too well what I'm thinking.****

Cloud froze. Wasn't he supposed to find all the great stratagems? After all, he was the leader. However, no one but Eclipse knew where the plan had come from, so it would appear to be his idea. If the plan worked, he'd get credit; if it failed, he'd blame Eclipse. For once she was right; he told himself that accidents could happen. Besides, she was actually asking him to help her, saying she couldn't do it herself. Cloud put all his sincerity into his voice. "I'd really like to hear your story, Victoria. If you'll tell it...Please? We'll tell ours later, OK?"

Sure, Victoria answered. She allowed that you could like telepathy, given half a minute to adjust. **Sure. Besides, Dad and Mom would never believe what I did.** She tried to order her thoughts, not protesting when Pickering shepherded them to a collection of lawn furniture. This was a long tale, easier told sitting down.

It started with birds, Victoria announced. **I didn't know that. Not then. I found out later. But it started with birds. Perhaps it started with Donny Martin, which means it started with the Martin boys. They're half-way reasonable—for boys, anyway—or would be, if their parents hadn't let them bother birds with their air rifles. Not that they shot anything; these were the air rifles that only made loud noises.** Victoria caught the slightest giggle from Comet and Aurora at her reference to boys.

Mr. Martin wanted to protect his apple trees. The boys' idea of protection started several blocks away. I told Timmy and Tommy Martin to stop. They were frightening my cat. When they didn't, they got to hit me back first. Of course, being able to beat up on either of them, even when they happen to be a grade or two older, helped. I play basketball and soccer; they just sit in front of a TV set like overstuffed potato sacks. Dumb!—like my older brothers, though Mom hardly lets my brothers watch TV at all, at least by comparison with most kids. Professor Pickering, of course, says television broadcasters are no different from dope pushers—that's a bit much.

At least dope pushers hesitate to praise the virtues of their own product, an acerbic Pickering emphasized.

Once, a year and a half ago, Timmy and Tommy realized they outnumber me two-to-one, Victoria explained. **Their younger brother*

Donny promptly pitched in on my side—"Just to make it fair", he'd said.

Why did birds matter? I'm not sure. Professor Pickering tells all the kids Indian stories about the Spirit of Table Rock, who did not allow violent death near her mountain. Certainly Indians never hunted on Table Rock. Now the mountain is a wildlife refuge. But Indian stories, probably stretched a bit, don't answer my question. Of course, the County Historical Society has a genuine true-to-life painting of the Spirit, made a hundred years ago by the state's greatest artist. I've seen the painting. When I first saw it, I thought it a bit strange. The Spirit wasn't an Indian girl in leather and moccasins. She was a white girl, red-haired, wearing a long cape, chain-mail armor, and a sword like one of King Arthur's knights. Later? Later I found out why that painting is important. Victoria realized that she could feel Star's disbelief. He couldn't see how an old painting mattered.

Last Spring was Donny Martin's accident. I almost got into a lot of trouble over it. And I didn't do anything wrong, only looked guilty at the wrong time. Donny had been playing on the Majelski bridge—General Ignatius Pavel Majelski to my history teacher—during Spring flood. It was a stupid thing to do, and Donny knew it.

In Summer, the St. Olaf river burbles gently, flowing through its stones so you can wade from one side to the other while schools of minnows swim by your toes. Playing on the bridge then is one thing. But in Spring, the Saint Olaf roars icy-cold off the mountains, raising white foam as it sweeps over boulders, on its course into the lake. If you fall into the Saint Olaf in Spring, you could get hurt, even if you're the county swimming champion. Well, maybe you guys can get away with it, being bulletproof and everything, but I can't. During spring flood, I cross the bridge carefully, keeping well away from the edge.

Donny Martin had to be different. She remembered him clowning on the railing, while she and her older brothers watched from downstream. Her brothers thought it was funny—boys could be awful stupid.

Not that stupid! Star objected, his tone shifting to shocked disbelief: *Are boys dumb now, instead of girls?* His sisters choked down laughter. Star tried to hide his disappointment: he'd just found the biggest change in history imaginable, and his sisters thought he was being a clown.

Some boys, Victoria answered. *Not you. Back to my story. Donny slipped.* Victoria drifted deeper into her story, so her descriptions of herself became the deeds of a third party. Ever so slowly, like the first leaf of autumn, he went over the edge toward the water. Her brothers ran for help. What could she do? She couldn't possibly go after Donny, not in that current, not in water chilled by mountain snow. She sprinted for the water's edge. Donny's head was above water. Someone was in the river supporting him. Despite the wild rush of the current, Donny and the other moved closer to shore.

Victoria reached the bank as they stood up in the shallows. Donny was white as a sheet, coughing and shivering from the cold. The person with him was a girl—a girl who didn't look much older than Victoria. Who was she? Victoria knew everyone in her class at Ford Middle School, and most of the kids in the next two grades. It was no one she had ever seen, and the girl would have been difficult to forget. She was tall, if not growing-up tall. She had to be a real athlete. Even if the river hadn't proved it, you could see how much muscle she had on her arms and legs. Her hair was a brilliant red-brown, now plastered to her scalp, matched by blue-violet eyes and a rosy complexion.

Donny didn't have the strength to walk to shore. Forgetting the danger, Victoria stepped into the shallows and pulled him over one shoulder. The girl held Victoria's hand as they dragged Donny out of the river. The girl's fingers were steely-strong. Whoever she was, she was breathing heavily, but not gasping for breath. She certainly wasn't shaking with cold, even though she was soaked to the skin.

You could've done that, Comet, Star added.

Yes. But I wouldn't've been soaking wet. And I'd have landed on the bank. This girl swam, not flew underwater. Sorry, Victoria, Comet said.

Victoria remembered very clearly what happened next.

Victoria had hauled Donny up onto the bank in a fireman's carry, just like they taught in Girl Scouts. The other girl, who still hadn't said anything, had kept him from swallowing too much water. When Victoria set Donny down, she took her eyes off the stranger, just for an instant. There was a sound of tearing silk, so soft she wasn't sure she'd really heard it. Then there was a stillness in the air, the absence of deep breathing. Even before she turned around, Victoria knew that she was alone, that when she looked back no one else would be with her.

So I was alone with Donny. Moments later two neighbors came running down the path. My brothers had found help. The neighbors thought I went in the river to rescue Donny. My clothes were pretty wet, after all. If that story got back to Dad and Mom, I'd have been in real trouble. Donny said I stayed on shore. Then Donny asked where the girl was, the one who dived into the river to save him.

No one had seen the girl leave. One neighbor said that the girl might have fallen back into the water. After all, she must have been on her last legs when she staggered to the river bank. Who was it? he wanted to *know. What was her name? For an second, I had a terrible sinking feeling. I was about to have an argument with a grownup, the kind you can never win. I had no idea who the girl was. It was someone I'd never met, but the neighbor wouldn't believe me. Grownups never believe children don't know each other's names. When I opened my mouth to try to explain, knowing it wouldn't work, I found I knew the answer. Suddenly, I had a vivid memory of looking into the other girl's eyes while she introduced herself. 'Adara'", she had said.**

Except the other girl hadn't said anything. I had vivid memories of every moment, from the instant I reached the river bank to the instant when she vanished. There was no time to have looked into her eyes, no time to have heard her speak. There was just an extra memory, like a piece in the box after you finish a jigsaw puzzle.

Telepathy? Cloud asked.

More like teletransfer, Eclipse answered. **Oh, sorry, Victoria. In telepathy, you hear my voice. But if I'm careful, I can leave you a memory, without you hearing me put it there. You remember the memory, but you don't remember learning it—it's just there. That's teletransfer.**

That's what it was, Victoria agreed.

That sound, Aurora said. **That's [sound of ripping cloth, muted, vanishing in a few instants]. That's Them. Them!** Her thoughts were tinged with fear.

Them? Victoria asked. **Giant ants? [Images of 1950's vintage film, USA saved by heroic FBI agents, watched on late-night TV with all the outside lights on.] Her disappearing—you did that in the shuttle, in reverse, didn't you, Eclipse? The astronauts said you appeared from noplace, like with a transporter beam. [Recollections of a television classic many decades old.]**

Them, Star answered. **The folks who invaded South America.**

Transporter? Teleportation. I don't use a machine, Eclipse said.

"Adara called it gating. There's more later," Victoria explained. "Anyhow, the rescue squad and a reporter arrived. Donny got an ambulance ride with police escort all the way to the County Hospital. He looked all right to me. I think the grownups were bored and wanted to have some fun. After all, the last crime in Table Rock had been three weeks before, and that was a purse snatching. That was all last Summer, before the troubles started."

"At a neighbor's insistence, more policemen fanned out downstream, looking for Adara. They didn't find her. No one knew who Adara was. The police wanted Adara's last name. I didn't know, and said Adara must be visiting from someplace. After all, I know everyone at Ford Middle School, and Adara didn't go to school there. I couldn't shake the feeling that I'd seen Adara before, even if we'd never met. But where? I couldn't remember. The reporter listened politely. He pretended to believe every word."

"He asked hard questions. I hadn't seen Adara dive off the bridge, but Adara must have, to reach Donny so quickly. She hadn't been wearing jeans or sweats or anything common. She had trousers and a tunic, woven in dark and light green, with yellow thread—gold lace, I thought, not saying it—on cuffs and collar and waist. There was a pin—a golden sun-disc—on her chest. Where did Adara go? I hadn't seen her leave. She was just gone. Adara was a heroine. If the reporter could find her, her picture would be on the front page of every paper in the state."

"Finally I told him to stop asking. If Adara's parents learned she dived into the St. Olaf, never mind why, they might get angry with her. She could have died. Maybe Adara wouldn't want people to find her. The reporter stalked off, leaving me to walk home. At least Mom didn't notice my clothes were wet."

"I think the next important part was the calendar," Victoria inserted. "Up on Table Rock Mountain is this vertical sheet of stone covered with strange inscriptions. If you stare hard, they look like they were melted into the rock. If you ask about people who wrote in spirals, Professor Pickering talks about 'the unique example of the Phaistos disc'. No matter what you ask him, he knows the answer. But Phaistos is on Crete, six thousand miles away—I looked it up—so it couldn't have to do with Table Rock. The inscriptions were supposed to be an ancient Indian astronomical clock, just like Stonehenge."

Aurora almost but not quite suppressed Pickering's pride at Victoria's characterization of him, even if he didn't know quite absolutely everything. Whispers of thought passed across the audience. Pickering caught names, Leaviork and Tsolrin and Goetica Arcana, all ancient nations known only to his visitors. *The Phaistos disc,* Pickering inserted, *is unique. [picture-memory: a blond-brown terra-cotta disc, carefully mounted, peculiar glyphs pressed into both sides by long carved styli.] We associate it with no known civilization, and ought to be able to.*

Victoria resumed her story. "I went to photograph the shadows as they lay on Mid-Summer's day. If it was a clock, it must have been used in Mid-Summer. The guidebooks said it was used in Winter, to find the year's end, but that's silly. It rains all winter. There aren't any shadows. I set up my tripod on top of Chimney Rock, fifty feet above the parking lot, and waited for noon. Then a group of high school boys arrived. I listened, horrified, to what they were saying. The inscriptions are used in my school's insignia—the Table Rock Titans—so the boys wanted to blow them up for a prank. 'My dad checked,' prated—another Dr. Pickering word—one of them, 'Them cuttings is all a big fake, not something worth money.' I had checked, too. The first explorers in the valley, two hundred years ago, had seen them.

"I carefully took pictures of the boys and their car, then hid the film under a stone. Even if they grabbed my camera and searched me, I'd have proof. Finally I stood up so they could see me. 'I heard what you said,' I shouted, 'I've got a camera if you try it.'

"The boys shouted back, using words you aren't supposed to know, let alone use. They tried climbing after me. Chimney Rock has one very steep, narrow approach, the chimney of its name, and sheer walls you need ropes to climb. Well, I'd need ropes, not knowing how to fly. I threw two big stones down the chimney. The first was a warning. The second they had to dodge. The boys retreated, cursing. They gathered dry wood. 'Come down,' they called, 'or we'll burn you out.' That wasn't clever of them. The flames would keep them away from me. The smoke would lure Forest Rangers. I called them names and begged them not to burn anything. They put a match to the wood, just the way I wanted.

"Safe, I took my pictures of the sun's shadow. Doctor Pickering was surprised to learn I used solar noon, not wrist-watch time, as if he hadn't told me the difference himself. Sirens in the distance announced the Volunteer Fire Department. The boys took off in their car. I told the firemen what happened, then persuaded them not to scale the cliff to rescue me. After all, stone doesn't burn. After the Sheriff caught the boys and found their dynamite, the firemen gave me a ride home in a real fire engine."

"Now," Victoria announced, "we reach important part. It was a bit frightening." Her memories sharpened, so they all saw it as if they were there watching. *[Last Summer, Victoria and classmates Kelly Pierce and Penny Deering had marched off on a picnic, not knowing that the county was in an uproar. Five hardened criminals had escaped from State Prison, robbed the Fifth National Bank of Centervale, and headed for Table Rock State Forest. It had been the start of the troubles, though absolutely no one knew that at the time.*

[Her recollections were confused. Five strange men found the picnic and invited themselves into the conversation. Kelly, whose mother regularly told her not even to think of talking to strange men, stood up to leave.

['No!' one man shouted. 'You come with us!' He drew a knife. Victoria bolted for safety, but was tackled by a second man. Roughly, the girls were dragged into the trees. 'We won't hurt you,' the man announced. 'We need hostages.' Kelly and Penny took his words at face

value. Victoria had watched too many news stories about hostages. How could she escape?

['That will be quite enough!' came the voice. Adara! Wearing the same green fabric, but a different outfit, with long sleeves, a full-length over-shoulder cape, and green-brown leather boots. Adara stood upon a low stump, her back against an ancient Douglas fir, one foot propped on a protruding lump of wood. The men still towered over her. 'You will let them all go!' Her voice sounded of absolute determination.

[Two convicts grabbed for her. Adara punched one in the jaw. Incredibly, he toppled over. The second she pivot-kicked in the stomach. He sailed back, rolling to land behind Victoria. 'Get her!' a third convict shouted. The remaining men jumped on Adara, pushing her back in a flurry of struggling limbs. They couldn't pin her, but she didn't have enough room to throw a good swing. Victoria knew what happened to girls kidnapped by criminals. This was life and death, right now, her life and her death. She grabbed a melon-size rock, brought it over her head, and hit one of the prisoners. She had all her weight behind it.

[The distraction gave Adara the moment she needed. Two men fell to the ground. Autopsies revealed multiple shattered bones. The remaining prisoner whipped out a knife and plunged it at Adara's face. There was a cling of metal on metal. From someplace, Adara had pulled her own dagger—really a more-than-girl-size sword, noted Victoria—and blocked the prisoner's blow. He stepped back. Adara went after him, her blade a flicker of silver light. He parried once, raising blue and pink sparks. The prisoner fell to the ground. Heart attack, the coroner's report read. Victoria was positive he'd taken a sword thrust to the chest.

[The second prisoner, still clutching his stomach, drew a pistol. 'No witnesses means no trouble,' he announced. He took aim at Victoria. Or was he aiming at Adara? Victoria blocked the line of fire. The barrel loomed enormously wide, a black mouth swallowing her every thought. She was too frightened to dodge.

[Suddenly, without seeming to move, Adara stood between Victoria and the pistol. The man snarled and fired. For the shortest fraction of an instant, Victoria's eyes insisted that Adara was gone. Then she was back, seemingly unhurt. The prisoner deliberately squeezed off two more shots, equally without effect. Each time he fired, Victoria was sure Adara vanished. The prisoner cursed. Victoria heard a burst of shots, one blending into the next. At the last, Adara staggered backwards, gesturing intricately with one hand. The prisoner's eyes glazed. Adara looked around. Her face was dead white. Victoria could see blood splashed on Adara's tunic. Before Victoria could say anything, Adara vanished, disappearing like a light bulb that had suddenly been switched off.]

Teleport, Star thought. *No flare, none at all, either! She must be real good! What was the bullet trick?*

Double, Eclipse answered. *Teleport out; take bullet with you. Teleport back; leave bullet someplace else. Needs real sharp timing. You're right on flare, Star! She must be real good. Lots better than me. You could double, Comet, if you learned teleport. You're that fast. Faster-than-light is almost the same as teleport. You should learn; it beats sneaking away from miscreants. Or the bullet could have been dephased. That's not the same as double; it means the bullet just passes through everything without harming them. That's tricky, especially fast.*

Adara got caught at the end, Victoria noted. *After she got shot, she knocked the man out.*

The early part. That wasn't Manjukuoan hand-fighting, Cloud noted. *She was using a lot of muscle. Almost the way I would. Are you sure there aren't personas here, Alex?*

Reasonably, Pickering answered. *Present company excluded. Her gifts have another source. You could say she was our world's one persona, though.*

That big sword, Star added, *that's what Anachronists call a bastard sword, a hand-and-a-halfer. Someone let me swing one at Morgaine's Fair last year. Swinging them one-handed needs a real good wrist. I couldn't. The hand waving at the end?*

Magic. Adara told me so, when we met, Pickering inserted. *Continue, Victoria.*

The law was drawn by the gunfire. The Sheriff had little to do. Three of the men were dead, a fourth had a broken jaw and was unconscious, the fifth was in a coma. Kelly and Penny and I gave three different stories. They saw Adara, but completely contradicted each other about what Adara did. Five bullets were found in a tree. The sixth vanished. Professor Pickering told Dad and Mom that the bullets were terrorist munitions, packed with deadly nerve poison.

Dephasing, Eclipse interpreted. *Double teleport makes bullets vanish. Dephasing lets them go through things. Through you, Victoria.*

They put me in the hospital, with neighbors and relatives—people I ordinarily see once a year—trooping through to check I was all right. I'd rather have been at home. The parade was enough to give me nightmares, Victoria said. She returned to her story.

CHAPTER 17 VICTORIA ON TABLE ROCK

And I had nightmares: hazy dreams of being trapped, neither here nor elsewhere, unable to move. The dreams were more horrible than terrifying. Not enough to wake me up so I'd run crying to Dad, but enough that I remembered in the morning. I dreamed I was at Table Rock, looking at the sky, and I had a terrible fever, enough I saw things I knew don't exist: Giant bugs. Flying dogs. In my dreams, I knew I was seeing through Adara's eyes. Night after night, the dreams repeated, the Moon taking its slow course through the sky. If I look at the Moon, I think of a faded Christmas ornament or the ball of stone first visited in prehistoric times—before I was born, even—by astronauts. To Adara the Moon signified a gate slowly swinging open.

Not prehistoric, Pickering objected. *Within my lifetime.* Aurora felt a sharpening of Eclipse's interest when astronauts were once again described as Modern Americans, not as AutumnLost's ancient mariners.

Victoria resumed. [With the dreams came pain. A tearing agony was a great spike driven through her shoulder blade. There was someplace she wanted to go, but with her shoulder pinned that someplace was an uncrossable distance away.]

In the dreams, Table Rock was a glowing opal pillar. Around the pillar, some tens of yards out, hovered a ring of light—a warding circle. I looked up 'ward' in the big dictionary, and found that a ward could be a protection from magic. The dictionary scared me. How could I know things in my dreams before I knew them when I was awake?

The ward made Adara invisible, so picnickers saw in Table Rock a cold black stone. Beyond the circle massed the lurkers in the darkness, those who waited to shatter the ward and claim Table Rock. Adara was sure she could beat the lurkers, yet terrified of what else would happen. I couldn't tell what frightened Adara. [Adara's thoughts came shrouded in a shower of brilliant grief, the end of a goal Adara had pursued for longer than Victoria could understand. Adara was maybe a little older than Victoria; in the dreams, she had waited for something through vast impossible eons.]

Then, Victoria explained, *I knew Adara was in trouble, and I had to help her. It was impossible. It didn't make sense. How could I know? I owed her my life. My life! So I had to help her.* She returned to her memories.

A full moon floated above the mountains, shining brightly into Victoria's bedroom. Her watch chirped once, softly, to be swiftly stifled. It was time! Quickly, she pulled on jeans, navy-blue sweatshirt, and black ski mask. Not quite garb, Victoria noted, but it worked.

Her sleeping bag, already rolled to the proper size, went under her blanket, the bulge giving the illusion that she was still in bed. Ever so gently, she eased open the latch on the screen, pushed it away from the house, and slipped out the window. Her parents were sound asleep. Older brothers and sisters were still watching TV. This was not the moment to be caught. She'd never be able to explain what she had to do, not in time.

Victoria froze recollections in mid-frame, realizing that everyone had seen what she remembered, down to the tightness of her watchband and the soft rasp of metal against metal when she opened the screen latch. This was telepathy, but it was so close, so complete, so well-controlled that they might all have been there.

Thanks, came Aurora's response. *It's the way it's supposed to be. If I do everything exactly right. You've been meshing into it for a while, now.* She felt Victoria's acceptance of the mentalic link.

Great job, Aurora, Eclipse added. *We were there with you, Victoria.*

Victoria resumed her tale, swiftly forgetting where she actually was. Her thoughts drifted out of first person, so the six heard the tale as told by a distant storyteller.

In time! The nagging pressure which had filled her dreams for the past week was more insistent than ever. There, up at Table Rock, her friend was waiting for her—needed her badly. Her friend could wait no longer, not with the full moon a skull-white galleon floating over the Pacific Range.

The yard was empty. She slipped from shadow to shadow, locked in a very real game of hide and seek. You can't, she told herself, be seen when you aren't moving. Not after dark. Not when everything you wear is dull black, darker than the very shadows that hide you. She reminded herself of hide-and-seek games played in moonlight. She had lain still on rough ground, her brother's toes not three inches from her nose, without his knowing she was there. If she had to, she could do it again.

The cold dew soaked her feet. But she'd foreseen that. Extra socks and all her hiking gear waited in the treehouse at the end of the lot. She'd hidden them there earlier. If someone found her now, she might be able to explain why she was outside at this hour—"I'm memorizing a constellation for the Science Fair" would fool Dad—but if they spotted the pack, they'd be sure she was running away.

Parents will believe almost anything, Cloud inserted. *So long as it sounds like something you should be doing.*

If they'd caught me, that would've been the end of the rescue expedition, Victoria continued. *And the end of my friend, too, I

175

somehow knew. * Grimly, she switched from sweatshirt to looser clothing, laced up her boots, and pulled on her jacket. Table Rock was five miles away, and 3000 feet farther up. She had a long climb ahead of her. This far into autumn, most of it would be cold. She couldn't chance a flashlight, not for much of it, though there was a good trail. With a full moon, a clear sky, and some caution, the climb still ought to be possible. Getting back home in time would be hard. She'd worry about that later. Maybe her friend could help.

Her family lived right at the edge of town. The path took her by only one other house. If she met Dr. Pickering, its eccentric resident, she would just tell him the truth about where she was going and why. He wasn't a grownup, not really, no matter how old he was. He'd believe her. He might even come along.

Perhaps optimistic, * Pickering interjected. *Your tale was a mite hard to believe, except that I trust you completely, until I met the evidence.*

Town lights faded behind her. Under the pines, it was pitch dark. A few stumbles, taken with her alpenstock, reminded her to raise her feet. Dr. Pickering, of course, wouldn't have an alpenstock, he'd have his walking stick, a beautiful piece of dark wood topped with a tiny silver gargoyle.

The trail began to curve upward, not enough to slow her down, but enough that she began to breath more deeply. The lightest of breezes shook the branches, setting fuzzy moon shadows shimmering at her feet. That was good, she told herself. If someone saw her, they would think it was only the wind shivering the pines.

Real sharp, * Star noted. *Like a FedCorps Commando, when he can't use his invisibility.*

FedCorps? * Victoria wondered. She sank deeper into her recollections, so that they were there, walking with her, inside her body.

She finally came out of her reverie. The easy path was at its end. The rest of the climb was a series of meadows, separated by steep, rocky pitches through which rough steps had been cut. Great-grandmother had done this walk in daylight. She could do it at night with the full moon behind her. The air was crystal clear. The breeze had blown itself out. Despite the full moon, constellations burned bright in the heavens. They were familiar friends: Andromeda and Pegasus and Cygnus. She was climbing briskly. Soon the ocean would be visible to the west.

There was a sudden rustle and crackle behind her. Victoria started, swallowing an outcry, then froze in place. If someone was following, she couldn't move. She looked over her shoulder. In one small group of trees, branches swayed heavily, as if stirred by an unfelt wind.

Something must have flown into them, she thought. An owl, she told herself, only a big owl.

The climb to the next meadow was short, but so steep she was almost on hands and knees. Now she heard more creaks and groans, and saw trees shudder, though the air was completely still. She wasn't afraid of the dark, but her ears insisted that something was following her. She tried to believe that she had spooked herself, that the sounds were all in her imagination. Finally she stopped and rummaged to the very bottom of her pack. Her great-grandfather's hunting knife, carefully sharpened, buckled to the side of her belt, placed where she wouldn't fall on it if she tripped. A visiting aunt from Los Angeles had left behind a canister of tear gas. Victoria slipped the can into a jacket pocket. You're being very silly, she told herself. You're afraid of shadows and little noises, at the time of day when you should feel safest. After all, if you can't see it, it can't see you.

She glanced at her watch. It was well after one. Despite the darkness, she had travelled nearly four miles. She leaned back against a rock and sipped at her canteen, peering all the while into the shadows. She didn't see anything. Not that I'm afraid, she said out loud. I'm bigger and meaner than any wild animal left in the state.

Meadow followed meadow. The air was so chill that her breath formed little clouds which sparkled with trapped moonlight. She was only cold when she paused to catch her breath. She heard the snap of breaking twigs behind her. Something large and heavy was following. Or perhaps two somethings, one which climbed and one which flew. The twig-snappings and the branch-wavings lay in different directions. She stopped once and again to look. They only moved while her back was turned. She tried turning suddenly to surprise them. Once she caught a hint of motion. Her stomach knotted. The shadow looked very big, too big to be real. She felt at her knife, and at the can in her pocket.

Then she laughed at herself. She was behaving like a little kid, afraid to go to bed because she had seen a horror movie, full of vampires and witches. There couldn't be anything out there, so there was nothing to fear. Well, maybe a bear, but they slept at night, didn't they? She was being frightened by her own imagination.

It didn't matter. Even if something were out there, out where nothing could possibly be, she had to go on. She had a debt to Adara, one impossible to repay. Besides, she told herself, whatever they were, they were behind her. If she turned around, she would be walking toward them.

Victoria's daydreams were interrupted by a light. Up the mountainside she could see a pearly glimmer, rosier than moonglow. It was the opalescent color from her nightmares. At first she was heartened. She wasn't chasing shadows; something was really there. Fear took slightly longer to arrive. What was she doing? Here she was, miles from home, climbing a mountain in the moonlight because of a dream. Suddenly her climb became absurd, like the astrology column in the paper. Telling the future from dreams was for stupid people from a hundred years ago, not for sensible girls who went to school and watched movies and helped their fathers wash the dishes. But she had really seen that eerie glow ahead of her—seen it!—while she was sound asleep, before she saw it in real life. That wasn't possible except in make-believe.

If you thought they were just dreams, she asked herself, why are you hiking up a mountain? It's the middle of the night, when you should be safe in bed. Victoria asked herself what her parents would say when they found out. That scared her a lot more than anything else. They really let her do a lot, compared to some other kids. Kelly Pierce's mom wouldn't even let Kelly play softball if there were boys on the team, let alone coed soccer or basketball. But if she went beyond her parents' limits, and this had to be beyond the limits, Mom and Dad were pretty rigid.

Your parents and mine too, Cloud offered. *Yours may not know about personas, but someday mine are going to learn I went up against Emperor Roxbury, one-on-one.*

Two-on-one, Star corrected. *And he went down in flames.*

Guys! Comet objected. *Before time got changed around, people did things like, well, like what you did, like stopping Emperor Roxbury and arresting the Supreme Illusionist, but no one does anything like that any more; they don't have a hint you can, so what Victoria did is a lot farther out of line. From her parents' side, I mean; we'd say it was gifttrue. Wasn't it, Victoria?*

Of course it was, Aurora answered. *You were great, Victoria! Going up alone. We stayed together. Besides, doing personas is something people do. At least, it was before we went to the Tunnels and came back. We get gifts in dreams. But running away from home because a dream told you to, that's a lot harder to explain, isn't it?*

Harder? Victoria responded. *Impossible? I still don't believe I did it. Except the dreams were so convincing.* Victoria kept a thought to herself. Something she'd said about Kelly Pierce's mom had rubbed the five very much the wrong way.

Dreamshaping, Eclipse suggested. *To someone who didn't know, the dreams would be totally real. You were really brave, braver than I'd ever be.* Eclipse's words carried complete sincerity.

"Eclipse?" Cloud questioned. "You did the Maze. You told off the

League of Nations. How can anyone be braver than you?"

She shrugged, wishing he didn't always pick arguments with her. "I knew what the Maze is. I had to do it. I did it. What Victoria did, not knowing why, was lots harder."

Victoria regained her train of thought. The final slope was piled with boulders, forcing her to test her footing with each step. Halfway up, she stopped to catch her breath. The sounds behind her had drifted away. She looked over her shoulder, and immediately wished she hadn't. Not more than a hundred feet behind her, a black amorphous mass crept along the ground. At the front floated a pair of emerald lights. Eyes! came the unbidden thought. Eyes! Her flashlight, unused until now, hung on her belt. Desperate, she grabbed it, hoping light would reveal some harmless trick of shadow. So what if she lost night vision! The flashlight would last the two hundred yards to Table Rock. She pointed and pressed the slide. Four D cells worth of light stabbed out.

It was the size of a small van, with glistening blue-green shell, two dozen fine multi-jointed legs, and a ridiculously small head that turned up to stare, bedazzled, at her flashlight. Below the eyes things moved from side to side. Like a spider, she recognized, it has the fangs of a giant spider. A shriek died in her throat. Just as in her worst nightmares, she was too scared to speak. Her knees sagged.

The tale-telling was interrupted, the telepathic link swirling in chaos. Aurora, at the verge of panic, clutched her brother's hand. "Sorry," Victoria said, "I forgot how frightened I was."

"Oh, wow," Star said. "And you don't fly, or disrupt, or throw lightning bolts, or anything useful. And there was this thing even uglier than a Lemurian almost close enough to touch. You didn't faint. Or scream your head off like a silly girl. Or anything dumb like that. That was really frigid!"

"Did what I could, I guess," Victoria answered. If she hadn't been in the middle of her story, and Star had been someone she knew better, she told herself, she'd need to have a little private talk with Star. Scream like a silly girl, indeed! She wasn't some twit escaped from a 50's horror film, all mouth and no brains. What was it with these five, that the boys and girls kept cutting each other down? "Are you okay, Aurora? I'm sorry I scared you. I forgot what it was to be there and see that thing."

Aurora smiled and restored the link. Victoria continued. *I didn't have time to scream. So I turned and ran.*

Memory carried Victoria ahead. She scrambled up the slope, jumping from rock to rock. No matter how fast she moved, she knew the thing would be faster. It was chasing her. It had to want to eat her. Things like that always ate people.

She scampered to the hill crest. Table Rock was as she had dreamed, an enormous unfaceted opal whose luminescence outshone the full moon and threw shadows up at the sky. "Adara," she croaked, too frightened to do more than whisper. "Adara? Where are you? Please!"

Silence answered her.

"Adara?" she called again, almost in tears. Shivering with fear, Victoria stumbled toward the rock. Perhaps the ward from her dream would protect her. Near Table Rock, she saw Adara, slumped on the ground, head propped against a small boulder. Victoria felt her legs buckle with relief. Somehow she managed to keep walking, sinking to the ground only when she reached her friend. Adara's face was pale. Her tunic was streaked with dried blood.

"Adara?" she asked.

"Victoria?" Adara's voice, when it finally came, was high-pitched and remote. "Have I your name aright? I wasn't sure you'd hear my dreams, or that you'd be here in time."

"Of course I came!" Victoria answered. "I owe you. I owe you my life." Then Victoria realized what Adara meant by 'hear'. "You sent the dreams? But how? That's impossible! Come on! We've got to run! There's a thing chasing me." Victoria slipped an arm under Adara's shoulder. Adara's hands were cold from the Fall air, but where her cloak had sheltered her, her skin burned.

Dreamshaping, Eclipse suggested. *Depth-of-power requirement is a real bear.*

"A thing?" Adara asked nonchalantly, shrugging off Victoria's aid. "Large and green? Oh, don't worry. Kreesha can't climb stones. It'll have to circle around."

"But...besides, you need a doctor. I can feel the fever." Victoria calmed down slightly.

"One of your shamans...that's all I'd need. Victoria, there's no time to talk. I know what to do. I've had a week of lying here, stumbling no farther than the spring while I maintained the Shield, to think about it." Adara gasped for breath. "Unless you want armies of Kreesha crawling around. The ones in the trees are worse, when there's lots of them."

Victoria was baffled. This wasn't like anything she'd studied in school. It didn't match the plot of any movie she could remember. Her Dad's gentle lessons on choosing the right didn't seem to matter. What was she supposed to do? "I owe you my life, don't I? Those fellows would've killed Kelly and Penny and me. Can't we call the Sheriff? No. He's a grownup. In movies grownups don't believe kids about monsters until it's too late."

Adara sat up. "There are three things to do. Third, I stop the Kreesha.

Second, you delay the Vandamond—the flying things. I can't, not and get the tool I need. Don't worry. Vandamond aren't tougher than the boys on your street, only uglier and dumber. First thing is the hard part."

"You're going to fight that green thing? But it's the size of a truck. And it's got teeth like crowbars."

"Mandibles," Adara corrected dreamily. "Mandibles. Teeth are fixed in bone, and go up and down. Those are held by cartilage, and go side to side. No, the first part is worst. The bullet is still in my shoulder. You have to take it out."

"Adara, we've really got to get you to a doctor. I mean it. Those bullets were poisoned."

"I noticed," Adara said coldly. "The metal is worse. It keeps me from gating home. I'd take it out myself, if I could reach."

"What do you mean, gating? Where is home?" Victoria asked.

"It's easier to show you. I'm not imagining things, though I've had a week of lying here to try." Adara was stiffly matter-of-fact.

"Here? For a week? Through night and rain? Didn't anyone help you?" Victoria was appalled that people would ignore someone lying in plain sight, close to unconscious and obviously bleeding.

"Within the ward, I cannot be seen, save when I will elsewise. Passers-by think me a tree stump, one too rough to sit upon. The rest was not—pleasant. Days were nice and sunny, so I slept then. Nights, and this high it was sleet, not rain, I endured. My cloak helped some. I didn't have a choice. If I walk away, the Kreesha have the Gatestone. When the full moon reaches the zenith, they may yet take it. Now, slip off your pack and belt. There's too much metal in them. Even so, I can't do this for more than an instant, nor gate far enough to get what I need. Not against the metal in my shoulder." Adara was grimly insistent.

Victoria felt the hill tremble under her knees. It was early evening again. They were surrounded by acres of luminous flowers, blue and violet in the twilight. The air smelled of lemon and nutmeg. Victoria stood, still holding Adara's hand, and stared into the distance. A flock of brilliant-orange birds with impossibly long, billowing wings glided out of the sunset. Gentle hills rolled out to the horizon. The mountains, the whole Pacific Range, were simply gone. Victoria's hand tightened around Adara's. They were back at Table Rock, the moon floating unperturbably overhead.

That's the place you saw, Eclipse? Aurora asked.

Check, a stunned Eclipse agreed. **When those folks teleported.**

Victoria continued, unaware of the background conversation. "Do you believe me now?" Adara asked. "That's gating. You do it enough times, you learn how. If you're human. You saw me do it before, when I left your picnic." Adara trembled with exhaustion. Her voice was nearly gone. "I'll tell you what to do. Don't be afraid. I won't bleed to death. Please? You're my only chance."

Victoria wanted to argue, but there as nothing to say. If it was a dream, well, what you did in a dream didn't matter. If she was awake, she had to trust Adara.

"Victoria, my other way of stopping the Kreesha. If you won't take the bullet out, I'll do it. But it will kill me. I don't want to die. Not here. Not yet. Please?" Adara begged, her voice a hoarse whisper.

Numbly, Victoria propped her flashlight behind them, then did Adara's bidding. Adara looked grimly into the distance, showing no sign of pain while Victoria followed directions. Despite the depth of the incision, there was very little blood. Only at the very end, as Victoria fumbled to pry out the bullet, did Adara's guard slip slightly. She squeezed her eyes shut, not quite holding back a gasp while tears streaked her face. Victoria ransacked her pack for a bandage, while Adara distantly described the Vandamond. Adara's voice stopped. Adara was gone, here one instant but not the next, like a coin in a magician's palm. Where was Adara? Victoria wondered. That disappearance? Was that what she and I did, when we went wherever we went? Adara had vanished like a ghost to a half-heard rustle of tearing cloth.

Victoria loosened the sheath of her knife, and put on her heavy leather gloves. She was terrified. She had never been in a fight before, not in which someone was actually supposed to get hurt. She had to stay. She didn't have a choice. All she could do was wish she was back home, safe in bed where she belonged. Adara had told her a dozen things not to do, as though she were in fights like this all the time. Perhaps she was. For Adara everything seemed possible.

Victoria peered into the darkness. Where were they? She stepped back against a tree the way Adara told her to, grateful for the solid wood. The creatures couldn't fly in tight circles. They'd have to come more or less straight at her. They were cowards. With any luck, Adara had promised, she'd fight them one at a time.

One? she asked herself. Only one? There shouldn't be any. I'm not supposed to be here. She tried to squeeze back tears. Her gloves were harsh against her eyelids. The flashlight beam caught something in the trees. Blood red eyes stared in at her. She looked away. One would attack while others watched. There was movement to her right. The flashlight beam lanced out again.

Seeing a monster fly out of the dark was not nearly so bad, the second time you did it. She had run in blind panic from the Kreesha; she only wanted to run from a Vandamond. Vandamonds were miniature winged lions with human faces and fingered paws. She had seen stone-cuttings of one, in a picture book about Parthia or Prussia or someplace like that.

Persia, Pickering noted. *Actually, Assyria, but Assyria has been gone for three millennia. [Image of a winged lion, man-faced, crowned, carved in a stone cliff.]*

Victoria wondered if the artists had drawn from life. Except for the wings, it really was pretty small. It swooped in on her. She brought up her alpenstock like a club.

She hadn't expected it to hit so hard. The impact tore the pole from her hands. The Vandamond tumbled, recovered, grabbed a tree limb, and threw itself straight down on Victoria. She screamed, put up a hand to fend it off, and grabbed her knife. Its hind claws dug into the wood as it thrust ahead. The weight pushed her off balance, away from the tree. She slipped sideways, started to fall over, and stabbed blindly upwards. A wild screech filled the air. The Vandamond's front paws were little pincers reaching for her eyes. Its jaws clamped excruciatingly around her arm. Teeth worried away at her heavy coat; wings beat at her head. She stabbed once and again. The jaws went limp as it fluttered to earth.

Victoria's heart pounded. Where were the others? If they both rushed her at once, she wouldn't stand a chance. She picked up her flashlight. There were so many places for them to hide.

The second creature took her in the small of her back, knocking her to her knees. Too late, she remembered Adara's warning to stay against a tree. She tried to catch herself, and dropped knife and flashlight. She reached around, grabbed a section of wing, and tugged. The creature worked its way up her back towards her neck. How could she fight something behind her? She got one leg under herself and tried to stand. The Vandamond was hideously strong, but almost weightless. As she rose, the third came gliding across the field at her. Despair tugged at her heart.

With a final surge of strength, she pulled the creature from her back. Claws slashed through her jeans into her legs. She slipped one arm around its neck and held it in a hammerlock, oblivious to the slices its claws dug into her thighs. Her free hand located the tear gas. She held her breath. The flying Vandamond took a blast of Mace. It dropped from the air, paws pulling at its eyes. She pushed the can into the final creature's face and squeezed the release. It screamed and flopped convulsively. She threw it down and jumped on it, once and again, listening to bones crunch.

Adara stood next to her. "I finished off the last one," Adara announced. She carried in her right hand a long silvery sword, which gleamed wetly in the moonlight. "I suppose I should put this one out of its misery." She stabbed once. The battle madness faded from Victoria. She noticed that the tear gas had vanished, looked down at the creatures, saw what she had done, and threw up. Adara held her gently.

"I tried my best," Victoria said. "I'm sorry I..."

"Victoria, you beat them. By yourself. They were good as dead when I returned."

"Can I help against that bug? I'm pretty much out of tear gas, but I have a knife." Adara had somehow found time to change to clean clothes. "You look better than when you left."

"Time passes faster there than here. I feel like a worn-out dish rag, but don't look the part. The Kreesha is mine. Cold steel won't help. But it can't win. I won't let it. Just stay behind the Gatestone...behind Table Rock." She pushed Victoria into position, obviously favoring one arm.

Victoria peeked around Table Rock. Adara stared in a single direction, as though she knew exactly where the Kreesha was. After a few minutes of increasingly anxious waiting, the beast rose over the hill-crest. Behind the Kreesha loomed another and another. Except for the first, they were ghosts through which the stars shone. Row after row of the creatures could be seen, phalanx after phalanx. An army of Kreesha filled the sky, then another and another. Their ranks were mind-numbing.

The united will of the Kreesha drove palpably through the air. They wanted Adara's Gatestone—Table Rock. To take it, they had only to force away its single sorely-wounded defender.

Adara stood like a tree. Her arms were straight. Despite her shoulder, she held her sword out before her, its point a waiting lightning rod. Gradually she let her grip slide. The sword shook slightly. Her head sank. She shifted her stance and straightened her back. All was the same as before. Except, realized Victoria, that Adara had yielded half a step.

Victoria watched impatiently. Could Adara possibly win? She had done impossible things before. The real Kreesha hunched unmoving, carefully back from Adara's reach. How were they fighting? The contest must be elsewhere, some hidden place which Victoria could neither see nor feel. Adara's head began to nod. The very tip of her sword fluttered. She pushed it back up and shook her head, as if trying to clear her thoughts. She had lost another fraction of a step.

Minute followed minute. Once and again, more and more often, Adara's strength flagged. Each time, she managed to recover, but not before losing another bit of distance. Initially, she had been twice her height away from the stone. Now she stood next to it. Another half-pace back, and the stone would be exposed. Adara was trying desperately to hold her place. Victoria could see the strain on her face. However strong

Adara might be, the union of millions of Kreesha was stronger.

Victoria had been told not to interfere. But watching while a friend, if a very strange friend, lost a fight was foreign to her. Besides, only Adara stood between the Kreesha and the whole world. Victoria picked up a stone, noted its heft, and looked for another. She wasn't the superstar of the softball field—there were too many more interesting things to do, like reading, and going on picnics, and looking through the microscope Mom had given her—but she had a pretty mean throw. "Adara?" she called.

An answer whispered across Victoria's mind. **When you removed the bullet, the favor bond passed into your hands. I cannot ask your aid again,** Adara explained. With the phrase favor bond came a precise concept, a ritualized exchange of beneficial deeds, birds for Donny Martin for the calendar for the kidnappers for a block of stone against felon's back for bullets deflected for bullet surgically removed. Adara was in debt to Victoria, and could ask no aid of her.

Adara glanced at lakes below. Moonlight danced from the water, forming a beckoning silvery highway summoning her to infinity. There was her escape, if she wanted it. Her friend, who had protected her mountain's peace and come through the dark to rescue her, could come with her. She had needed to shield the Gatestone until dawn, but that deed had proven beyond her power. The Stone was lost. Only the manner of its passing remained to be chosen.

"No!" Victoria shouted. She pitched rock after rock at the Kreesha's glowing eyes. The first two clattered off Kreeshan hide. The third struck its target. The Kreesha jerked back, its concentration broken. In the heavens, the Kreeshan host wavered out of focus.

Adara's delight soared around Victoria, exultant as a thousand wedding bells ringing across cathedral naves. Their thoughts were suddenly linked. Victoria felt Adara as a hollow shell of pain-etched consciousness, holding steady against bitter fatigue. Adara set her hand firmly against Table Rock. The opalescence flooded out of the stone into her. Adara's flesh glowed from within. Saint Elmo's fire glimmered over her sword and sparked from the top of her hair. The air crackled and shimmered. The energy of the Gatestone, disciplined by Adara's uncompromising will, displaced her utter, bone-aching exhaustion.

Night turned to day. The Kreesha, exposed in all its malignant beauty, reared back. The Gatestone's opalescence coalesced into a single blinding drop of liquid light, which floated unstoppably through the images above. The Kreesha, a stringless puppet, fell to earth. Steam poured out of its carapace. Its ghostly supporters dissolved into fiery chaos.

GEORGE PHILLIES

"We did it!" Adara shouted. "We did it! This day they'll surely rue."

"They're all dead?" Victoria asked weakly. Now she felt the pain in her legs. Her jeans were soaked with blood.

"Enough that the rest will learn a few manners." Victoria's last sharp thoughts were of Table Rock, reduced to powdery gravel. Then they were someplace else, someplace warm and bright. Victoria remembered fragments of images: An alabaster tub filled with steaming water, Adara dressing her wounds with an astringent cream, a bed softer than goosedown into which she sank in a dreamless sleep.

~~~~~

Morning. Victoria awoke, still dreamily sleepy. Sunlight streamed through one set of windows. Outside were tall mountains. Snow covered the heights; pine trees perched like brooding owls on the slopes. Another set of windows was dark. Pressing her nose against a pane, she found that she could see a night-lit field. Why, it was Table Rock State Park, just as she had left it. Table Rock was shattered to gravel. Or was it a photograph? The steam from the Kreesha's joints did not rise. A bat floated in the air, wings frozen in mid-beat.

Victoria felt rested, so it had to be morning, no matter how Table Rock looked. By now, Mom and Dad would be in a complete panic. She had to get home. Her clothes must be a mess. Then she realized that she was wearing her own nightgown. Her regular clothing, mended well enough that even Mom probably wouldn't notice, at least on an old pair of jeans and older coat, hung by her bed. Vandamond claw-marks on her legs were barely-visible scratches. Her memories of the Vandamond seemed oddly distant. She could remember what she did, and remember feeling afraid then, but she didn't feel afraid now. Adara had somehow managed to fix everything.

Telediting, Aurora critiqued. *Find memories, take the sting out of them. Like a tranquilizer, except permanent. Well done, too; you remember the name of the fear when you want to, so it's not lurking in your undermind.*

Victoria stepped from the bedroom and wandered through marble-paneled corridors, her toes sinking into richly patterned Oriental carpets. Paintings and tapestries lined the walls. On an inset shelf nested a swarm of bees cast in gleaming gold, sipping from bejeweled silver flowers.

She was drawn by distant, gentle sobs. She found Adara sprawled on a couch, her face pressed to a pillow. Adara hadn't changed her clothes from last night. What was wrong? Last night, Adara had been deliriously happy.

186

Adara looked up. "Victoria? You slept well?" she asked. Adara's eyes were bloodshot. Her complexion had recovered a little of its rosy hue. "We'll get you back before people notice that you're gone. You saw the windows, didn't you? While you slept, time passed here. It didn't pass as much at home, so it's still night there. I'm just sad about Table Rock. It took so long for me to build. I destroyed it. I needed its power to stop the Kreesha."

"You destroyed Table Rock, when it meant a whole lot to you, to save me?" Victoria asked.

"The Rock was doomed. I made too many mistakes. Killing that thug, never mind he had a knife at my throat, upset the Rock's balance. Once I was hurt, I couldn't get home—here, I mean—to fix it. Fixing would've been easy, except I had to be here, and I couldn't get here to do it, no matter how hard I tried. The iron in my shoulder—iron won't easily gate—was too much, once the poison in the bullet hit. The unbalance let through the Kreesha and the Vandamond. With the rock gone, they can't return. That's why they wanted the Rock; it would let them gate freely from plane to plane. No, Table Rock was doomed before you came to me. Either I used it against the Kreesha or I used it to run away. That's no choice—I was bound by the favors we traded. You started the bond with the birds. After the birds, there was the boy in the stream, my stone clock, and those men. Finally there was last night, so I owed you."

"What if I hadn't been there last night?" Victoria asked.

"I'd have done the same. Though with three Vandamond at my throat, a chunk of iron in my shoulder, and no gnothdiar—my sword—to handle the Presence, well, I'd have lived through it. I think. I'm not that fragile," Adara announced. Victoria thought that Adara did not sound convinced, but it seemed impolite to say so.

"Couldn't you get help someplace? I'm not that dense. Those things were from outer space. You must be, too. How did you get here? A flying saucer? You must have a dad and a mom someplace." Victoria was more and more confused.

"Not another planet. The True World is all about us, like the place we saw. It's just farther away. Farther than any star you can see. But there's no flying saucer, only the trick I showed you for stepping from plane to plane. And I'm not a Martian, I'm a...peri," Adara explained.

"A Persian elf?" Victoria questioned.

"I've been to Persia; the carpets are Persian." Adara pointed around the room.

"An elf! The Spirit! No wonder I recognize you! You're in the County museum painting—'The Spirit of Table Rock'." Victoria choked in disbelief. "That's impossible! That painting's a hundred years old!"

187

See, Star, I said the painting was important, Victoria observed primly. *Yes, it was a detail. But why shouldn't boys get details right?* She returned to her tale.

Adara explained, sinking from energy to despondency. "Yep. That's me. But I'm not much older than you, not where things count. We just grow up slowly. In calendar years I'm older. But I'm not a grown-up. I'd rather be home, with friends and brothers and relatives. But I can't! I can't! I ran away. I had to."

"You had to run away? Why?" Victoria asked.

"My people were doing wicked things. I said they were wicked. And I'm old enough I can't be hushed like a baby. The wicked people killed my friends. They tried to kill me, too, with thugs and soldiers and monsters. The hrordrin makes a Kreesha look like a field mouse. I got away by the skin of my teeth." Adara gestured at a suit of mail hung carefully on the wall. Deep circular patterns were etched across its silvery rings. "I ran as far as I could. I ran so far that I've never seen one of my people again."

"You must be lonely," Victoria said. Adara's wistful muteness was her answer. "Maybe if I asked my parents, you could come live with us. Would you like that?"

"Me? Oh, Victoria, it's not I don't like you, but—we really are very different. It wouldn't work. Perhaps I could visit, if your dad and mom didn't know who I was," Adara answered gracefully.

"They'd know. They know your name already, and what you look like. And Mom knows everything. She knows if you're thinking something bad before you think of it yourself. And Dad knows, too, just as fast, but he'd only smile if it's not too bad." Victoria wondered how she'd ever explain her current escapade.

"Victoria, you have to go back now. An hour here is an instant at your home, but your mother is approaching your bedroom door." Adara took Victoria's wrist.

They stood in Victoria's room. In her palace, Adara had been exotically remote. In Victoria's bedroom she looked more like a girl visiting overnight from Centervale.

"Can we have a picnic sometime? Kelly and Penny want to thank you. For saving them," Victoria said.

"Sure. Give me a week? I'm a bit tired. But I'll be there." They paused awkwardly.

Victoria's door swung open. "Are you having a nightmare, Victoria? Oh!" It was Mother, settling her insomnia by looking in at her children. Adara smiled and vanished, leaving behind an afterimage of violet flowers on a rolling knoll.

"I was just looking at the stars, Mom. Is something wrong? You shouted." Victoria glanced around the room. Her bed was open, the knapsack again under the bed. She was in her nightgown. Her other clothing was back in the closet, almost where it belonged.

"There is someone else in this room, and she vanished like a ghost," Mother announced.

"Oh, Mother, there are no such things as ghosts. And no one is here. Maybe it was a peri." Victoria giggled.

"Yes, dear. Now go to bed. What's a peri?" Mother asked.

"Persian for 'elf'. Crossword puzzle clue. In the Times every single Sunday. Goodnight, Mom." Victoria yawned and slipped under her coverlets. Her mother straightened a corner of the quilt, then looked beneath the bed. "Is there a monster under there?" Victoria asked matter-of-factly.

"Now, why should I think that? Nor one of your friends, either," Mother answered. Mother's thoughts were obvious: Someone else had to be hiding in the room, but where?

"Don't worry, Mom, I'll protect you from monsters," Victoria promised.

"I'm sure you will, Victoria." Mother pulled the quilt up to Victoria's chin. It must have been a shadow.

"I'm sure I have." Victoria, having told her mother the complete truth about what she had done, and Mother being uninterested, closed her eyes. The terror on the mountain seemed so long ago it hardly mattered. Adara had done that, healing Victoria's mind while she healed Victoria's other wounds.

"Yes, Victoria, I know. Happy dreams." Mother's thoughts remained absolutely transparent: Children made such wonderfully implausible promises.

~~~~~

Victoria, her story at its end, sat back in the lawn swing. Aurora was leaning against her shoulder; the others clustered at her feet.

"You did great!" Cloud said to Victoria.

"Thinking of rocks was stark ice," Star added.

"But I was frozen. Sitting in the dark waiting. I didn't know what to do. All I could do was try to hide." Victoria looked at the ground. The terror of those moments came back to her, so she saw nothing clearly except her fear.

You're all right now. Eclipse's thought was sharply screened from the foursome's awareness. To Victoria, Eclipse somehow felt very close and warmly supporting, the way her dad and mom tried to be. *You're here with friends, and you won.* Victoria felt her terror fade, this time for good, vaguely knowing that Eclipse was responsible for the change. "For a first time, you did very well. Better than most of us, first time. Honest. We knew what gifttrue is. We knew what a public persona is. Your first warning was turning on your flashlight."

"That was really great," Comet said. "Most of my friends, not persona types, if they met a Kreesha they'd faint or curl up in a ball, and they've all seen pictures of monsters and rogue personas, or even met one. You never have, and you did something good. I just feel sorry for Adara, to be so alone for so long; even if she's old enough to be a grownup, she didn't sound like one, and it'd be lonely no matter who you were."

"Professor Pickering?" Comet continued, "you said your world had no personas, no people with garb or gifts? But Adara had strength boosts and teleport and something to let her swim in ice water, not to mention the tricks with Table Rock and the sword."

"Comet, those teleports were cross-time," Eclipse added. "The change in time flow, slow here and fast there, is a dead giveaway."

"You ever been there?" Cloud challenged. "You teleport crosstime, too?"

"Me?" Eclipse giggled. "Teleport crosstime? No. Not me. I can't. OK, I haven't learned how to yet. Just like you."

Pickering answered. "But Adara was not a persona, not from this world, and she's gone. I think forever. Everyone who knows about her, everyone except Kelly and Penny, is right here. She visited Dragon House, sat in my kitchen, slept in the very bed Eclipse now uses, and told me her version of her tale."

"Could I see one memory again?" Aurora asked. Victoria nodded. Aurora took them back to Adara's home, looking at her armor, looking carefully at the circles etched across them. *How? She said 'hrordrin'. I got a flash of a picture—something big with tentacles.*

She said 'monster', too, Victoria thought. *Is that the flying jellyfish you described, Professor?*

"Indubitably," he answered. "Adara's tale, the once I met her, was all too explicit on the hrordrin's dietary proclivities. They're urbanivores. They eat cities." His mental image of Adara, sitting in his breakfast room, brought stares from six children.

Victoria glanced at her watch, consternation on her face. Her story-telling had consumed several hours of real time. "Oh, no. Oh, no! I had to be at a party cross town. Five minutes ago. I'm dressed okay. We're playing soccer. But it's miles from here."

"No trouble," Comet answered. "A few seconds flying time. No one will see us. Invisible is only a little tricky. I owe you for your story. It was really ice."

"Where?" Eclipse asked. *Victoria? All I need is a sharp impression. Where are we going? Aurora, please, scan for where I can drop us?*

"It's" *here*, Victoria said. [A picture of a path, two short legs.]

Got Eclipse, realizing where the path went, lapsed chokingly into speech. "it." *You don't need my help, do you?* Her words were more a statement than a question.

"I..." *Oops. I did give it away, didn't I,* Victoria answered. *I haven't been doing it long. I haven't told Alex. I haven't told Mom and Dad. I haven't told anyone. I don't know how to tell them so they don't freak out. Now I've given it away. I might as well do it.*

Pickering finds out if you tell him, Eclipse's firm answer rang loud and clear. *I'm not talking. After all, you're the only persona in the world—the world now that it's been rearranged. But take me along? Please!* Eclipse's mind trembled with urgency. *Please? If I see which way it is, I might be able to copy it. I mean,* [Images of ruined towns, masses of people fleeing in terror into the Brazilian rain forest.] *you're the only hint I have.*

Victoria nodded assent. *I've never taken someone else. What if it's not safe for you?*

It was safe for you, right? Eclipse answered. *If I want safety, I stay home. [A shower of memories from personae alive or long-dead, choosing their duty to their gifts over safety, over love, over life itself.]*

Aurora cut in. *WHAT are you two TALKING about? WHERE do I SCAN?*

No problem, Aurora. Eclipse answered. She took Victoria's hand. The two girls disappeared, here one instant and gone the next.

"Well, fine," Aurora grumbled. "First ask my help, then ignore me."

"They shut you out, too?" Star asked. "You see how it feels?"

"They did not shut me out. I heard them fine. They didn't make sense. They understood each other. But 'you don't need me to help you?' and 'Alex doesn't know,'? I don't understand what they meant," Aurora fumed.

"Of what have I not been informed?" Pickering asked.

"Victoria said she'd started doing something," Aurora answered. "I don't know what. Eclipse saw at once. Not even from words. A picture was enough. And said Vicky didn't need her help. Golly, Eclipse is sharp."

"A puzzle. Interesting," Pickering remarked. "I thought teleport came with flashes and sounds, a light show and carillon."

"Depends who's doing it," Cloud said. "But you're right, Eclipse is bells and blue light."

"Didn't you see her? Didn't you see them?" Comet asked impatiently. "It wasn't that fast, was it? I wasn't calling my gifts, not then." The group looked at her quizzically. "When they vanished, for a second they were someplace else. I could see it! Someplace where plants are purple. The place Aurora showed us, the place Adara took Victoria. Someplace crosstime."

"I saw it, sister. Didn't believe it," Star answered.

"Now she's doing that?" Cloud groaned. "Ten minutes ago, Eclipse swore she didn't have a clue how to go crosstime. So she does it. How can you trust her about anything?"

"Oh, Cloud! Will you just cease downing her! Eclipse is more gifttrue than anyone else you'll ever meet in your life!" Comet snapped, her cheeks flushing. "She must have figured out how. Girls do that, you know; figure things out without someone telling them every detail of how, the way boys need." Cloud bristled.

"She did not! Not yet." Aurora shouted. "Eclipse asked Vicky 'take me along'. That was Victoria. She did the vanishing."

"Victoria?" Cloud asked. "She can teleport? The whole world doesn't have a single persona any more. And we meet a teleporter? A cross-time teleporter? By accident?"

"I'm sorry," Pickering said, "surely that must have been your friend Eclipse? Victoria is bright, athletic, and well-raised, but she is a normal girl, not a persona or a gatemage."

"Like, they don't have personas any more, remember?" Star said supportively. "Except us five. Of course we're great public personas, but they don't know yet."

"Wait," Cloud said. "The StarCompass took us to Victoria. This could be why."

"Cloud! You're right! I know! I know what Vicky meant! When she showed the path," Aurora answered. *[Two legs, each a few steps. The separation: a pause, a stroll across a rolling sea of purple violet foliage, the stroll compressed to the sparest of mental shorthands.]* "It's what Adara said. You get gated, and you learn how. Victoria was. She did. All that magic Adara did, Victoria just standing there, mayhaps engifted her so she learned faster."

"Certainly, Victoria has not told me that she could do such a thing," Pickering responded. "But that's what Adara said to me, a tale I'll someday tell. Adara did say that one could learn to gate. Indeed, that fact made her a political outcast."

A watery shimmer cut through the air. A few paces from the group, there appeared a vertical disc, a circular hole showing utter black laced with fluorescent spider webs, through which stumbled a shaken Eclipse, her screens flaring laser-bright around her. Disc and screens vanished. She staggered across the lawn, her knees folding under her.

"Eclipse!" Comet's frightened cry came. Cloud set his hand on Eclipse's shoulder to cancel her weight; she sank slowly as a falling leaf to the lawn. "Eclipse, what's wrong?" Comet asked. "Is Victoria all right?" The children crowded around their stricken friend.

Eclipse gasped for breath. "Fine. At her soccer game," she answered. "Gating. It's a teleport. Inside-out. Once Victoria showed me which way, it's not complicated. Goddess! The power level!" Eclipse cradled her head in her hands.

"Victoria carried both of you with no ill effects?" a worried Pickering asked. "Yet you by yourself were stricken?"

"Her? Sure?" Eclipse answered. "She, ummh, it's hard to explain. Think of sawing wood with or across the grain." She paused, her breathing gradually slowing. "She went with the grain; I found across. She went here to there in a step. I forced my way back. There's space in between: really weird place, black as night, full of sparks and rainbow curtains. Not vacuum. Something my body screens did not like, even maxed out. Moondark! I'm cold to the bone."

"Guys?" Star asked. "Give her a chance to rest? You remember manifesting new gifts? What it can feel like at first? Before it feels so great?"

"I guess," Cloud said. "You can catch up on raking later, Eclipse." Comet propped her fists on her waist, eyes steel-bright in his direction. "Sure, sure," he corrected, "We'll do it for you."

"It wasn't that difficult," Eclipse mumbled to herself. "Victoria made it look so easy. I just undercharged." She stared at the grass. "Then I had to dredge very deep to compensate. That dark place, that's where the sky octopus hides. I don't know what good knowing that is. I don't know how to target there. It'd be real hard to break anything. The place is...big, in a very strange way." She forced herself to her feet. "Could I talk later? I'm half-frozen. I need to warm up for a few seconds. Weren't we supposed to rake a lawn?"

"We're raking," Comet answered, "and you're going to go and lie down until you feel well; I mean, you rescued me, so now it can be our turn to do something for you." Eclipse looked uncomfortable at the thought of not working while others did, but allowed herself to be led off to a hammock. She was asleep before Pickering finished folding a blanket over her.

"I think," Cloud whispered to Star, "we're lucky we didn't go along. Her screens—they were so bright they hurt to look at. And stuff was getting through them. Enough to hurt her."

"Cloud," Star answered, "You let someone else pick a fight with her. Screens like that you can't break. No matter how hard you try."

"Brains, Star, brains," Cloud whispered. "She can't hold them that high. Not for long. You saw how wimped out she got. Just be patient, and she gets tired. I mean, she's a girl. She runs out of breath after a couple seconds."

Star nodded, politeness masking his doubts. His sisters didn't get winded, not hardly, not from using their gifts. Not even from playing lacrosse, not more than a boy would. What was Eclipse going to be doing to you, he wondered, while you waited for her to get tired? Something violent, he expected, something personally violent.

His reverie was broken by a salmon blur. Comet! His sister, gifts engaged, had whizzed by, passing above the lawn at near supersonic speed, her flight field entraining grass and leaves so that the lawn had an orthodox raking completed in fractions of a minute. Sedate columns of leaves rose from Pickering's ivy beds, branches and leaves and debris being driven cleanly skyward by the winds raised by Cloud's gifts. Aurora's gifts trapped everything solid that the wind raised, shredded leaves in neat segments, and dropped them into a mulch pile. They'd almost missed their promised schedule because they'd used Aurora's gifts to hear Victoria's tale. Now it was fair to apply other gifts to keep their promise to Pickering. Star applied himself to his hand rake. His gifts, he told himself, awaited more spectacular applications.

CHAPTER 18 A QUIET SUNDAY AFTERNOON

"ATN, New York, Affiliate News Support. I'm Jane, how may I help one of our fine affiliates?" Jane Goldstein kept on her best smile. It was late on a Sunday afternoon. The news cycle was asleep. The call was from KZOH-TV, western New York, someplace near the end of the universe.

"I am Howard Maynard, News Director, KZOH, North Lockport, New York. My authenticator is Omega Omega London Batavia Jakarta." The screen showed an older gentleman, his name on the chyron.

Goldstein froze. Omega Omega was the total disaster priority. "One moment, please." She tapped the touchscreen, put her thumb in the bioconfirm block, and typed "Omega Omega". "London Batavia Jakarta" came up on the screen. "Yes, Sir, I confirm."

"North Lockport Middle School has a Saturday noon TV news club, run entirely by students. They put it out tape delay on Sunday. We get the feed. Today they interviewed three of the Koster children, Heather, James, and Rebecca. That's the astronaut's kids. The kids claim Eclipse—the girl who rescued the space plane—showed up at their house. To return Marge Koster's clipboard. They have a stack of photos, them with Eclipse. Eclipse says she and friends were sent here to save the world. If they fail, everyone in the world dies. The Middle School program is already viral. We're running it as a special news bulletin. My International Press message went up...yes, they just approved my nine-bell alert."

"Just a second," Goldstein managed. She activated her split screen. "Argus, connect me to Ms. Windemere. Three-way. Emergency-nine!"

"Connecting," the AI answered. The connection formed.

"Yes, Jane? Make it quick? Working lunch." The screen showed Jennifer Wyndemere putting down her sandwich.

"IP Alert. Nine bell. Eclipse from the Space Plane says she's here to save the world. She wins, or we all die. Everyone. Video on line 978. I haven't seen it. Mr. Maynard WZOH North Lockport is source. I'm third hand," Goldstein said. "Please talk direct. I've suddenly got ten, no fifteen calls incoming."

"On it!" Wyndemere dropped Goldstein out of the link.

Goldstein stared at her call list. At least it was affiliates, not her superiors at the Scarlet Pinnacle. "Argus," she said, "I want a group kaffeeklatsch. Me and everyone calling. Everyone except me muted."

"Opening," the AI answered. Twenty-two faces appeared on the screen.

"Hello from ATN, New York," she said. "I'm Jane, Affiliate News Support. There are now 22, no, 28 of you trying to call in the same minute. I'll try to get to you each as quickly as possible. Please text me with your issue, as few words as possible." A new window covered part of her screen. Phrases like Koster kids, Lockport School, Eclipse, and apocalypse filled it. "OK," she said, "If you are calling about Eclipse appearing in North Lockport, please stay there. If it's something else, please email me ASAP." The text window began scrolling.

"OK, I'm going to unmute one of you at a time. You all get to hear. Please keep it short." This was not, Jane thought, in our emergency plans. She tapped a point on the screen. Bill Murray was always to the point.

"Cable 27, Cleveland. KZOH says end of the world possible, with this Eclipse superhero as source. Network position is?" He stopped.

"I just passed Howard Maynard, KZOH, up to Jennifer Wyndemere." She's our solidest news anchor, Jane thought. "I gather it's a ten minute video?" Heads across the screen nodded. "We haven't had a chance to listen to it yet. We'll move as fast as possible. Has anyone seen it?" A hand waved near screen bottom. Jane unmuted it.

"Channel 9, Worcester, Mass. Just finished watching. Looks to be the real Koster kids. Student newscaster/moderator was rock solid. Even blue shirt and scarlet tie. The interview was 'they rescued your mom'. Came out by accident: Eclipse showed up last night at their home. The real Eclipse, outside in minus twenty wind chill in a light blouse, not even cold. Eclipse told the Kosters, matter of factly, she and friends were sent here. There are 'dooms'. Either they beat the dooms, or we all die. Oh, Eclipse said she expects to die when she defeats them. No, she didn't say what the dooms are."

"How charming," Jane Goldstein responded.

"Private link, please? Channel 9 News exclusive?"

Goldstein winced but tapped the authorization. "One minute max!" she said.

"Channel 9 says: I've notified our man in London. That's London, England. Eclipse had a coin purse with weird coins. Morgenthaler coins. Cyrus Morgenthaler, the man who vanished? She's likely selling them, likely Monday, through Southwards. I'll have men in place covering the entrances. That's it."

Goldstein wondered how an obscure local affiliate could have reporters in foreign countries. "Noted," she said. "Returning to Kaffeeklatsch."

"When will ATN be interviewing Eclipse?" Murray asked.

"First we have to find her," Goldstein answered. "Perhaps tomorrow in London someone succeeds." She spent another ten minutes fending off questions before a text message appeared.

"WLA-TV. We have a contact who can arrange an Eclipse interview for tomorrow evening. Contact sent her here. It's legit. Eclipse is standing in front of me. Amazing. I saw someone teleport! It's exactly like that TV show. We have the interview. If Windermere wants to be here, Eclipse says she'll fetch her." The text message followed with an image, WLA's lead reporter standing next to a young girl who appeared to be Eclipse herself. Goldstein scrambled to interrupt Windermere, who really disliked interruptions, again. Forwarding the message image appeared to be the safest alternative.

~~~~~

Night. Perched on the stairs to the upper widow's walk, a tired Aurora wrote in her diary. She'd described events of the day, from the interesting (Pickering's wonderful friend Victoria) through the boring but dutiful (more medicine smugglers, the fellows who supplied the man they'd arrested yesterday) to the surprising.

"Dear Diary,

"Cloud is being very gifttrue. He even went after Star for saying a bad thing about Eclipse. When we arrested the next medicine smuggler, the one Salvadore remembered as a customer, the smuggler had guards. They had flameguns. Or beam pistols. They set Cloud's clothing on fire. They tried to hit Comet. She was scared. I don't blame her. All she can do is duck. I put a wall in front of Comet. We put out Cloud, who didn't flinch no matter how much fire hurts. I questioned the guy who ran the place. Star shot back at the guards, because they were shooting at him. First Star politely asked them to stop. They were trying to kill him. They didn't stop, so he did it back, except they didn't have screens so they were dead right away. Being cut in two does that. But Star did it heightwise! On purpose! Euuwh! But now we know exactly where to go for the next step up the ladder. And we salvaged their guns. The guy we arrested didn't have money to salvage, not in the building, but we found it elsewhere and salvaged it.

'So, after we questioned the smuggler, and Cloud washed the smoke out of his hair, Comet found a church, a real church with Sunday evening services. Comet and Star and me snuck in. Cloud didn't want to. He thought using gifts to sneak into a church wasn't gifttrue. It helped us, not them, even if we left a donation. Not much of a donation; we're almost broke, not counting Eclipse's money or what we salvaged. That's our League's money, not ours.

"Did we ask Eclipse along? No. Why would we? She's an Illuminant. They worship the moon, pray to stars. No, get it right. Illuminants pray to constellations. We hid in a choir loft and listened. It wasn't good as downstairs. We don't have dress clothes, so we didn't dare let people see us. We didn't dare sing, not even a whisper. Someone might have heard us. But it was a church, and it was Sunday. I didn't tell Comet or Star about the Bible I found. The New Testament was there, but the Further Testaments were gone. There wasn't a Book of New Miracles anyplace. Things just stopped at Revelations. I peeked at the priest's mind, very carefully, looking only for an explanation. No hint. A whole chunk of the Bible is missing. I'll tell Eclipse tomorrow. She'll never think to look at religions.

"Then we went back to the camp site, just for a couple minutes, to do a post. Cloud started bragging himself up. Eclipse told him off. He'd told Comet to be in the front line, when she has no combat gifts. Eclipse completely totally lost her temper. She used all those words Dad would kill me for using, and a bunch of others I've never heard before. I could tell. Cloud knew what they meant. For a moment I thought the two of them were going to have a fist fight, gifts off. Cloud thinks he is taller and heavier than Eclipse, but doesn't realize how much training Eclipse has, not to mention how much weight she lifts. Instead, something good happened. Cloud agreed Eclipse was right. He even apologized to Comet. There's no more Book of New Miracles, but there was a miracle.

"Then, late evening, Alex Pickering persuaded Eclipse to appear on video in Los Angeles. She goes tomorrow. The Koster kids had been interviewed about our rescue. The reporter thought he was asking about Eclipse and their Mom on the Space Plane. He stumbled on the big news story. The kids told him: Eclipse showed up at the Koster House. She described the dooms, didn't ask that dooms stay secret, so now the whole world knows. We win or they all die. The world is not taking it well. Worse, now the dooms know we're coming for them.

"Love,

"Janie."

~~~~~

Pickering returned to his desk to work through his thoughts. Some obvious safety precautions were mandatory. This situation could be an elaborate blackmail scheme. If one believed Comet's story, one would believe that she was from another world, a world almost identical to this one, a world so close that the language was the same, the city names were the same, half the buildings were the same, but at the same time people could fly and read minds. That conclusion was patently absurd. There are, Pickering recalled, only a trillion or so stars in a galaxy, and rather fewer visible galaxies than there are stars in our own Milky Way. The likelihood of such a planetary duplication occurring by chance was negligible. Comet's story could not be true.

His contacts in Washington were confused. He blandly proposed asking Comet to visit Edwards Air Force base and demonstrate her talents. Would there be interest? His contacts said they'd get back to him.

An old murder-mystery principle brought clarification: was there a woman or money involved? Not a woman, surely, but he did have money. Could it be a plot, someone trying to prove that he was insane to separate him from his wealth? Such things had been done. He would have to be very careful to record everything in a way that proved he was sane and never believed his guest's stories. The record would show him playing along with a practical joke. Whenever the special effect appeared impossible to fake, the magic phrases 'laser hologram projector' and 'resonant scattering by metallized aerosols' would be invoked.

Suppose the children were what they appeared to be, namely people with unusual talents. Where had they come from? He had a small group of very strange acquaintances. The acquaintances knew Earth was not home; they were from elsewhere. These children expected to go home to Boston. Comet appeared to be acutely upset that her Boston was not to be found. There were then two issues: where did the children get their powers, and where did they get their ideas about geography?

Aurora's telepathy was seriously inconsistent with modern science. There were perfectly sound group-theoretic proofs that nature didn't have room for additional long-range forces, such as the one needed to explain telepathy. Flight was in principle lawful, but where was the momentum going? A wormhole could simulate teleportation, but his library manifestly had not been shredded by the associated tidal forces.

Rumor said that the New Empire of the Great Inca, or whatever they were calling themselves this week, had unconventional weapons. Could these children be examples? Certainly no one had expected the Empire to conquer Peru overnight until the evening they stormed every major city in the country. Nor, four years later, had they been expected to win the war they had provoked, overrunning Bolivia, Ecuador, Columbia, and Chile in a few days while America was lost in the impeachment crisis. Why, though, would the Great Inca be interested in him? His inventions were well-described in patents; licenses were readily available. Indeed, the Empire appeared to be scrupulous about paying him royalties, unlike three dozen other so-called countries he could name. There was no rational reason to suspect the New Incan Empire.

Pickering continued to ponder alternatives. Having eliminated the obvious ways in which the children could be from this earth, he was left with the possibility that the children were not from this earth, or were from an earth that had been changed. That was what Eclipse had said: 'Someone changed history, and we need to fix it'. Pickering had slight reservations about Eclipse's ideas for 'fixing' history. If Eclipse, *et al.*, succeeded, his world would disappear. Even he, the world's greatest intellect, might cease to exist.

It seemed more reasonable that someone had tampered with the children than with an entire planet. The children might be not human at all. They might from someplace completely different, and have been given false memories. Why, though, should children from wherever have been given memories that were consistently slightly wrong? Why give them memories of Roger's Institution and not MIT? What motive would lead to children with consistent wrong memories? Malice? Confuse the five of them so that they finally suicided, or did some mischief? This might work in a story, but not in real life. Incredibly convoluted plots seldom turned out as their designers planned. Once the children became confused, as was now seemingly the case, their acts would be virtually unpredictable.

Pickering tried to summarize his wanderings. A hoax might be a practical joke or a blackmail attempt. If the children had real talents, they might be deceived or lying about their background. If they were telling the truth about their background, they might be from another world, or they might be returning to a world that had been manipulated by time travellers. Of course, there were also fantasy possibilities. For example, they might be illusions or fugitives from near-parallel timelines.

Pickering entered notes in Telzey, both his remarks showing he knew that the children were a hoax, and his hypothetical notes, prefaced "If I had fallen for this practical joke, I might infer...". The latter, prefatory remarks deleted, would be his gift to whichever friends had made the joke. Pickering's librarians in New York had made an extensive search. Even if the police report omitted flight, teleportation, and other powers from the description, there were no missing children resembling the five. His friends on the Potomac, after an elliptic description of his guests, their gifts, and their connection with the Lemuria, had arranged legal protection for him against suit by the five's hypothetically irate parents.

If the children had run away, and the parents complained that they had not been reached immediately, he would wrap himself in the cloth of piety. He would claim he had given the children shelter, an opportunity to telephone their parents, and had sought to turn their minds to their duty to return to their family, a duty they were more likely to perform if they did not feel that every adult threatened them. He had also reported their presence to the authorities. Sending them away might have risked their lives. No matter what was happening, he would be prepared. A variety of outcomes threatened his physical or legal safety; adequate contingency planning shielded against each of them.

Meanwhile, the nation was deeply troubled. Unidentified reconnaissance aircraft were making regular sweeps over North America. Daily terrorist attacks and bombings left hundreds dead and law enforcement agencies flailing blindly for clues. Rumors of war swept the world. The Washington permanent bureaucracy was in a state of turmoil. There was silence from the White House.

Telzey's news service listed the day's events. Bomb explosions dropped two major bridges into the Mississippi. Black-robed terrorists appeared in a Minnesota shopping mall, spent several minutes blazing away with automatic weapons, and disappeared without a trace. Anti-tank rockets disabled a California oil refinery. The list was long. Pickering directed Telzey to make hourly cycle tests of the intrusion detectors, confirming that the region's most extensive set of burglar alarms still protected his estate.

Tomorrow he would have to persuade Comet to demonstrate her powers—gifts, he told himself, gifts, use their language—to the Air Force. The demonstration would convince the Air Force that the Washington object was not a crisis. The alternative looked dismayingly like a major war, an alternative seriously bad both for his royalties and his tax bills, or, worse, the possibility that there would be attempts to interfere with his studies.

The more the five said about their world and its history, the less believable their own history sounded. Multiple coexisting civilizations? Historical men, none of whose motives could be understood? An amusing possibility suggested itself to Pickering. Perhaps there had been temporal intervention twice: Once to change the real world into his guests' world; a second time to restore normalcy. On this interpretation, the children were a remnant from moments during which the earth's timeline staggered along some utterly irrational path. Of course, for this interpretation to be viable, one would need working time machines, a scheme for predicting how changing the past would change the present, and a motive.

The time machine. That was the important theme. If the past could be altered, then he too could find the means to alter it, to arrange that certain events came to pass. Aurora had shown him memories, the appearance of the stars as one passed the speed of light. Every detail was not yet pinned down, but once one saw the remarkable effects visible near c the alterations to special relativity were almost obvious. Obvious, he decided, if contemplated by one of his genius. Undoubtedly the modifications would be inapparent to men of talents more limited than his own. The time machine would take a while yet to complete, but would undoubtedly follow. Then that which had not been would be made to have happened, and his life's sole ambition would be fulfilled.

~~~~~

Eclipse stood on her balcony, listening to the breeze caress the tree branches, staring into the starry gulfs of the night. The sky was utterly still. Before she awoke she'd been standing on her balcony back at her own house. The sky had been talking to her. In her sleep she understood what the sky was saying. Her mother's faith venerated the heavenly names, teaching you to speak your challenges to the appropriate constellation, but mother had never expected the sky to reply to her monologues.

Eclipse told herself that prophetic dreaming was an extremely rare gift, one she'd have known that she had. Other dreams were interpretations of things she knew. Here, the sky was silent. The contrast between this silence and home had been important to the dream. Here she could be one with the night. In her dream the sky spoke with the voice of the Adversary, chattering mechanically with a twisted logic that mixed true and false, history and fable, so that all who listened to its whispers became ignorant and foolish. In her dream she'd consciously heard its voice and learned the names of its lies, names she could not remember.

What did the dream mean? Was she on the verge of penetrating the deceptions that had so altered the world? Perhaps her reading was about to make sense, so her under mind had found the mistakes of the time pirates, slicing through the tissue of lies they had woven. There was a gap in that logic, though. Her dream had been very clear. Here the sky was silent. It was the sky from before the change that susurrated with a thousand ill-heard mistruths. Dutifully, she wrote down her memories of her dream.

CHAPTER 19 THE NATIVES ARE FRIENDLY

Comet sailed over northern California, the morning sun bright over her left shoulder. Alex had been very convincing. She'd frightened people. Another visit would calm them down. Pickering's friends in the Army Air Corps—no, they called themselves the "Air Force"—had agreed to his suggestion. They wanted her to visit them and let them examine 'the vehicle that passed over Washington'. He'd told them they could only examine the vehicle if they promised not to dissect its pilot. They'd happily agreed. She hoped they wouldn't be too disappointed when they learned that the pilot was the vehicle.

Having Aurora track her, with Star and Cloud and Eclipse ready to teleport to her rescue, made her feel a lot safer. That was what friends were for, after all, to stand behind you when you put your neck on the headsman's chopping block. Besides—something she hadn't told Alex— while he spoke to the Air Corps on the bell, Aurora had traced the bell lines and read the Army men's minds, enough to be sure they weren't thinking of hurting her.

She glanced at her map. You couldn't miss Mount Shasta. Its snow-capped cone was visible for hundreds of miles. The big body of water was Shasta Lake, with Reading on the far side. Route 5, the bridge across the lake, led straight south to Sacramento. There she would meet an Army Air Corps escort.

Alex had lectured her about manners near fighter planes. He hadn't quite thought that he was giving a lecture on manners, but manners were how you behaved with other people, so he was talking about manners. Local pilots were very nervous if you flew directly behind them, where you could shoot at them and for some mysterious reason they couldn't shoot back. She should stay in front of them. That would be very easy, she thought, if Alex was right that Army aircraft couldn't pull more than eight or fifteen gees any more. Route 5 rolled south, two wide strips of concrete separated by a continuous hedge of rose bushes. Once she dove from the black sky of seventy thousand feet to skim thirty feet off the ground, checking that she was following the right highway. She could read the road signs from altitude, but there was no reason to advertise how good her vision was. At fifty feet the air felt smooth and slick as olive oil, giving a warm syrupy resistance to her steady three thousand knots. A faint hiss marked molecules being dragged to the side and pushed back into place, her sonic boom squelched by side effects of her flight field.

Comet spent minutes daydreaming, admiring farm fields, olive trees,

and fresh spring grass. The next town was Woodland; the big city further
ahead was her destination. She focused attention on the sky, looking for
the aircraft, a pair of specks that should be orbiting over Sacramento,
thirty miles away. There! The design was strange, squarish with split
tails, but those had to be F-42s. Alex had shown her a picture. She rolled
upward.

Comet? Her sister had been following her progress. *The Army Air
Corps people started tracking you. I'm following tesla links to their
airplanes.*

What're they saying? Comet asked.

*'Delta Tango Two Niner, Bogey at az Two Eight Zero, range three
zero miles, Angel one four thousand feet, incoming at two nine hundred
knots, climbing now to angel two two thousand feet.'* chanted Aurora.

The airplanes were turning ever so slowly toward her, control
surfaces flaring, wings almost vertical.

*'Delta Tango Two Niner, bogey at angel three five thousand feet,
range now two three miles, incoming at two thousand four hundred
knots. There is a single, repeat single target. No trace of missile
launch.'*

I should hope not, Comet answered to no one in particular, *they
promised not to shoot at me!*

Comet? said Aurora. *They mean you're not shooting at them.
They are aiming at you.*

Oh, positively wonderful. Comet's thanks had a sarcastic tinge.
Pickering had sworn it was safe, hadn't he? What was aimed at her? She
edged sideways and hit the brakes, shedding her thousands of knots in a
few seconds. Now she was flying parallel to the fighter planes, scarcely a
hundred feet from their wingtips, keeping a constant station in their
formation. She waited patiently while their pilots—fast for ungifteds, she
noted—realized she had joined their flight.

'Delta Tango Two Niner,' repeated her sister, *Radar shows bogey
matches your az and alt.'*

The pilots didn't look frightened. *'Star Leader, Delta Tango Two
Niner copies and confirms.'* Aurora repeated. Comet flitted towards
them and forced her flight field water-white, making it clear as glass.
Pushing her field clear while maintaining Mach One needed
concentration; she'd only learned the trick recently. The pilots stared in
wonder. They had been joined by a sparky tangerine ball that bore no
semblance to anything except a crayon sketch of the Great Comet of
2020. The ball had suddenly faded into transparent air, revealing a
human figure flying without visible means of support. Comet waved.

'Star Leader, this is Delta Tango Two Niner.' Aurora passed to

Comet the flight leader's words, snatched by Aurora from the pilot's microphone cable. *'I have visual contact. The bogey has joined our formation. Bogey matches the Washington sightings. The bogey pilot has waved and I am acknowledging.'* The pilot waved back at Comet. *'That's a real small fuselage she has. Estimate no go on radio to the bogey.'* The flight leader decided not to try explaining that the bogey appeared to have no fuselage at all.

'Star Leader copies. Bring her home.'

The pilot waved to Comet again, gesturing for a turn south. *'Delta Tango Two Niner turning home.'* Comet effortlessly followed the aircraft, her flight field slipping back to its natural salmon-orange as they boosted through Mach two.

A fraction of an hour brought them to the southern California desert. Salt flats glistened in the early spring sun. The wide expanse of Edwards Air Force Base stretched beneath them. The fighter aircraft landed in precise formation; Comet kept pace, staying a few feet above the runway as the fighter planes taxied to a distant corner of the airfield.

That was a reception committee, she decided, military officers, technicians, and gaping black-painted hangars. Only if you looked carefully did you notice soldiers hidden here and there, machine guns and rocket launchers trained in her direction. She decided not to worry. They were frightened, not angry.

Aurora spoke to her, mind to mind, repeating what her escort told their controllers. The pilots innocently advised ground control that Comet appeared to have VTOL capacity, and probably would not need a tow to the hangar. Comet floated over the concrete, hovering while technicians took photographs of her flight field. The field folded in on itself, depositing her on the ground a few yards from the officer who was obviously coordinating operations.

Comet could see the tension in the air. She was visibly not what they had expected. Or were they looking at her clothing? They seemed to be. Was something wrong with it? Her garb was fresh-ironed, every stitch in place. The whole gang had looked her over, Aurora combing her hair until it fell properly over the straps of her domino. Nothing could possibly be wrong there.

She tried her warmest smile. "Hi! I'm Comet." She took a quizzical General's hand. "Alex Pickering said I owed you an apology for scaring you over Washington, I mean, when all I was trying to do was visit my friends, except they're not there any more because someone changed history so the real world got turned into your world." That explained everything, and was so simple that everyone would know exactly what she meant. She reminded herself not to emphasize that, once Eclipse and

Aurora worked out the details, the five would be putting history back the way it belonged, altering time until her reality prevailed and their reality ceased to exist.

"Comet? I'm General Wilkerson. Welcome to Edwards. We're all pleased to meet you."

They strolled across the concrete into a hangar. Comet tried to ignore the hum of cameras. She decided she was happy she'd worn gloves and domino. All those people staring at her would have been a bit much, if she'd had nothing to hide behind. Wearing her domino, she could pretend they were on the other side of a fence, while she stared at them through the knotholes. She was positive she was blushing, cheeks a match for her carefully combed copper hair.

"Will you need refueling?" the General asked innocently, hoping she'd reveal which fuel was involved. There wasn't the least sign of flight gear on the woman anywhere, he noted. Most of her clothing was skintight. Miniaturization or not, you certainly couldn't hide anything as large as a rocket engine under her costume. Indeed, you couldn't hide anything at all under most of that costume. Wilkerson forced himself to reject the impression that Comet, as Professor von Pickering had named her, was no older than his oldest grand-daughter. Some women, he told himself, were more trimly built than others; this one had presumably taken physical conditioning to an extreme. Her mask, gaudy green and gold crossed comets with the profile of a giant butterfly, hid eyes and cheeks but left her nose and mouth free. As an oxygen mask, it appeared ineffective. Nonetheless, there had been a radar track. The pilots had been ordered to push her flight envelope, seeing if there were altitudes or speeds at which she couldn't match the Air Force's hottest fighter plane. She'd followed every maneuver with no sign of strain, including a sustained run at altitudes at which blood under unprotected skin would boil.

"Refueling? Oh, lunch? Sure, thank you. Though I really just had breakfast so you don't need to put yourself out of your way for me, I mean, that's very kind of you, if you'd like to have lunch I'm happy to join you." She tried a deeper smile, wishing they wouldn't crowd quite so close. Her back was ramrod straight; the boots in her garb gave her an extra inch of height. She was still looking steeply up at all these people. Logically she knew she could be airborne before they could grab her. Her heart said she was twelve, they were grownups, and they had her surrounded.

"I'd actually been thinking of JP-4, or whatever, for your flight gear," he responded.

Comet managed not to giggle, then launched into an extended

explanation of gifts and personae, ending with her experiences over Washington. She found herself sitting on a workbench table, surrounded by a cluster of enthralled men and women, one of whom thoughtfully presented her with a mug of hot cocoa and a sour-cream glaze donut. They had to be good people, she decided; they were giving her chocolate. There was an occasional background whisper, people comparing notes with what Eclipse had told the Lemuria's crew. Asked how she knew so much about Washington's antiaircraft defenses, Comet noted that they'd all fired at her, concluding "Well, sure I'm speeded up when I'm flying, so I can see things like bullets and rockets moving fast as me; it'd be real inconvenient to be flying a couple thousand miles an hour right off the ground and not be able to dodge if a fence came along."

"You can see what's coming, sure. A jink is a turn. How many gees can you pull?" the seniormost fighter pilot asked.

"I don't feel gees, because a flight field keeps you from feeling them; it pushes on all of you at the same time so there's no pressure, not like there is in a roller coaster," she answered. Then she understood the question. "Oh, how many will the flying gift deliver? Ummh, there's a girl I know in New York who got supersonic inside a base ball nines stadium. That's like seventy-five gees (her older brother the science whiz figured it out and I checked his math to make sure the details were right) and I'm faster than she is—course I'm a half-year older than her—I can do a hundred and then some gees." Comet sank into herself for a moment, reminded of yet another friend she'd never see, not until Aurora and Eclipse solved everything.

"A hundred gees? That's more than a Sprint." There was a tone of disbelief.

"I don't suppose," asked the General, "you could be persuaded to demonstrate?"

"Sure! Would someone like to come along?" she asked. "I absolutely positively never drop anyone ungifted. You'll be inside the field. You won't feel a thing. Honest. I promise." She hadn't expected such a scramble of volunteers, a scramble lasting until General Wilkerson noted that rank hath its privileges.

~~~~~

Star balanced teapot, boiling water, cups, and plate of sweet biscuits on a silver tray. Had he forgotten anything? Milk, sugar, spoons, napkins? No, he had it all. It was nice of Pickering to let them use his kitchen, but at breakfast Comet insisted they buy their own cups and saucers and teapot and tea. Using Alex's dishes was rude. She hadn't told them where to get the money, just announced how they should spend it. Cloud even agreed with her. Thanks to yesterday's criminals, their League even had money.

Comet made her trip to California, then took the Army Air Corps General to Washington, so people could say they were sorry they shot her. A short side trip got him moon rocks for his grandchildren. The Air Force people apparently thought Comet had a rocket plane. They were unhappy they didn't get to take it apart. They'd taken lots of pictures of her flying, but taking pictures wasn't as much fun as taking a machine apart. Star knew just how they must feel. He'd taken enough alarm clocks apart, and even put most of them back together well enough that they worked. That was a lot better than talking with someone.

The Army had told Comet they wanted to do experiments on her while she was flying. She told them she had errands to run first. She didn't explain: Alex might be rich, but he was already letting them sleep in his bedrooms. He kept pretending that he didn't expect them to pull leaves from the gutters, wash outside windows, or other things personas could do without a clumsy ladder. There had to be a trade for guest privileges; giving him a new tea service was one of them.

Eclipse was seated in the gazebo, head buried in the third of a large stack of books. She'd disappeared early morning, recalled Star, returning later with huge wads of local money, the books, a tea service with tea and biscuits, and changes of clothing for the whole group. Almost everything fit, too, and what didn't was too large. Comet had taken in Cloud's trousers, the only really bad fit of the lot. Asked where she'd found the money, Eclipse said she'd traded currencies. Also, she added, Leaviork had made windows of synthetic ruby and sapphire, emerald and diamond, so two millennia later large gemstones were both beautiful and common. Now Leaviork had never existed. Large gemstones had become beautiful, rare, and valuable. Star hoped Eclipse hadn't sold anything she really liked. She wouldn't say. It wouldn't have been gifttrue to say, and to Star's eyes Eclipse had a wonderful concept of being gifttrue, no matter how totally wrong she was about the Namestone.

Eclipse wore a simple rose-gray jogging suit, collar zipped tight, with long sleeves covering her wrists. The breeze tugged at her hair, blowing stray silver curls back and forth across her ears. Her face was a relaxed smile, her attention entranced by whatever she was reading. When Eclipse focused on thinking, he decided, it was like Aurora playing City of Steel. There was her mind and its prey, like a hawk stooping over a rabbit. Eclipse had to be drawing on her body field, he told himself; the breeze was too cold for someone to sit unprotected. It was chill and dank; blocks of darker clouds kept drifting across the sun. A golden shimmer at his wrists betrayed his own call on his gifts, enough to keep him warm despite the weather.

"Eclipse?" he said. She looked up at him, her steel-gray eyes radiant. "I thought you might be cold out here," he explained. "Besides, there's nothing for me to do. I'm waiting. I know you'll find the hints."

"Oh, Star, that's lovely." Her gesture encompassed tea and sweet biscuits. "For me? You really didn't have to. But thank you!" He shrugged in embarrassment.

"What else could I do? I can't help anyone, not you or Comet or even Aurora," he observed sadly.

"Star, you're doing fine. I haven't done more than you have." She pointed at the table. He set down his tray and began to make tea. Eclipse gave him her undivided attention. A solid pour of boiling water heated the pot and cups. From the pot he spilled six drops of water on the tray, one to each of the cardinal directions. That was another change, she thought; Alex would not recognize northeast and southeast as two of the six cardinal directions, to the great dismay of the Lords of the Hexagon. The rest of the waste water went between two rose bushes. A dry spoon put tea leaves into the pot. Carefully, Star poured the rest of the boiling water, first slowly to dampen the leaves, then quickly to fill the whole pot. A wire whisk, strokes carefully matched left and right, dispersed the leaves. The whisk went on a towel; the lid went on the pot. A ceremony older than Atlanticea completed, the two inclined their heads to each other and waited for the tea to steep. If it had been the three girls having tea together, Star noted, they would just have dumped the tea leaves and water in the pot. The tea would have tasted practically the same. But he was a boy and Eclipse was a girl. There was a right way for a boy and a girl to behave when they were being polite to each other. Ultimately, Eclipse poured tea for the two of them and gestured at the third cup.

"Alex said he'd join us," Star explained. They sipped their too-hot tea, talking of little things until Pickering came. Star dragged the conversation toward Eclipse's reading—languages and cultures of the ancient world, places about which he knew almost nothing. The hints could be right in front of her, he thought, but how could she find them?

"Oh, I've found lots of hints," Eclipse answered. "No pattern. I dropped all the hints on Aurora. She's very good at finding hidden patterns—that's what a gamesmistress is, after all, a pattern finder. There's something you and Cloud could try. Cloud got dragged through seventh-grade Historics—I remember him complaining about it on our flight. Not that I blame him for complaining. He read about all the different countries in Massachusetts and Washington two thousand years ago. They were all there at once, and didn't notice each other. Proving history is all fairy tales, he said; no one could be as stupid as these people were. Could you two check out Washington? Look for ruins from Sarnath or Marik or Leaviork or, well, there should be lots of ruins, almost as many as Massachusetts. See which ones survived?" Eclipse suggested. "I tried Pickering's library. He's got lots of books on deciphering old languages. The same languages, but only five or ten of them, places that usually hardly get mentioned 'cause their people were real primitive. Egypt—the pyramid builders. Babylon. But no place where people did machines, no ships or airplanes."

Pickering, now seated across the gazebo from them, recounted a story from a graduate of the local college, one who'd gone into English and foreign languages and found herself teaching near one of the Great Lakes. Her experience put a new scale on ignorance. She proposed teaching a foreign language in high school, something not previously done, to meet resistance from the school board. A board member's definitive contrary argument had been 'English was good enough for the ancient Romans, so it's good enough for our children.' Pickering caught the look of his guests, slightly puzzled by a tale they knew was supposed to be amusing. "Of course, everyone knows that in ancient cultures people spoke their own language, never English, the Romans speaking Latin, a school board containing an ignoramus who thinks the Apostles wrote in English rather than Hebraic, Aramaic, or the Koine Dialectos being amusing." They looked baffled. 'Perhaps humor doesn't translate, for all that your language appears to be English."

"I didn't see that!" Eclipse put hands to cheeks in horror. "Those languages—Latin, Greek, Sumerian—not a single ancient country spoke Historic English! How could I be so incredibly blind?"

"Don't get zapped, Eclipse." Star tried to be reassuring. "Seeing what's missing is hard." He launched into an anecdote, him fighting one of Emperor Roxbury's robots when the robot went invisible, finding the robot because the robot's perfect copy of the building behind him lacked the flicker of declining fluorescent bulbs. While he spoke, thickening clouds darkened the sky, threatening the approach of rain.

"Forgive me," Pickering intruded. "Am I to understand that some of your ancient cultures spoke English?"

"Of course. Of course they spoke English. Not Modern English like us, but Historic English. I learned it in school," Star said. "Sarnath and Marik spoke Historic English. Atlantis and Rome didn't. Even I know that. Of course, everyone knows history is just a bunch of stories. So why shouldn't stories make people speak English?"

"It's unreasonable," Pickering announced. "It's impossible! Languages don't just appear. They descend from each other, so English and German and Dutch came from the same roots, like children from one family. If you're clever you can trace them back thousands of years. The ten-thousand-year reconstruction—Nostratic—is controversial. But you can see languages change into each other."

"Languages are related?" Star asked. "Like people?"

"Yes," Pickering said, "so father came from vater or pitr or whatever, so learning French is easier if you know Latin and Spanish."

"Gee, you should tell Cloud that," Star said. "He always says it doesn't matter what languages you know to learn a new one. A new language is new."

Eclipse gave Pickering a deeply penetrating look. "Loan words. Latin helicopterum, Atlanticea but not Rome having them."

"Not loans, ancestors," said Pickering. "We have, we appear to have, documents going back five thousand years. Don't you? You can line them up one after the next. You can see how one language became another, how the Latin V became U and V and W. I and J became two letters only a couple hundred years ago. And my history makes sense. All of it. That's more believable than your history, where, Cloud mentioned, ancient men had incomprehensible motives. Rationally, it's your memories someone changed, so you believe in places like Atlantis that never existed." Pickering asked himself if he believed his own arguments. Time travellers? Children who flew? It was all unreasonable.

Star was taken aback. He could remember touring ruins of Sarnath, his father showing him murals and inscriptions. How could Sarnath not have existed? How could languages descend from each other, when he'd seen inscriptions on those ruins and mostly understood the ones in Historic English? It couldn't be true.

"And who was I, before I became me? A runaway from your local orphanage?" Eclipse said, not expecting an answer. "Wherefrom came my gifts? You could telehypnotize someone until they believed they were a persona. But if you mindwiped an ungifted, she was still ungifted. No matter how much she believed she could fly, if you threw her off a cliff, she would fall straight down, terminal bounces not counting as flight." Eclipse knew she agreed with Pickering: She could be someone else, not Eclipse at all, no matter how loud her memories shouted the contrary. But if no one here were gifted, there was no one who could have been mindwarped into someone who flew.

~~~~~

It was late evening in Pickering's home. The five's minds were elsewhere. Not three hours ago, Eclipse and Comet had disappeared to

Los Angeles to be interviewed on a national video net. Their garb was freshly washed and ironed. Eclipse had rolled and clipped her hood so it formed a steely halo behind her frost-white hair.

Aurora linked Eclipse with Pickering, so that Eclipse saw how an adult of Pickering's America heard her. Aurora and Star hadn't realized that Eclipse ever felt the least apprehension. When they'd watched her on video, coming out of the Maze, she'd appeared the picture of total certainty. Linked with her, mind to mind, they felt her unease at facing a half-dozen possibly hostile adults, no matter that the adults had been most cooperative at planning demonstrations of her gifts.

The panel included the station host, correspondents from the Times and the Journal, a matched trio of noted liberal, conservative, and libertarian columnists, and one of the country's leading science writers. Unlike the viewing audience, the panel had known in advance of its guest and composed appropriate questions.

The interviewers were fascinated by the dooms. Questioners were frustrated by one difficulty: Eclipse and Comet didn't know what the dooms were. Comet tried to be reassuring. The Wizard had selected them as the best people in the world to beat the dooms, so the odds were much on the world's side.

A suggestion that Eclipse was a hoax was swiftly eliminated. She teleported the science writer and a cameraman to geosynchronous orbit, allowed them to broadcast from outer space, and returned them and an obsolete communications satellite to earth. Eclipse provided air but no gravity; the columnist reminded viewers that two minutes of zero gravity was impossible to fake. Waiting engineers from the satellite's manufacturer confirmed that the hulk had indeed been launched into orbit and only minutes before had been 23,000 miles above the Earth, precisely where the remote broadcast had been transmitted.

Half the panel wanted to know where she and Eclipse had obtained their powers, whether they were mutations or a secret government project and, if so, whose government. The remainder of the panel had concluded that their guests came from another timeline, one almost the same as our own, and wanted to know why personae had had no effect on their history. The panel ignored Eclipse's clear explanation of Einsteinian transitivity, and how you could change the present by tampering with the past. They were even less interested in Comet's assurances that gifts had no genetic component.

Final minutes mired in questions of ethics. The panel asked how people could allow ten-year-olds to risk their lives in outer space. How could anyone let children go off by themselves when they might die? Eclipse responded by asking how anyone could expect a persona not to

212

honor one's duty to one's gifts. Pickering jotted down Star's whispered question "Why does everyone get our ages wrong? Eclipse, her garb makes her look practically grown up. These guys think she's ten or eleven. The shuttle crew, they did the same."

The conservative columnist's parting shot, a tribute to comic-book ethics preached by comic-book heroes, drew amused smiles from his fellow panelists and bemused glances from Eclipse and Comet. The audience's final view of the program showed Eclipse and Comet dissolving into a blue haze as they teleported out of the studio.

CHAPTER 20 DREAMS AND SHADOWS

Eclipse leaned back in a window seat, her shoes neatly stacked by the baseboard radiator, her feet primly tucked under her. She stared intently into her book, pausing once and again to write on a legal pad. A sheaf of overfolded pages hid notes from other references. Her face held a gentle grin; her eyes focused solely on the text she was struggling to understand.

Earlier, the sky had been bright and sunny. Then a heavy rain had pounded on the gazebo roof, driving her indoors and leaving puddles on open porches. Now gray blankets of cloud had given way to a watery blue sky. Once and again, the sinking sun forced her to shift her seat to retreat from its glare. Finally she noticed that Comet had entered the room and was sitting quietly, waiting for her concentration to break. Eclipse peered up from her reading. A bright smile flashed across her lips. Steel-gray eyes gleamed.

"I didn't want to interrupt," Comet apologized, "You said you wanted to talk. Privately?"

"You're not. Interrupting, I mean. I'm going in circles. Not that I know what I'm doing. I'm looking for a hint. It has to be there. The sun room down the corridor? Let me put these away. I only need a minute." Eclipse began shelving books, carefully, each to its original location.

The sunroom was house-long but narrow, barely wide enough for several outward-facing couches. A wide window seat with two rows of book shelves underneath, two stair-steps lower than the couches, ran the length of the room. Three walls of the room were almost completely windowed, large sheets of glass hiding behind a delicate diamond lattice of walnut strips. The fourth wall was hung with wooden objects d'art, paintings, and two large tapestries depicting the settlement of the West. Comet considered the window seat, generously furnished with large pillows, folded quilts, and a paisley object that might have been a sleeping bag except that its fabric obviously didn't belong out-of-doors. She choose the couch, giving her a view of Pickering's formal gardens.

Trees and evergreens, still traped in winter's grip, formed a pattern, arranged to lead one's eyes to a single magnificent Japanese maple, perfectly framed by the rest of the garden. Except, she remembered, she had looked out the window when she first entered the room, and again when she looked at the sculpture above the window seat. Each time, she had had a different point of view. Each time, a different aspect of the garden had been framed, the maple to which she was now drawn having then been an accent rather than a centerpiece. It was a terribly subtle set of plantings, so arranged that a move of a few yards gave a new perspective.

Eclipse took the couch's other end. "I promised to explain your dream. I couldn't with Star and Aurora there."

"You thought it was very important, didn't you? You were awful fast to change the topic," Comet said.

"It's important to you. Did anyone ever tell you about dreams and planes?" Eclipse tried to make her question sound matter-of-fact.

"Planes?" Comet answered. "No. Wait, there was this fellow I met the first time I visited Washington, who (when he wasn't busy telling me that I couldn't really be a persona because I was way too young so I couldn't possibly really have any deep gifts, as if I weren't obviously lots older than Star and Aurora) was busy talking about complete nonsense. Munin, his persona-name was; he seemed to remember an incredible lot but couldn't get it out in any order that made sense, so you just had to listen and put it together for yourself afterwards, like he was all memory and absolutely no common sense in between anyplace, let alone any paying attention if you asked a question. I remember. He talked about the sky, the breaking wave, the sea of grass, and said those were how strong I am."

"The shallowest planes. They aren't really places. I think." Eclipse shrugged. "They're a symbol. Ask someone whose gifts just went down a level: What did they dream the next night? Almost everyone has the same dream."

"I keep dreaming of green rolling hills, a place I've never been. On one hill I always see a temple." Comet remembered the vivid dream, grass the brilliant hue seen after spring rains, marble a flawless white with bright-hot smokeless flames gusting out between deeply fluted columns. "A Greek temple like in American Geographic. Except it was burning, flames coming out from every entrance. I'd always see it in the distance, but if I tried flying to it I never got there, in fact I never got closer, it being that sort of dream."

"The temple is the next plane. Or its symbol. When you were awake, your gifts hadn't reached the Temple plane, so dreaming you couldn't fly to the temple," Eclipse explained.

"Last night I was inside, marble walls glowing white-hot and fire beating around me, except I didn't feel warm," Comet said. "It didn't hurt. Well, it was like doing wind sprints until your arms and legs burn, except you know you really haven't hurt yourself. In one corner of the room, there was a ball of light, painful bright to see."

"That's the Temple," Eclipse said. "You got down another plane all at once. Some people get closer and closer in their dreams. Then a bit at a time they're inside, because slowly they can reach down another plane with their gifts."

"Everyone has the same dream? Every persona?" Comet asked.

"I don't know every," Eclipse answered. "Some people don't dream. Some forget. Why a dream? I don't know. Why are there personae? It really doesn't make sense. Evolution, you know? Fish to dinosaurs to birds?"

"Of course I know about evolution," Comet said. "I mean, I'm not that dumb, for all you think circles around us whenever you try, but daddy put that sort of thing in front of us, every morning when we were having breakfast, so we'd always start the day by thinking about something."

"You're not dumb at all! You're smarter than me," Eclipse countered. "You outwitted Speaker Ming and Morgan Le Fay. I just knew a couple extra facts. Had extra time to think. That makes me look smart. I'm not that smart, not really. So, where did personae come from? Evolve, I mean? Do monkeys fly? Do baboons shoot lightning bolts from their eyes? No, not at all. But the dreams come from someplace. The same place as personae, so people who do public personae get dreams. The dreams signify you moved down in your levels."

"They do?" Comet felt baffled. Where did Eclipse learn her facts? You could count on her being right, but where did she learn all these things? Not in any library Comet had ever seen, and she had a library card at her father's Institute. It was like Eclipse knew people who saw the world as a big stage play, and they knew how to press the buttons and move the scenery.

"You'd forgotten Munin, yes? He probably told you the next ten planes. Munin'll talk on forever. But you won't see a plane. Not until you're ready. Almost everyone can't even remember a plane's name. Not until they're ready to use it." Eclipse looked thoughtful. "Wait. You saw the Sun? The fiery ball in the temple? You're sure?"

"Sure." Comet smiled.

"That's the gate to the plane below the Temple. Would you promise absolutely not to tell Star or Aurora? It's very dangerous. Star really is too young to know. No matter how sick I am of people telling me I'm a little girl and should do what I'm told, like all other good little boys and girls, and Give Them That Goddess-Cursed Namestone Right Now, there really is such a thing as too young." Eclipse's tone bespoke her annoyed contempt for her hordes of enemies.

"People tell you?" Comet asked. "Gee! I thought it was only me. After the Maze, you were treated like a grown-up. Such as, the whole League of Nations did have meetings about you, though you're right, all they said was 'Give us the Namestone right now, and don't expect us to say please, you little slink, or we'll beat it out of you.'; they could've at least been polite; but if I promise not to say, do you promise to tell Star and Aurora someday?"

"Done. If something happens to me, so I can't, it's your call what to do," Eclipse promised.

"Deal!" Comet answered enthusiastically. "What can happen to you?"

"Oh, little things. The Peace Police catch me. The Manjukuoan gold gets doubled again. The Italians put up the Sistine Chapel as a bonus. No, they did that already; they could put up the museums of Florence. Little things like that." In Eclipse's voice, the enmity of the world shrank to a minor nuisance. "Anyhow. There's a trick, a way to get extra power. Find the Temple. It's in your mind. Reach into the Sun. Deep. Oh, it'll hurt like heck. It's not safe. You're overloading. You'll get sick later. People don't usually die that way."

"All those planes you named; I can do...four. Five with your trick. How deep can you go?" Comet asked. "If you don't mind saying?"

"I'm not sure I can tell you. Until you use a plane, it's hard to remember the plane is there. I know how far I went at the deepest. If I'm careless, sooner or later I'll go too deep and not surface. The Sun, the Matrix, the Fall of Crystal, the Tomb, the Hall of the Lidless Eye. I could go on. Don't even think of trying them. Stop with the Sun," Eclipse warned. "Well, unless you're for absolute sure going to die elsewise; then it doesn't matter. If you have time at that point, find and read a copy of the *Presentia*."

"I hear you...I heard what you said about hurting yourself," Comet said matter-of-factly. "I mean, it's not like I'm a boy always having to be bragging myself up, no matter whether it makes any sense, or whether anyone with any sense would see that bragging up doing something dangerous is just plain stupid, like that stupid boy Adara saved."

"Sorry." Eclipse shrank back into the crook of the couch. "You're right. I should have trusted you. Boys are the problem. Always showing off and bragging themselves up. They have to prove something. That's another reason not to tell Star. He's a boy."

"You don't have to apologize. I know you were protecting me, because..." Comet tried to cover over Eclipse's embarrassment.

"I've gone too deep. More than once." Eclipse peered out the windows. "I hurt myself, was sick for days until I could..."

"...you care about us, no matter what my slink brother keeps saying, though if he'd stay away from Cloud he'd be a lot better, but you're totally right about Star; he thinks nothing can hurt him," Comet finished.

"...put myself back together," Eclipse continued. "Cloud is a pain. He just wants everyone to do what he says. He never listens to anyone. No matter what they say. When he's talking about me, he just echoes what he heard on the video." She looked wistfully at the garden. "I had to do the Maze. I had to! The League was going to solve it. They didn't understand the Namestone. They wouldn't listen. Not to me! Not that I tried very hard. Why bother? They're boys at heart, even Krystal North." Eclipse threw up hands in disgust.

"Did you try? At all?" Comet asked. "Not that I blame you, if you didn't, because you're really right; the League wouldn't have listened, not until you took the Maze, because until then to the very limited extent they noticed you they thought you were just another kid like Aurora and me, except you were very cautious about meeting people, and cared about getting your rewards in cash, even when they mumbled about putting your money aside for college, except like mayhaps all of once they said you were very good for being our age after you took out the three Emperor Roxbury robots all by yourself at the same time. They didn't even figure out that Joe was a girl."

"The disguise worked!" Eclipse nodded happily.

"But you did it. You took the Maze. You did," Comet reminded. "And I don't care what anyone else says, you proved you were the greatest persona in the world up there with Plasmatrix and Prince Mong-Ku and Solara-the-Desolation-of-the-Goddess, because none of them ever tried the Maze, but you took it all alone." Comet's eyes glowed with admiration for the fantastic thing her friend had done by herself.

"I did do it, didn't I?" Eclipse looked at the garden. "I must have. I remember holding the Namestone. I cradled it in my hands: A frozen piece of sky polished into a ball. And that last climb? Out from the Tomb into the sunlight? It was wonderful! More wonderful than anything! Even if I still get nightmares." She saw Comet's worried look. "Not a big trade." Her tone hardened. "I almost never get them unless I've pushed too deep."

~~~~~

Pickering padded the round of his widow's walk. This evening had repeatedly been frustrating. Yesterday Comet had shown him faster than light flight. That revealed fragments of Einstein's Transitivity. No, he told himself, he had part of the forms for von Pickering's Theory of Universal Transitivity. The one true Einstein died believing in general relativity. Transitivity was his alone. He still needed to eliminate a few minor lacunae in his analysis.

His contacts in Washington were confused. On one hand, Comet's talents presented them with enormous opportunities. On the other hand, for a Federal Agency to retain without parental consent the services of a minor child—who apparently had no guardians—raised novel legal questions, especially when the child could detail the legal process that made her an adult. Pickering wondered if his informants had been infected by the White House's indecision.

He had not been entirely pleased with the results of the last Congressional elections, even given the Impeachment Crisis, but the present situation was unreasonable. Legal order seemed to be collapsing. Since Election Day, scarcely three months ago, the National Guards of half of the states had been called to the colors by their governors. It appeared that tomorrow morning the State Legislature of New Hampshire was going to mobilize the state's unorganized militia—the armed adult citizenry—an act with only pre-Civil War precedents. Washington made vague calls for peace and calm. Admittedly, he noted, the past four years had demobilized most of the Armed Forces, the Army and Navy dipping towards numbers last seen under Herbert Hoover, but the Federal government could still try to do something. Even with stock markets shaken by reports of dooms, the White House was largely silent, putting out brief pablums telling the public that all was well.

~~~~~

Aurora sat at the wonderful desk in her bedroom. It was her size, not for grown-ups. This whole room had been laid out for children. The boys slept in long grownup beds, but she had something that matched her four and a fraction feet. She set to writing.

"Dear Diary,

"Today I stayed here at A__P__'s home all day. Comet went to California yesterday. I read their minds, the Army people in California, and made sure she was safe. If she wasn't, Star and Cloud and E__ would have rescued her.

"P__'s computer plays chess. We played. It's very good at tactics. Its book isn't that great, but no one's book is good any more. They've only played chess for hundreds of years, not thousands and thousands, so they've got things wrong. The computer has an opening book with commentary. I made the computer go through all the openings it knew, even bad ones like the Glorious Shield of Sarnath, and say what people thought of them. When I went after its mistakes, it lost. When I stayed with openings it had right, it beat me. I played A__. He has no idea how to play chess. Games aren't important now, not like the way they used to be. I told A__ I wanted to be a Mistress of Games when I grew up, and he smiled. He thought I was good to be ambitious. Then he asked what a Mistress of Games was. After I told him, he tried to be polite, and still tried to say I should do something serious. Like anything in the world could possibly be more important than being a GamesMistress. Even Star agrees about that. Well, I guess I could become a High Programmer, or the Analyst Supreme.

"I should have been searching for clues, but there was this absolutely unique chess opponent sitting there. I peeked at the Sea of Glass. There really is a country there. They play bichrome Stones, two liberties, except only a 19x19 board. The Lemurians and everyone else must have been studying Stones longer than these Taiwanese have studied Go, to want a bigger board and more rules. Telzey only plays 19x19 Stones, and doesn't know polychrome or other-liberty rules.

"Star and Cloud went for a walk in the State Park. Lots of trees and grass and quiet. E__ spent all day studying. I watched her. She was going through books and taking notes, working harder than Comet does for school, the day before an exam. She was looking for the answer. She hasn't found it yet. She will! She did the Maze. She can do anything. I know she can.

"Love,
"Aurora."

~~~~~

Cloud and Star lay in their beds, unable to sleep. The harshness of their predicament had reached them. Their homes were gone; their parents were gone. All they had was each other, and the three girls, none of whom could understand about a person being lonely.

"You think we'll ever have another trolley series?" Cloud asked.

"Next year," said Star, pulling the covers tighter around his chin. "The Doves need a couple more trades, that's all, and they'll be ready for the Brahmins. Wasn't the last one great?"

"Sure was," said Cloud. "Great to know, no matter what, the Summer League champion will be in Boston."

"You could even say the champs were in Roxbury. Half the stadium sticks into your home town," said Star. The layout of Ruth Stadium was dreaded by opposing pitchers through all the major leagues, Summer and Winter. "Can we talk about something else? Every time I talk base ball nines, I remember dad, and skipping school for a game. Now, no school. And I study because I've got to, not because I should." Cloud forced himself to keep his voice even, hiding how he felt.

Star choked down an answer, too close to tears to keep his voice level, not about to reveal that he was crying. 'Good night," he choked.

"Good night," came Cloud's whispered return.

~~~~~

Aurora stared distantly at the ceiling. Her room was dark, the faint glow of a blue-violet nightlight sparking from blinds and lamp shades. Why was she awake? There wasn't an obvious reason. She always slept like a log. There hadn't been a noise. Her sister, her twin brother, and Cloud were all asleep. It must have been the tap to Eclipse. It was all right now, but something had nudged her across the twilight demarcation between asleep and awareness. Did Eclipse have another nightmare, a very bad one? Eclipse would never say. If you asked her, she would say 'no'. She was painfully polite; she always pretended to be grateful you asked. Inside her mind, if you watched very carefully, she would be incredibly upset that you'd asked, like she didn't want to think anyone ever cared about her at all. It was better not to ask. Aurora faded into deep sleep.

CHAPTER 21 A COURSE OF ACTION?

The day was bright and clear. Pickering broke his fast alone in the west tower, tea and melon and toast competing with the morning papers for table area. The national and international news was truly dreadful. Threats of war spread across the globe. At home terrorists disrupted the tranquility of half the Union. For a moment Pickering considered asking his guests to apply their gifts to the world's problems. That wish had to wait; Transitivity, and with it the ability to manipulate time, were not yet completely within his grasp. Until his theory was complete, he would do nothing to drive away his resident experts on faster-than-light travel. Until he could alter the central event of all history, replacing his virtual image with eternal reality, minor local disturbances would have to be endured. Of course, his guests said they were here to prevent dooms. Perhaps they did not need to be asked to prevent wars.

His guests had made themselves a solid breakfast, washed their pans and dishes, and left the kitchen cleaner than they found it. He had caught Aurora washing the floor, using strands of amber light to send soap and water swirling across the tile. Her work cleaned every irregularity, even the most inaccessible nooks and crannies, leaving the faintest traces of moisture. Eclipse had excused herself, announced that she needed quiet to read, and disappeared, taking with her a large stack of books she'd purchased someplace-or-other. He'd recognized Wells' World History, Spengler and Toynbee and Sorokin. He had suggested that the last of these held more sense than the first three put together, at least if you knew enough about chaotic dynamics to recognize a historian's description of strange attractors, penned before anyone had heard of chaotic dynamics. He'd also suggested that Sorokin was not the lightest of reading. What was she looking for? He couldn't imagine.

Comet marched the boys through several changes of trousers, precisely marking cuffs and waists. Pickering considered offering the use of a sewing machine, then saw that her hand-stitchery was faster and more precise. Later, he wondered if she found it subjectively faster. Perhaps she would have welcomed the sewing machine after all. Cloud asked about general libraries—public libraries, he seemed to mean. His main interest was library manners: how you behaved, what resources a library had, what not to do.

Aurora had discovered that Telzey played chess. Her twin brother suggested, perhaps more pointedly than was entirely tactful, that she should be looking for clues, not working towards Mistress of Games. He told her that whoever changed time had made gaming unimportant. She had to fix time, before gaming would be the most important thing in the world again. Before she became a Gamesmistress, she agreed, she would need to restore the title's central significance. Pickering later found her in the meditation room—a cylindrical maple-lined chamber lit by narrow stained-glass windows. She'd been standing on the central carpet, arms outstretched, eyes blank, seemingly not breathing, surrounded by a glowing pyramidal nimbus. Pickering decided that he might eventually learn which of her gifts she'd been using, and left her in peace.

Star was obviously bored. He tried to be very polite, but he had nothing to do. His gifts didn't lend themselves to finding clues. Finally he announced he'd go for a walk, if it wouldn't cause Pickering any trouble. Armed with a neighborhood map and a bag of cookies, he set out into the woods.

~~~~~

The five straddled benches on the lower lawn. They'd all performed morning errands, thanked Eclipse for appearing with store-bought hot sandwiches, and found a quiet place to picnic. Light from the noontime sun warmed their faces and danced over ripples in a brick-lined ornamental pond. Behind them, Pickering's house was a looming wall of Neovictorian lacework, wings and towers framed by trees and ornamental plantings.

"We're doing something wrong," Star finally announced, "with our gifts, us being gifted. Not 'not finding the hint' wrong, but 'right or wrong' wrong."

"Morals?" asked Aurora. She stared meaningfully at Comet, who shrugged patiently. The two sisters had concluded that every so often Star found a strange idea rattling around in his head, and you had to wait until it fell out. From their perspective, it always did.

Star looked at Eclipse, sure that she'd not care about his notion of wrongness, finding to his surprise that he had her absolute attention. "Are we failing gifttruth?" Eclipse questioned.

"Hey, mayhaps I'm wrong," Star explained. "You'll know. You've got lots more practice deciding what you do. I mean, lots of people say you're wrong about the Namestone, but they say wrong, not giftfalse."

"So what is it?" Aurora asked.

"It's us staying here," Star said. "We aren't paying. If we were ungifted, just runaways, Pickering would give us to the bailiffs—ummh, sheriffs. He doesn't. Because we've got gifts."

"Got it," said Aurora. "Interesting gifts. Watch him. Mention time travel, he lights up. Translight, same thing. He wants them himself, I can tell."

"Translight I can understand, so he can go to all the places he sees in his telescope, but time travel?" Comet wondered. "He wants time travel for himself, when absolutely no one in the world does time travel, not even Corinne or Solara—well, I know you said you might, Eclipse, but that doesn't make it like the most common gift there is, not really, does it?"

"I said I might—might!—pull it off. Once. And I touch your debit card for my funeral," Eclipse said. "Pickering wants transtime for a reason. A lifetrue reason, a reason more important than death. Star's right. You are, Star! Pickering wants us here because we've been gifted. That's us being given dinner, bed, bath for our gifts, just because we have them. That's practically stealing."

"It could be a trade," Cloud countered. "I saved that rocket plane. Me and Comet and Aurora."

"One night was okay. We raked his lawn and washed all his windows," Star said. "No, Comet, I know you could clean his whole house in a few hours, but don't. That's what Dad and Mom made you do—all the housework. That was terrible, and I should have said so. I didn't. I was wrong. I don't even know how to apologize. Not for all that. But move in with him? We've been here for days. No way that's right. We need a base. Like Prince Mong-Ku and the Palace of Celestial Eternity. We get a base. Then figure out how to put things back, back how they were before, so we can go home." His final words brought him almost to tears.

"You're right, Star," Cloud said. "We've got to get a base. Now. Then we kill all the time pirates. And crush the dooms. That's the only moral way."

"He's rich," Aurora said. "Very rich. Something he invented. He has gardeners, maids, even a tailor. Here a day a week. Other days he has peace and quiet. He thinks we're company. I asked. We talked, mind-to-mind. I tried explaining gifttrue. He thinks he owes us 'cause we took him translight. But you're right, Star." She almost bit her tongue on that admission. "We have to go. So we need a base. Now. Before we can catch the time pirates, we need a base. And pay him back for having us."

"We took him translight?" a surprised Cloud asked.

Comet explained. "A couple times. Short flights, once to Mars and back, once to Alpha Centauri. I gave him air and temperature while I flew, and besides he really liked the trip even if he was too busy taking pictures, with this funny looking camera that only had one lens, to lean back and enjoy the view."

"Frigid! So he's paying us for something you did. That's fair," Cloud said. "Like when you and Etherbourne took that fellow to the Eye last month. His money went in your College Savings Account."

"CSA? Cloud! Thanks for reminding me! I forgot! That's now my money," Comet said.

"Is it right? Us here? For more than a couple days?" Star was not convinced.

Aurora understood his doubt. "You're right. But for a base we need money. Are bases easy to get? You know that, Eclipse. You built a base. You know how to buy armor and screens and secret weapons and laboratories and everything."

Eclipse swallowed. Aurora's notion of building a base seemed to be missing the more interesting steps. "You need a lot of money. Then a base, if you want. I think it's easy to get money now. There are lots and lots of criminals. No personae chase them. Only bailiffs."

"Only bailiffs chase criminals?" Comet asked.

"You got it!" Star and Eclipse chimed in unison.

Eclipse continued. "But Star is right. About gifttrue. We can't stay here. I'll settle for a tent. You guys want a base, don't you?" Four pairs of eyes gleamed. "So first find crooks. Salvage money. Get a base. When you put time back, it's like it never happened, so you can take as long building a base as you need, just so long as you fix time in the end." She tried to avoid grinding her teeth. First it would be money, then a base, then something else—they'd never get around to helping her find the time pirates. She'd have to find the dooms, too, whatever they were.

"How do you find criminals?" Star asked. "Criminals with money?"

"Supreme Illusionist. Emperor Roxbury. They were just there. Stacks of Aztecans. Bullies at school. They were just there," Aurora said. "Finding criminals is hard. Isn't it? How many murders were there in America last year? Two hundred? Surely not a thousand? That's not many out of a hundred million people. We could wait a long time and never see one."

"I found the answer," Cloud announced. "Criminals with money. It's smugglers. People smuggle tens of billions of dollars a year, bring stuff here from South America and Burma and Afghanistan. And take paper money the other way, out from the USA."

"Frigid! Are these the medicine smugglers? Or is it Mayan statues?" Aurora asked, a rush of enthusiasm bringing her to her feet.

"It's drugs. Not doctor drugs." Cloud rose, fingers waving as he made his points. "Chemicals. Things that warp your brain. People pay money for them. It's against the law, like Rectification made chocolate illegal. So, 'cause it's illegal and you can't hardly get the stuff otherwise, you pay lots of money. The fellows we arrested, they were very small-time businessmen, and we salvaged from them a big wad of money. I went to the town library and read about it. I said I was from out of town and reading was instead of school, which was sort of true, and I was looking up about criminals who made lots of money, and that was completely true."

Eclipse strained though her memories, looking for a half-forgotten analogy. "Chemicals. It's like being engifted. Do you remember? First time you get a gift, how great it feels? The best possible feeling in the world. Right? Everyone knows that. Pickering's people use chemicals to feel the same way, well, half-baked the same. That happened in Sarnath. Bankers used chemicals so they wouldn't need dreams or flower gardens. I read about it." At least, she thought to herself, I also read about it. The person who gave me memories of glorious Sarnath, its austere banks and blank-faced counting houses hiding the greatest trading empire of all time, showed me.

"It can't feel the same! Can it?" Aurora sat down again, legs angling under her so she sat on her ankles.

"I read it can't," Eclipse said. "Not really. Not for a healthy person, someone who enjoys getting things done. After all, everyone gets little gifts, and it feels just as great getting a little gift as getting translight. But what about someone lazy enough to watch video two hours a day, lazy enough to stuff themselves until they're a hundred pounds too heavy? That's lots of Pickering's people. Lots of them are very lazy. Lazy enough not to vote or get a job or finish school. Incredibly beyond-belief lazy. Alex said some people watch video four hours a day, but he must've been exaggerating. For effect." She smiled. "Plus some people have minds like scrambled eggs, so they enjoy breaking laws. I'd say it was little boy fun, excitement of doing something you shouldn't, but the boys I know," she looked at Star and Cloud, "are way too smart for that." The boys looked sheepishly at each other.

"I found another way to get money," Comet added, "mayhaps it won't make as much money but it makes it very quick. All we need is a good camera and finding something that flies over the USA every day."

"Where's the money?" Star asked. Cloud let Comet talk first.

"I read in Alex's Sunday paper, there's these things that fly over the United States, been going on for months, and the Army Air Corps, ummh, Air Force can't shoot them down 'cause they can't get close, so at first they hid that these flying things were up there, and then some journal in Virginia published it, and now everyone is thrashing about like beheaded dodos. The money is me sneaking up on one and taking pictures and selling them to this Virginia journal," Comet explained. "I mean, it's only a silly machine, so it can't hardly manage to turn inside me or outrun me, whatever it is."

"And my money?" Cloud said. "There's this island. A real rich person bought it, and built an aerodrome and refrigerated warehouses and lots of guards and neat stuff like he was a persona. Smugglers go there. It's all illegal. If we go and turn smugglers over to bailiffs, the money is all criminal and not stolen so we could salvage it like we salvaged Emperor Roxbury's treasury."

"Real frigid," Star said. "We must've gotten a couple thousand each from Emperor Roxbury, all four of us. That was great." He remembered what else had happened and glanced guiltily at Eclipse.

Eclipse leaned her wide, square shoulders against a tree, waiting for Cloud to finish his story. "Need more than thousands for a base," she said matter-of-factly. After destroying the Emperor Roxbury's replicants, she'd dragged herself home and fallen half-conscious on her bed. In her absence, the four had searched Emperor Roxbury's fortress and salvaged his personal wealth. They had searched his base, she told herself; it was their money.

"These criminals," Cloud announced, "they've got hundreds of thousands of dollars. Mayhaps even more. They're illegal, but they pay governments not to see their base. That sounded impossible. Until I figured out what no telepaths means. No telepaths means you can't tell if government people are honest." Aurora covered her mouth in horror. Telepathy was the basis of good government; everyone knew that. How could Pickering's world work without it?

"Frigid!" an exuberant Star chortled. "We'll have so much money we won't know what to do with it!"

"You need a lot of money for that," a skeptical Eclipse said. "Prices now are way higher than before. And real evidence," she continued, "that this fellow is a smuggler, this being a Regular Action at least you're proposing." She was gratified that Cloud gave her an instant thumb's up when she said he'd need evidence first.

"So where is this base?" Aurora asked.

"That's where Comet comes in," Cloud answered. "This airplane journal near the Federal District? We get them pictures and they'll tell us which island. Checking all the islands in the world is a lot of work. But they're an airplane journal; their computer must know every aerodrome in the world."

"The silly thing," Comet said, "is I heard about these flying things from the Army, ummh Air Force in California, and after I said I could catch them real easy because they only do four or five thousand knots they sounded about to ask me to take pictures, except right then someone asked me how old I am and after I said thirteen—which is plenty old enough to use a camera even if it's one you've got to adjust and focus yourself—they said they'd get back to me about pictures. They haven't."

"You know," Star said, "even with a little money we could get a simple base. No armor or rapier mines or anything. But a base. Or we could camp out in Antarctica." His sisters nodded supportively.

"Star, can you take a bath with your body screens summoned?" Eclipse questioned primly.

"Of course not," he answered. "I wouldn't get wet!" Eclipse waited, smiling coyly. "Oh. No screens means I get cold," he added. She inclined her head approvingly. "Unless the base is someplace warm."

"She didn't say no," Aurora said. "Just cold. You learned that the hard way, didn't you, Eclipse?"

"I knew in advance. You can take a cold bath. If you want a bath enough. I did. Or you can zorch water till it's hot. But," Eclipse added, "there's a shortage of empty places. To hide a base, I mean. When we left, the world had a whole billion people, and then some."

"Too many." Cloud shrugged. "It's a world problem."

"There are now seven billion people. Some starve, no surprise. Nice places are full. You'll have to be smart to find a place for a base," Eclipse added.

"Seven billion! Eclipse?" Cloud asked. "Can I ask an unfair question? Could you use the Namestone? To make people? Someone made them, if there are six billion extra."

Eclipse stretched, hands clearing silvery falls of hair from rounded ears. "Never tried making people. Never had a reason. It sounds real difficult. Lots harder than paving streets with gold, rebuilding a school in marble, gold roofs and diamond windows. I did that twice! To show myself I could."

"Even a few new people?" he asked.

" 'Hard' is 'complicated', not 'big'. Six billion anything sounds like a chore, if the anythings are all different. But ask yourself! Why did someone want six billion extra people? No matter how they got them. Why?"

"Eclipse? Could you use the Namestone just once? Please? To build us a base? A small base?" Aurora asked. Eclipse's frown and crossed arms terminated her line of thought.

"So we get the money from the medicine smugglers?" Star asked. "Frigid! Something to do!"

'Let's go after that airplane journal, OK? Before they close for the day?" Cloud said. "League cheer!" The four stood and formed a square, hands firmly linked in a quadruple rosette. "Greater Medford!" the four shouted. Eclipse, momentarily ignored, waited patiently, chewing absentmindedly on a strand of hair.

~~~~~

The northern Virginia woods waited for spring. Sunlight dappled the edges of the clearing. The fivesome hid behind bushes, staring at a highway rest stop and untended telephone booth.

"We've got the Journal," Star said. "And their Bell number. We figured out how deposit bells work now. We make sure they're home. You fly. What can go wrong?"

"What if I say the wrong thing?" Comet asked, "So they absolutely positively don't want to talk to us. Then what do I do?"

"Remind them we've got that other journal's Bell number," Cloud answered. "It's like taking a story to Base Ball Nines Daily, and saying if they don't care you'll go to Batsmen. It's foolproof. Even for a girl!" Comet, a firm look to her face, crossed her arms, considering her best retort to Cloud. "I mean, you'll do it, don't worry," Cloud added. "Even a boy could do it." Comet giggled.

"Comet? You take tea with the Wizard of Mars? You argued with the Guardian of the Tunnels? And won? Now you're afraid of a journal annotator?" Star challenged. That argument worked once with Eclipse, hadn't it? It should work on his sister Comet, too. Comet looked away.

"I'll call," Eclipse announced. "They might recognize my voice." She strolled across the clearing, no one protesting, dropped coins into a slot, shook her head at the eerie whine from the earpiece, and pushed oddly-arranged buttons.

"Aerospace Science Weekly," came the distant male voice.

"Editorial Office? I'd like Mr. Parkhurst, please." Eclipse hoped she understood their indicia correctly. Parkhurst appeared to be their expert on ultratech.

"May I ask who's calling, please?" the voice answered politely, "Mr. Parkhurst is very busy today with the Lemuria and Washington stories. I can take a message for him."

"Would you please tell him that Eclipse called? I'm the persona who boarded the Lemuria. Comet and I want to meet him. But if he's busy..."

He interrupted her last sentence. "Please stay on the line. I think he's just stepped out of his meeting. One moment, please." The line went quiet. Eclipse waited patiently.

Another, older, voice joined the conversation. "Hello? Miss Eclipse? I'm Hubert Parkhurst. Aerospace Science would be delighted to meet you and Miss Comet."

Eclipse beamed. "Great! This afternoon? We have a map to your office." She listened to an acknowledgement of place and time. "One little thing? Could you tell your antiaircraft people we're coming? Comet is a bit put off about being fired on." She listened intently. "Not the Shuttle. Washington. A couple days ago. I don't care, but she could get hurt. That's great! See you then."

The foursome joined her by the phone. "No trouble," she announced. "He agreed to everything. Except he was awful fast to say his office building doesn't have antiaircraft guns. Awful awful fast."

Cloud looked thoughtful. "It could be a trap. We'll sit in the woods, half a block away, line of sight on the building, ready to help."

~~~~~

Late in the evening, the same five sat in a clearing near Pickering's lake. The interview with Aerospace Science had been exciting, though Comet had been asked the strangest questions. Parkhurst hadn't batted an eyelash on being offered a trip to the Moon. He even knew a landing site, one that set them near the Landing Module of the Apollo 11. Comet forced herself to stay superficially calm while being told that she was looking at the first manned spaceship to land on another world, and it had been launched a half-century, not thirty-four centuries, ago. Parkhurst took his photographs and let Eclipse take several of him and Comet hovering near the American flag.

Asked about pictures of the new flying objects, he'd promised information and other support. The objects flew to a schedule; they showed up every day, starting over Florida.. He listened to Comet describe medicine smugglers—Comet let him call the smugglers 'narcoterrorists'—and promised to recover from his files a series of interesting maps.

CHAPTER 22 ECLIPSE AND PICKERING

The grandmother clock on the front stairs tolled the hours. One! Two! Three! It was pitch dark. Eclipse, shuddering, forced herself to look over her blankets at the darkened room. All was quiet, even Pickering having drifted to sleep. Nothing moved. Nothing seemed out of place. She gestured with one hand, drawing faint sun-yellow light out of air until hints of color could be seen in drapes and walls and carpet. Nothing was there. Nothing was creeping at her, closer and closer, nothing like the Maze's solid shadows that haunted her dreams until she sprang to terrified awakeness. Nor was she frightened by the voice that was not speaking, so she heard its silences as gaps in her thinking. She knew that lying back in bed would not get her back to sleep, not quickly. She released her light, rolled noiselessly out of bed, and changed from nightgown to her winter-weight garb.

Eclipse tiptoed down the stairs, stepping lightly on the end of each tread. The loudest sound was the rustle of her cape, the soft hiss of fabric against fabric. Teleport? she asked herself. No! She would not become slave to her gifts, unable to act without their support. When she crossed the kitchen, a soft click marked the back door unlocking itself. That had to be Telzey, she thought.

"Thank you, Telzey," she whispered. "No lights, please?" She wasn't sure what the machine understood.

The moon, waxing, was low on the horizon. Her breath made little clouds of smoke. She pulled her cowl over her ears and shrugged her cape's broad folds forward onto her arms. Drawing on her gifts, she had set foot on Triton. Now, gifts grounded to zero, she felt the chill as deeply as the most humble of the ungifted.

She slipped across the lawn, hoping the stillness would reach her quaking heart and quiet the fears that came to her every night. She'd walked the Lesser Maze, come to the tomb of its alien creator, and taken his Namestone. Then she'd climbed a flight of stairs, ascending into the bright sunlight, a smile of joyous triumph on her face, the Namestone's song alive to her heart. At night, what came to her was not triumph but terror. When it wasn't the Maze, she dreamed of the League of Nations, the Manjukuoan Ever-Victorious Army, loneliness....She took a deep breath and exhaled slowly, watching the condensation swirl away into the moonlight. Her feet brought her to the lake.

The winter sky was brilliantly clear, stars thick as the blooms of a blanket flower drowning out the skeletons of constellations. There was absolutely no breeze: The waters of Pickering's tarn were still as black glass, a mirror in which the brighter stars were frosty white blurs. She had learned the constellations from her mother. Now she remembered the warmth of her mother standing behind her, one hand on her shoulder while the other traced figures across the sky, Pegasus and Unicorn and elusive Merlin. That was a past gone forever. She stuffed her hands into her cape's inner pockets, staring hard at the water, using the flickers of the stars to trace an unseen ripple's progress across the lake. Reason said that she trusted her mother's inexplicable decision to send her alone into the world. Her heart still ached.

Sand grated softly underfoot. The stars were majestic in their watchful solitude. She took one step after the next, letting the night's beauty relax her. Finally she paused, arms across chest. She had walked far enough for one night, been outside long enough that she was downright cold. Now she could retrace her path to her bed, drawing on gifts but once: The swiftest flicker of screens wove around her feet to deposit beach sand outside the porch.

Her return to Pickering's home brought one surprise after another. The garden was faintly illuminated, a trail of pin lights marking the path around Pickering's maze. Other lights shone in the breakfast room. The kitchen door was slightly ajar. She stepped inside and hung her cape in the vestibule.

Pickering sat at his breakfast room table. A dish of cookies and a steaming carafe waited on the sideboard. "I thought you might like some herbal tea," he explained. "Nothing to keep you awake. Or do your gifts keep you warm?"

"I've taken pictures on Titan, ankle-deep in liquid methane, and not been chilled." Her defensiveness faded. "No. I'm only warm if I use them. Elsewise I get as cold as anyone else. I was trying to get away from my gifts, not be their slave."

Pickering poured her a mug of tea and set it in front of her. His hand brushed her cheek. "Would your pride be offended if I gave you a blanket? This was a raw night for a walk, even if you leave no footprints on my vestibule tile."

"Screens," she explained. "I pushed the sand off my feet before I came inside." Pickering held the blanket, gently folding it above her. She stiffened. "I'm not used to people doing things for me. Not kind things. Not any more." She looked determinedly into the mug, briefly hiding her face. "I suppose you wouldn't know about that."

"There is no difficulty," a sympathetic Pickering answered. "None at all." Encountering no resistance, he finally draped her shoulders in the soft fabric.

Eclipse found herself at the verge of tears, sharp and hot as blood from a slashed artery, not knowing why. She clutched for her pants pocket, snatched out her handkerchief, and tried to pretend to blow her nose, almost masking her crying. In a minute it was over. "Sorry," she apologized. "I shouldn't drop my past on you."

"Eclipse, I know very little about your world. Let alone you. I hear bits of a story from different people with different prejudices, so it is non-trivial to winnow truth from error. But you've been a charming house guest. And cleaned up after two almost-teen-age boys, no one saying a word about it. So why should you be surprised at minor kindnesses in return?" He nudged her upwards, swaddled her stomach and thighs in the blanket, and pushed her gently back into the chair.

"Thank you." She had to force the acknowledgement past clenched lips. "Are you asking my version of what I did?"

"Only so much as you may wish to tell," he answered. He slipped around the table to sit facing her.

Now Eclipse was deeply homesick, wishing that she were in her home, guesting Pickering in her own kitchen. She managed to speak. "You heard about the Namestone. It could make imagination into reality, bring heaven to earth. It could actually change things into each other. I could've used it to pave streets with gold and make deserts into gardens. That's telekinesis. I did. A bit. Namestone could make criminals into honest men, bring people peace and contentment, now until the end of time. That's telepathy and mindlock. Mayhaps don't mention mindlock, OK?" Eclipse cautioned.

"Everyone knew what this Namestone promised? Thousands died trying to reach it?" Pickering inserted, giving her a chance to drink her tea. "It was hidden in a maze. A maze you solved. Having gained the Namestone, you kept it, to others' dismay."

"Close enough. Some parts of the Maze you could solve by being smart. Some places I used brute force. It allowed that. Sort of. You could be somewhat smart and somewhat tough, instead of all smart. You couldn't be all tough. I think. I think someone who was smart enough could have solved it by being very clever. The Great Maze is like that; you only solve it by being clever, but it only gives you things for yourself. I'm not that bright; a bunch of places in the Maze I solved by getting violent," she explained.

"One of our leading lights once asserted 'violence is the last refuge of the incompetent'. To this, his critics added 'the competent having resorted to violence at previous instants, whilst hope yet remained of its successful application'," Pickering said.

"I earned the Namestone," Eclipse said, pausing to sip more tea. "I almost died, but I got it. I had to. If I hadn't, The League of Nations would have had it. It was a mind control projector. They'd have used it to cram their idea of a utopia down everyone's throats. So I took it, and everyone knew I had it. The League of Nations Peace Executive had a big meeting. They wanted me to give them the Namestone. I'd told them *sub rosa* why not, but their computers proved I was wrong. Morally wrong. That's what they said," she explained.

"I told them they couldn't have their toy," she continued. "I told them to make their own utopia. By doing honest work with their own hands. That didn't go over well. The League went through the ceiling. They invented a new crime for me, even though every country voting for the crime, every single one, had a law in their constitution saying you can't make something a crime after you did it. The only big country voting no was Austria-Hungary. OK, America boycotted the meeting. The Satsuma Daimyo abstained. Foreigners had pestered Emperor Otto about human freedoms, when he had trouble with his parliament. He got his talk-backs. He told the Prussian and Aztecan and Manjukuoan Ambassadors that Austria-Hungary was a civilized country, and no civilized country ever makes an ex post facto law. He quoted their own Constitutions at them."

"Manjukuo put a hundred tons of gold on my head." Eclipse rolled her eyes. "France offered a lifetime loan of the Mona Lisa. Almost every country in the world put all their best computers and High Programmers and personae into finding me. They haven't. Yet. At the time we left, they were having a civil war about who should run the League. There were also a bunch of national wars. America was invaded by the Aztecans."

"I think," Pickering responded, "that what you did is less important than why. You're how old? And you risked your life. Why?"

"Twelve. By a bit. Namestone was my birthday present to myself, a couple months late. Why?" she asked. "The Namestone. What it does is horrible. With the Grand Master—the ruler of Tibet—using it, everyone would have turned into machines. No hate. No fear. No anger, no passion. If you didn't like what was happening, you'd be unhappy. The Namestone stops unhappiness. By changing you until you're happy, if that's easier than changing what you're unhappy about. I kept that from happening." Her last sentence held a stubborn pride for her deed.

"I understand," Pickering said. "I'm more surprised that your friends don't agree. Are you people accustomed to obeying higher authorities without question?"

"I think our people trust governments more than yours do." Eclipse shrugged. "And you (forgive me, Telzey, nothing personal) you don't trust computers the way we did. The League's computers proved the

Namestone was morally perfect. That settled everything."

"I see," a bemused Pickering mumbled. The notion that her governments trusted moral decisions to digital computation was seriously alarming, or would have been, if their governments had ever existed. There was only one immediate solution: he helped himself to another sugar snap. "I want to know why you did it. Not why it had to be done, but why you—twelve years, somewhat more than five feet, not more than a hundred pounds, felt you personally had to challenge this Maze deathtrap. No one told you to, did they? So, why you?"

"Why me? I told you, didn't I? I said why Namestone was wicked." She wrinkled her brows. "Or did I? Oh, you mean, why me, not Comet or Krystal North or the Screaming Skull?" She waited for Pickering's acknowledgement of her words. "I keep wanting to say 'of course I did'. But 'of course' is real rude. It's what you say to little children. It's not I think you're a small child. But usually it's children who ask very hard questions, questions you answer by of coursing them."

"Why you went. We're talking about something ingrained, aren't we? Something so obvious that you never doubt it?" Pickering asked.

"Let me explain? I have gifts. Flight. Mentalics. I had a choice. I could sit back, let the League grab the Namestone, and watch them turn the world into Hell. I could grab the Namestone myself, because I could see clear and honest what would happen if I didn't. If I let them grab it, knowing what would happen, I'd be guilty of wrecking the world."

"There is a distinction, presently, between sins of commission and sins of omission," Pickering remarked. "Between evils you actively perform, and evils you fail to prevent. The former are said by some to be more serious." He reached for another sugar snap.

"But I have gifts!" she said. "I don't have to spend my time looking for trouble. But lots of gifted people do, which is why the American Republic had fewer murders last year than your Washington had last winter. What if I saw someone about to murder you, and didn't stop him? Wasn't it just like I murdered you myself? Sitting and watching is doing something. If I don't act, knowing you're about to be murdered, I did something that meant you got murdered. Not using my gifts, when I have gifts and know they matter, that's as bad as doing the wicked things myself. Or worse. I know what's right and what's wrong. Your murderer mayhaps didn't."

Pickering reached for another cookie. "I think I understand your point of view. Local children would say, they saw where you were coming from. You have gifts. You saw this horror swift approaching. A horror you could prevent. Perhaps even a horror most other people could not have prevented, you being, ummh, stronger? more gifted? smarter? than others?" Her cheeks, rosy from recovering warmth, reddened further. "So you stepped into the breach, put your own life at risk, because you could. Whether you absolutely had to or not: you could, so you did, automatically. Because you do what's right. You didn't ask if someone else would do it. That didn't matter. And you expect everyone to act the same way."

"Got it! I saw what I had to do. I did it." Her smile was suddenly luminous. "I think others would have done it. If they saw why. Mayhaps if someone else started first, I'd've waited. Of course, if I met someone else doing the Maze for the same reason, we'd've helped each other."

"You'd've felt guilty? If you didn't, I mean?" he asked.

"Guilty? Ashamed?" She took a lemon butter cookie. "You know, I found guilt, when I looked for personae here. I looked for why people did good things. I thought I'd find memories, inspirations from seeing personae do the right thing, how great it feels to do what's right. That would've let me find your personae—hey, it sounded clever at the time. After all, that's why history is all about deeds of heroes and heroines. So people remember it feels good to do right." She let Pickering think about her words. "I found people who felt guilty. I found people who were afraid. People who thought that doing wrong felt unbathed. I found people who'd do something wrong if they thought they could get away with it." A quarter cup of honey-lemon tea disappeared in one swallow. "I found people who thought like Lemurians, only caring about themselves, only real toned down, not black and white like a Lemurian but gray-shaded. I found people who thought they'd always get away with everything. But not often did I find someone who did right because she enjoyed doing it."

"You do things because they make you feel good? Not because you feel bad if you don't?" Pickering probed.

"Well, mostly." Eclipse shrugged. "Holding the Namestone, knowing I'd done it, saved the world from itself? That was great. Absolutely incredible! Like nothing else you can imagine. You're half-right, though. I wouldn't want someone asking me why I didn't use my gifts, when I could have."

"You aren't bothered that people say you're wrong?" Pickering asked.

"Why? Of course not! Not at all. I use my gifts. As deep as I can call them," she answered happily. "In the Maze, that was: Use no gifts at all. What I did with the Namestone, that was right and wrong. I say right. They say wrong. There are more of them than me. That doesn't prove anything. Right isn't counting. Everyone knows that. Well, everyone used to know that."

"I think you're correct," Pickering answered happily. "Some might demur. America, my America, tends to browbeat its girls until they're no longer brave or clear-sightedly honest or firmly moral, until they're women who prefer consensus to justice. Most Americans would ask what your parents thought of all this."

She wilted into herself, the blanket's warmth and late night exhaustion finally taking their toll. Her answer came as a choked whisper. "Please don't tell anyone. Except Comet knows. Six months ago, my mom threw me out of the house. Rather, she packed my stuff into storage, made the house disappear as if it had never been, disappeared, and told me not to try finding her. I didn't."

"Oh, dear," a staggered Pickering managed. "The authorities didn't help you..."

"If I asked for help, they would have wanted to know who my mother is," she answered. "If I told them, they would have tried to kill me. Note I said 'tried'. Then I'd've had a way more difficult time fading into the woodwork." She yawned, very deeply. "I'm sorry, but this is too far past my bed time."

"In that case, go back to sleep," he said, standing as he did. Her sleep, once she was back in her nightgown and buried deep under the bed quilt, was dotted with gentle dreams of rolling fields, hollyhocks and daisies waving slowly in the breeze.

CHAPTER 23 COMET AND MISSILE PHOTOS

The Florida sky was the palest of roses. The rising sun limned a point of horizon with incandescent ruby fire. Comet and Aurora perched on a split-rail fence, listening to the calls of morning birds and roll of the surf breaking against the Florida Keys. Aurora monitored interceptor aircraft communicating with ground control. A half-dozen fighter planes covered a line east and west from their location. Very soon, the interesting target was expected on tesdri. Aurora reminded herself: 'radar', not 'tesdri'.

She suppressed an occasional yawn. 6AM here had been 3AM at Pickering's home. When this was finished, she was very definitely going back to bed. The people at Aerospace Science Weekly had been oddly indirect about helping Comet take photographs. They'd been happy to supply flight times and flight paths of the unknown aircraft. They described how the Air Force ran missions. They had been somewhat reticent in their description of Air Force hypervelocity weapons, which they expected would finally be tried against the intruders. They had pointedly not been willing to supply Comet with a contract. That, decided Aurora, was related to Pickering's ideas on lifeboats. They'd buy a photograph, but didn't dare ask thirteen-year-old Comet to take it. Pickering had lent Comet his old camera and a good pair of lenses.

"Comet?" Aurora said. "They've found it. That way." She pointed to the southwest.

"Wish me luck," Comet answered. Aurora gave her the thumb's-up gesture. Comet's flight field flickered to invisibility as she began a leisurely climb. There was all the time in the world, and no sense in revealing where Aurora waited.

'Baker seven two, come to zero one zero.' Aurora began echoing messages from the fighter planes to Comet. *'Contingency Alpha. Execute. Execute.'* Aurora's clairvoyance revealed a turning aircraft, its pilot bringing its engines to full throttle and firing up the afterburners. Where was the target, wondered Aurora? The aircraft, supersonic, brought its nose up in a thirty-five degree climb. Aurora flashed the location to Comet, now level with the fighter aircraft.

'Baker seven two at angel six five thousand, az zero one zero, mach one point five.' 'Copy baker seven two. Target overtaking you at angel one five five kay, your az one seven five, mach seven point four.' 'Baker seven two: detectors scanning.'

Comet had been even with the interceptor, looking for a target in front of them. Nothing was there. But if it were overtaking.... She looked over her shoulder. There it was, thought Comet! A great hulking flat-black torpedo, easily seen by its infrared glow and the heated contrail behind it. Her flight field turned its natural chalk orange as she rolled up and away from the fighter.

'Baker seven two, autofire handshake is green. Fire in ten. Mark. Nine. Eight.' 'Baker seven two! That's a premature fire! Premature!' 'No fire! No fire! I say again, I did not fire! Awaiting autofire.' 'Baker seven two. Fire in two. One. Fire.' An air-to-air missile, a modified satellite killer recently wheeled out of mothballs, dropped from the fighter's wing. Its rocket engine ignited.

Far above, Comet closed on the mystery aircraft. She told herself she had tens of seconds to take her pictures before the antiaircraft missile was close. Well before then, she'd be on her way to safety.

Aurora continued to pass messages to Comet. *'Baker seven two, this is Homestead GCI. Do you see another aircraft? Over.' 'That's negative, negative. Where?' 'Baker seven two, we showed another missile, almost on top of you a few seconds before you fired. We did not acquire a launch aircraft. Over.' 'Ground, this is baker seven two. There's no one else here.'*

Far above, Comet closed on the unknown. Matching speed and altitude had not been difficult; her target lumbered along with constant speed and direction. She forced her flight field toward invisibility. No one had said anything about the target being armed, but there was no sense in taking unnecessary chances. A look downward revealed the intercepting missile, still remote, now moving considerably more rapidly than she was. She accelerated and closed on her target.

A hundred yards from the target, she began taking pictures. A wide barrel roll took her around the missile, giving good profile shots from all sides, nose, and tail. She hoped they'd come out properly. She dropped back, staying to one side as the missile closed. Her camera clicked as fast as she could trigger it. Half automatically, she cycled through a series of shutter speeds. She reminded herself that the makers of her new camera might be very clever people, for all that they lived in a country that didn't even exist until history was scrambled, but surely they had not designed her camera for the photography of flat black objects against the black of space.

A fraction of a second before impact the intercepting missile exploded, a series of spines expanding umbrella-like from its nose. Pieces of metal slashed into the hull of the torpedo, some recoiling from armor plate while others penetrated deeply into its avionics. The unknown rolled clumsily, lost control of attitude, and plummeted for the ground, its engine still at full power. Comet pulled hastily away as the unknown blew apart.

CHAPTER 24 STAR AT THE HARPSICHORD

Strands of Bach's Goldberg Variations echoed across the living room, soaring from corner to corner of the great spiral stairs until they reached Pickering's ears. Who was playing, he wondered? A fair hand: Clearly a student's, if a far better hand than his own. He descended from the master suite to find Star dutifully practicing the harpsichord.

The boy glanced over his shoulder and froze in surprise. "Hello," he finally managed. "I thought you went to town for the morning."

"Went and returned," the older man answered. "I go very early. I don't mind your practice; I said you could, and you're better than I."

"It was something to do. Mom insisted I learn to play, to accompany Comet's singing. Please do not ask her about singing. It's one of the reasons she divorced Mom and Dad. I'm not real good at playing. Else it's real boring. Here is boring, not the music. Eclipse keeps reading, says she's working hard. I can't tell. Cloud is supposed to take me up north when he gets up. He was awake real late."

"I'm surprised you study the harpsichord rather than the piano," Pickering said.

"Piano?" He hesitated quizzically. "Piano? Do you mean pianoforte? Oh, wow! You know someone who owns one? I actually saw one being played once." Star pivoted gracefully on the harpsichord bench, turning to face Pickering. "Are they common now? They used to be rare, rarer than panharmonicons. Don't tell my sisters? I don't know what to do."

The sound of footsteps cut off the conversation. The rest of the children poured into the room and clustered themselves around the harpsichord, waiting for Star to finish whatever he had been saying. Star pointedly said nothing.

Breakfast dishes were done. It was time for action, starting with politeness to their host. He said he'd had questions for them. Pickering urged them to a long couch. A swirl of motion left Comet against one arm-rest, Aurora leaning into her sister's shoulder, Star and Cloud sitting a foot apart, and Eclipse seated stiffly at the far end.

"If it's fair to ask, your parents aren't personae, are they?" Pickering asked.

"No," Star answered. "Why'd you wonder that?"

"Why?" Pickering asked. "I thought the alterations—whatever they are—the differences that make you a persona might be hereditary in nature. That is, even as parents with dark, curly hair tend to have children whose hair is dark and curly, so also one might expect parents who fly to have children who fly."

241

"Mom and Dad aren't personas," Aurora answered.

"Mine aren't either," Cloud added. He suddenly paused and looked thoughtful. "I think they aren't. They know I'm a persona. Mayhaps they're putting off telling me."

"You mean, mayhaps Dad and Mom are personas," Comet interjected, "so just like we didn't tell them right off, they didn't tell us, so we're all doing public personas? They know about us, but we might not know about them."

"Right," Cloud added. "We don't know means we don't know."

"It's uncommon," said Eclipse. "Lots of people say they descend from Prince Mong-Ku. Almost none are personae, that I've heard. And open personae," she caught Pickering's upraised eyelid, "people who don't have their private and public personae separated, so you know they're gifted when you meet them in the ultramarket,are common in Manjukuo and Mongolia and Tibet. But people looked at gene sequences. They couldn't find any genes for flying."

"Where do gifts come from?" Pickering asked. "If you're not born with them, do they simply appear when you get older?"

"It depends," Cloud said. "Some people just have gifts turn on. Other people have gifts given to them."

"Given?" Pickering questioned.

"Given. By someone like Solara or Plasmatrix-the-Desolation. It's not real common," Cloud explained. "One of the great personas appears and gives you a whole slew of gifts all at once. That's why they're called gifts. Someone gave them to you. Of course, you have to learn how to use them." Cloud focused on Pickering. "That's how gifting's done. You're asleep. You dream. Aurora? It'd be easier if he saw my story."

The girl's powers brought minds together, so all experienced Cloud's memories. *[It was deepest night. Cloud lay in bed, looking over the covers, unable to move. There, right at the foot of his bed, stood someone Cloud didn't know. The stranger was dressed in flat black—black pants, black tunic and vest, black mask and wide-brimmed floppy black hat. He leaned on an ebon walking stick. Cloud tried to call out and found that he was paralyzed.*

Ahh, came the figure's voice. *Th* A burst of static, Aurora hiding from Pickering's hearing the name of Cloud's private persona. *This is your time. From all whom I might choose, I have chosen you. The powers of the air are yours. No matter where you stand, [In the dream, Cloud found them floating in outer space, then deep under the ocean.] the breath of life is yours. You may call the powers of nimbus, so your foes are cloaked in obscurity. [They stood on a playground. A gesture of one hand brought the thickest fog, fog that blinded all around them, cloud* *through which Cloud could clearly see.] Yours are the roar of the winds, the Hammer of the Thunderer, [The dream brought blasts of air, pinning the playground's occupants in place, followed by a flash of light and crashing roar as a lightning bolt toppled an oak tree.] You may ride among the clouds, carrying what you wish. [Cloud, stranger, and bed floated effortlessly over the ocean, glorious puffs of cumulus floating around them like a second sea.] You may take such additional powers as you find within you, for that is the gift of all gifts, the realization of the self.* *

They were back in Cloud's bedroom. Cloud managed a whisper. "You trust me? With that?" The stranger inclined his brow to Cloud. *I err, once and again. I do not believe I err now.* * The stranger faded into the room's darkness, leaving Cloud staring at the doorway, through which the night light could again be seen.

"That's it," Cloud concluded. "This fellow showed up, and I was a persona, all at once."

"That was frigid," Star said. "No matter how often you tell it."

"Who was the giver?" Pickering asked.

"The walking stick?" Eclipse answered. "That was the Screaming Skull himself, gifts masked. He does not engift people, not hardly ever." Cloud stared at her. "You must've done something really gifttrue before he'd notice you. Before he engifted you."

"I don't have a fancy story," Comet said. "We were in the country, and I climbed this very old apple tree, and went out too far on a limb, and the branch snapped. I remember thinking it was twenty feet to fall, so I lunged for another branch, knowing it was too far, and felt my flight field cut in—for the first time, all at once, it was wonderful, getting a gift is the most wonderful feeling that there can ever be for anyone—and it carried me skyward, so I missed the branch, missed the tree, and was two trees over before I landed. I knew what it meant. I didn't become a public persona until Star and Aurora found their gifts."

"I almost burned down the Summer cabin," said Star. "I was supposed to start the fire for a cookout. I had the papers set up, and the charcoal on top, and the lighter fluid applied. I kept snapping matches in two, so they wouldn't light. I ran out of matches. I was so mad. Suddenly the fire came! The paper was on fire. The charcoal was on fire. The grill got real hot, glowed, burned all the gunk off. The lighter fluid bottle exploded. It was on fire all around me. Then I knew. Lucky I was out on the concrete pad, so I just scorched some grass. I hid what I'd done. Dad was real surprised, when he came back, that I'd edged the patio, tossed the edgings away, and cleaned the grill.."

Aurora shrugged shyly. "You guys all had something very frigid happen. Nothing frigid for me. I just found my first gift. I was up very late, when I shouldn't have been. Up in the side attic looking out the window. For an aurora. You almost never see them where we live, but the swift video news promised one. Then I saw one, very bright. It was all around me. I could see the attic, dim and dusty. I could see aurora, all around me. I was seeing from up in the middle of the sky, someplace where the ground's covered with snow and there's no city lights. *[A flash image, a place of stars and darkness filled with ethereal fire that rustled like stiff silk, ground many miles below glinting from auroral flame.]* It was so beautiful. Mindreading people and computers came later."

"What about you, Eclipse?" asked Aurora. "If you don't mind telling."

"My story's a bit different. And I don't remember it. Not as well as you guys do," Eclipse apologized. "It was a long time ago." Seeing her apologies accepted, Eclipse locked minds with Aurora.

[Eclipse, as a small child, sitting in her mother's lap, being held while her mother read to her. On her lap reposed a well-remembered book with large print, and sketches of a boy and girl riding ponies east day after day toward the rising sun.] *Sorry it's blurry,* Eclipse explained. *I was barely four.* Eclipse let her memories unfold. *[A growing feeling of impatience. She'd heard the story many times before. Where were the words hiding? Why couldn't she see them? Mother did. 'Mommy, I want to learn to read.' 'You will, dear, you will.' 'I want to know now! Not someday. Please? Please, mommy?' 'You want to start today, dear?' 'Yes, please?'] [Feelings. Eclipse's mother, reaching ever so gently into her daughter's mind to supply the first bit of the answer.]*

These are the letters, dear. Thorn, like a toy top...

In Eclipse, a rising hunger to know, a reaching out, a ravening demand for information. A burst of confusion, so she was sitting in her mother's lap, and at the same time she was her mother, holding her beloved daughter. Letters transformed from mysterious blotches to the alphabet to letters and syllables and words and sentences. A flash of concern, mother recognizing that the flow of learning was not under maternal control. An all-consuming reach for knowing, Eclipse memories and Mother memories interlacing until neither could tell which memory was whose.

*[**Mommy? Mommy! What is it?**]*

[Mother's reaction: surprise, and the calm certain knowledge of what each should do to unweave their thoughts, washed with deep love and pride for daughter's precocious deed.]

The listeners realized that Eclipse remembered her manifestation solely as a minute of fear, fear that her mind was being buried in strange concepts. Her mother's reactions remained in Eclipse's memories, embedded like a magnificent flying insect trapped in an ancient amber bead, but Eclipse herself recalled the panic, not her mother's reaction. *[Panic fading, the world returning to normal, memories safely separated. But when Eclipse finally dared to look at her book again, the words were all there as words, mysterious squiggles having been replaced with a comprehension of printed words as readable entities.]*

"That's it," Eclipse said. "I didn't do anything. No falling out of a tree, no standing in a sea of fire—that was frigid, Star—no one visiting my dreams, certainly no vision of the heart of the aurora. Just—I learned how to read. All at once. I must have scared my mom half to death, even allowing mom is seriously real hard to frighten."

"Thank you," Pickering said, "Thank you all for trusting me with your pasts."

"I've got to go inside," Aurora mumbled. "It's cold here." She rose to leave.

"Be chill, Aurora. Stay!" Cloud ordered. "We're not done talking yet. We're still working on time pirates."

"Cloud, I want to be by myself. You have a problem with that?" A flicker of amber was the first trace of her wall.

"Oh, come on," Cloud grumbled. "Don't be a quitter all the time. We need to solve this, and you have to help me!"

"Cloud? You just leave her alone!" Comet was on her feet shouting at him.

"Oh, big sister's playing mommy!" Star teased. "Little sister can't even hear happy happy stories without getting frightened." Comet fumed. Aurora ran from the porch.

"Little girls!" Cloud smirked. He made to follow Aurora. Eclipse blocked his path.

"Let her alone?" she asked calmly. He took a step forward. She moved not at all, her voice staying completely calm. "This is hard for her. She's away from home. She's never done it before."

"She has to stop being a little girl all the time," the older boy snapped. "I need to tell her that. Right now!"

"It's his job," Star answered. "He's our League's leader. He gets to tell her things like that, because he's supposed to."

"Yes, Cloud. She'll stop. But you're thirteen. She's barely twelve. Right? Give her a chance?" Eclipse asked. Besides, Eclipse noted to herself, *unlike Cloud, Aurora has the brains to realize we should all be terrified.*

"Yeah. You're right. I guess. But she's just so, so little-girlish," he said. Eclipse struggled to keep a straight face as she nodded agreement, then turned her head, enough so only Comet saw her wink.

Pickering looked in dismay at the group. "Might I ask," he intoned, "that before you have an all-out brawl, gifts and thrown lightning bolts and what-not, you move someplace where you will not damage the surrounding terrain? Say, the Nevada atomic testing range?"

The four remaining children stared at Pickering, appalled looks crossing all four faces. "Oh, no." "We'd never do that." "No, never!" they said.

"Guys?" Comet asked. "Mayhaps we pack and go? If he doesn't trust us. I mean, he's ungifted and we aren't allowed to upset him by arguing, so if we upset him with our gifts it's his house and we've got to go, so shall we pack and clean up the mess we made?"

"My sense of humor is perhaps slightly dry, but you need not decamp," Pickering stressed.

Star had a flash of insight. "Wait. They don't have personas now. So they don't know gifttrue. Right?"

"Oh! Right!" Cloud said. "Of course. I'm so dumb. Apologies, Alex."

"So they—Alex, I mean—doesn't know how terrible it would be," Star said, "if we really used our gifts to hurt each other, us all being one League. We aren't a bunch of Lemurian Racemasters, off to plunder and fight each other when we feel like it."

"Were my words that harsh?" Pickering asked. The children nodded.

"Alex," Comet said, "You wouldn't know. Being irresponsible with your gifts is worse than anything. We'd never ever do that. Never ever. The Supreme Illusionist and Emperor Roxbury used their gifts to change things or kill people, but they did it on purpose for a lifetrue reason. The Master of Airships would have killed almost everyone in the world, but it was for a good reason. Well, he thought it was for a good reason. Those villains, they didn't break things because they happened to get mad."

"May I apologize?" Pickering said.

"Why?" Star asked. "The world changed. You don't remember what was before we took our trip. You didn't know. It's different now. We'd never hurt you. It's your house. We're supposed to protect it. And we all promise not to shout at each other again. If you're around to hear us, I mean." The others nodded assent.

"Apology happily accepted," Cloud said.

Pickering noticed that Comet held a shadowy piece of gold in her hand. The object swirled in the light, wiggling like a living thing. She saw his upraised eyebrows.

"The StarCompass," she announced, as though the name explained everything. "It was supposed to bring us to the hints the Wizard of Mars promised. Then it was supposed to take us home again, but it brought us home with no hint and no home either; every so often it gets all agitated, like it was changing its mind which way to point, but all it ever does is point around town jumping back and forth and then back here, so we're home except home is missing, except once instead of pointing half the time at town and half the time here, it started half the time pointing here and half the time spinning in circles like it was lost, and then it stopped pointing at the town very much."

"Agitated?" Star asked.

"It starts wiggling in my pocket, and I take it out because it tickles," Comet explained.

"That peculiar object of indefinite shape is a star compass?" Pickering remained confused.

"Right, that's the StarCompass," she answered. "It brought us to the Tunnels and back; and it's only got one shape, but it's not three-dimensional, so it look like it changes shape when it spins."

"Comet," Pickering asked. "This star compass. It's not three-dimensional?"

"Well, no," Comet answered. "It's, ummh, quadrudimensional."

"Is it safe to see?" Pickering asked. "For someone who's not a persona or elsewise accustomed to the sight of the fabulous?"

"Oh, sure," Comet answered. She passed Pickering a tangle of golden plates. "This is it."

Pickering fingered it gently, deducing in a few moments its true shape from the three-dimensional cross-sections.

"You have all these wonderful gifts," Pickering persisted, "yet you need a compass?"

"StarCompass," Comet continued . "We went all the way across the universe, billions of lightyears. Finding our way home again, finding the right galaxy, finding the sun after we found the right galaxy, I could never ever possibly think of doing that, even with my vision. There are just billions of galaxies, and trillions of stars, so I had to have the StarCompass. Without it, I'd've found the Tunnels, but I'd've been lost and never found our way home, not before the end of time. Without it, we've had to stay on Earth, our Earth; we've been there when the world got changed. So I keep looking at it, hoping it takes us someplace else, even though I know this has to be Earth, except someone wrecked up history, so I know it'll never point anyplace else."

It has to change, Comet prayed silently, it has to tell me where to go. I'm the fastest persona there is. I can go any place in the universe, any place at all, in lickety-split. But I don't know my destination, so all I can do is stand here. Lost in her mournful thoughts, she looked blankly into the distance, waiting for her friends to finish what they were saying so she could leave.

~~~~~

Aurora sat on the long couch of the solarium, a blanket pulled over her legs. Her stare took her out across Pickering's garden. The first crocuses were in flower. She was scarcely aware of the splashes of green and violet, deep purple and white. Certainly this wasn't the first time she'd read a friend's mind, the friend having asked her, and learned something unpleasant. There were only a few ways to explain what she had seen. She didn't want to face any of them.

The sun made its way down to the western ocean, the house's shadows being thrown longer and longer, first over the garden, and then, the garden being swallowed in gloom, into the glade beyond. The palest of glimmers, falling from Aurora in all directions, marked her call upon her gifts. Aurora's inner eye reached across the Pacific Northwest, searching desperately, one hilltop after the next, hoping beyond hope that she would find ruins left from ancient Atlanticea or glorious Marik, or the eldritch towers of Goetica Antiqua. She found natural uncut stone, deep-green firs, the soughing of wind as it whispered through the branches and needles of Douglas pines.

"Aurora?" Her sister's voice called her back to here and now. She shuddered to awareness, finding she had lain so long in one position that she was cold and stiff.

"Comet?" Aurora answered. Comet pulled a blanket over her sister's shoulders, covering her from neck to toe.

"You were gone a very long time. Is everything OK?" Comet tried to hide her concern.

"I was looking." Aurora stared out the window, afraid even to look at her beloved sister. "Looking for Atlanticea. Looking for anything except America. It isn't there. I even looked at Crater Lake. Wizard Island was empty, no buildings, no glass towers, no hidden tunnels, nothing. Lost Ship Rock was a rock. It must've been like that before Marik carved it into a real ship."

"I know, Aurora," Comet answered. She slipped under the blanket, hoping Aurora would take some comfort from her presence.

"I couldn't sit. Sit and wait and do nothing. I want to go home! I, that must seem awful mean to Alex, who's been such a wonderful guy, but this is all too strange. I want..." Aurora pulled herself together.

"You did a great job, showing Alex how we got our gifts," Comet said, "that was very well done; Alex hasn't ever met a telepath before and doesn't realize just how incredibly good you are, linking all of us at once and showing pictures."

"I try," Aurora answered. "Sometimes I do better than some other times."

"Aurora," Comet said, moving even closer to her sister, "I was there in your projection, and I don't know what you thought you did, but I didn't see a mistake at all, and even Eclipse didn't see it, and she always sees my mistakes even if she never gets mad at me when I make them. I think. Well, she never says she's mad, and she never acts like she's mad, except sometimes she gets terrible disappointed at her own tiny mistakes, and after you left she only said nice things about how well you projected memories."

"Huh?" Aurora forced herself to think, freeing herself from the web of her emotions. "What I did wrong? What do you mean?"

"I mean, you were very polite, but you left as fast as you could, and of course Star and Cloud were mean because they're only boys, and Eclipse said she didn't know what was wrong with you and thought mayhaps you wanted to be left alone because you were unhappy about what happened to the world, but I could tell it wasn't just that, that you did something during the projection and it wasn't right, except I couldn't tell what you thought you'd done wrong." Comet told herself it couldn't be anything important. Her sister was very good at mentalics. She simply judged herself too harshly, even harsher than she was judged by the people she gamed against.

"Oh," Aurora responded. "Oh. It wasn't: I did something wrong. It was: I saw something scary. Something I wish I hadn't seen. I knew what it was. I got frightened. Then I did want to go home. I wanted to find something from the past. Anything to show there was a past, AutumnLost or any place. I couldn't find it. No matter how hard I looked."

"Aurora? What frightened you? We're all here! We'll protect you," Comet reminded. "It was while you were telling Eclipse's story, and I know that four years old is awfully incredibly young to manifest your first gift, especially something complicated like telepathy, but it happens. I guess. Besides, Eclipse is interesting because she's so different and so nice to people, and she really is nice to everyone, even Star when no girl in the whole world in her right mind would be nice to him."

"Well," Aurora answered. "First, her gift wasn't telepathy. That rush? The ideas? Her mom's mind? Eclipse learned how to read in an instant. That was mind merge. That takes incredible depth on your gifts. Most FedCorps mentalists can't do it. Eclipse's mom had screens—good ones, too—mayhaps better than Eclipse's. Even if they were mostly not summoned when Eclipse manifested."

"Eclipse being that strong? Was it that frightening? I mean, she did take the Maze," Comet reminded. "What was so frightening, sister?"

"Numbers," Aurora said. "During the mindmerge, when Eclipse's mind and her mom's were all mixed together. I saw their minds. There were lots of numbers."

"Numbers? Bell numbers? Bank accounts?" Comet asked.

"Number numbers," Aurora answered. "It's, I can't show it even if I do mentalics. It's like someone blind. They don't see colors the same way a sighted person does. Not even when they look through someone else's eyes. Or it's like the stupid things grownups do by themselves that don't make sense. But there was an avalanche of numbers, like snowflakes in a blizzard. There were numbers like the mind of a big computer. There were so many numbers I saw the avalanche, not any particular number."

"Numbers? Inside someone's mind?" Comet remained puzzled.

"Numbers," Aurora answered. "Part of a mind. Eclipse's or her mom's. It was numerical. Made of numbers, not likes and wants like a human mind. There was a computer in her mind. It was a cyborg mind. It had to be."

"Oh, Aurora! There's no such thing as..." Comet leaned back into the couch. How could she doubt her own sister? "...you saw the numbers, right there? I believe you. Even though there's only one cyborg, and she's the worst villain there is?"

"Right. Except it's Eclipse who's the worst villain of all time, not the Silver General, if you listen to those twits at the League of Nations. Boys! Every one of them! Brains like boys!" Aurora grimaced in disgust at what the League had said about her dear friend. "I asked how could it be true? How could Eclipse or her mom have a cyborg mind? Unless Eclipse lied about how she manifested. And she's not good at reading machine minds, not like me. She couldn't fake a machine mind. Besides, I was so deep inside her mind I could hear her crying—deep inside, where she refuses to listen to herself—when she remembered her Mom. That's why she's always so sad. She's always crying, all the way inside. She won't admit it to anyone, even herself. She didn't fake the numbers."

Aurora waited for Comet's agreement. "But numbers. Eclipse or her Mom has to be a cyborg. How? One of them has to be the Silver General."

"Eclipse's mom is the Silver General?" Comet wondered. "The Silver General is completely crazy and kills people because she enjoys it. How could she be a mother?"

"No way," Aurora answered. "Could Eclipse be the cyborg?"

Comet sat quietly, looking out at the garden. "Eclipse can't be the

Silver General. The Silver General fights with Solara about whether countries live or die. Why would she have tea in my treehouse, play chess with you or base ball nines with Star or anything like that? But, oh wow, I mean, the Silver General's a lot more powerful than Eclipse. When the Silver General fought Solara, they destroyed the star cluster that got in the way. When Eclipse fought Emperor Roxbury, which was a lot easier, she got hurt."

"What if she were a different cyborg?" Aurora asked.

"Eclipse a cyborg?" Comet questioned. "But she's twelve. No one's made cyborgs for thousands of years."

"When was Eclipse four years old? Eight years ago? I don't know. Her book wasn't in any language I know," Aurora said. "If Eclipse were incredibly good, she could pretend she's twelve. She just has to look twelve. She could be that good because she's a cyborg. Then her manifesting story is true. Except it happened thousands of years ago."

"Eclipse is a thousand years old? I don't believe it!" Comet protested.

Aurora continued. "That's when I got frightened. She says she's twelve. She acts twelve. When I'm in her mind when she wakes up from a nightmare, she feels twelve, not even old as you. You feel more grownup because you know we're right here. You're not so frightened of things, because you know I'll help you, and even Star and Cloud would help you, if you needed. Eclipse only has herself for family. I think she's afraid to go home. It's too dangerous for her Dad and Mom. She's scared to take chances, because no one will help her if she gets hurt, because absolutely no one in the whole world cares if she gets hurt. Except boys who want to hurt her more. She's afraid, so it's like she's younger than us. But she's gifttrue, so she takes those chances no matter how scared she is, even when she keeps getting hurt."

"Oh," Comet managed. She bit her tongue. The truth about Eclipse going home was even worse than Aurora suspected.

"But if Eclipse is twelve, and her mother's in her right mind, neither of them can be the Silver General. So how could they have machine minds?" Aurora asked. "Finally I realized. Another cyborg is left over from the High Technarchs, still alive after three thousand years. Except this cyborg, the one who's Eclipse's mom, is totally sane. I know; I felt how much Eclipse's mom loves Eclipse."

Comet, stricken by Aurora's words, stared at the Japanese maple, its first leaves not yet in bud. How could she tell Aurora? Except, how could she not tell Aurora, since if Aurora didn't know she might repeat to Eclipse what she'd just said. Then Eclipse would be impossibly hurt. Aurora was very quiet, sensing her sister was deeply troubled.

"Something?" Comet asked. "Something absolutely never to tell Star?

Or anyone! Don't tell Eclipse you know! Promise?"

"OK. Absolutely. I promise," the younger girl answered.

"When Eclipse says she can't go home, she doesn't mean it's too dangerous for her parents," Comet said. "Well, it would be, but that's not why she can't go home. She can't go home because six months ago her mom threw her out from her own house, told her never to come back, burned the house down so no home was left, and vanished. If you tell Eclipse her mom loves her, she's going to get awful confused." Suddenly frightened, the two girls hugged each other. Eclipse's secret was the most terrifying thing they had heard in their lives.

CHAPTER 25 COMET SHOULD DO BERMUDA

Eclipse looked out the window. This was the second floor guest study, above the sunporch, with enough room for the five of them to spread out what they were doing. She'd drifted to sleep with a book in her lap and Star and Aurora rattling chess pieces. Comet and Cloud, sitting head to head at the far end of the room, had opened pocket lessoncomps and were doing homework. They sounded to have settled on Editing, something they could do together. Earlier they'd done math and languages. Comet was so far ahead in math that only Alex could have helped her; they'd agreed not to bother Pickering. Cloud had to do his Atlanticean and Lemurian declensions himself.

Eclipse was so tired she wasn't learning from her reading. There could be a separate hint on each page of Wells' world history; she'd miss them all. Now she was lost in a description of China. The thought of east Asia as a single country was odd, as odd as a single country filling Europe or Hindustan, but now two of those were united and the third was uniting.

That was a possible hint, one she carefully wrote on her 'hints' pad. Before the timeshift, there'd been crazy people who wanted to put all Hindus or all Catholics under one flag. Some did violent things, even in America. That was the second time she'd met Comet and siblings. Their father had been kidnapped by Christian Democrats—a group neither Christian nor democratic, and too small to be dignified as a party.

Suppose someone rearranged the past to unify the Han. They might have found a clever way to do it, changing the odds so you got large silly countries, not small sensible ones. Her idea explained personae, too. If you wanted to take over a country, it was a lot easier if they had no personae to stop you.

She folded her notepads and stacked her books. She was going to go to bed. There was no point to continuing. Twinges across the back of her head warned that sound sleep was unlikely tonight.

"Leaving?" Star asked, looking up from the chess board. "Sleepy already?" His voice was not quite a sneer. Her answer was a distracted yawn. She was too worn out to argue, not that she cared what Star thought.

"Girls!" Star grumbled. "Get a little tired and go to bed." His sisters grimaced. "There's a way you can make up, Comet. A way that puts time back. Besides, I found it," Star announced triumphantly. "I know how to fix everything."

"There is?" Comet responded. There might be a way to fix something, she decided, but her younger brother wouldn't see it before it hit him in the face. And if he kept riding Eclipse, the thing that hit him in the face wouldn't be a plan.

"A plan?" Cloud asked.

"All we have to do is agree. We have to do something we did before. Of course, it's a bit dangerous. But that's what gifts are about. You were given, you must return to be gifttrue. Then everything will be back. Will we?" Star waited for agreement. Cloud and Comet were vigorously enthusiastic; Aurora nodded in half disbelief. What had her brother come up with now? Finally Eclipse gave her silent acquiescence.

"Sure. Comet, all you need is a short flight. Out over the Atlantic," Star announced. "That'll make up for everything." Comet's jaw tightened.

"She flies over the Atlantic? And makes up?" Aurora asked. "Oh. Right! Star! Absolutely brilliant!"

"What, Aurora?" Cloud asked, finally peering up from his lessoncomp. He'd really wanted to study before he got totally behind on homework. Did the three have to lay into each other quite so much, he wondered? Sure, Eclipse said she was tired and quit all the time, but she was a girl. She for sure was working hard on trying to find clues; there just didn't seem to be any. No one could claim she hadn't gotten thoroughly pounded on, hard enough to have killed the rest of them, just to get here. Why did Star have to get all excited about Eclipse acting like a girl? After all, Eclipse was a girl. That's how girls were supposed to act. And why did Star have to nag his actually-pretty-frigid sisters until they had hissy-fits?

"How could you know?" Star challenged his sister. "I haven't told you my plan. How do you know it's brilliant?"

"Your plan's obvious," she answered.

"Sure. It's a boy's plan. It's got to be great. But I could have made it dumb. On purpose. To fool you," he smirked.

"No," Aurora said. "It's brilliant. She flies out and back. She takes you to the ocean's middle and drops you. You wouldn't change. You're all wet already," she continued. Not, she considered, that being all wet made him different than every other boy.

Star hadn't expected her answer. "No. I mean it. I've got a plan. Honest."

Cloud interrupted the spat. "What sort of a plan, Star?"

"A real plan," Star said, "If you agree, Comet. If you think it's dumb, then we need another plan. The past is changed, back thousands of years, right? No Atlantis? No Mugglewuggles?"

Mugliuvianu, Aurora and Comet mouthed.

"Go to the Bermudas," Star continued. "Find St. Brendan's Isle. Find the Maze. See if it has the Namestone. It must. The people who changed time didn't leave Eclipse behind. So no one did the Maze. Tell Eclipse to fetch the Namestone. Mayhaps it can't fix the world. But it 'knows the illness in mens' hearts', so we can use it to find the time pirates. It can do that. Then we use it to make them fix history. Or if Eclipse has a double here, one that no one knows about, like the Rogers Institution has this MIT place as a double, and the double did the Maze and got the Namestone, tell Eclipse to find her double, beat the double up, and take her Namestone back. After all, she did the Maze in the real world, so the Namestone is for sure hers, not her fake double's. See, it's completely simple," Star answered. "So simple even Aurora understands."

"Eclipse? Do the Maze? Again?" Aurora was horrified. The Maze left Eclipse with nightmares so she woke up screaming, and Star wanted Eclipse to go back and walk its halls? Again? The worst thing about Star's idea was that if Star asked Eclipse, and had a good reason why Eclipse needed to fight the Maze's solid shadows one more time, Eclipse would do it. Aurora decided she didn't want to think about Star's suggestion that if Eclipse's double had the Namestone, Eclipse should fight her Namestone-armed double.

"Of course, first Comet's got to find St. Brendan's Isle," Star said. "It might be a mile deep in the Atlantic. That's why we need Comet. That's why," he turned to his other sister, "we need you to take a flight."

"Me?" Comet complained. "Why always me? You and Cloud sit around all day, leave things for me and Aurora and even Eclipse to clean up, don't make your own beds or anything, let alone try to find what happened, and always come to me whenever you want something done, no matter how tiny. Why don't you go look for clues yourself? Daddy took you to Seattle twice so you know what it should look like, at least if you ever looked up from eating long enough to notice you aren't in Boston, so why don't you go see if the time pirates left hints like an extra castle someplace? Just because we didn't find anything in Boston doesn't mean the time pirates got every little detail right everywhere. Or do boys get to sit all the time, because they're too tired, exhausted by complaining about how tired we girls get?"

"Hssh!" Cloud whispered. "Alex will hear! People? Fight time pirates? Or medicine smugglers? Not each other! You give Alex terrible ideas about how personas behave." The three quieted. "Okay, tomorrow Star and I go to Washington."

"Sure," Star echoed. "No problem. Glad you thought of it, Cloud."

"Besides, we four did a great job on the other smugglers this morning. Even if I got a bit scorched. How would I know they had flamer pistols?"

Cloud asked. He wished he knew how to lead people. Great leaders never had subordinates who fought each other. They all worked together. He wondered how it was possible.

"We remember!" Comet answered. "We remember. You didn't flinch, even when your clothes were on fire. That was very frigid of you."

"Look at the bright side," Aurora continued. "You weren't in garb. You don't have to replace it."

"I can't replace it," Cloud groaned. "I asked Alex where a local tiergarten with a dodo is, to pluck a new feather for my beret. He said dodos became extinct four hundred years ago! He was real grateful when I gave him the old feather. He even promised us a big cut of the profits— if he can grow more dodos from it."

"Tell Eclipse," Star said. "Tell Eclipse about dodos. She's listing all the hints we find. Even dumb ones like Aurora's Pirc book."

"*The Complete Pirc* is more than you found, Star," Aurora said.

"Comet?" Star asked. "We do Washington? Tomorrow? You check the Maze? Trade?" His older sister gestured agreement.

"Only one thing, Star," Aurora said. "It's not your move any more. Your clock ran down while you were jabbering."

"My clock? Aww! Aurora!" Star groaned. He had had a half-even game for once, and now had thrown it away by berating Eclipse. "Another?" he asked, knowing the answer. Dad had given them a strict rule: No more than one long game a night. Aurora began putting away pieces. Her next book was waiting. She never did posts with her twin brother. He might learn something. Aurora remembered that she never dared tell that to her girlfriends. Girlfriends would all be horrified to learn that she, Janie Wells to them, thought her twin brother could learn something complicated, like walking or throwing a ball, if not both at the same time.

"I tried something else," Cloud said. "I thought, instead of reading up on ancient places, I'd find an expert in details, and ask her. Not a regular expert. These people think for sure there was no Atlantis, no Marik. So I looked for an expert in wrong facts, facts people don't believe in. Facts about places like Marik, places that Alex's people can't remember."

"An expert in wrong facts?" Aurora asked. "They have one?"

"Not wrong facts. Odd facts. Remember that home they found in the California desert, a forty-year old ranch house buried in a hundred feet of sand? And its radium-ray age was fifty-five thousand years? That sort of fact." Cloud deliberately paused. Experience told him not to get too far ahead of the people he was trying to lead. "So I looked for the Order of Gow."

"Yes! Of course!" Comet squealed. "That's positively absolutely brilliant of you, Cloud! That's wonderful!" She hugged him. He blushed.

"Whoever changed the past would've left hints, facts that don't make sense any more, and Gowists would scoop them up for their temples. I found a list of world museums. There's no Order. Not under that name. Not under some other name," the disappointed boy confessed.

"Good try," Aurora said.

"Then I asked Alex about telepathy," Cloud said. "First he said it should be impossible for some physics reason I don't understand. He thought a long time. He asked Telzey questions and found the precedent. Three hundred years old. In Massachusetts there were women—I think a witch is a type of persona and we should remember to look that up—who got convicted with spectral testimony. Spectral is telepathy with funny realizing."

"Realization," Comet corrected under her breath.

"And finally the Supreme Judicial Court of Massachusetts said spectral wasn't admissible. Because you couldn't cross-examine the specter to find out if it—the realizing—was from God or the Adversary," Cloud finished. He hoped no one would ask him how a Court could possibly think mentalic evidence had a theological component.

Comet crossed the air in front of herself. "Evidence from the Adversary? Here?"

"Back to my plan," Star said. "None of us were born, no personas at all. That includes you, Eclipse. But everything's the same a million years ago. Right?" Star waited for agreement. "Meaning the Namestone still got to Earth. I mean, there's no hint the Namestone's bearer knew the Wizard of Mars, so it can't matter that there's no Wizard. And because you weren't born any more, Eclipse, not since history got changed, the Namestone is still on St. Brendan's Island. It's still waiting for you." Star's pride in his wonderful idea shone through every word.

"Star," Eclipse said, "someone else? Someone who didn't get born until things got changed? He could have taken it."

"When there aren't personas? Could you do the Maze if you didn't have gifts?" Star challenged.

"Me? I very carefully didn't use any gifts. No! You're right. The Maze stopped lots of real smart people." Eclipse yielded gracefully.

"That's it," Star said. "All you have to do, Eclipse, is walk the Maze again, get us the Namestone, and use it to put history back. See? Easy!"

Eclipse collapsed back onto a chair. "All?" she managed weakly. Wasn't once enough? she asked herself. The others looked first at Star and then her, hope bubbling in their eyes.

"We'll help," Aurora announced. "That'll make it easier, won't it?"

"You mean we can have dad and mom again?" Comet asked. Eclipse sank further down, head cradled in her hands.

"You will, won't you?" Cloud asked. "You did promise."

Yes, Eclipse told herself, you did promise. She closed her eyes and leaned her forehead against folded hands. "I did," she admitted. "I did. But do the Maze? Again?" You can't, she told herself. Not now. Last time you were in tip-top shape. It nearly killed you. Right now you'll die trying.

Eclipse? Aurora's question was tight-focused. *Can you, this soon after the last time? Star doesn't understand. He won't ask you to kill yourself. Not if it won't do any good.*

Be very close. Eclipse answered. Did Aurora mean that Star would happily ask her to die, if he thought her dying would solve his problem? It seemed likely. "I can try," she announced. She shifted her position, mostly-healed bruises from the Tunnels protesting. Joining up with the Medford League brought her into the most interesting predicaments.

"If you aren't ready, we've got to wait," Comet said, "because it's for sure that you're the one that has to walk the Maze, not us. If you fail, we can't do it."

"Except it won't work. I'm sorry," Eclipse apologized.

"Why not?" the crestfallen boy asked. "It's right there, isn't it? And it does anything you tell it to."

"The Namestone isn't that powerful," she answered, "Not for what you want. I mean, it could do frigid things. I could've used it to make every ancient Chinese legend of California true, paved every street with three inches of solid gold. I could've changed the winds so every desert flowered. I know. I've cradled It in my hands."

"Sure!" Star said.

"It would make what I wanted," Eclipse explained. "Exactly what I wanted. Only what I wanted." Cloud nodded. "So if I wanted Alex's garden, I'd have had to imagine it, one bush at a time, or have his gardener imagine it for me. I could find people and make their house your house, and make them into your parents. But it's my memory of your house. They'd be my memory of your mom and dad, not the real thing. I could change the world. But I didn't memorize the world. I could use the Namestone, but I couldn't get the world right."

"You're sure you're not afraid?" Cloud asked. "Afraid you might muss your hair? Afraid this time you'd get a scar or two?"

"Cloud!" Comet snapped. "That's an awful terrible thing to say!"

"But it's true, isn't it?" Cloud challenged Eclipse. "You're afraid. That's why you won't do it, Eclipse! You don't have the guts! Even when your gifts say you can, you're too frightened."

"Of course I'm afraid," Eclipse answered calmly. "Do you think I'm a complete and total idiot? Last time, the Maze almost killed me. My legs still hurt when I land hard." Don't complain about the dreams, she thought; he won't understand. "That doesn't mean I won't try." Eclipse folded her hands. "Find St. Brendan's Isle. Tell me a sensible use for the Namestone, and I'll get it. But knowing evil? It does, but its focus doesn't work that way."

"This is silly," Cloud said. "Star, why not just ask her to loan us her Namestone. The one she already has."

"I said it was lost," Eclipse reminded. "Lost forever, one with the Crown Jewels of Mugliuvianu. Try something else." Star looked downcast. He had been so sure that for once he'd found the answer before his sisters did. With a shuffle of stockinged feet, Eclipse slipped around the chess players and closed the door silently behind her.

CHAPTER 26 TRAVELS

Southern fields were covered by a verdant haze of freshly-sprouted plantings. The dawn was almost cloudless, with a few scattered cumuli clustered like grazing sheep, mottled grey-white against green haze. Comet flew far above, carefully inspecting the first burst of spring plantings. Cities buried for two millennia left their mark on surface growth, so the parade grounds of long-lost Marik and buried canals of ancient Leaviork revealed themselves to fliers as faint shades of darker and lighter ground. Pickering's people might not be able to remember the past, but that didn't mean it wasn't here. All she had to do was find it.

Why me, Comet asked? Why am I looking? Eclipse was buried in her books. That was where Eclipse should be. Eclipse might say that she wasn't as smart as Aurora, would even claim that Comet could think, not just fly, rings around her, but if a puzzle could be solved by putting together obscure facts, Eclipse was incredibly good. Today Cloud and Star were supposed to go to the Pacific coast and search for ancient ruins. They might search; they might sit on a lonely beach and build sand castles. Either way, they had something to do besides pick on Eclipse and complain they were bored. Here, spying out the terrain from above, Comet was truly in her own element.

Flying cross-continent meant she couldn't have another argument with Star and Cloud. Baby brother was really getting on her nerves, and Cloud was egging him on, no matter he pretended to be completely innocent. Star was absolutely positively completely sure that everything could be fixed by the Namestone. All they had to do was to persuade Eclipse to use hers or to get it out of the Maze again. Every time Star mentioned the Maze, Eclipse looked distraught. He must have noticed, but he didn't care. Boys never cared about other people. All he thought about was himself, not what would happen to poor Eclipse when she tried to solve the Maze for a second time. Besides, flying cross-continent meant she got to stop in Virginia and pick up the money she was being paid for the missile photographs and the moon spaceship photographs.

Cities and towns rolled under her, larger and more numerous than those she remembered. Pickering's America had thrice the population of her own, not to mention a tendency to cluster in cities so dense-packed that she found them unnerving. She'd overflown New York, finding Central Park contracted to a narrow strip at island's center. Central Park's east and west shores were paved over. Its edges were lined with great huge shadowcasting skyscrapers.

She was supposed to be looking for ancient ruins, not admiring modern architecture. She'd done this before, a year and ago, soon after she'd manifested her first gifts. It had been so easy to find the ruins of a half-dozen ancient civilizations, intertangled with no regards to each other's existence. Now she found nothing. Once and again, she saw patterns, lines and circles. Closer examination always revealed an irrigation device, buried gas line, or some less common artifact. A particularly strange set of shadows proved to be an abandoned set of Army Air Corps—no, Air Force, use their names—rocket projectors.

She retreated before the rising sun, moving ever westward so that morning shadows would accentuate the patterns she sought. When the unceasing waves of the Pacific Ocean were breaking under her, she conceded defeat. The ancient history of America had been tracelessly erased. A swift vertical climb hurtled her into the ionosphere, her destination the Bermudas. If someone had changed the past, Eclipse had never been born, so the Namestone had never been recovered from the Maze. The Namestone must still be in the Lesser Maze, waiting for someone smart enough to take it. All she had to do was to prove that Saint Brendan's Isle still existed, and that the Maze remained unsolved,

The Bermudas were a blur of surf-ringed green. Northward a carefully counted number of miles brought her to vacant ocean, the place where St. Brendan's Isle had to be. Endless waves marched rank after rank across wind-touched sea. The Isle could hide itself beneath the waves, remaining dry and sunlit though two miles of water blanketed it. If you searched the sea bottom the Isle was not difficult to find, if only because it was so large.

Comet dropped vertically from the sky, coming to a hover fifteen feet above the waves. Her gifts allowed her to fly directly into water, but hitting the surface at flight speed hurt, gifts or no. She looked down, vision fading many feet below into the murky green depths of the Atlantic. Confident that the water beneath her was deep enough for a safe dive, she started a forward somersault, then killed her flight field. Arms outstretched, body straight as an arrow, she plunged in the water of the Atlantic, her passage raising the slightest of ripples.

The sharp snap at impact jarred locked wrists and elbows. Flight field cut on. The water was pleasantly cool against her hands. Garb stayed dry behind her body field. Ripples from her wake cascaded against back and legs. She dove deeper and deeper into the ocean, flying vertically downward, watching while the water faded from aquamarine into stygian black. Her flight field gave more than adequate light, letting her see hundreds of yards in all directions. Beyond that distance, the improbable lights of hundreds of fantastic luminous fish bobbed in the darkness.

Finally she reached bottom, more than two miles beneath the waves.

Her body field protested softly, reminding her that like Verne's public persona and his submarine she could visit the deepest of depths, but definitely ought not to overstay her welcome, not with water pressure well above a ton to the square inch.

She'd gone a lot deeper in the Pacific during the Lemurian invasion, stayed a long time, and paid the price afterwards: piercing headaches lasting for days. She didn't regret it. There had been a war, and her country had briefly needed her, even if most of her now-missing countrymen hadn't a hint of her existence. That included her former family; she'd never told them what she'd done. She began a spiral, relying on her sense of direction to guide her above the bottom, looking for traces of a sunken St. Brendan's Isle. An hour's time, over a hundred miles of high-speed submerged flight, revealed only mud and rock. Satisfied that St. Brendan's Isle had truly vanished, she guided her flight upwards, shallower and shallower until the water above brightened to sapphire blue, a color almost as rich as Eclipse's screens..

~~~~~

Star refolded his map, its edges catching in the breeze that leaked through Cloud's flight field. Their overall motion was a gentle bobbing. If he closed his eyes, he could almost convince himself that he was on a raft in the middle of Waltham Pond, not sailing windborne over Washington State. Star's father had taken him to the Cascades last Summer, a side trip after one of his science conventions. Their swing today over the North Cascades had revealed a few lonely towns and vast empty forests, but no sign of ruined towers or shattered halls, the stone and concrete and petrified timber that should have dotted slopes and mountaintops.

The memory of his trip through the Cascades with his father, miles rolling by as he peered out the car window, brought him to tears. Where were Dad and Mom? What had happened to them? The Glorious Hall of the Master Accountants, whose grotesque facades memorialized Sarnath's vanished scholars, had disappeared from remote Twisp, its place being taken by an old high school housing the tourist bureau and library. A remarkably friendly staffer had been delighted to help him choose a good map, though she had had to apologize that the North Cascades Highway would be snowed in for months yet. Star decided not to try explaining that he and Cloud did not use roads.

After the Cascades they'd flown south, Cloud summoning patches of haze to hide them from prying eyes. Seattle and Tacoma and Olympia passed beneath them. Star wished he had a map from before the change.

He thought he remembered the bays and islands, but some of them seemed to have moved. Now they were closing on the Hood Canal, its mile-plus width of icy-cold glacier-fed water lined by dark woods. Cloud slowed until they were moving scarcely faster than the cars on the coastal highway.

A quarter-hour later, they stopped for lunch at a primly clean rest area. The tide was out. Star and Cloud walked across a beach covered with rounded rocks and the shells of long-dead mollusks. Lines of ripples sectioned the sky's reflection into thin slats. They spent time skipping rocks across the water. Star remembered the Canal, if not the particular tidal flat. Leaviorkianu municipalities had once lined its shore, their ruins cluttering every beach with bright-colored shards from long-gone gem-encrusted windows. Usually the shards were easy to spot, but not now. They searched the tidal flats for gleams of color, finding no sign that the magistrates of Leaviork had ever set their great bejeweled pavilions near this place.

More rapid flight swept them by Port Townsend and Cape Flattery, then south to trace out the Pacific rim. Tree trunks, washed to the sea by spring floods, polished by wave and wind to the hue and finish of ancient ivory, lined the beaches. Once they paused. At the mouth of a narrow creek, a hundred yards out in the water, rose a gray pyramid of rock. Before the change, here and there along the coast one would have found lighthouses and watchtowers from ancient Leaviork, their heights reduced to stumps by time and tide. This rock was certainly not a lighthouse wall. Tourist signboards gave a more mundane explanation: sea stacks were especially tough sections of rock, left behind when the Pacific coast eroded inland.

They landed on the beach, carefully descending behind three tourists, man and woman and red-coated child. There was no sense in being noticed while they looked at the sea stack, even if it was clearly a natural formation, not a jagged remnant of floor and wall. A second little girl, her mottled-gray coat and hood having hidden her from sight until she moved, stared at them in wonder. They'd landed almost on top of her, but her cloak so completely matched the ground that she was virtually invisible until she stood. She stared at the two boys. They could fly! Star smiled and put finger to his lips. She grinned. Meeting the new Peter Pan and a real Lost Boy was clearly a wonderful secret to keep from her parents.

By late afternoon, they'd flown the Washington and Oregon coasts, never finding signs of the ancient world. Hours on a lonely Oregon beach, building a sand castle and watching until the rising tide swept it away, was good fun. Star made a note to himself. Comet would kill him if he didn't tell her about the Hoquiam Castle, which had proven to be not a last remnant of the Goetic Knights but instead a red-painted turreted home, its interior stuffed with every variety of elegant Victorian furniture and bric-a-brac.

CHAPTER 27 ECLIPSE AND VICTORIA

Maxwell Park spread across a low bluff. In mid-Summer it would fill with playing children, running dogs, and couples strolling along the walk above the lake. In early spring, school having just let out, it was deserted. An astute observer would have realized that Victoria had reached the park faster than should have been possible, given city speed limits. A dodge into a closet, gate to the purple sea, careful check that her target point was unoccupied, and a second gate had taken her in moments across the width of Table Rock.

Victoria hoped that Eclipse would actually be waiting when she arrived. Eclipse had promised she would. What, though, did a promise mean to a girl who flew and read minds and shrugged off bullets?

? An interrogatory incised in water-white crystal, so cleanly formed that no trace of its maker's other thoughts were heard.

"Eclipse?" Victoria spoke out load, louder than she had intended. "I mean," *Eclipse?* Actually using telepathy was so strange. Where was Eclipse? The answer came as a sketch, a seldom-used path leading to a low wall at the water's edge. *I'm glad you came!*

I said I would, was the cheery response. To Victoria, Eclipse sounded not at all offended that she'd been doubted. *Oh!* Eclipse added. Victoria realized that her words had carried traces of her doubts. *Well, sure I'd keep my promises to an ungifted. Same as to anyone else. Besides, you are gifted, for sure, same as Star or Comet or me.*

I am? Victoria challenged.

Gating? That's a very frigid gift. And you even met the person who gave it to you. Eclipse relaxed slightly, so Victoria could feel her sitting on a stone wall, back against an ancient tree, her seat accommodating to ripples in the fieldstone while feet trailed inches above the shallow water. Victoria edged her way down the path. For a moment she didn't recognize Eclipse, whose silver-white hair hid under a ruddy-brown wig. She pushed through overgrown brush, finally to sit on the wall besides Eclipse.

"I thought my classes would never finish," Victoria said. "Usually they go by so fast. Today dragged and dragged. Is it like that for you, too, sometimes?"

"I live by myself," Eclipse said. "So there's no school."

"You live by yourself?" Victoria hesitated. "You live completely by yourself? All the time? No school? Doesn't anyone try to put you in an orphanage?"

"Plenty of people want to put me places, but not an orphanage,"

Eclipse answered. Perhaps, she thought, I shouldn't explain that 'six feet under' is not an orphanage.

"It sounds hard," Victoria said. Had she hurt Eclipse's feelings? "Maybe I'm sorry I asked."

A trace of sadness crossed Eclipse's face. "Sure," she said. "Sometimes it's a real bear. Lots of times, it's incredibly frigid. I can swim or ski in the middle of the day. If I'm reading something, I can stay up late as I want."

"Right! Sounds great!" Victoria agreed. "What about school?"

"You have to make yourself study," Eclipse said. "It's easy to do what you want, and skip what you should. I try. School work by yourself is...different."

"You never have to wait for someone else to catch up," Victoria said, trying to accent the positive. "Or have people get tiffed at you because you did homework and they didn't."

"It means you figure everything out yourself. You can't ask for help. That's better than never trying hard. But books with wrong answers in the back get powerful frustrating," Eclipse said. "We have better computers than you, I think. Mostly not as good as Telzey. It's like having someone kibitz. And fair-test, so I know how I'm doing."

"Does, does mind reading ever help?" Victoria asked. "So you know exactly what a teacher is thinking when she says something?"

"It can. I learned how to shoot that way, sort of. But I can't take that chance. Not any more. The other four? They share thoughts all the time," Eclipse noted.

"I guess that's why they all think completely alike, isn't it? Sharing thoughts all the time. They're even more alike than me and my brothers and sisters, except we always all get along really well," Victoria said. *Still there? [Images of two older brothers and two older sisters, similar faces and builds, touches of four similar personalities.]*

Alike? THOSE FOUR? [Star and Cloud sniping back and forth at Aurora and Comet, boys and girls bitterly divided.]

"That cat-sniping-and-snarling? It's all the same, all four of them," Victoria said. "It's all us and them, and us is better than them, no matter what. Different us and them for Comet than for Cloud, but it's all us and them. If I didn't know who was a boy and who was a girl I couldn't tell them apart."

What?! Eclipse jumped, almost falling off the wall, toes touching the water and sending circular wavelets spreading across the lake. Victoria saw boys' and girls' thoughts as completely similar? Eclipse thought that the four's constant quarreling back and forth was a little silly. The notion that the back and the forth were practically the same still made her skin crawl.

"They're exactly opposite! Boys and girls! Because, because..." Eclipse found that she didn't know. What was different once you said 'us' and 'them' and not 'boys' or 'girls'? It should be totally obvious, like colors in a rainbow. Everyone knew boys and girls were completely opposite in everything until they grew up, and decided they liked each other after all. The way Victoria saw them, boys and girls were practically the same. That couldn't be right, could it? Where was the mistake in Victoria's thinking? Eclipse couldn't find it, but it had to be there, didn't it? "I never thought about it that way. It's a different war to see things," Eclipse temporized.

"Star and Comet said they play soccer. There's a bunch of us that play," Victoria said. "So I invited them. It was fine until they realized we play boys and girls in one game. Not leagues, just games. They weirded out, though they tried real hard to hide it. Boys and girls together like that was too much for them."

"Hmmh?" Eclipse was momentarily baffled. "Star's and Aurora's teams played each other, before the change. 'course soccer's mostly a game that girls play for keeps, and boys don't, but lots of people play." Her voice trailed away to a whisper, as though she were afraid someone might hear her say something impolite. "Ohhhh. You mean boys and girls? Both on the same team? All the time, not a pickup game?"

Victoria nodded, afraid that she'd offended Eclipse.

"Yes," Eclipse agreed. "That would 'weird them out', is that how you say it? I wouldn't mind. Even if my team was more boys than girls. But neither of them ever thought of boys and girls playing regularly on one team in a real game. Never in their lives. No matter that Comet and I joined Star's friends to play pick-up against the school base ball nines team."

"I see." Victoria said. "But they all like you. Even Star, and you're a girl. That sounds real silly to me, not liking someone because they're not a boy. I mean, there are plenty of boys I can't stand, but that's because they're complete jerks, not because they happen to be boys. But Comet and Aurora dislike boys for being boys, and Cloud and Star dislike girls for being girls. Except you don't do that, not at all."

"Except me?" Eclipse said. Someplace she'd heard of a group of eccentrics who wanted to bring up boys and girls in mixed groups, so they'd get along with each other before they were teenagers. Boys and girls now got along well. Could that group have played with time? It would have been no more one-minded than Master of Airships' scheme to make dirigibles practical: Transmute half the Indian Ocean into krypton gas while using biologicals to change living things so they could survive the Earth's new atmosphere.

"The four argue," Victoria said. "All the time we talked and raked, they argued. Except deep down, they agree on what's important. And deep down you disagree."

"Deep down?" Eclipse asked, wondering what more she'd missed. She shifted her weight slightly, so that her weight conformed better to the slopes in the fieldstone.

"When you thought about Solara and Silver General, it was all different. Completely different. Their Solara is a name in a book. You know how strong her powers—her gifts, right?—are. You had a real fight, you against her, and she's a grown-up. Didn't you?" Victoria was frightened by that. Having a serious fight with a grownup was crazy, no matter that she'd done it herself. She'd simply hit a man on his back of the head with a large rock. Eclipse must have faced her opponent.

"Is there one Silver General? Or more? Your image is opposite to theirs," Victoria intruded on Eclipse's reverie.

"Well, sure there's only one. I mean, there's dozens of Colonel Dixies, but important names you don't copy. There's one Solara. When DreamStorm became important, people stopped taking DreamStorm as a persona name. But...Great! Just great! Am I doing that?" Eclipse, upset, withdrew into herself, reflecting on her patterns of thought. "You're right. I am. Thanks a lot! I never notice what other people see in me. That could cause trouble."

"I don't understand," Victoria said bluntly. "How can your world be so close to mine and so strange all at once?"

"I don't know. Whoever changed history removed one billion people and made seven billion new ones. Why? Something wicked, but what?" Eclipse remembered that Victoria had wanted to talk about something important. Not this, for sure.

"I'm still glad I helped you. Gating, I mean. You're a real friend I can talk to. So I won't ask about the Silver General," Victoria said.

"No. It's all right. Besides, if I tell, you know what not to say," Eclipse said.

"Secret?" Victoria asked.

"Secret! Before the change, our age—history age, like Rome or Sarnath—was Solara's. Cloud and the rest are good, so they took her side," Eclipse said.

"And you don't? They had bad thoughts about the Silver General," Victoria observed.

"They're good. The world's more complicated. That's not why I see her differently," Eclipse explained.

"The Silver General's a her? Not a him? Is that the secret? I promise not to tell." Victoria looked earnestly in the other girl's steel-gray eyes.

"The Silver General. This villain Cloud wants to kill? She's someone I knew. And I trusted her. And she's wonderful." Physical tears were matched by mental agony. Eclipse's rational thoughts broke into chaotic sadness.

"Oh, Eclipse! That's terrible. I didn't know you'd feel like this." Victoria hugged Eclipse and produced a handkerchief from one pocket. "And the rest of them give you a hard time about your parents, too? Not being able to go home? That's awful."

"Not all of them." Eclipse's voice was broken by sobs. "Only Comet knows about my Mom. They don't know it hurts me..."

"That's still awful. Awfully awful," Victoria said.

"...and Aurora's half on my side." Eclipse paused, drying her eyes. "We're telepaths. She knows exactly how I feel. She just doesn't know why." She paled, clenching one fist, eyes focusing at the distant shore, waiting for breathing to steady, for clamped muscles to relax. "You still haven't told me about you. Your problem."

"You saw the Purple Sea. I took you there, right?" Victoria gestured vigorously.

"You showed me gating. That's really a chill gift to have! All those incredible and strange places you can visit!" Eclipse's voice was completely sincere. Victoria was a persona. She had gifts! If the time pirates meant to warp history so there were no personae, they'd failed.

"I can gate. So I'm a superhero, I mean, a persona. Something out of a comic book. No one does that. Not for real," Victoria objected, her words falling one on top of the next.

"There's lots of things people do for the first time," Eclipse said reassuringly.

"I haven't told Dad and Mom! I haven't. I'm being terrible. I never keep secrets from them!" Victoria groaned. "After all, did you keep it secret? That you have gifts?"

"My Mom knew right away. She was there when I manifested for the first time. Before I knew what a persona was, she knew about me. But being a persona was just something I did, like reading or playing with blocks or riding a horse." Eclipse decided she wasn't helping her friend at all. "I don't know what to say. I never had secrets from my Mom. Not big ones."

"Great! Just great! If I tell Dad and Mom, they'll want to know why I didn't tell them sooner. Then they'll get mad. If I don't tell them, they'll find out. Then it'll be worse. If I stop gating, I'll forget how. I don't want that, either," Victoria added.

"If something had happened to me, and I kept it secret from my mom for a good reason, it would have been okay. My Mom trusted me, right until the end. I think your parents trust you," Eclipse said.

"She didn't worry, when you were little, you'd give away you have gifts? When you went to school?" Victoria asked.

"I never went to school," Eclipse explained. "Not regular school. I had playmates. Not where we lived, way out in the country. My mom took us places. There were kids I knew. Most gifted. Not all. When I was nine I learned how to go myself. Teleport, I mean. So I had friends in far places. None of us ever visited the other's house."

Eclipse considered how lucky she'd been on the last. After she'd been driven into the wilderness, after she had a base of her own, she'd almost invited some old friends to visit her in her own home. After all, it was her house, paid for with her own money, and she wasn't a fugitive from justice or a runaway or anything like that. She really hadn't needed to hide from other personae, not before the Maze. But if anyone now knew where she lived, she would have had to abandon her base for a new one. "That's not answering your question. Is it?" she asked.

"You're being nice to listen. I never ever had things happen to me, not the sort of things that happened to you. I don't know what's right. If I knew what's right, I'd do it," Victoria said.

Eclipse leaned against the tree, her gaze wandering from her friend to the brush beyond and back again. "You really don't want to mention Adara. Not casually. That gets you deeper into trouble. Even if it all worked out right. You did tell your Mom what you'd done, right after you'd done it. Remember? She didn't believe you, but you did tell her. Say anything now, and it all comes out." Victoria looked pensively out across the lake. How did she get out of this? "So tell all, or say nothing."

"What you did was right," Eclipse continued. "Before the world got changed, you did what a good persona would do. What was needed, that's what you did. Before the change, you'd do what was right, but sometimes you couldn't tell anyone. Because telling would uncover your public persona. People would learn your," Eclipse struggled for a word, "your secret identity. Sometimes you had to hide in your heart what you did."

"I guess," Victoria answered dubiously.

"What you did was right!" Eclipse emphasized. How should she say it? If you thought about what Victoria had done, remembering that Victoria had no gifts or weapons, what she'd done was fantastic. "You saved Adara's life, saved your town, saved your world. You were gifttrue, completely gifttrue." Eclipse made a mental note. The Kreesha had been the size of a truck. Had Adara disposed of the corpse? Pickering's world had some astonishing blindnesses, but a dead giant insect, where no one had heard of giant insects, ought to have made some impression on the collective awareness.

"I didn't know I was right," Victoria protested. "Not before. I guessed. No one else will ever believe my guess made sense, except it turned out right."

Eclipse looked Victoria firmly in the eyes, steel-gray meeting blue-green. "I would have believed you," she said. "Even if I didn't, I would have gone up that mountain with you. Because I know what sort of person you are. You're good as you can be. Besides, if you decide something, you most-times don't know every fact. You guess, try as hard as possible. Hope for the best. I did the Maze. The Four think I had it all mapped out, every detail solved. I didn't. All I knew was I was ready as I could be, last winter. So I went. I only almost died. You did the same. It worked. So you made the right choice." She smiled, waiting until she was met by Victoria's tentative grin.

"Thanks. Really thanks!" Victoria said. "It's great to have you to talk to. You understand. I guess I could tell Penny. I think she wouldn't freak out. Except she would want to learn how to gate. But you answered my question."

"That's what friends are for," Eclipse said. "Listening. Saying when the same thing happened to you, so you share it."

"I might have asked Adara what to do," Victoria continued. "I wish I'd seen her after, more than once. Just to talk. She must be really lonely." Victoria looked carefully at Eclipse. "Lonelier than you, maybe even."

Eclipse spread her hands, her face taking the aspect of remote tranquility. What was there for her to say?

"I told Adara she could visit us, except I knew it really wouldn't work, because Mom knew Adara did things. Impossible things. Swimming the St. Olaf." Victoria paused. "Are they expecting you for dinner?"

"Well, no." She paused. "The four are over the Pacific. Aurora says they all say hi! to you."

"You talked to them? Right now? That was telepathy again?" Victoria asked.

Speed of thought, Eclipse answered.

"I'd invite you to dinner. I need to phone my Mom. Ask if it's okay. I'm sure, but I've got to call first."

"Sure. I understand. My Mom was the same way. Well, she would have been, if I'd ever wanted guests. But am I wearing," Eclipse tugged at corduroy pants and tan sweater, "something half-way decent?"

"You're fine. That's great," Victoria said.

"One favor," Eclipse said. "When we go there? Could we walk to your house, and you let me see the town through your eyes? So I see what signifies? Thanks!"

CHAPTER 28 ONE CAME TO DINNER

The two girls walked up the driveway to Victoria's home, Eclipse carefully matching her pace with Victoria. Victoria came to a sudden stop. "Wait! What do I call you? I mean, what name are you using? If you're not, ummh, who you are?"

A smile crossed Eclipse's face. "Oh, right. I'm not in public persona. I haven't done that in ages, except when I was in disguise. But 'Jim' or 'Joe' won't work.' Except I don't have a private persona."

"You disguised yourself as a boy?" Victoria asked.

"You remember the boy-girl thing you pointed out? Before the change, absolutely no one would suspect 'Jim' of being a girl."

"Oh. Right. You don't have a secret identity? Your parents' nickname? No, sorry, I forgot." Victoria was terribly embarrassed by the oversight in her last question.

"Let's use my real name," Eclipse announced matter-of-factly. There was no one who knew it any more, no one in the whole world. "Glory."

"Glory?" Victoria asked.

"Short for Gloriana," Eclipse explained. "Except you've never heard of Edmund Spenser or *The Faery Queen*. He's this poet who wrote this very long poem hundreds of years ago. But his poem still exists, even after time got scrambled. I looked it up, and Gloriana is still there."

Victoria choked. She barely fought off a laughing fit. "Oh, yes. Oh, yes, I've heard of him. I've had the whole thing read to me. Several times."

Eclipse's eyebrows rose. Spenser was an incredibly obscure poet, invisible to the tesdri screens of most college English departments.

"My mom was an English major," Victoria said.

To Eclipse, Victoria had suggested an obscure possibility. Could history have been scrambled by literary fanatics? Her own mother's literary tastes came to mind. What if Marlowe had no longer been rescued by Philip Sidney? What if Marlowe didn't live to ninety, and so never wrote his great late plays, the ones Mom so loved? What was it she'd said when we saw the Elizabeth Regina? 'Silver thatch purged gold of dross'? That was it. Marlowe, white-haired, finally learned to separate well-formed work from material fit only to be discarded. If Marlowe had died young, the great Elizabethan playwright would have been who? William Shakespeare? She remembered disappearing to New York, one of the few times she had done something mother might not have liked, using her gifts to sneak into a performance of King Lear, a play so wickedly conceived that children were forbidden to see it. It was terribly depraved, but terribly sad at the same time. She couldn't remember anyone who both liked Shakespeare and was powerful enough to reform the world around that obscure playwright.

Victoria, wondering what had distracted Eclipse, continued her explanation. "My middle name? The one I never tell? It's Britomart. After the knight." The two girls giggled in mutual recognition. "That mindreading trick? Can we use it while we're eating? Without them knowing?" Eclipse nodded. "Might be convenient if they start talking about something everyone knows. Except you don't, because it didn't used to be true?" Eclipse gave her a thumb's up.

Victoria's parents were delighted to meet one of her friends, even if it was someone she'd never mentioned before. Victoria didn't say how recently she'd met Glory. She couldn't very well explain that a day with a telepath was worth weeks with someone who only talked. Brothers James and Charles, and older sisters Anna and Karen were on their best behavior.

"Glory? Did I follow that you're one of Professor Pickering's nieces?" Victoria's mother asked politely over the dinner table. Clarissa made a point of knowing about all of the relatives of all of her neighbors, or as close thereto as she could manage.

"Not exactly," Eclipse answered. "We're more friends of the family than close relatives. He doesn't talk much about his close relatives," she added, hoping to deflect the line of conversation.

"He doesn't talk much about much of anything," Victoria's father James said in a brief emergence from taciturnity. "He is friendly, especially considering he is the wealthiest man in the state."

"Did you meet his guests? The girl who flew over Washington? Are they nice guys?" Anna, Victoria's older sister, ended her question by helping herself to more roasted potatoes.

"Meet them? Sort of more than that. They were at his house yesterday. They're good people, I believe," Eclipse said defensively.

"Those satellite pictures they replayed? From when they took that TV cameraman into orbit, all in a flash? They were totally out of this world!" James, Junior, added.

"A shade under three planetary diameters," Eclipse corrected. "Hardly far from our Earth." She didn't notice the sudden sharpening of Clarissa's eyes.

The main course was replaced by dessert, a raspberry pie topped with caramel crust. "I suppose I shouldn't pry," Clarissa said off-handedly. Victoria rolled her eyes. Mom not prying was like a cat not going after sardines in cream. "Before I met Jim, before I went into English, I was in linguistics." Clarissa realized that Glory was studying her face more attentively than most twelve year olds attempted. "And those young people, when they spoke on television, they had an accent like no English accent on this Earth."

"Well," Victoria intruded, hoping to head off her mother. She didn't know what mother was about to ask, but it would require a lot of fast talking. "Why should they? It's not on this earth, not any more. Professor Pickering said so, on television even, and he's a great scientist."

"Especially the way they rolled the r's and flattened the a's. Like 'sort of more than that'," she continued without deviating from her train of thought, precisely duplicating the shadings of Eclipse's tone and accent. Her husband, who had been casually buttering an ear of corn, stared for an instant at Eclipse, smiled, and went back to his buttering. Victoria's brothers and sisters looked back and forth between their mother and their sister's guest.

I think you'd better tell her, Victoria thought. *She figured it out.*

"That accent used to be Modern English," Eclipse admitted.

"You mean, you're from there, that other world, too?" Karen asked. "You must be really incredibly cool."

Eclipse flushed. *She didn't mean THAT! Did she?* Eclipse asked Victoria.

Mean what? Victoria sensed which word had triggered Eclipse's reaction. *'Cool' is, she means she thinks you're something good. Or interesting. Or she likes the idea,* Victoria suggested.

Got it. Same word. Very different meaning. Star'd say 'frigid', not 'cool', Eclipse noted, trying not to wince when she used the word herself.

"Now, Karen," Clarissa intruded, "it's not polite to pry. Is it?" Her voice tended towards the firm.

"As it happens," Eclipse interrupted, coming to Karen's rescue, not quite admitting who she was, "What Professor Pickering talked about, it's not another world. It's this world. Except things were all switched about. I don't know who did it, or why. Or how."

"That must be terribly strange," Anna said, still not suspecting that Glory was one of Pickering's exotic visitors. "For Doctor Pickering's guests, I mean. Coming home. And home's not there. If that happened to me, I'd completely freak out."

?freak out? Eclipse asked.

run in circles, scream and shout. go crazy. not be cool, ummh frigid, or calm and collected, like you always are. Victoria translated for her friend.

"I had practice," Eclipse admitted. "The others were very upset, even if they're frigid in public."

"Sure, practice always helps." Anna did a double take. What did Glory mean 'others'? "Was that your friends on NightNews?" Her parents and siblings were dead quiet, some waiting for Eclipse's acknowledgement, others realizing for the first time that sister Victoria had brought an international celebrity into their midst and neglected to warn them.

You did say your mom would spot me, Eclipse said to Victoria. *I didn't used to have an accent.*

"As it happens," Eclipse said, "that was I last night. Comet and Cloud were with me this morning on Washington Life."

"You were on TV? I saw you?" Anna asked. The girl sitting in front of her couldn't be one of the children she'd seen on television. She didn't look like any of them. Did she? Perhaps that sweater made her look a little chubby, when she was only square-shouldered, but her hair certainly wasn't coppery or white blonde.

"Garb makes a difference. Plus this is a wig." She tugged at her hair. "We walked through town, and I didn't think you'd want a hundred video annotators on your doorstep, the way Alex Pickering has. Do you?" Eclipse asked.

"Oh, no," Clarissa answered swiftly. "Not at all."

"Hey!" Karen objected. "It'd be fun. All those TV reporters, every single one wanting to interview us. And put me on television."

She was drowned out by the united voices of her whole family: "No, Karen!"

"Okay, okay! I was just suggesting it to think about."

"You said video, Glory," James, Junior observed. "That's the old name, like the tellie. Did you ever call TV television?"

Eclipse considered for a moment. "Television is a gift. It's seeing places where you aren't. Aurora does that. And a tellie, ummh, a teles is an artifact, something you draw on to deepen your gifts. Those are old words, from before Edison and Swift invented video." The conversation dissolved into a whirl of questions, Victoria's family all trying to satisfy their curiosity at once.

"I had a simpler question," Victoria's father finally asked. "How do you buy a costume? Did your parents buy them? If everyone sees you buying, a mask isn't going to help keep your secret."

Eclipse turned to Victoria. *Costume = garb(?) Mask = Domino [Comet's facepiece, garish green and gold crossed comets with eye slits](?)*

Domino? [Small black blocks with painted dots.] Oh! The masks! Got it. Yes!

"It depends," Eclipse said. "My persona is open, so people know who

I am if they see me, whether I'm wearing garb or not. To buy my garb, I walked into Neurath's—a garbmaker on the Ringstrasse in Vienna. Comet made her own and Aurora's and Star's. I don't know about Cloud. I think Comet flew Cloud to Mauritius for the dodo feather." She decided not to explain the details, nor to say what a good persona chandler did to cloak its customers' identities.

"Can you show us flying or something?" Karen asked. Her parents glared in her direction. "Please?"

Eclipse looked thoughtful. "Flying? I think I know something better." She looked at Clarissa. "You liked Spenser? The poet?" The children laughed.

We each, Victoria said, *have a middle name, Guyon or Florimel or Britomart, from the immortal's work.*

"How'd you like to hear him read?" Eclipse asked.

"That's impossible," James, Junior, objected. "He's been dead for hundreds of years. Even Mom never heard him speak. Or did you, Mom?" He was rewarded with a maternal glare.

"These aren't my memories," Eclipse answered. "They were passed to me. If you want to stop seeing them, think of stepping back. The link will fade." The family set down silverware, waiting with intense curiosity, only Victoria knowing what must be about to happen.

[A distant smell of wood smoke, the harsh crackle of a fireplace burning in the background. A short man, dark, with close-cut hair and ruffed collar sat in a high-backed wooden chair at a longish table. Clarissa recognized the period of dress with a gasp of astonishment. The man read from a hand-written manuscript.

"...No word they spake, nor earthly thing they felt,
But two senceless stocks in long embracement dwelt.

Had ye them seen, ye would have surely thought,
That they had been that fair Hermaphrodite,
Which that rich Romane of white marble wrought,
And in his costly bath caused to be site:
So seemd these two, as grown together quite,
That Britomart half envying their blesse,
Was much empassioned in her gentle sprite,
And to her selfe oft wisht like happinesse,
In vain she wisht, that fate n'ould let her possesse."

The image dimmed, the man's voice fading to incomprehensibility.]
"That's it," announced Eclipse. "That's all I have."

"You remembered all that," Robert said. "You're really cool." Eclipse managed to avoiding blushing.

"My mother gave me those memories. It was a birthday present." She said it was because the verse signified for me, Eclipse remembered. Eclipse decided she still didn't understand the importance of reuniting two people. She had never reunited a pair of lovers, had she? Eclipse hadn't expected the sweep of applause from Victoria's family, let alone the tears she had brought to Clarissa's eyes.

"Okay," Clarissa said, "Dinner is over. You all have schoolwork for tomorrow, right? Go do it. Glory, could we talk more?"

"Happy to," Eclipse answered. *Victoria has a bit to add, for the two of you. Victoria, stay here.*

"Four older siblings, on your way," Victoria's father said. *This is about the teleport?* he asked Victoria. *Can you hear me? Is this Eclipse doing telepathy?* Victoria nodded. Victoria's brothers and sisters marched dishes to the kitchen, then headed upstairs.

Exactly, Eclipse answered.

Eclipse, can you take four of us to someplace private? James, Senior asked.

Done. Eclipse answered. They fell into a blue waterfall, finding themselves near benches in the city park. "So long as we stay close, I can keep you all reasonably warm."

"Let's hear it," James, Senior said.

"Mom, Dad, There's something I have to tell you," Victoria said. "I should have told you way earlier. Except you wouldn't possibly have believed me."

"We always believe you, dear," Clarissa responded.

"This is way less believable than the teleport," she countered, "but it's true. Eclipse wasn't the only superhero at the table. Last month, I became a superhero, too. Not on purpose. But I did," Victoria said, not quite calmly.

"You did what?" Clarissa asked.

"Well, you see," Victoria paused. "Eclipse, could you please do the telepathy thing again?"

I'll do it, Aurora said, *if you don't mind, Eclipse. Oh, hi,* she said to James and Clarissa, *I'm the other telepath in our group. People haven't seen me yet.*

She's the better telepath, Eclipse corrected, *by a lot.*

"I'd better show you, first. I think one at a time. Dad, hold hands?" Victoria asked. She and her father vanished and reappeared. "Mom?" Victoria and her mother disappeared and returned.

"Where was that?" James, Senior asked.

"Not our earth," Eclipse answered.

"Now I explain. Please let me finish before you ground me until I die of old age. Please?" Victoria said. *Ready, Aurora?* She felt a nod. *You see...*

CHAPTER 29 AURORA AND ECLIPSE

Aurora padded quietly along the beach of Pickering's lake, each step made deliberately and carefully, trying her best not to make a sound. Eclipse was ahead of her, taking her midnight walk; she'd never said a word about the walks to anyone. Aurora had needed a few nights to figure out: Eclipse was waking up with nightmares every single night, waking hard enough that she had to get completely awake before she could sleep again. Eclipse never complained, never said anything about feeling tired, but you could feel the strain, an eldritch veil cast over her every thought.

At least, Aurora corrected herself, you could feel the strain if you were a telepath and went tight mind-to-mind with her. Eclipse hid her feelings really well if you stopped by looking at her face and listening to her voice. Only the slightest sag of shoulders betrayed her inner hurt, a hurt compounded of bone-deep exhaustion and the pain of rejection. If you asked, Eclipse would say everything was just great, except the whole world was missing, but she promised she was working as hard as she could on solving the mystery. If you listened carefully to Eclipse, Aurora decided, everything was not well at all, Eclipse's good cheer masking burdens no one in the whole world, let alone a girl not a year older than you, ought to carry alone.

The silly boys, Aurora thought, only cared about their own troubles. They went to bed at night, not caring at all how anyone else felt. Even if they knew that Eclipse was out here, night after night, they'd never say anything to her. After all, they'd think, she was a girl, she wasn't supposed to be able to protect herself the way a boy would. Boys! It was Eclipse who lived alone, took care of her own hurts, and did the Maze by herself; it was Star who was so afraid he'd never get home again that he could hardly think straight.

She spent half a minute entrapped by memories of home, of mother and father and house and friends and her collection of chess and stones and game books. Someday she would be a Grandmaster, perhaps even Supreme Mistress of Games. Meanwhile, the challenge was just such wonderful fun. One foot followed the next, but her mind was strange aeons away.

Aurora had decided. The time had come to try to help Eclipse, if she could. She suspected she'd have to sit and listen, and tell Eclipse about how the things, that had happened Eclipse, had happened to her, too, and hope that sharing made it better. It sounded easy, except what had happened to Eclipse had been so awful. How could she find something that showed she understood—from her own experience—exactly how Eclipse felt? With other people, people who really hurt inside, sometimes she could do something to their minds, something that eased the worst of the burden. Eclipse hid behind mind screens like polished steel, letting you see little except what Eclipse wanted you to see. To help Eclipse, she'd have to rely on voice and good sense. Comet would do the same for Eclipse, if she knew what was wrong, but Comet did everything else. Comet needed to sleep. It was her own turn to do something for the group.

Down the beach, Eclipse peered into the depths of the constellations. The patterns, the magnitudes, the names given each point of light by Arab and Greek and half-forgotten Goetic astronomers, all things she'd learned from her mother's soft but firm voice, came to mind. Whatever had happened here on earth, however someone had reached back in time to change the past until most of history was simply cancelled, the stars were unchanged. Some of Pickering's names were different, the Blessed Unicorn being now the Big Dipper—or was it the Bear?—but the stars themselves were exactly the same.

"Eclipse?" Aurora reminded herself to project her voice.

Eclipse whirled on one foot. "Aurora? Have you been following me often? Not that I mind."

"Just this once. Sorry to intrude," Aurora answered. "Apologies. I'm sorry. But I thought—you've helped us so often. Mayhaps I could help you."

"I," Eclipse turned away, just for a moment, squeezing tears from her eyes. "That's very kind of you," she finally answered. "My Maze nightmares? I finally found what was causing them. You're allowed to take the Maze over several days. For anyone who does, there's a nasty dream-trap. So I deleted the trap."

"You're still out here," Aurora said.

"But my nightmares—those nightmares—are gone. Honest!" She looked back at the constellations. "But there's something else. I can't figure it out. It wakes me up. It gives me bad dreams. But I keep thinking, edge of my mind, if I could hear it, the dreams would go away. But I can't. And I'm not sure I want to hear it. When I'm awake I'm sure I'm not hearing anything."

"The Maze nightmares are gone?" Aurora asked.

"Completely. My new nightmares are wrapped up in Christian symbolism and High Programmer Cult nonsense. And I've never been very interested in either of those," Eclipse said. "So I come out here to look at the stars and think. Except sometimes I get very cold."

"Mentioning cold," Aurora said, "I'm calling my body field to stay warm. You could, too."

"Could. I don't want to become a slave to my gifts," Eclipse answered. "But I won't make a fetish of not using them. Not when they're useful. Shall we go back inside?"

CHAPTER 30 SILENCES FROM THE SKY

The sun passed the zenith. "This morning," Comet announced, "the folks at Aerospace Science Weekly had for me this huge packet of information about medicine smugglers, and all the accusations made against this guy who lives on St. Dominick. That's an island in the Caribbean. Here's a map of Saint Dominick." She hesitated before taking one of the sandwiches Eclipse had bought someplace or other. "I flew over invisible and sketched all the buildings that aren't on the map, and Aurora looked and listened and read minds."

"The packet said this fellow was safe because he bribed judges," Aurora announced. Cloud shuddered. "They're public officials. So I read their minds to prove they're innocent. They were totally guilty. So this fellow and his minions were fair game for having their minds read."

"You read all their minds?" Cloud asked. "Great work!"

"I tried," said Aurora. "Can't see inside those warehouses. It's not line-of-light to someplace. And I've never been there. But guards and foremen and that accountant knew plenty. These buildings," she pointed, "are refrigerated warehouses. Those two are hangars. They have underground fuel tanks and a repair shop. The little low buildings are rented. They're very thick reinforced concrete with steel doors and firing slits. Each one has its own guards. Only its own guards go inside."

"Is there lots of money? From smuggling medicine, so we can salvage it?" Star asked. "Can we count on it?"

"I think so," said Aurora. The boys' eyes lit up whenever salvaging money was mentioned. She told herself that money was why they were making an action against these particular crooks. Other crooks were closer. But these crooks had money, lots of money, money that could legally be salvaged. "Anyhow, the guy who owns the place lives here. That's a swimming pool, except the bath house is a disguised helicopter." She marked a rise of sand facing the end of the runway, "That's a bunker with jet plane, always fueled and ready to fly. A getaway plane."

"Are there many guards?" Cloud asked. "Where do they live?"

"Two hundred?" Aurora answered. "Those orange dots, they're firing positions. They've got machine guns and antitank rockets and mortars. It's a big secret, they think. They've got antiaircraft rockets. I marked disguised places that can fire rockets at ships. Big rockets, enough to sink a cruiser-escort. Lots of tesdri. Video cameras. Motion detectors. The place where the guards sleep is buried. They've got this part that looks like beach houses. That's where they relax. They've got lots and lots of tunnels."

"That's good. Really good," Cloud said. "We can beat them, because we're smarter and stronger."

"Only guns and rockets?" Eclipse asked. "What about lasers? Particle beams? Lemurians? Something weird?"

"Guns and rockets. No Lemurians. What's weird?" Aurora answered.

"Poison gas? Privileged band attacks?" Eclipse smiled.

"Who has gas?" Star challenged.

"Salvadore, remember him?" Aurora answered. "So it was a powder; it still killed you if you inhaled." Gas weapons, for all their crudity, were effective against that large fraction of persona who needed to breathe. She and her fellows didn't have that problem, at least if they kept their minds on it. She hoped Comet would remember this time. Last time, Comet's heart had stopped beating, which could be very bad in almost no time at all. Fortunately, Star had been there to save her.

"Seriously? Those warehouses are full of poison? Screens up all the time! Don't breathe!" Eclipse emphasized. They fell into a discussion of approaches. Defenses would be flattened. The island's owner would find himself trussed, gagged, and deposited in an NOJ, no, FBI office back in the United States. Hoards of money would be salvaged and put into lawful service by public personae, namely Comet and friends.

"People with guns," Aurora said. "I can't knock them all out. Some I can't reach. Is this a regular action, or full?" Cloud and Eclipse looked at each other, their thoughts moving in parallel. A regular action, arresting ungifted criminals without hurting them more than absolutely necessary, was routine. A full action, constraints on violence and deadly force removed, was much more serious, not something you did because you felt like it.

"This is only regular, isn't it?" Comet proposed, "them all being ungifted and us being gifted and them only being regular criminals who smuggle things and have guns, though once we start doing things they'll be shooting at us for sure, so Star and Cloud can shoot back, so long as you can tell exactly which ones are really shooting at you."

"Frigid," Star whispered. Action at last, something to do instead of sitting and waiting for Eclipse to find the dooms. He told himself not to be impatient with her. She was working as hard as she could, doing things he couldn't match, but waiting was so boring.

Cloud waited for Eclipse to say how she felt. He was tired of being second-guessed. For once, he'd make sure no one else had the last word.

Eclipse's voice was entirely matter-of-fact. "The owner was brought to trial there. He," she hunted for an unfamiliar word, "bribed judges. He paid judges money to forget their duty to their community. Aurora asked me to check. I read his mind and the mind of a judge, and I am a witness. And Aurora checked and agreed. He did it on purpose. So," her pause let them all focus on what she'd just told them, "so he is a corruption upon this earth. He and his servants?" She lapsed into the near-archaic Sarnathi formula she knew by heart. "They are a corruption upon the earth; they are to be removed, cut out from the body politic, excised from the span of creation."

"You sure, Eclipse?" Cloud challenged. He'd heard of corruption of the earth, people who warped governments so they didn't do their job. He knew what to do about those people—learning how to tie that knot was something you did to pass sixth grade—but he'd never seen done, even on video.

"Sure I'm sure." She sounded absolutely confident. "Besides, there aren't personae any more. We have to do what's right. We have to figure out what's right when we're the only personae in the world. Locals mostly let smugglers shoot each other. If bystanders don't get hurt when we shoot up the smugglers, locals don't care."

"Full action, gloves on," Cloud said.

"Really frigid!" Star agreed. He hadn't done a full action since Emperor Roxbury.

"Kill them all?" a dubious Aurora asked. "Must we? All couple hundred of them?"

"Nab the fellow in charge," Cloud said. "If his people escape, so what? The guards, they do it for money. Warehouses and money are fair game."

"They truly are bad people," Aurora said. "And I checked the judges. Eclipse is right. Besides, the accountant had opinions about those medicines and people's minds. He didn't know that we know, there being no telepaths here, and his ideas were pretty weird, but he had an opinion. He thinks those medicines fry the brain. He was paying people, people who write magazines, people who do video and music, and putting thoughts in their heads. They'd write stuff to make his medicines sound interesting. And harmless. And fun. So more people would try them. He thought it was funny."

Comet spread her hands. Eclipse and Aurora thought these people were wicked. They'd have to be almost bad as Lemurians, before you could make a full action against them, but bribing a judge? That was really incredibly revolting, something even a Lemurian wouldn't do.

"I've got a plan," Cloud announced. "Eclipse, be high cover? Keep planes from leaving? Shoot up stuff on the ground? Aurora, stay off in the distance, read minds, give us a wall if Star or me needs one? Star and I land at one end and walk through, shooting everything up. Comet? The gravel trick you mentioned? Will you do that? Wreck buildings, burn the medicines, salvage the money, send the chief crook and his accountant to the Federal District. OK?" The foursome noted refinements to his plan. "Have to do this tomorrow. We want it to be night there."

~~~~~

"I had an idea," Star announced. "Mayhaps it's wrong, but it's an idea." He paused, the crackle of the fire and hiss of the night surf punctuating the silence, to nibble at his marshmallow. Comet had found this deserted island, he thought, which was even for sale. One way or another they would move here.

"You aren't really going to tell them that one, are you?" Cloud prodded. " 'Silly' is too nice for it."

"Hey! It's an idea!" Star snapped. "It's more than you've got."

"Let him talk," Comet said. If Cloud thought it was a bad idea, there might be some sense to it. "Sometimes you can polish an almost idea into a good one." She returned Cloud's glare.

"Sure," Cloud said. "Why not?" After all, he decided, if Star put his foot in his mouth as hard as he was about to, he wouldn't be able to challenge for leadership of their League. His sisters obviously couldn't challenge because they were girls, and Star's foot in his own mouth would keep him from challenging The Great Cloud for a long time.

"Anyway," Star said. "It's got to do with time travel." Aurora put another marshmallow onto her stick, pointedly not interested in still one more time travel discussion. "Instead of people changing the past. Perhaps they changed our trip. So we left, and now we've come back, except it's thousands of years ago. We can't find Sarnath or Atlantis or AutumnLost because they haven't happened yet. All those places that spoke English, they learned it from, wherever here is. What Alex said about languages having families is right. America, his America, this is the original place from where people spoke English. The place everyone else copied."

"But Alex's history has ancient countries," Aurora countered. "Egypt. Rome. If this was three thousand years ago, Egypt and Rome would be now, not three thousand years back." Star's newest suggestion, she decided, seemed to have gaps.

"But all that history stuff is a fake," Cloud supplied. He agreed with Aurora: Star's suggestion was really incredibly dumb, but he wasn't going to let Aurora pick another boy's ideas apart, not so long as he could pretend to find holes in her argument. She still wouldn't believe Star's idea, which was fine, but he'd have proved he was smarter than

Star and Aurora put together. "We read that those places were three thousand years ago. Suppose they were six thousand years ago. Then we're three thousand years ago, and Rome and Egypt are still three thousand years in the past."

"Is this the past?" Eclipse asked. "When we went to Mars, it was in the same place as last week. The Moon is the same phase, almost. Well, except it no longer has a dark side. But planets move. A year ago, Mars was way across the sky. If all the planets are where they belong, this is now, not a long time ago."

Comet soared into the heavens, vanishing for several minutes, and returned. "You're right, Eclipse," she announced. "I looked over the horizon. There was Pluto and Charon, right where they were a week back, almost. The star in the Unicorn's horn that's a triple star? All those stars are right where they were last week. Either it's now, or it's so long ago that all those planets and stars got back to the same place again, which is very hard, 'cause they all take different times to run in circles."

"Suppose someone left us at now and moved the Earth three thousand years futureward," Eclipse proposed. "We'd be in the past, according to someone on the Earth we came from, but we stayed in the present, and he'd be in the future. Moving the Earth forwards is time travel to the future, which supposed takes a lot less power than time travel to the past."

"Huh? Of course!" Star sounded enthusiastic.

"Moved the Earth?" Cloud asked.

Aurora looked puzzled. Then her face lit up. "She means someone left us in the present," she repeated. "They grabbed the whole Earth. They moved its complete time line three thousand years to the future. Think of a time line on a wall chart at school, Rome and King George's Armada and the Summer War and Now in order left to right. Next to the timeline is a cutout that's you, next to Now. You and the timeline are tacked to the corkboard. Regular time travel is picking up the cutout that's you. You take it off the corkboard and put it down on the board where Rome is. You time travelled. History stays put and you move." Cloud nodded understandingly.

"Moving the earth is leaving you on the corkboard, pulling the time line off the corkboard, and putting it down on the corkboard again. With Rome now next to you this year and the Summer War 2000 years in the future out at 4000 A.D. You didn't move. You're still in this year. The planets didn't move. They're all in this year. But the timeline and Planet Earth moved, so the Summer War was moved to 4000 A.D., not 1908 A.D. Now do see, Cloud?" Aurora asked.

The older boy nodded. Eclipse's idea was so strange. He couldn't say the idea was wrong, not and appear to defend Star, but her idea was so strange. A time machine was something you got into, and it flew you through time like an airship flew you around the world. Now she proposed a machine that left you alone and moved the world around you.

"That sounds like the Astonishing Displacer," Cloud said, "the mythical Astonishing Displacer, whose sole gift was to teleport the whole universe by ten feet while leaving himself in place. But can you move a planet in time, Eclipse?" Cloud asked. "Let alone a time line?"

"Time travel? A time line? I can't," Eclipse stammered. "I can't even time travel me." That's a slight exaggeration, she thought. If I drop to the bottom of the Well of Infinity, tread the square circle, and am very careful not to disturb things too much, I should be able to do it. Once. And mayhaps even be alive afterward.

"They could speak English three thousand years ago," Comet said. "But Sarnathi cities were places like Kilantroarpejio and Radicciobellieau. Besides, I mean, I went home and our house looked just like it did before we left except mayhaps the paint was different and the wrong people lived there. If this was three thousand years ago even if they spoke English they'd have different-type houses, like Sarnath traders always put their homes above where they worked. If the houses were the same at home and now and we were in the past it'd be us before the change living in houses copied from places three thousand years ago, and no one I know copied a house from Sarnath or anyplace like that."

"Oh, right," Star said. "Someone want another marshmallow? Chocolate-filled?"

"Star?" Eclipse waited until the others' attentions were distracted with juggling too-hot marshmallows stuffed with slabs of half-melted chocolate. "It was a good piece of an idea. Honest! It's better than mine." Star shifted uncomfortably. Eclipse always talked to you the same way, saying good things about you if you had a good idea, no matter who you were, as though she didn't care if she were speaking to a boy or to another girl.

"I had another idea, but it was even dopier," Star apologized. "What if the Tunnels don't just take you to anyplace in the universe, but someplace else? What if takes you to some other universe, someplace where all those countries we can't find never existed." He looked away shyly. That really was a dumb suggestion. The universe was everywhere that existed, wasn't it? You could look that up in the dictionary. He had. He'd even asked Alex Pickering, who was a real scientist. How could there be someplace else, Alex had asked? Especially someplace that was almost a perfect copy of Earth? Aurora had listened, when he'd tried to explain, and she'd almost made the wisecrack about boys straining their one brain cell whenever they remembered how to breathe. Usually she'd never say anything like that, not to her own brother, anyhow.

Eclipse sat there thinking. It was a fiercely alien idea. Finally she spread her hands. "How can we tell?" she asked. "Changing the past, or going someplace where the past is different?"

"But the dictionary says the universe is everything. There can't be an elsewhere. I checked a big dictionary after I heard Star," Aurora said primly. "The dictionary proves it."

"Can you trust a dictionary?" Cloud asked. "It might be wrong. About universes, I mean. They don't do space travel here."

"It might have been written by a woman," Eclipse noted.

"See!" said Cloud. "Even Eclipse agrees it might be wrong."

Comet raised her eyebrows. Written by a woman? That meant it was wrong? That was a boy's argument! Why had Eclipse said that? Whose side was she on? "Well, of course a dictionary would be written by a woman," Comet said, "because it has to have all the details right, so of course it was written by a woman, because men can't get details right. That's why Daddy's pre-docents are almost all," Comet choked on remembering where they were not, and who was no longer her father, "women."

"Or perhaps by a computer," Eclipse added.

"See," Aurora said, "Only a boy would believe something because a computer said it."

"Of course it's right! They used a computer!" Cloud shouted. "That's why the League and Congress and every country in the world uses computers, and appeals to High Programmers and Analysts Supreme, because computers are fair and don't get mad and you can trust them to tell you what's good or bad!"

"This argument's getting really stupid," Star said. "The universe doesn't care what someone wrote in a book here on earth."

"You're right, Star," Aurora agreed. "And I should have kept out of it. I apologize."

"Happily accepted," Star answered. "Besides, at first I thought it was a good reason, too."

"That's what Eclipse said!" Cloud swallowed the rest of his words. What had Eclipse said? If someone other than Eclipse said something was written by a girl, you'd know it was another girl saying it was good, or a boy saying it was bad. If someone else said a computer said it, that was a boy or a grownup saying it was right, or a girl saying it was wrong. But with Eclipse, you couldn't tell. She sounded as if she didn't care whether a boy or girl had said something. She sounded as if she only cared if something were true, not who said it. That was so strange.

"No," Star said, "And I keep meaning to say this, and don't. We keep having these stupid arguments, about whether something's right or wrong because a girl said it. Or a boy said it. Before we left, that made perfect sense. Now, I remember some of those arguments. And they don't make any sense at all. How can words stop making sense? And the other thing," he continued, "I didn't say enough. Comet, I really truly apologize. When Dad and Mom started dumping on you, and grounded you, I should have told Dad: If you ground her, you have to tell her why. You didn't. None of us understood. A parent needs to make sense. But before we left, Dad said you were grounded, so I agreed, automatically, like a clockwork marionette. And before that, I should have done my share of the housework."

"And I believed Mom and Dad," Aurora added, "when they said I didn't need a sleeping bag, which was totally stupid of me."

"Aurora," Cloud said, "Half the good stuff I packed, I only packed because Dad told me to. So don't feel bad about believing your parents."

Aurora smiled at him. "But now it makes no sense. And Star told me this earlier, so I thought 'mayhaps we're being mind controlled now, subtle control, so we don't automatically believe our parents.' But I can't find anything. It's like there's a quiet in the sky, where I should be hearing something."

"Those are the dreams I told you about, Aurora," Eclipse inserted. "And it's 'something is missing and I can't find it, and I can't figure out what it is.'"

"What?" Comet asked.

"I can't check until we fix the world," Eclipse said. "It's like 'before we left, someone was doing mind control very subtle on everyone, so you believed your dads and moms, automatically. And made boys and girls think the other side was full of idiots."

"Eclipse," Cloud said, "find the dooms first. Fix the world. Then you can track down the mind controllers." Eclipse gave him a firm thumb's up. "I'm one hundred percent available to help, if that's what was going on. And you're right, Aurora, I can remember Dad and Mom telling me things, and I did them automatically, not thinking. And saying things about girls, that includes the three of you, and now that I remember them, what I said was really dumb."

"Ditto me," Comet said.

"But not you, Eclipse," Star said, "at least not often. Not ever that I remember. That's why I kept getting confused; you only cared about if something was right, not if a boy or a girl said it."

"Oh!" Eclipse added, "If we're in another universe, if the past's just different because it happened that way, then there's no one who changed the past. It just happened that way, all by itself. If no one changed the past, I can't find him. He's not there."

"Unless we do like the Czar's Internal Security," Star joked, "and prove someone was guilty, no matter if the crime was committed or not."

"Wait a moment," Cloud asked. "Didn't we know there's cross-time? Places you can go, but you can't fly to because they're not connected to here and now?"

"Cross-time is an expression," Comet said. "My geometry book says so. Cross-time is directions different than x or y or z or t or u or v. If you go to cross-time places, they're really weird, so laws of nature aren't the same, like in a privileged band attack."

"Comet is right," Eclipse announced. "There are places where a day there is a second here, places where the privileged bands are different. It's not a privileged attack, but if your atoms decide they're little cubes, you still die. That purple place you gate to is safe cross-time, I think."

"Oh, yeah?" Star said. "Why do you think that?"

"I've been there," she announced. "Places where time is different, places where nothing is the same. My," memories rose to her consciousness, rising from the deep of her under mind like the dorsal fin of a hungry shark, "I had friends take me there. Excuse me." She walked away from the fire, jaw set, back rigidly straight.

"What's with her?" Cloud whispered.

"She's about to not cry," Comet whispered back. "Her parents. They must've been who took her cross-time. The only time she gets about to cry, all at once, is when she remembers them, and if you say a word, so help me, I'll..." Comet stopped, seeing the stricken look in Cloud's eyes when he remembered his own father.

CHAPTER 31 WAGING PEACE THROUGH OVERWHELMING FIREPOWER

The waters of the Caribbean lapped gently across a shell-strewn beach. The sky was dark. The two guards covering the end of the runway dutifully scanned waves and sand, alert for unexpected visitors. Their faces were masked by night-vision goggles. Automatic rifles were at the ready. Their post appeared to be a circular wall surrounding a picnic table and umbrella. Close inspection would have revealed that the umbrella was an inch of steel, the table lacked chairs, and the artistic holes in the wall were firing ports. Sheltered by the parapet, a glimmer of lights was an LED display reporting seismic and motion detectors, all quiescent in the evening stillness.

These was a wonderful hire, the senior mercenary noted: You got to pull guard duty at incredible pay. Of course, he knew where the money had to be coming from, given an all-weather airport used almost exclusively at night, private stealth submarines that only docked after dark, and an interesting set of bunkers that he made a point of not noticing. He'd asked no questions and been told no lies. Living quarters were excellent; recreational facilities were superb. The boss ordered him to go sailing three times a week, hours picked so he would meet tourists on neighboring islands. He'd been told what tales to tell, tales obviously calculated to lull local curiosity. He'd neglected to mention to his employers about one particular tourist—more a long-time resident enjoying the benefits of the local concept of tax-free government—he'd met. Melissa was a private matter.

A flicker of amber and scarlet passed across an LED panel. Motion detectors responded to something two hundred yards from the position, well inland from the shore. The guards peered into the darkness, their goggles repainting the night in eerie shades of green. A patch of fog masked their line of sight. All quiet, noted the senior, except that he had scanned that area, not one minute ago, and no fog had been present.

"Center," he whispered into a tablet microphone, "Post nine. Delta three: motion and seismic. Fog or smoke—wasn't there one minute ago."

"Copied, post nine," Center answered. "Hold your station. Patrol Two to investigate." A brief pause. "Y'all watch your rear, hear?" was the friendly encouragement of the Officer of the Watch. The guards waited the minutes, nervously switching between covering their perimeter and eyeing the patch of fog as it drew closer to their position. LEDs flickered softly, the area of active seismic activity moving in unison with the fog patch.

"Center?" the guard called. "Post Nine here. Patrol Two? Where?"

"Should have been on the fog patch, a couple minutes ago." The guards peered up the runway. The guard touched finger to lips, felt the air, suddenly recognizing the obvious. The patch of fog now almost on his position was moving into a steady breeze. "Center, Center! The fog. It's moving upwind." Mechanical clinks were rounds being chambered.

"Center copies, post nine." At Center, the Officer of the Watch discovered he had lost touch both with Patrol Two and with the observation post nearest to the patrol's last-reported position. With only the slightest hesitation, his finger lifted a safety cover and threw the switch beneath.

At the watch post, the guards dropped to prone positions, weapons poking from firing ports. The patch of fog was now seaward of them, in a direction into which they could safely fire. The gentlest mechanical rasps marked two shot selectors switching from safe to full automatic.

"Halt and identify yourself!" the senior guard called. In the back of his mind, he noted that he was still following SOP from his former, more conventional but less munificent, employer. Silence came from the darkness. Wisps of fog began to flow over the parapet. "Halt or I will open fire!" The wisps became a torrent, air thickening until the guards could scarcely see each other.

The junior guard panicked and began shooting. Silencers dampened the sharp crack of firing. With no visible target, he hosed the darkness, tracer rounds fading almost instantly into the cloudy opacity.

"Center, Center. Post Nine! Fog is totally opaque. Can't see ten meters." The junior guard, first magazine exhausted, suddenly realized that smoke might hide tear gas or some less gentle agent. He doffed his helmet and donned a gas mask. As he did, the senior guard opened fire. Another thirty rounds sailed into the darkness.

The guards realized that they heard people talking, not far in front of them. "I think that counts as trying to kill me," one said, voice a girlish soprano.

"Yeah," the other answered, "those were real bullets. I felt them sting."

"Ahoy!" a voice called. "Drop your guns! Come out. You have to ten to quit and run away. One. Two. Three." The guards opened fire again. Surely some of their rounds were reaching the voices? "Ten." The fog suddenly flowed to one side, revealing a figure clothed in glowing sun-yellow.

"Who are you?" the junior guard cried, leaping to his feet to stare over the parapet. "What are you?"

"Center, Center, Post Nine. Visitor is, is,"—What was it? the senior guard asked himself—"a burning man. Covered with yellow flame."

The guards' snapshots were returned by a glowing beam of gold set at waist-height. The beam went off to their right. It pivoted side-to-side, an immense broadsword swung by the burning figure. The parapet's reinforced concrete dissolved in a flare of sparks. "Center, heavy weapons attack. Bunker being destroyed!"

The more senior guard had already vaulted the parapet to drop into his foxhole. Management had maintained that reinforced concrete was more than enough, but made no protest when his shovel improved on their work, creating a narrow but deep slit in the adjoining sand. Further combat was obviously pointless. The younger guard continued to fire, weapon at full automatic, tracers confirming that his aim was true. Suddenly there was quiet.

The senior guard lay flat, eyes closed, while the light passed over his position. He concentrated on playing dead. Very dead. Two pairs of footsteps passed his position and faded toward the main complex. He could hear their voices. They seemed to be discussing baseball, but the teams were...wrong. The guard remembered that his sailboat was anchored in the south lagoon, with a certain young lady on board, waiting for him to finish his week's sentry rotation this midnight. A decade of increasingly generous paychecks, seemingly from a perfectly legitimate party, had passed through his Cayman Islands bank into a series of stock funds. If he lived another ten minutes, now was very definitely the time for early retirement. Providing security against human beings, even his former employer, was one thing. Providing security against things that crept from fog like escapees from a late-night horror flick, things that shredded ten inches of concrete and steel like so much tissue paper, was someone else's MOS. He wasn't being paid that much. He almost stood to flee before remembering that soon the fog creatures would reach Post Eight, at which time the air above his head would be filled with masses of fast-moving, if ineffective, lead.

Center noted that Post Nine had encountered something violently destructive. Contact with Post Nine had been lost. Its last words were obscure. A burning man? Something was destroying motion detectors, too, cutting a swath of silence across his electronic net. He lifted two additional switch covers, pressed two additional buttons. Alarms sounded across the island. The airport's excellent approach and ground radar system ramped up power and scan rate. A trample of feet and gasps for breath were Center's command staff entering at a flat run. Center glanced at his pocket watch. From the first alarm, their time to reach their posts had been truly excellent. He'd have to remember to commend them afterward.

Across the room, Center's silent counterpart from the foreign shareholders stared at a television monitor. The counterpart wore camouflage suit and combat boots. A stylized gold-brown cloth sunburst on one collar tab was the only mark of his loyalty. He began whispering into his throat microphone—another gift of the foreign shareholders— giving a description of events to third parties.

The intruders were out in the open, advancing along the main landing strip. Center cut on the landing lights. Television showed a patch of fog, moving faster than a man would walk. Lightning dropped from the clear night sky, bolt after brilliant bolt, striking at lamp towers, shattering searchlight bulbs and sending towers crashing to earth. Yellow-white lines of light, like tracer rounds packed so close that each could not be distinguished from the next, sliced into concrete to section the runway. Moments after each sectioning an explosive bang shattered concrete, so broken runway sections lay stacked askew.

"Radar clear," Center's electronic warfare expert, a middle-aged woman whose hard face and black hair matched her flat black jumpsuit, began. She turned to the on-duty radar operator, who had shifted to the support console. "James? Our navy friends doing anything?"

"No, ma'am. Same racetrack course as ever. Signal burst after I ramped up the radar." On an auxiliary screen, the radar operator flagged a U.S. Navy frigate sailing a few miles southeast of St. Dominick.

"No, kill that, stationary target directly over the tarmac at 1800 meters." The EW expert had the slightest London accent to her alto voice. "No other targets, no new radar sources, no radio on military or other bands, only our navy friends and a few sailboats across the channel."

"Above? Where?" the foreign shareholder's representative whispered. He made passes over a second console. "I have visual lock and laser scan," he announced. "Why did alarms not sound? Why did they not trigger on its approach?"

The specialist examined her displays. The optical image looked like a grain of rice dyed the color of a good sapphire. The laser scan reported a target a meter and a half tall, no more than a half-meter across. "Size," she announced. "Size. That thing's smaller than a gooney bird. And not moving. Radar shows no doppler reflection from drone props. AI filtered it out. That's a program feature. You don't want an alert for every bird that overflies us. We get alarms for something small as an ultralight, not smaller and stationary, or we'd be living here."

"But this is not a bird," the foreign shareholder's representative hissed.

"So what is it? A kite? A tethered balloon?" The representative's manners grated on the specialist's nerves. The target matched poorly anything in her very extensive experience. "The ground fog," she observed, "I'm getting radar reflections—that stuff's full of metal. Can't penetrate it with this gear."

"Show me?" the shareholder's representative asked.

Center ignored the discussion, focusing his attention on his defenses. Patrols one and three were converging on the cloud. His mercenaries were racing for positions around the hangars and storage areas. The battle management specialists in the bunker tracked their advances, keying fixed-point automatic defenses to the mercenaries' motions. The island was a fortress. Two decades of careful engineering, weapons imported through a dozen illicit channels, and the generosity of the foreign shareholders gave security, even if no defenders did anything above ground. The battle managers had the specialist task of coordinating automatic devices and human actions.

Center didn't feel himself above taking risk. To command men, there was no substitute for leadership from the front. He knew he wasn't good at it. He'd hired the best he could find to provide that leadership outside, leadership he wished he could provide.

On the surface, skeleton positions were always manned. Outside parties attempting a helicopter assault would get a very hot reception. Center reached for a dialless telephone, its handset boldly labelled "Owner". It was time to advise his one superior of the situation.

"Target! Target! Aircraft azimuth one zero zero range two zero miles, altitude three hundred meters. No incoming scheduled until 0200 hours." Electronic warfare tapped fingers across her console. "Closing— Lookitthat!—two thousand knots. Accelerating. Two three zero zero knots. Arming SAM. Am I cleared?" Her harsh half-question brought Center's attention back from the phone. "Center! Impact trajectory! I have an impact point. Central complex! Impact in twenty-four seconds." Her finger stabbed at the monitor.

Center raised one hand. He gave himself three seconds for thought. It was night, almost midnight. Whatever was happening was unconventional, unexpected, but had to be an attack. Something had killed two guards at Post Nine. Something was demolishing a runway thick enough for large four-engine aircraft. The incoming was highly likely to be hostile. To the further islands the ground-to-air systems would appear to be a harmless fireworks display. He nodded.

"Locked. Firing one, two, three. One through three fired. Reloading. Dispersed phased-array coming up." The specialist smiled. Her main radar system was half-a-thousand small antennae spread across the island, waveguides deep-buried, dispersal of antenna sections making the system immune to conventional anti-radar missiles.

"Three?" the foreign shareholder's rep questioned. "Expensive."

"Pushing the intercept envelope. Mayhaps we score a hit. Incoming at three thousand knots." Labelled points of light floated across the radar screen. The specialist praised her private gods for advances in AI technology. A decade ago, her system would have demanded a team of specialists to run; now one person—and some first-rate maintenance techs! she noted—did everything.

"Observed acceleration is not possible," the rep whispered. "Speed is not possible."

"Cruise missile," the specialist suggested. "Ukraine model. Solid fuel booster for impact phase. More gees than I expected. Didn't know they were deployed." Points of light closed on each other. The incoming target jinked sideways, turning inside three top-of-the-line surface-to-air missiles. Ranging indicators on the missiles noted that their target was receding and detonated their warheads, sending circles of metal links ineffectively into the air.

"Navy friends increasing illumination. No sign they are firing! Point defense antiaircraft now engaging!" The specialist reset a dial, fixing the engagement distance to its maximum. The speed was outside the specifications for the aiming hardware. Getting hits would require luck, even against something with several square meters of radar cross-section. Seeming air conditioner units on warehouse roofs shed camouflage panels, revealing multiple autocannon underneath. The foreign shareholders had made real contributions to the equipment here. The target dipped to sea level, three dozen autocannon tracking and firing as the target came in-range. The specialist noted that if the visitors had been the anticipated fifty military helicopters, rather than three-and-a-heaven-help-us-half thousand knots of surface-to-surface missile, very soon the visitors would have been conditionally available for use as dog food.

Events of the next two seconds came so quickly that only in retrospect did Center understand what had happened. The flying target dropped to sea level and zoomed along the runway. A mile out it jinked up, banked down, and disgorged—something. A shotgun burst of incandescent points of light spread from the intruder, travelling almost parallel to the ground while spreading laterally. Autocannon continued firing. No hits were apparent. The target made an incredibly sharp zoom climb and retreated zenithward, autocannon futilely tracking a target fleeing faster than their muzzle velocity.

Outside microphones near the complex reported an enormous clatter, the father of all hailstorms battering at every tin roof in the Caribbean. To judge from status monitors, a remarkably large portion of the exposed gear in the complex area—detectors, monitors, radar, lights, autocannon—had just gone non-functional. Performance of the phased array was noticeably degraded. In the same moment radio channels went quiet. Center had been listening to squad and fire team leaders transmit orders to their men's helmet radios. Now nothing was heard. Battle managers scrambled to re-establish contact with ground forces.

"Target receding at four thousand knots and accelerating. Straight up," the EW specialist announced. "No, repeat zero, anomalous EM: no radar or radio except navy target."

Center spoke into the telephone. The situation was not developing according to plan.

"The stationary target," the foreign shareholder's representative's voice rasped, "destroy it!"

Electronic warfare stared. The rep was an advisor, not someone to be giving her orders. However, it was a reasonable request, all things considered. "Reloads on line." Cursor locked onto target. "You springing for one missile, or two?" He'd complained about price before. Let him take the decision this time. He held up three fingers. She set all three systems to 'ARM'. "Recorded, you're paying. Firing one," she announced. "Firing two. Firing three."

Trails of flame sprang upwards from the island. Radar showed the fast target had rolled over and was receding eastwards, far faster than any weapon could pursue. Radar screens reported the stationary target and three rapidly-closing missiles. A remote telescope, a detector system lifted from American fighter aircraft, tracked the missiles, so the specialist saw exhaust flames closing, then a sudden disc of luminous smoke marking impact. "Hit," she announced. "Second apparent hit. Third apparent hit." Smoke and fragments of missile masked the target's location. There was no sign of a burning aircraft plummeting to earth.

The battle managers began reassessing their assets. Something had devastated the main complex. Three aircraft parked near the warehouses had blown up. One hangar, its broadside to the attack, had collapsed. Warehouses reported fires and loss of pressure in sprinklers and refrigeration systems. Men in the open, save a few sheltered by very solid walls, were off the radio net, dead or badly wounded. The mortar team leader, his position well emplaced and heavily camouflaged, reported that the camouflage and top half foot of his berm were gone. Lower down, the exposed face of the position's berm was badly eroded. Mortar team leader had recovered pieces of red-hot gravel from the walls of his position. Automatic mortars, those still below the surface, remained available.

"The mobile attacker?" the representative asked.

"Receding east," the specialist replied. Her voice remained perfectly calm. "Trajectory analysis coming up. The zoom climb, that turn was one hundred thirty, repeat one three zero, gravities."

"Impossible," the representative answered. "It must be ECM. We're being spoofed by some electronic illusion."

"Awful lot of property damage for ECM," the specialist noted blandly. The representative looked at the ceiling, then nodded his agreement.

The fog patch crept along the ground. Center saw that Patrols One and Three had engaged with 12.7mm machine guns. Other sentries were using their individual weapons. No particular effect was apparent. One battle manager tied the mortar team to the best-placed observer. HE and white phosphorous rounds began sailing towards the unknown. The second battle manager gestured to the specialist. Three of the still-working autocannons redirected muzzles groundward and started sweeping bursts across the shallow bank of fog.

"We'll have IR and UV on target in a few moments," the EW Expert said. It might be good military smoke, but it couldn't be opaque on every band, not without blinding whoever was inside. The first phosphorous rounds exploded, the cloud glowing like lightning within a distant thunderhead. The representative and the electronic warfare specialist compared notes. In the sky above, the stationary target had reappeared, seemingly unmoved by three near-direct hits. Electronic defenses, the representative proposed, had detonated surface-to-air missiles well short of their target. The specialist disagreed; the telescope with side perspective showed hits. Telemetry was inconclusive. The foreign shareholders had supplied missiles equipped with contact detonators. The specialist reprogrammed the next trio of missiles, disengaging proximity fusing. Against a stationary target at this range, design specs indicated that true impact detonation was attainable. Another trio of surface-to-air missiles left their launchers. The telescopic scan, displaced well sideways from the airfield, remained locked on the target. From its angle, contact or non-contact would be readily apparent.

Two missiles clearly struck their target. The third rolled and plunged earthwards. To Center's dismay, rollover failsafes failed to detonate the warhead. The missile continued earthward at full thrust until it struck Owner's cabana, reducing his helicopter to flaming wreckage. The foreign shareholder's representative, uncharacteristically droll, spoke softly. "Scratch my bonus this quarter," he remarked.

Outside, the patch of fog swerved away from the phosphorous, leaving on the tarmac a single figure. Center recognized the burning man of Post Nine's anguished call. Tracer rounds closed on it from all directions. The figure responded with streamers of flame, striking first at patrol vehicles and then at individual firing positions. Each jeep exploded in a bang, followed instants later by a billowing fireball as vaporized gasoline caught fire. A pair of guards engaged the burning man with hand-held antitank rockets, failing to hit a very difficult target.

The second battle manager continued his survey of rear areas. Passive acoustic arrays bordering the island showed no unusual activity in the surrounding waters. Motion detectors, those away from the explosions, remained static. Monitoring of radio bands found the Navy frigate, clearly broadcasting in response to changes on Saint Dominick, but no other increase in traffic, indeed, no traffic at all from the direction of the invaders. The island's fire service had deployed to the Owner's cabana. The helicopter's remains were being extinguished.

The first manager found that patrol vehicles carrying designators were out of action. Someone had reached the runway with a laser designator and the nerve to point it at the mystery target. The designator acquired the burning man. The battle manager marked a trail with a light pen. Whoever it was, the burning man had good bulletproof armor. No body armor, the battle manager told himself, competes with a properly designed antitank round. A mile away, hatches popped from well-camouflaged buildings. A distant boom marked the cold pressure-launch of a heavy anti-tank rocket, motor igniting after it safely cleared the rails. The rocket sailed a few tens of meters above the ground, climbed to acquire the designator beam, and hurtled into the burning man.

To Center's dismay, the explosion dropped the burning man to his knees, but failed to destroy him. Even hunched over, the burning man managed another volley of attacks at the nearer quonset huts, which slumped into rubble. What was he armed with? wondered Center. That was a human figure, Center told himself, so the weapon had to be man-portable. Or did it? Vague references to experiments with power-assisted armor came to mind.

"Anti-tank! Volley fire," Center ordered. "I don't want you to hurt him, I want you to kill him. Daid! You hear me, girls? Daid!" Battle managers managed not to wince at the sudden reappearance of Center's deep Texas accent, something he only voiced under extreme stress. Another half-dozen antitank rockets, followed for good measure by a pair of surface-to-surface antiship missiles, were readied for launch.

Center took a few moments to review his position. He was under attack by complete unknowns. Despite commitment of reserves, he hadn't scored one clear kill. Perhaps he had the burning man now, but that left him with the fog bank, the lightning from a clear sky, the impossibly fast flying object, and the stationary flying object, which at least hadn't shot back. Yet. He ordered automatic mortars to engage the fog bank to keep it on the move.

Secret weapons, he concluded. Those had to be secret weapons. The fast flying object was the Aurora reconnaissance plane he'd read about, operating at a slightly lower altitude than previously reported. It had to be remotely piloted, notwithstanding popular report. No human being could survive the turn it had just made. The lightning was a particle beam weapon. Only one country in the world had secret weapons like this, no matter that their warship floating right off-shore was not participating in the attack. Perhaps no one had told them about the impending battle. He'd seen worse communications failures with previous employers. Center picked up the telephone. It was time to speak to Owner again.

The second battle manager reported another alarming trend. Across the island, watch post after watch post was falling silent. Local sections of the electronic security net were going down. He'd managed to get technicians to one site. Guards were stone cold unconscious. Circuits were systematically burned out, with wires melted, circuit boards charred, and holes blown in integrated circuits. Someone had sabotaged the regular phone and power systems. Only security's optic fiber network was working. Across the island, backup generators and batteries gave power and light.

"Center, that plane is incoming again," the electronic warfare specialist announced. "My active jammers are maxed out, Hertz to millimeter region. I can't find anything to jam. It's like those guys out there never heard of radio."

The foreign shareholder's representative brought a suggested set of detonation specs up on the specialist's console. "At three thousand knots," he remarked, "it can have any armor it wants. We put enough metal in its path, and it falls out of the sky." He stared again at the stationary aircraft, which had ignored everything they'd thrown at it. He told himself holograms couldn't give laser reflections. The stationary aircraft had to be a solid object. But what was solid, less than two meters across, flew, and ignored direct SAM hits?

The first battle manager launched antitank rockets. He'd concentrated autocannon fire on the visible target, not with apparent success, then switched autocannon to the hovering target. There he was at least scoring obvious hits, even if they didn't appear to be doing anything. Missiles reached the burning man. Multiple explosions raked the tarmac. Shaped charges and copper-core penetrators were brilliant green stilettoes; the two-ton HDX warheads of the antiship missiles made substantial craters. The burning man was blown head over heels, landing tens of yards away. His flames guttered, as if on the verge of going out. Battle manager shouted orders across the radio net. "All units! Final protective fire! Runway tarmac sector dog mike three three." Automatic rifles, machine guns, mortar fire, grenade launchers, hand-held anti-tank weapons, automatic cannon, and another volley of anti-tank rockets came into play. He noted to his dismay that the guards were rapidly being depleted by lightning strikes. He was pleased to note that the autonomous security units, the crews inside the protected vaults over which he had only negative authority, were not only active but cooperating with his orders.

Something that to Center resembled a giant black fishnet appeared over the burning man, something that deflected rifle fire and detonated missiles before they reached their targets. Each missile hit reached closer to the man than the last, but none reached the target. Now the stationary aircraft opened fire on ground positions, dropping air-to-surface missiles of unconventional design—spinning discs like incandescent frisbies— into firing positions. The mortar crew was wiped out, ammunition detonated. Automatic mortars ceased to respond. Active missile launching silos exploded, anti-tank missiles being rolled onto launch rails detonating when hits exploded inside their silos. Fire team positions erupted in flame. Something from the stationary aircraft, something vaguely resembling an A-10's strafing attack, began destroying autocannon and punching holes in warehouse roofs. The fog bank rolled back to cover the burning man. Missiles exploded in mid-air, wove drunkenly out of control, or crashed.

The fog bank moved back to the water, leaving empty tarmac in its wake. The burning man was gone. The surviving guards engaged the fog bank. The battle managers reported that they were losing guards, those with more initiative, to desertion. The less serious problem was men who dropped their weapons and fled. The more serious problem was men who kept their weapons and shot NCOs who tried to stop them. Center consoled himself with the observation that the fragmenting squads appeared to have taken 50 percent casualties dead to incomprehensible causes before breaking up, a creditable achievement in any man's army.

The electronic warfare specialist fired another volley of missiles at the fast aircraft, watched the reload sequence begin, and lost all contact with her missile launchers. Surveillance cameras showed explosions at SAM launch sites. The stationary aircraft had struck again. The specialist wracked her brain, trying to recall references to air-to-surface missiles with sapphire exhaust flames. Her first missile volley, twenty miles out over the water as it closed on the fast target, detonated and spread clouds of shrapnel. The fast aircraft jinked and boosted toward the island. Her second missile volley was no more effective than her first, the incoming aircraft having meanwhile accelerated from three thousand up through four thousand knots.

The formerly stationary target was engaging two fast-moving aircraft. Where had they come from, she wondered? There hadn't been any inbound. Replay of the radar tape implied that they'd come off the ocean surface, from the deep water just to the west of Saint Dominick. The specialist realized that she not only couldn't tell who was winning, she didn't know who up there was fighting whom. The two fighter aircraft had to be American or British, no one else having fighters in possible range. Why were they engaging the obviously-American aircraft that had just bombed her positions? Worse, she couldn't recognize the weapons they were using. Missiles? Ball lightning? Apparently sourceless explosions?

She glanced back to her other screen. The fast aircraft was almost on top of them. "Aircraft incoming," she noted. She shifted to the general communications band. "This is Center! All defenses! Immediate deep cover! On my authority! Now!" She turned to face Center, who always said he encouraged that sort of initiative in a real emergency. She faced a wide-toothed grin, and two hands with upraised thumbs.

Center watched in horror while the reputedly unarmed spy plane swept north of the runway and released another cloud of tiny incandescent missiles. In its path, vehicles and buildings exploded. Trees crashed to earth. The facing side of the water tower detonated, a wall of water slumping groundward. The radio net fell to near-silence. Center began speaking to Owner again, telling Owner of the collapse of his defensive precautions under the attack of a foreign government. He didn't need to say which foreign government; there was really only one possibility. The implications for Owner were obvious. It was high time and then some for him to flee for his life.

The fog bank floated a few miles out to sea, paused there for half a minute, and returned to the south shore. Moments earlier, Center had had the cloud surrounded, gun and missile fire dropping into it from all directions. He'd failed to take it out. Now the cloud was outside his perimeter, destroying one position after the next, while he was unable to concentrate return fire. Battle managers noted the fog's location and began firing directional mines. Results were not apparent.

The battle continued in the air overhead, moving gradually to higher altitudes. Monitors lit up; night was transformed to day. The sound took moments to reach them, a series of explosions without obvious end.

The monitor saturated from a monstrous burst of actinic radiation. When all was clear again, the sky was empty. "No EMP," the EW specialist reported. "Strong X-Ray pulse. No gammas or neutrons. Two plasma clouds on radar. That has to be nuclear, doesn't it?"

"Actually limited for a fission explosion," the shareholder's representative mumbled. "The structure is not a conventional fireball." He gestured at a repeater.

"Someone got one, Ah see," Center drawled. The stationary aircraft had to be out of action. His further words were interrupted by a sudden shock that cracked two-foot-thick reinforced concrete walls, toppled computer consoles, and sent concrete dust steaming from the corners of the room.

"Circuit room one does not respond," the first battle manager observed. A second explosion came hot on the tracks of his words. "That's circuit room two." Almost all the consoles in the room went blank. "Switching to local control." He pressed a button. His console burst into flames, sparks leaping from every ventilation grill. The second battle manager grabbed for an extinguisher, turning his back to his own console just before it exploded. Sparks and burning debris flew across the room. Before the second battle manager completed his turn, lines of fire burned their way across the ceiling, etching tracks into the concrete wherever signal cables had run. Room lights flashed and shattered, to be replaced after a few moments by the glower of chemiluminescent emergency lamps.

"That's not a conventional systems failure," the EW specialist observed. "EMP from a high-altitude nuclear airburst would do that." She gestured at burning consoles. "Except you expect nuclear EMP to take out everything at once."

Nothing useful was left of the control facilities. Not, Center told himself, that much was left to control. Air attacks had destroyed his ranged weapons and mobile forces. The fogbank had destroyed the southern fortifications and occupants. Antiaircraft batteries around the warehouses were gone. The autonomous security units, safe behind feet of steel and concrete, were still in action, but simply didn't have the firepower to affect the outcome. House security was in place, but their heavy weapons support was gone. Owner and his personal bodyguards were conducting their strategic advance on previously prepared positions. It was now time for him to do the same.

Center looked at his crew. "Gentlemen," he said, "Ma'am? It's been a real pleasure working with you, all such quality folk. But we're out of business." He gestured at stilled television displays, inert keyboards, smoke creeping through the unframed blast doors. "We're out of contact, out of ammunition, out of reserves, and, unless you have something worth a truly Texas-size bonus, out of opportunities. The emergency exit is behind the snack dispenser, I believe?" Center was completely unsurprised that his crew spent the two kilometers of exit tunnel beginning a postmortem. He was entirely surprised when the foreign shareholder's representative, a man who previously had shown no indication of personal courage, strapped a pistol to his waist and indicated that he would lead the last stand of the autonomous security units.

~~~~~

Owner fled along a hidden path to his private beach. His run was the fastest sprint he could attain, a full breath taken mechanically with every pace. Two paces ahead and two paces behind ran his Japanese bodyguards, a gift of his Tokyo business associates, their speed effortlessly matching his own. The path was smooth paved, lined by small pin lights that flickered to life as he approached. Clever gardening had walled the trail with a profusion of tropical plants, the sweet scents of their flowers filling the air. If he had not been fleeing in abject terror, the stroll would have been a tropical eve's delight. Behind him, his carefully disguised helicopter and jet aircraft were piles of burning metal. Fortunately, he told himself, he had always allowed for unexpected contingencies, so the cigarette boat and submersible were still in place. The present circumstances remained inexplicable. He knew who in the American government accepted his retainers. He couldn't have been taken by surprise, not by the one country on earth that could deploy the weaponry used this evening.

"That's far enough. You can stop now." A boyish voice came from the trail before them. The point bodyguard screamed, launching into a forward sweeping kick which impacted crushingly on the figure's stomach and chest. Further screams were the bodyguard's. The figure had moved not at all. The bodyguard, braced for impact against a human target rather than unmoving stone, had broken both legs. While obviously taken by surprise, the figure had nonetheless grabbed the bodyguard's feet and was shaking him vigorously up and down by his broken ankles.

Owner stopped. His second bodyguard passed to the front. Owner considered a retreat to the last branching of the trail. While he did, a second figure, burning flame-white, appeared by the first. A third could now be seen in the second's illumination. All three were garishly dressed in clothing of brilliant colors, masks hiding faces and ears. Their dress did not hide their lack of height. These had to be dwarfs in front of him, noted Owner, no matter how bizarre their costumes.

"Yeah. You're all under arrest," the second figure announced self-importantly.

Owner reached for the .357 Magnum pistol in his coat. His bodyguard sent throwing stars whirling at the trio. A sky-blue-clad hand released an ankle and palm-slapped the first star earthwards. A further shuriken struck the yellow flames wrapping the second figure, eliciting a burst of pyrotechnics before falling, smoking, to earth. The third figure blurred, shoulders and butterfly mask dissolving into colored smoke, then reformed, a pair of shuriken clasped in delicate green-gold gloved hands. The bodyguard, pistol half drawn, peered into the space above the figures' heads. He shrieked in terror and fell unconscious. The owner was confident that he too had seen something there: a lidless eye whose merciless gaze had fortunately been directed elsewhere.

The owner levelled his pistol. "Arrest? For what?"

"Corruptification on this earth," the first figure answered. "Did I get that right, guys? Or is it 'corrupticification'?"

"Close enough," butterfly-mask agreed, "close enough for Federal Service."

"Federal? Oh, no. No way I surrender to a bunch of undersize escapees from a comic book!" Owner squeezed on the trigger, once and again, observing to his dismay that the two lead figures ignored his shots, while the third dissolved into a green fog through which bullets passed harmlessly. A sudden pressure on his neck, small hands coming from behind to clamp on his carotid arteries, dropped him unconscious.

"Frigid, Eclipse," Star said. "You practice that much?"

"Mom taught me," the older girl answered. "TK boost on pressure points helps. I can do it by brute strength. If I have to. I think. Probably. Comet? You and Cloud take him to Washington? I brought rope to tie him. We'll clean out the bunkers."

"He said 'comic books'," Star said. "That's the third time someone's said that to us."

"We should look them up," Cloud said, "whatever they are."

Manga, came Aurora's thoughts, Aurora remaining perched miles away on an offshore spire of rock. *Someone said it to me and I looked. They're like those silly Manjukuo picture books you boys read. The ones full with things getting broken.*

"They're not silly! They're great art. From a foreign country, even," Star said. "It's a three thousand year old classic art style. Besides, in them they don't break that many things, not like we did tonight."

"Three thousand years old? What about the ones you've been buying since we got here, Star?" Comet asked.

Cloud winced. What had Star been buying? Why hadn't Star mentioned? Aurora had other concerns. She knew all too clearly how much damage they'd done, how many people lay dead across St.

Dominick. They'd been involved in violence before, some events even more violent than this, but other times the other side had started things. This time, she'd gone along when they initiated a full action. It was on her say-so, she reminded herself. She and Eclipse had found those people bribing judges. They all deserved to die.

"So now we clean out those bunkers and salvage the money?" Star asked. "Frigid. We did real great!"

You did not! Aurora countered. *Brian Wells, you were almost killed! You just walked up in the open like you were a stupid boy who didn't know about cover! They shot you!*

"Hey! It worked." Star shrank from his sister's ferocity.

It almost didn't! she snapped. *Brian Wells, if you get yourself killed, I'LL NEVER SPEAK TO YOU AGAIN FOR MY WHOLE LIFE! Is tHaT cLeAr! If you get yourself killed being so stupid, I refuse ever to speak to you again, no matter how much you apologize!*

"Okay, okay. So I'll be careful, all right?" a chastened Star responded. Somewhat late, he realized he should have asked if his sister's threat was a firm promise that he could collect on. That wouldn't have been nice, he decided; she was angry because she cared about him.

CHAPTER 32 CARIBBEAN AFTERMATHS

Washington, D. C. The newly-remodeled headquarters of the FBI was an imposing slab of NeoAmerican Gothic. The guards at the night desk talked quietly with each other. Outer doors swung open and whisked softly shut. The guards tried to appear sharply alert. Motion detectors reported no one outside. Clearly no one had entered the vestibule.

Eyebrows rose. Why had the doors opened? Apparent practical jokes had a way of turning into security tests. The more senior guard rose and started for the door, the junior guard covering him from behind the desk. The senior guard had covered half the distance when a female voice came from behind him. "Pardon me. Is this where they arrest people?"

The senior guard whirled. The junior guard, still clean-shaven after six hours of duty, pointed at empty air.

"I mean, if I'm supposed to take him someplace else," the voice continued, "I know it's very late at night. I'll be happy to do it, I mean, I'm not trying to cause any trouble."

"I hear her," the junior guard said. "I don't see her. The boys in technical seem to have outdone themselves."

"Oh, sorry!" the voice apologized. The air curdled and cleared. Standing between the guards were two strangely dressed children and an adult caucasian male, early 60s, brown hair, clean-shaven, three-piece tailored suit, no obvious scars, securely trussed by a substantial length of heavily knotted rope. "Forgot I was still invisible."

"Don't worry, ma'am, it happens all the time," the older guard said. "Is the older gentlemen a friend of yours?" The younger guard wondered if this qualified as a hostage situation. Rules on what could be called a hostage situation were much more restrictive than ten years ago. The two children wore fancifully trimmed costumes and elaborate masks, but appeared to be unarmed. The older guard pointed covertly at the outer doors, the younger guard nodding in response. Electronic locks were now set.

"Star arrested him for corrupting the earth, but we brought him here because the American government had warrants for him, and we're Americans," Comet explained. We? She could perfectly well have brought the prisoner herself. Cloud had insisted on coming along, because he was the leader of their persona league, more or less. Except this place was belonged to a strange foreign government, for all they called themselves Americans and saluted the Stars and Bands. Sometimes strange foreign governments did odd things to real Americans, so perhaps it was comforting that Cloud was along and the rest of the gang was on tap through Aurora, in case this FBI proved less polite than FedCorps.

"Yes, he's a famous criminal." Cloud decided to start at the beginning. "This is Mr. Arturo Romansch. We brought him from the island of Saint Dominick. A grand jury said he helped smuggle medicine." Cloud had the rapt attention of both guards.

"Romansch?" the older guard asked the gentleman in the three-piece suit. The prisoner nodded feebly. "Medicine?"

"Illegal medicine," Cloud explained politely. "So he almost got put on your most-wanted list."

"Has he been Mirandized yet?" the older guard asked.

"Mirandized?" Cloud repeated dubiously.

"Civilians, Jim," the younger guard noted.

"When you arrest someone," the older guard explained, "you read them their Constitutional rights. Just like on TV. So they know they're don't have to say anything until they have a lawyer. Did you do that?" Mr. Romansch, he thought, undoubtedly knows criminal procedure to a T, and will hit us for the least deviation from proper procedure.

"When we arrested him he was, like, totally unconscious," Comet explained, "because when we stopped him on the trail he started shooting at us until Eclipse came up behind him and knocked him out."

"Do it now, Bob," the older guard directed. While the younger guard incanted the legal formula, the older guard picked up a telephone. Romansch was not actually on the most-wanted list, but the indictments were spectacular. Fingerprinting and booking someone who was claimed to be a notorious criminal was thoroughly unexceptionable, even if he later turned out to be a hoaxster.

The younger guard finished his litany. "The two of you say you arrested Mr. Romansch here? Was he alone? Didn't he have guards?"

"Arresting him was afterwards. First we took care of his guards, and wrecked all their machine guns and rockets and fighter planes, and blew up his runway and we're burning all the warehouses full of medicine," Comet said, "ummh, illegal medicine. We'll send you a report."

"Fighter planes? Rockets? Who is 'we'?" the older guard asked.

"We're the Greater Medford Persona League," Cloud said. "Saint Dominick was a base. Two hundred guards, machine gun nests, anti-aircraft rockets, antitank rockets, fortified bunkers. All sorts of real frigid stuff like that."

"Illegal Medicine?" the younger agent asked.

"Marijuana," Cloud answered. "Cocaine. Heroine. Extasy. Orgasmin. Borgiabizin. I looked it up. They're illegal. You know, illegal like chocolate was illegal under Rectification. I know Rectification never works, but it's the law."

"Chocolate?" the younger guard asked. He was sure he was awake. What was the kid talking about?

"Chocolate," Cloud repeated. "It was illegal under Rectification."

"Antiaircraft cannon," Comet added, "better than the ones here. I know that for sure since they both shot at me, and I can tell his were better than the ones at the Capitol, and he had fighter planes, too, good ones."

The younger guard looked thoughtfully at her garb. "Aren't you Comet?" he asked, "the Comet who rescued the Lemuria?"

'That's me," she answered. "This is Cloud. And the rockets and machine guns, they mostly fired at Cloud and Star."

"Eclipse took out his fighter planes," Cloud said quietly. "She can be real frigid. Especially considering she's only a girl."

"Eclipse? Another one of you costumed folk? Wasn't Eclipse the sweet little girl who appeared on the Lemuria?" the younger agent asked. "Mr. Romansch went after her with fighter planes?"

"Those were not my aircraft," inserted Romansch, "I am a peaceful, law-abiding, reputable international businessman, falsely indicted for the purely political needs of the previous, justly-impeached administration. I don't have any fighter aircraft. Furthermore, these rapscallions have kidnapped me from St. Dominick and slaughtered dozens of my employees. I have not been convicted of anything, and I attest that these two hoodlums have committed a variety of crimes—murder, arson, kidnapping, assault, criminal trespass, breaking and entering, strategic bombing without a permit—while on the territory of a friendly sovereign nation. Please arrest them. Also, I want my attorney. His card is in my wallet."

The junior guard decided not to emphasize that it was the immediately former President who had pursued the indictments, not her justly-impeached-and-removed spouse. "I'll dial the phone for you, Mr. Romansch," the junior agent announced. "And we'll get you out of the ropes as soon as we can." Romansch was momentarily surrounded by a flickering green haze. When it receded, Romansch was free, the coiled rope now being looped over Comet's shoulder.

"Arrest them? I'd need a foreign warrant for that, Mr. Romansch," the senior agent said, "St. Dominick not being our jurisdiction, especially considering that these two are clearly not even juveniles." Comet pouted. She wasn't some kid off on a lark; she was a known public persona doing her civic duty. If she consistently behaved like a grownup, she had the right to be treated as one, even before her Heinlein divorce..

Cloud continued with a description of the battle, stressing his and

Star's contributions. Several additional agents, multiple recorders, and the lobby's video monitors noted his every word. Comet added what she had seen and what Aurora had shown her, summarizing Star's lack of caution as 'What do you expect? I mean, he's my brother.'

"Anyhow, we have to be going," Comet said, "it's well past my bedtime, and I have things to do before I sleep, so if you can take care of him, we'll be on our way." Romansch, surrounded by a half dozen FBI agents, peered tremulously at the two personae. Life had been almost perfect on his island utopia. He'd had wealth, security, luxuries, companions, everything he desired. A few minutes' violence had reduced him to a prisoner whose sole prospect was old age and eventual death in the confines of a Federal penitentiary. His millions had bought him safety from local justice. Against the Federal judiciary they would avail him naught.

"I need to give you a hand receipt," the older guard said, "for one prisoner." The kids were perfectly well not going anyplace, he knew, not until they and their parents answered a lot more questions. After all, they had been accused of robbery and murder, and appeared to admit it, no matter that a freshly minted attorney trying his second case could get them off on self-defense. The receipt would give other agents time to position themselves in case the kids made a break for the locked door. He pulled forms from his desk, completed a three line description of the item being transferred, one Arturo Romansch, signed as the recipient, and passed the document across the desk.

Comet's signature, using the fountain pen she drew from a pocket in her cape, was in sharp Spencerian copperplate. Cloud put the paper between his hands, microscopic bolts of lightning passing from palm to palm, leaving behind the image of a thunderhead with 'Cloud' superposed. Cloud handed the second copy of the receipt back to the guard.

Comet's flight field flared to life, shrouding her and Cloud in chalk orange. The space they occupied became clear as glass. Agents surged forwards to grab the duo, finding empty air. Doors swung open, just as they had when the twosome had entered the room, then drifted shut. The younger guard checked his security panel. Something had overridden the electronics and released the locks. Trembling glass on the chandelier betrayed the escape route: Comet had turned herself invisible and flown over the heads of the agents.

~~~~~

Well after midnight. The senior sentry made a cautious

311

reconnaissance of the west anchorage. Far out on the water, the *Eternal Sunset*, his forty-foot sailboat, rode on gentle ripples. Buying the *Sunset* would have significantly dented his savings. Fortunately, poker had poor but honestly improvable odds, especially when you stayed sober. Binoculars and night goggles revealed Melissa's dinghy, floating at anchor beside his larger craft. Knowing her habits, she had come on board at twilight, fallen asleep, and not heard a thing since. She'd slept through an Atomic Metal band. Sleeping through a battle three miles away was a lot easier. As usual, almost everyone else had anchored on the north cove. Anyone looking for a boat to flee the island would be there, too. His own dinghy was at the small dock, a dilapidated wooden structure of a half-dozen pilings, rounded logs, and a few cross beams. He stared very carefully. Someone was sitting on the dock, leaning back into the pilings to be inconspicuous. If the sentry hadn't known the dock like the palm of his hand, the figure would have passed unseen.

Checking that his rifle held a full clip of ammunition, the sentry eased closer to the shore. The figure was looking out at the horizon, three suitcases stacked at its side.

"Ahoy!" the sentry called. "You on the dock!" The figure put hands overhead and slowly looked over one shoulder.

"Yes? You want the dock? Take it. I just wanted quiet." The figure slowly rose to its feet, careful to keep hands in sight. "Sergeant-Major Wright, I believe?" it asked.

"That's me, all right, and my dinghy there in the water," the sentry answered. The sentry saw the speaker was not wearing night goggles, but had recognized him anyhow. Furthermore, the dinghy was anchored but not locked, and the figure had not stolen it, though he obviously was looking to leave.

"It is I, Doctor Engelmann," the figure said. "I had hope of rescue."

The sentry recognized the foreign shareholders' representative, someone to whom he'd been introduced. Engelmann knew Wright's former rank, and made a point of using it, a courtesy that management often neglected. Engelmann and Center's staff, who did not view themselves as management, knew of Wright's arrangements with Melissa. They could hardly have overlooked her dinghy, given the sonar arrays around the island. Wright suspected that the electronic warfare specialist had bugged his sailboat, listened carefully for evidence of espionage, and—knowing the specialist—been totally disinterested in their personal activities.

"Engelmann. I just want my dinghy. Could you drop your pistol?" Wright suggested.

"No trouble," Engelmann answered cheerily, "I'm out of

ammunition." Engelmann slowly reached to his waist and unbuckled his belt. "Used it all on the burning man. I could have used blanks. Annunzio was a friend of yours, no?" Engelmann finished removing the pistol and dropped it into the water.

"Sergio was a good merc. A bit frightened, but stayed on the line when death came. You sure you hit?" Wright remembered shooting into the fog until the junior guard died.

"When it took out the last bunker I closed to four meters. Even I am not so poor a shooter as that." Engelmann shook his head in disgust. "I should go. Leave you in peace."

"Four meters. You closed to four meters? That's guts. You looking for a ride? This looks like a great time to change employers," Wright offered.

"A little ways, perhaps. You're welcome to the two large suitcases. Nothing but money in them. Nothing important," Engelmann explained.

"Neighbor, get in the dinghy. You've got yourself a deal," Wright smiled. "But we split the suitcases. I don't leave broke the guy who tried to avenge Sergio."

~~~~~

The surviving guards had fled the island or hid in the brush. Toward morning, the survivors made one last counterattack.

OK, Eclipse, Aurora warned. *They're lined up behind that wall. The guy in charge is giving them directions. He's a bit baffled you're standing in plain sight on top of the wreckage of that building, where they have clear shots at you, not to mention glowing bright blue, but you're between him and the huge pile of loot.. His guys off to your left will be shooting at you and his guys to your right are going to charge and run you over. They think there are a bunch of us to your left. We're supposed to duck when they shoot at us, instead of shooting back. Then they grab boats and make a getaway.*

It's a plan. If I were ungifted, it would even work. Eclipse shrugged. *These guys defending the island were actually competent. They just couldn't solve this, what's that phrase, oh, yes, out-of-context problem.*

Here they come, Aurora warned.

A wave of gunfire, automatic rifles, heavy-duty sniper rifles, and two 0.50 machineguns opened fire. Tracer rounds sailed through the air towards her, the sharp ting of deforming metal marking the rounds ineffectively striking Eclipse's shields and bouncing off. A dozen men vaulted the wall and ran at her. She yawned. It was well beyond her bedtime. She summoned her plasma torch and swept it across the running men, then turned it against the wall the shooters were using for cover. In a half-dozen seconds, all was quiet, her attackers having advanced to the next plane of existence. Two men who'd stayed hidden when their fellows charged turned and run. Eclipse cut them down in their tracks. They were, she considered, as guilty as the rest of them.

They'd spent hours, Comet thought, examining bunkers and tunnels. Aurora had made a heavy-handed search of Owner's accountant's memories until all the secret vaults were located. As a practical matter, Comet had done most of the searching and heavy lifting, moving at a hundred times the speed her companions could manage. Every so often, Star had lent a hand, delicately slicing open doors to locked vaults.

The sun peered over St. Dominick's horizon. The five were finished salvaging money. The accountant had been delivered to the FBI in D.C. Paper currency was stuffed into the plastic garbage bags Cloud had thoughtfully remembered. Fragments of colored glass that Aurora identified as diamonds and rubies were double-bagged. A large cache of opals and pearls, white and pink and black as night, Comet had swept into the large cloth bag she'd tied to her waist. Satisfied that they had almost every dollar, trash bags heaped around them in a rude parapet, they let Eclipse teleport them to their secret haven.

They returned to the desolation of an abandoned seaplane hangar. It was time to count their loot. 'Salvaged funds', Comet reminded them, the money from the druglord's haven—the rogue persona Romansch's base, to say it rightly—were legitimately available only to further their persona league. The setting sun stretched their shadows along concrete slabs whitened by generations of nesting seabirds.

Most of the money came in wrapped bundles. Star, Cloud, and Comet stood in a circle, pulling bundles from the bags and stacking them neatly in cardboard boxes. The two boys, standing in the midst of more money—even if it was an odd shade of green—than most persona leagues salvaged in a lifetime, were delighted to agree that they should have the fun of counting.

"Besides," Star said, "counting is numerical, so counting the loot is boys' work." Comet shook her head. She decided not to point out that accounting was getting every detail right, so it had to be girls' work. In fact, anything with numbers was getting details right, so everything numerical was really girls' work, no matter what a boy said. She said nothing. After all, that was really a silly rationale. The boys didn't complain that she stood there and helped them keep count.

"I'm sleepy," Aurora announced. "I found all the money. You guys can count it." She headed for their base camp.

"And I'm hungry," Eclipse announced, not to mention being tired. "Can't counting wait until tomorrow?"

"But we can count it now," Star said. "It's so incredible." Eclipse ignored him to join Aurora at the base camp. The trio still counting didn't complain a half-hour later when she and Aurora reappeared to leave them with grilled steaks, pan-browned potatoes, and stir-fried carrots and snow peas with ginger and soy sauce.

Their mission of feeding the threesome properly accomplished, Eclipse and Aurora talked sleepily. The older girl lay back on a canvas deck chair, a blanket drawn over her shoulders, usually-sparkling gray eyes half closed, sipping at a mug of cocoa. The last fragments of the setting sun bejeweled the horizon, brightening Eclipse's cheeks and tinting her hair the faintest of red-blondes. The sight of someone almost her own age publicly drinking chocolate troubled Aurora. What if some grownup caught her?

"Are you OK, Eclipse?" Aurora asked.

"Me? Sure. Got a tad violent. For a bit. That's all." Eclipse tried to shrug off the question. She'd gone along with the Greater Medford League's ideas, given them air-to-ground fire support when they needed it, and been pounded on as a result. Doing things by herself always worked out far more smoothly than working with a group. If she'd been by herself, she could have backed off and changed her line of approach. With the League along, she'd had to follow through with their original plans. The ground fire had been marginally respectable. Two aircraft with UV lasers, directed energy weapons, and nonchemical explosives in their air-to-air missiles had been more challenging, even before the aircraft blew up. Pickering swore that his people knew nothing of energy screens. Either he was wrong, or the planes had a lot of armor, more armor than most caissons carried.

"You look very tired. I did what I could, but I was busy with Star, and didn't help you enough," Aurora apologized. "My fault. I was supposed to backstop all of us, not just Star. When we took Emperor Roxbury, I got left alone against three of his agents. I had to take them all. I was absolutely terrified. Completely alone. It was terrible. I left you like that. I'm so sorry."

"Aurora?" Eclipse forced herself to look alert. "You did great! You kept up your wall around Star when he needed it, knocked out the guys with the rocket launchers, took out their electronics, and repointed their missile at the helipad. All at once. That's multiple attacks. That's excellent! If I'd absolutely needed help, I could've said so. And you'd've found a way to help me, just like you found a way to dispose of Emperor Roxbury's agents. You were fine. I was busy, and got pounded on some.

But I knew I had them." She peered wanly into her cocoa. "After all, I've had lots of practice deciding whether to stand or to run."

Comet, now dressed in jogging pants and baggy sweatshirt, bare feet leaving footprints in the sand, joined their circle. "Star and Cloud said we should wash the dishes, so I did. And they're having so much fun counting I thought I'd let them count it all, every last bit of it. Accurately. Are you-all OK?."

"We're fine," Aurora said, "watching the sunset." Aurora yawned deeply. "But tonight we go to bed early. Or is it tomorrow already?"

Eclipse nodded her agreement and pointed Comet to the cocoa pot. "Oh, yes!" Comet said. "Thanks!" Aurora looked askance at Comet. "Heinlein divorce, Aurora." Comet shook her head. "I'm an adult. I can make adult choices. You know, choices like washing everyone's dishes. Not complaining about yours, Eclipse! Or yours, Aurora! You did all the cooking, for which I am really grateful. Thanks! Besides, I'm a persona. Chocolate won't work on me, even if I were old enough, which I'm not."

"Now we get a good night's sleep," Eclipse said.

"This Romansch fellow," Aurora said, "and his accountant, they knew a couple more people on the mainland who were selling this stuff. We should arrest them. Tomorrow."

~~~~~

The Eternal Sunset plowed through the Caribbean, sails taut, her wake a phosphorescent arrow. The sky was crystal-clear, stars sharp as diamond chips. Sergeant-Major Wright remained at the helm, Melissa asleep at his side, her bare legs sticking out from under a light blanket. Wright had decided to submit his resignation to Owner after reaching the next island group. Engelmann had gratefully offered to conn the ship. Wright had seen Engelmann trying to sail in the lagoon and knew better than to accept Engelmann's aid. Besides, sailing singlehanded was too much fun to miss.

Engelmann disappeared below decks. Now, in the darkest hour before dawn, he had reappeared. He began to undress, removing shoes and socks and fatigues. Wright looked at him closely. Engelmann was unarmed. He couldn't be planning anything, could he? Engelmann's attache case was at his side. Something tagged Wright's intuition. Was Engelmann suicidal? He certainly looked ready to jump.

"Engelmann?" Wright whispered. "You all right? I mean, hey, sit down. There's scotch in the locker. Help yourself. It's not the end of the world, losing a contract. Even though I thought so, first time I had a contract sour on me."

"Sergeant-Major? Don't worry about me. Everything is going to be all right for both of us. You will have the money, your friend, and your boat. And I will go home. Very soon now," Engelmann sounded completely at ease, not spaced out, not disconnected like the other suicides Wright had seen.

The boat rocked, forcing Wright to tend the tiller and take in the line on the mainsheet. When he looked up, he saw that the water had changed, silver-green phosphorescence being replaced with a blood-red glow that sent shadows of hull and mast up to suddenly-faded stars. Engelmann had slipped off his trousers and was leaning over the rail, the light making a macabre mask of his face.

The fathometer beeped. They were in deep water, but suddenly there was a response directly beneath them. The sidescan—a real electronic luxury, Wright noted, but you could find the strangest things in a merc poker game—showed deep water everywhere except directly below. Wright relaxed. They'd be off this pinnacle in half an instant. He waited one instant, and the next, and the next, and they were not off the pinnacle. Indeed, the water beneath their keel was becoming shallower and shallower, even though they were making ten knots, and the sonar showed deep water not a hundred feet dead ahead. Wright looked over the taffrail, straight down. The lights outlined a complex shape, something that moved with his sailboat.

"Engelmann? You see a sub down there? They friends of yours?" a suddenly frightened Wright asked.

"Precisely, Sergeant-Major. Friends. But they are your friends, too, because you saved me. And I leave the large suitcases. Both of them. I would appreciate it if you told no one of my departure," Engelmann rasped.

"Herr Doktor Engelmann," Wright hoped he got the German right. Engelmann smiled. "I couldn't pay someone to believe this. Yes, word of honor, you have a deal. My lips are sealed. A real submarine? That's only in spy movies. If I told anyone, they'd just lock me up with the guys who think they're Napoleon. Or Jesus. Or two for the price of one. But if you're jumping, it'll be safer if I come into the wind."

Engelmann saluted with a crisp hand motion that Wright couldn't match to any of the armies he'd knew. The boat came obediently about, Engelmann disappearing over the side when they'd slowed nearly to a stop. A minute later the glow faded, the submarine fading into the depths of the Caribbean. Only when the Eternal Sunset was under way again did it occur to Wright that submarines do not commonly have undersea running lights. On the other hand, he noted, Engelmann's people were clearly honorable men. The submarine could perfectly well have recovered Engelmann and then put a pair of homing torpedoes into the *Sunset*. They instead gave him two heavy suitcases, holding surely enough money that he and Melissa could retire for good.

~~~~~

Captain Terence Vincent Macaulay, commanding officer of the U.S.S. *Nathan Hale*, stood with his Executive Officer, surveying a well-lit, windowless Pentagon briefing room. There were more brass than he had expected, not to mention people from Justice, Treasury, Narcotics Suppression Administration, and several suited gentlemen who 'worked for DoD'. He wondered if the last group was interested in what had happened, or only cared how their electronics had functioned. He wished they'd been interested in months past. Naming a frigate after a recently decommissioned submarine had had interesting effects on logistics.

Not twenty-four hours ago, he had been sailing the waters of the Atlantic, nominally on a training mission but actually providing surveillance on dope traffickers. Now he was in Washington, whisked point to point by fast military transport. He told himself that, relative to twenty years ago, briefings were much more straightforward. A battle might be the height of confusion, but good recordings let you report exactly what you had done with a minimum of uncertainty. It also meant that your bad decisions were glaringly obvious and could not be covered up.

The evening before, his ship had witnessed a remarkable combat segment. Higher-ups wanted a full report, preferably yesterday. Raw data, radar, signal intercepts, and pictures from their overflying RPV had been transmitted as rapidly as the Nathan Hale's computers could encode them. His task was to reconstruct what they had seen, integrating observations into a coherent whole. Analysts from a half-dozen agencies were examining his ship's logs with a fine-toothed comb. Before he left for Washington, the ship's radar had recorded multiple flyovers by reconnaissance aircraft. Someone was suddenly extremely interested in a sleepy tropical island.

Nominally a frigate, the *Nathan Hale* had been extensively rebuilt and stuffed from keel to mainmast with electronic gear. The frigate's original mission was electronic reconnaissance of the Asian bloc. She now contributed to harassment of a narcotics transshipment point, namely St. Dominick. Narcotics surveillance was tedious in the extreme. Tracking civilian aircraft represented essentially no challenge to the ship's electronics suite.

By day Saint Dominick Island looked completely tranquil, the sort of

318

Caribbean paradise to which a billionaire and his family might retire. The billionaire's alleged lines of merchandise had attracted Washington's attention. Last night life had become interesting. Macaulay began his briefing, allowing recordings from the ship's Bridge and Combat Information Center to do most but not all of the talking.

"At 0130 local time, we recorded bursts of radio traffic from the island," Macaulay said. "The watch reported vehicles with police-style flashing lights advancing along the coast. We were at that time southeast of St. Dominick. We then observed air targets." He cued a recording from the CiC, letting his audience hear last night's events.

" 'Incoming aircraft. Incoming aircraft," the radar section announced. "Target one: Range one-two nautical miles, bearing zero eight two, speed two one zero zero knots. Repeat two one zero zero knots." The radar officer had managed not to show surprise. "Target two: Stationary aircraft over St. Dominick runway: range three point five nautical miles bearing three two seven altitude five seven hundred feet speed zero. Stationary aircraft just appeared—no track of previous locations."

"Two thousand knots?" Captain Macaulay had asked, leaning toward a presentation console. Silently, the Captain offered thanks to Bona Fortuna for putting him in the CIC at such a benighted hour.

"Now two five zero zero knots. Target one changing course. Now incoming, our axis." radar reported.

"Officer of the Deck, set General Quarters!" Macaulay ordered. He stared intently at the display. "Left full rudder. All ahead flank. ECM on. Arm chaff and flare dispensers, arm point defenses. Signal Washington Flash Priority: Ship has unidentified missile incoming." Macaulay stopped the tape. He remembered thinking that only one turbine was on line and that target one would be on them before the other could be fired up.

"The immediate response," he said, "was to present the ship's stern to the apparent threat, minimizing our target and giving the dalek an optimum field of fire. We had no apparent launch vehicle to engage." He restarted the recording.

" 'Sir, my rudder is full left, no course given, engines ahead flank,' the helmsman repeated. A distant whine marked gas turbines coming on line. The deck heeled beneath the men and women in the CIC.

"Saint Dominick radar ramping up," the ELINT officer reported. "Military power and sweep rate. Multiple sources. Hey, they've brought up a phased array there."

"Multiple missile launches from Saint Dominick," radar reported. "Three repeat three launches. Towards incoming missile. Profile matches Sandalwood. Still no, repeat, no indication of a launch vehicle for target one." The SA-35 Sandalwood was the newest Russian anti-aircraft missile, fully competitive in performance with anything in the NATO arsenal. The Russians firmly denied that there were non-Russian components in its onboard electronics, which were widely reputed to match the best French and Japanese designs more closely than was reasonably assigned to chance.

"OOD reports firing on island," the XO said. "Automatic weapons. A patch of glowing fog, on-shore." Fog? the Captain mouthed. Here? At this season? "Moving upwind," the XO continued.

"Target one evaded Sandalwoods," radar reported. "Target one dead astern, incoming. Now at three thousand knots."

"Fire chaff and flares," Macaulay ordered. "Signals: last radar report as update to Washington, flash priority." Automatic launchers released a barrage of precisely cut aluminum strips laced with burning magnesium. The metal decoys formed a cloud behind the Nathan Hale, a target larger and brighter than the ship to confuse the incoming.

"Visual track on missile," the XO reported. The tension on the bridge was nearly palpable. The room became deathly still.

"Missile is not tracking our turn," radar announced. There was a perceptible relaxation throughout the CIC.

"Captain, below-decks has a match on the missile," the XO announced. 'Below-decks' were the highly secret electronics sections that constituted the *Nathan Hale*'s raison d'etre. "On CIC screen one." The VCR paused.

"This was the best estimate at the time," the Captain explained to the briefing room. "The match was two sigma above next-best." Macaulay brought up the display for the attendees at the briefing. The screen was split, the left half showing a small chalk-orange disc labelled REAL TIME IMAGE/ST. DOMINICK, while the right half showed a much larger picture of a similar disc labelled WASHINGTON DC. The right-half image scrolled up, to be replaced by a still from Washington Life: Comet in front of TV cameras. There were nods from the audience. Macaulay returned to the CiC tape.

"Below-decks reports the island is doing massive jamming," ELINT reported. "No sign of what the island thinks they are jamming. They're ignoring SeaSpace Uplinks."

A reddish glow engulfed the island's center, followed twenty seconds later by a loud rolling clatter. "Air to ground missiles," radar announced. "Lots of air to ground." Radar tracked target one's climb. A section of the island had been reduced to burning rubble.

"OOD reports sound and light flashes: heavy ground combat on Saint Dominick," the XO said. "Automatic weapons, mortars, anti-tank rockets."

"Signs of a landing?" Captain Macaulay asked. "Who are they shooting at? Each other?"

"No aircraft or ships tracked earlier, Captain. Everything was dead quiet until a few minutes ago," the XO answered. "Someone's heavy weapons are chewing up the airstrip." CIC watched the ground battle on the video repeaters.

"Incoming aircraft," announced Radar. "Target one making a fresh pass. New targets three and four, bearing three two five speed five zero zero. Three and four appeared on the deck off western shore and are climbing. No track of them on earlier scans. SAM launches against target two."

"This little girl did that?" MacAulay had said during the battle, pointing first at Comet's picture and then at television repeaters of the island, which showed burning aircraft and collapsed aircraft hangars. "And I thought my twins were a wrecking crew!" Gentle laughter rolled across the CIC.

"Missile launches on island," Radar announced. "Antiship." A pause. "Not toward us. Multiple Sandalwood hits on target two. It's still there."

"Recognition on two?" Macaulay asked.

"Negative from below," the XO responded. "On CIC screen two. Cross section under one square meter." The Captain and XO stared at the TV repeater, which showed a featureless blue cylinder.

"One of her friends," the captain told the CIC, pointing at Comet. The blue image vanished from the repeater. "Not a fleaweight, to ignore direct hits from a Sandalwood. And I told the twins that UltraGirl is a story. All ahead standard. Course two seven zero and resume racetrack. XO, you have the conn. Put up the RPV. Prepare to overfly and observe as soon as firing dies down."

"That's foreign territory, Captain," the XO noted.

"Very true," Macaulay answered. "Territory of a friendly foreign government, some of whose American residents appear to be having a house fire, appear to have had a sailboat set adrift, and may need friendly assistance to save their belongings. Note it in the log. And keep up the reminders, number two, that's why you're here."

"Two accelerating," radar said. "Targets two through four in dog fight. A real furball—range between them under three hundred meters and staying there. Incredible climb: now at fifteen thousand feet. Eighteen thousand. Drifting east." radar announced. "I compute sustained accelerations of twenty-five gees. Two is clearly outmaneuvering three and four."

Instruments duly monitored the brilliance and duration of the final airburst near targets two, three, and four. The intensity had a well-known characteristic double-humped pattern, maxima being separated by a few milliseconds. The absence of prompt gamma rays was puzzling, but the intensity and residual fireball were definitive. "Loss of target on two, three, and four," radar announced. A pause. "Recovering track on two." The recording was stopped again.

"I would have to rate the events as a complete tactical surprise," Macaulay admitted to the review panel. "We had readiness against surprise attack by kamikaze cigarette boats, aircraft, or submarines, or ship-to-ship engagement with anti-tank rockets or 0.50 inch machineguns, but not the mid-air event. However, ship's hardware responded as designed."

Captain Macaulay restarted the recording. The *Nathan Hale's* threat analysis computer had spat out an interpretation. Macaulay had paused for several moments, considering what it was reporting. "Signals," the Captain had spoken, realizing he was about to send a message he had never expected to transmit, "To National Military Command Center Washington DC, ANMCC Ft. Ritchie MD. Priority LIGHTNING." Lightning, the signal priority above Flash, was limited to messages of the highest imaginable priority. "From: this ship, place, and date." Signals automatically inserted the ship's name, longitude, and latitude, and recomputed references to Greenwich Mean Time. "Subject: NucDetRep. Text: At 0315 hours local time, 10.2 nautical miles bearing 330 from this position, estimated altitude 4.5 nautical miles near St. Dominick Island, a bright flash and fireball were observed. Flash intensity satisfies NucDetRep definitions. No prompt gammas were recorded." He looked at a message from below. "Weak X-ray burst. Estimated yield: 0.2 kilotons. Detonation in proximity to air battle between three unknown aircraft, unknown types, described in Flash messages..." the signals officer queued a series of message referents on the screen, got the Captain's acknowledgement, and appended message ID numbers to the current message. "Append closer." The computer affixed the appropriate opening and closing statements, the Captain's name, rank, serial number, and ship, and presented him with the final text for his approval. The record ended.

"The actual message is Appendix A of my presentation," Macaulay explained. He paused while his audience riffled through their briefing books. The message was the formal reason for the Captain's presence in Washington. Certain messages were so critical to national security that they automatically resulted in the convocation of a review panel. "Appendix B is my casualty report. Three men flash-blinded, fortunately all temporarily." He reminded himself that he'd been through Bethesda early this AM, and would pass through again to see them before he took the flight back to his ship. "Six starlight scopes and two television cameras burned out. There was no loss of combat readiness to radar or other electronic systems. Degradation of electronic shielding is being assessed."

"At dawn, the local government authorized us to land a shore patrol to assist the island's residents. The patrol found bodies and wreckage strewn the length of the island." Captain Macaulay's memories were more graphic. The patrol found smoldering wreckage, shattered concrete, the stink of death and expended ammunition. Residents had fled in small boats. "We did rescue three badly wounded men, who are now getting the world's best medical care in a guarded hospital."

CHAPTER 33 VISIT TO A MINOR HOODLUM

Arthur O'Malley sat on his living room couch, feet buried in the litter of a proper bachelor's apartment. His uninvited guest, most notably the muzzle of her pistol, pointed directly at him, had his full attention. Her finger was on the trigger. He had no idea who the girl in front of him was, but the casual speed with which she had shot his two bodyguards proved she knew how to use the weapon. The bodyguards lay on the floor. The smell made it clear they were now answering, just like in the TV commercials, to a higher judge.

He kept his trembling hands well out from his chest. The boys had each emptied at least a full clip from their Mac-10's into her, to no visible effect. The piece he was carrying was smaller. Where, he wondered, could he buy her body armor? For that matter, where could he buy her pistols? He loved one-of-a-kind items, and didn't recognize the one she held, let alone the hand cannon at her waist.

The most frightening thing was that she was talking to him, telling him things he had sworn never to say, things he thought only he knew, things that would get him locked up for life if the honest part of the city's police force found out, and dead as a doornail if the other half of the police force found out. How could she know all this stuff? It was like she was reading his mind, learning what he knew and what he'd figured out about his suppliers and employers. But figuring them out was just smart, wasn't it? You figured out what the big boys really wanted, how they operated, what ticked them off, and you rose in the organization. You didn't figure out, you sank in the harbour. Every so often, he'd murmur "I didn't tell you that." or "I want my lawyer."

The side door crashed in. The boys upstairs had finally wised up. Louie One-Ear had his wire into the room, heard whatever got said, and was supposed to figure when things had gone bad, so that heavy metal was needed down here. Louie had taken his time about it. Of course, Louie had heard the Mac-10s, figured a deal had gone slightly bad, and likely assumed that the boys were busy cleaning up after the ex-customer. Only this weird one-sided conversation gave away things were not right.

O'Malley threw himself at the floor, hoping for a moment the kid actually was reading his mind. He was absolutely not going against her; he was just getting out of the line of fire. Then Top Hat, his girl friend, and their .50 cals got very, very loud. Only the puffs of smoke showed she was shooting back. It took O'Malley a moment to realize she should have been cut in half by Top Hat's machine gun. Instead, he could see

Top Hat's one-in-five tracers dinging across the room after bouncing from her body armor. Impossible, thought O'Malley. Impossible. Even a good hunting rifle goes through kevlar.

The firing stopped. Top Hat and girl-friend dropped their pieces, then sank to the ground. O'Malley's ears rang. Whenever he tried to remember what the girl had told him, his head hurt. If she'd been reading pages in his book, she'd been tearing them at the same time.

Sorry, came the voice inside his head. *But you don't get hurt nearly as much as...* there followed a list of unsatisfactory customers *...did.* "Now, about your supplier's contact information..." He shuddered as she repeated that list. When it got out that he'd told anyone those names, he was a dead man.

The rear wall bulged and collapsed in a spray of plasterboard. Out stepped O'Malley's suppliers' special present to their favorite wholesaler. O'Malley wasn't quite sure what it was, except 'illegal alien—Tin Man from Oz' was not a good bet. "Drop it, sister," said O'Malley. "You can't hurt my friend with a pistol, but he can for sure hurt you. And I have some friends who want to meet you."

The girl had already pivoted. O'Malley recognized the grip: hand horizontal, left hand bracing right wrist, left pinkie carefully clear of the travel, was a very special forces pose. Not that it would do her the least bit of good, as her first half-dozen shots revealed.

The one problem with Tin Man, O'Malley remembered being told, was that it was a teenie bit slow with unexpected situations. A ten-year-old girl in a running suit and a bunch of friendlies downed on the floor had to count as unexpected. Tin Man took two steps forward, giving O'Malley space to crawl behind it toward the tunnel exit.

He told himself the kid couldn't know what piece Tin Man was carrying. If she did, she wouldn't be giggling at a heat-ray pistol, like she thought it was some kind of joke. Not even the Army had them. Only his suppliers and their really good friends. Bright light and heat. A wash of flame surrounded her, set fire to carpet and curtains, and blew out the front wall. A few moments, though O'Malley, and her lungs would be charcoal.

Whoever she was, she was still standing there, not even her hair out of place. Except now she was holding her other pistol, the one with most of a foot of barrel and more bore than seemed natural. Tin Man fired again and again, this time setting fire to lawn, trees, and a parked car. O'Malley scrambled through the secret door in the rear wall, heading for the tunnel and escape. He never left kept anything incriminating around the place. Every so often, his suppliers gave him pieces of bugs someone had tried to plant. Even so, as a place of work his apartment was now out of business.

He more felt than heard her second pistol fire. Two rounds, he decided. He glanced over his shoulder. Two neatly spaced rounds. Grapefruit-sized holes had appeared in Tin Man's back. Tin Man froze up. O'Malley grabbed a hanger and began rappelling, fast as he dared, down the escape tunnel. He really did not want to be nearby if Tin Man had given up the ghost. His suppliers had told him what happened next. He hit bottom and started running, dropping steel doors behind him.

The blast knocked him off his feet. Whoever she had been, she wasn't there any more. He hoped Louie One-Ear had cued in to what Tin Man was doing, and gone out the back alley. He and Louie, no one else, knew about Tin Man, who had been brought in, all hush-hush, not two nights before. The explosion must have killed her. Naturally, he never kept any of his goods in the premises. Any payment reached him through cutouts.

~~~~~

O'Malley realized he had been lying on the ground for some time. What happened? His watch showed he'd been out cold for several hours. He'd have to report all this to the big boys as soon as possible He reached for his special cell phone, the one strapped to his leg. It wouldn't work down here, but he wanted to be ready to report just as soon as it showed a few of the special bars. The big boys did not like bad news, but the one thing they liked less than bad news was someone not telling them bad news as soon as possible.

The phone was gone! His trousers had been slit open. The very special hard-to-cut fabric of the phone case's strap was cleanly slit. The phone and its case weren't there. He checked his trouser pocket. The special coin, the one only he knew how to get out of its coin trap, was missing. The pocket had been slit from side to side. It had to be the little witch with her absurd pistols. Impossible. He'd dropped the doors behind him, and she'd been blown to smithereens by the Tin Man.

He paused and thought. The exit was two blocks down the street. His escape car was there. It was completely innocuous, every detail of its acquisition and ownership being entirely legal. He would drive very carefully to his safe house, and tell the big boys what had happened. They would not be pleased. However, the house was wired three ways from Sunday. They assuredly knew what had happened already. He'd just be proving his loyalty.

The car keys were stored in a hidden compartment, some feet before the tunnel exit. He popped the disguised door. There they were. One thing had gone right. He opened the door to the garage. How had he forgotten and left the car windows open? Was he getting senile? Was it time for him to pack it up and take retirement? He had an invite to retire in South America. He was no fool. He'd be retiring in Switzerland, as far from the big boys as he could get.

He opened the car door and swung into the seat. The dome light was out. No matter. He could find the keyhole in the dark.

"Arthur O'Malley?"

At the unexpected voice he jumped.

"Is this your car, sir?" the voice asked.

O'Malley turned the ignition key. Nothing happened. All the lights in the garage came on. A half-dozen members of the city's finest ringed the car. He knew each of them. They were all from the honest half of the Police Force. Several had insultingly large guns pointed in his direction.

O'Malley turned the key again and pumped the gas pedal. Still nothing happened.

"It works better when the battery is under the hood," the officer said, pointing at a car battery sitting on a work bench. "However, I have a search warrant, and a warrant for your arrest, Mr. O'Malley, the charge being conspiracy to commit murder. Please get out of the car and put your hands on the hood." A shattered O'Malley did what he was told.

~~~~~

Eclipse, crouching on a warehouse roof a few blocks away, watched through Aurora's eyes as the arrest took place. O'Malley's attorneys might wonder how the police had obtained the interesting photographs of his money vault and the boxes of illegal medicine, all in a house a block away. The live videos of his men trying to kill her were the basis of the arrest. The Fire Department, already on the scene, was baffled but not complaining as to how the explosion had reduced O'Malley's house to splinters and its cement block walls to fine gravel, with no damage more than three feet beyond its outer walls. The blast wave and flying debris had crashed to a stop, as though it had hit an invisible wall in the air.

"He gets tried and hanged!" Aurora said gleefully. "He tried to kill you!"

"Ummh, they don't hang people here," Eclipse answered. "No telepathy means they can't tell, usually, if someone is for sure guilty or not. So they just lock people up. After what they view as a trial."

"Oh. Right!" Aurora said. "Makes sense."

"I have his phone," Eclipse said, "operating instructions, and password. But where does the phone call go? It's a radio thing. I can't trace it."

"Read its mind?" Aurora asked. "Read the mind of the phone system. Trace the call."

"Can you do that?" Eclipse asked. "With this phone system? I can't. Not a bit. If it were a cyborg, I could read its bio part, not its computer mind. But it's just a chunk of metal. I can't touch it mentalically. Can you?"

"Not while it's turned off," Aurora said. "Can you turn it on?"

"I insert this coin—it isn't a coin—it turns on and makes the call. There's a bit of delay. Then I say the code words. Guy at the far end likely figures out I'm not O'Malley and hangs up."

"We won't have much time after you make the call. Please fetch Comet," Aurora asked. "I'll read its mind while speeded up. It helped a lot for reading Telzey's mind."

"On it," Eclipse said. A robin's egg blue haze enveloped her. She vanished, to reappear moments later.

Comet, in a short nightgown, yawned deeply. "It's, like, not yet dawn. Give me a few moments, please? She closed her eyes, her flight field keeping her aloft for two minutes. "Ah," she said. "Two-hour nap. Much better. Aurora, just be very close to me. Eclipse, please put a wall around us?"

"Wall? Can do...if I know why, I might do it better," she added.

"The house was booby-trapped. If the phone is booby-trapped, I don't want to get blown up," Comet explained.

"Oh. Right," Eclipse answered. Working with other personae, she thought, was just so strange. Ghostly shimmers marked shields around her and the two sisters. "It wants skin contact," she grumbled. "OK, force field right under my skin on that finger. When I insert the coin and poke the contact, the call begins."

"Ready!" Aurora's answer, her thinking done as slowly as possibly to cancel Comet's 1000-fold time speedup, held ghostly ringing echoes.

Eclipse shoved the coin, properly aligned, into its slot and pushed her finger against the sensor.

The phone rang three times. "Sunlight!" was the voice at the far end.

Eclipse chanted the code words. "Anencephalic. Poltroon. Infinibulum. Parcheezi."

She was interrupted. "Where's Art?"

"Laryngitis. Can't talk. I'm his new chief squeeze."

"Baloney!" Eclipse hoped the two girls next to her didn't hear the rest of his response. Her Jim disguise would have worked perfectly here, but too late. The telephone exploded, Eclipse's force walls trapping the blast.

"I tracked it! I tracked it!" Aurora shouted. "I've got an exact location. I'm reading his mind. And his mental pattern if he runs away!"

She transmitted those details to Eclipse.

"What did he mean at the end?" Comet asked.

"He meant, he expected O'Malley's son, someone like that, would call." Well, Eclipse thought, that was partly true. Eclipse hoped some evidence of those other crimes could be found. "OK, you two, back to the island. I jump this character."

"I'm still reading his mind," Aurora said. "He's not real bright. He has things he does, not exactly thinking about them. He gets those medicines from the New Incans and sends money to weird places across the country."

"Not to the New Incans?" Comet asked.

"No. It's seriously strange," Aurora answered. "It's a not-for-profit crime business."

"Ready for vacuum?" Eclipse asked.

"Ready," Comet answered.

"Give me a moment," Aurora answered. "He did something. I lost contact. But I know where he is."

The world shimmered. "Dark side of the moon," Eclipse announced. "No, I guess it's now the back side." Three more jumps brought them to the island.

"A lot of jumps," Comet said.

"These guys play seriously for keeps," Eclipse answered. "That phone explosion should have been impossible. Not enough weight for the explosives. OK, I have a villain to catch."

"May I come along? Please?" Aurora asked. "Body screens to my max?"

Eclipse nodded agreement. *Here's my plan,* she said.

I can add some extra mindscreens, Aurora said. She followed with an image.

Super idea. Ready? Let's go.

~~~~~~

Serene Master Rajul stared at his telephone system. Various screens, controls, and video feeds occupied much of a wall. Someone had procured Arthur O'Malley's special cell phone, extracted the code key and the voice code, exposed a hand, and then gave away that she was for sure not making a legitimate call. Detonating the phone was the automatic step. In a bit he'd have an image of the death scene, and see who he'd killed. Hopefully the decedent's friends had been crowding around to listen. That way the one he killed would go to the afterlife in the company of her friends.

Rajul tapped more buttons, forwarding the record to the Tower of Gold. O'Malley must have been brutally tortured, given how little time had elapsed between the war machine detonating and the phone call. Perhaps he should be surprised. Americans usually took their time about even considering the use of violent moral suasion. Mortals were like that. On the other hand, some mortals folded instantly when exposed to pain. On him that would not work, because his secrets were not in his mind.

He'd been lucky. A microbot was close to the crash scene. It forwarded images. The exact explosion location, within a fraction of an inch was known. He stared at the picture. There were no bodies. Worse, there was absolutely no damage to the roof of the building, an aged warehouse in one of O'Malley's city's less wealthy districts. The microbot sniffer took its time, then reported the expected trace chemicals, all that remained of the cell phone. Other microbots converged on the scene. The locals might wonder where the dragonflies were coming from, but there were not many of them, and they took paths that largely masked them from sight. They all found the trace chemicals. What was going on?

"What's going on," a high soprano voice behind him announced, "is that you are under arrest."

Rajul whirled around in his desk chair. He faced two little girls, both attractively built by his standards, if dismayingly overdressed. They were wearing clothing. What had gone wrong with his staff? They knew what they were supposed to do. Worse, the taller one was pointing a pistol at his head, and had her finger already on the trigger.

"Didn't your parents teach you firearms safety?" he asked. "Finger not near the trigger, unless you are about to shoot someone."

"You get a point for that," the taller girl answered. He'd heard the voice before. That was the girl on the phone. Why wasn't she dead? A ton of TNT, at pointblank range, should have reduced her to hamburger. "We had the same lesson. But I'm about to blow you away, so my finger is where it belongs."

Rajul tried to shift his weight in the chair. Jumping her, counting on her natural reluctance to kill someone to give him the moment he needed to grab her gun, might be a needed option. He found that all his joints were locked. He couldn't move, except his jaw to speak. Worse, he was surrounded by an invisible wall. His implants couldn't communicate with the house AI. His thoughts couldn't reach the Ascendance of God.

Wait a second, Aurora, Eclipse thought. *They're cleverly hidden, but he's got a half-dozen constructs surrounding him.* She followed with an image, his head with six tangled masses of colored thread orbiting it.

Oh, I see them now, Aurora said. *They're right there. I never thought to look. And he remembers what each of them does. They keep his memories for him.* She passed the information back to Eclipse.

Clever, Eclipse responded. *If he's about to be arrested and scanned telepathically, he can erase them. A shame you've put a mind screen right at his skin so he can't. He's got backup copies for them, someplace. Let's see. This one is 'Current Operations'. This one is a list of his bases, ones where he sends money. Here are plans. Here are, oh, yuck.*

What? Aurora asked. She looked, just for an instant, and threw up. *He does that to girls our age?*

Mostly younger. I lifted the list of names, Eclipse said. *And how he got rid of the bodies, well, what was left of the bodies.* She rattled off a set of criminal acts.

Are you sure he's guilty of all that? Aurora asked.

No doubt. Eclipse answered. *He remembers doing those things himself. These are really well organized, small structures. I've copied all of them. Well, not the yuck one, except to the list of victims' names and their faces at the start. Is there anything useful in his mind?*

A whole list of 'If this happens, do that.', Aurora answered. *I've copied that. That part of him is a robot. And the rest is all the gross things he does. It's weird, like he has three different minds.*

Shall I kill him now? Eclipse asked.

No. Professor Lafayette taught me what to do, Aurora answered. *Said I shouldn't unless I was sure he was guilty.*

OK. I trust her, Eclipse answered. And, she thought, I am not picking a fight with Morgan Le Fay if I don't have to. *He's 100% guilty.*

"You are guilty," Aurora said to Rajul. "You have been weighed, and measured, and found wanting, just as Marik and Sarnath were found wanting." She followed with images of his crimes, people being tortured.

Rajul's answer was a string of obscenities.

"Second death!" Aurora shouted. Rajul began to scream at the top of his lungs.

"OK, we can go," Aurora said casually. "And tell FedCorps, no, this Federal Bureau thing where to find him and this building."

"Aurora," Eclipse said, "I'll take care of notifying people." Three teleport steps brought them back to the island. "Out of curiosity, what did you just do to him?"

"Deleted his memories of the last half-hour," she said. "Exfoliated his other memories, crisscross, so he can't think. He'll have bits of thoughts, but not coherent, and he'll know his thoughts make no sense. Gave him an illusion, buried in his lizard brain, but mentalic—painkillers won't help. Not every heart beat, just most of them, so it's random, he thinks his every pain nerve fired, as hard as possible. Illusion, so his nerves won't wear out. It stops when he dies."

"He deserved that?" a doubting Eclipse asked.

"No, but it's the best I can do. He deserved much worse." Aurora sounded entirely sure of herself. Eclipse decided she very definitely did not want to have Aurora mad at her.

"Sounds good," Eclipse said. "I need to think about the facts in those structures. Can you be free this evening, west coast time? And tomorrow AM, early, we all need to be ready." She transferred to Aurora a set of Rajul's other memories.

CHAPTER 34 AN ISOLATED RANCH

Eclipse and Aurora peered cautiously through a line of pine scrub. A few lights below marked the house and buildings of an isolated ranch. The two of them knew differently. Serene Master Rajul...what a strange title...had known the locations of this terrorist base in the United States. The money came from selling illegal medicine. It went not to the people who made the medicine but to the people down below, crazies who blew up bridges and oil refineries and staged terror raids against shopping malls.

Eclipse shifted her gaze all around, regularly watching the area behind them. Eclipse reminded herself that Aurora was doing the hard part of the work. She was just covering Aurora's back. On the island, Cloud and Comet and Star were talking about building their base. First they had to buy the island, for which they had a surplus of money relative to the asking price. Now Aurora was ecstatic. Eclipse had asked her to help, to do something useful with her gifts.

Aurora completed her description of the fortress in front of them. "Sorry it took so long. They've got a half-dozen telepaths. I had to work around them. I didn't get as much as I wanted." Eclipse glanced at Aurora's notepad. Not only did it have a full description of the hidden fortress in front of them, it had a list of other terrorist bases around the United States, bases Rajul hadn't known about. "Except this place is the top-end base. Now I try their telepaths. One of them doesn't sound nearly so good as the others. Mayhaps I can get his thoughts."

Eclipse gestured for a pause. "We don't want to give away we see them," she cautioned.

"OK. I'll be very careful. I promise." Aurora sent her thoughts out again, setting a pattern as soft and strong as a spider web. Eclipse waited patiently. She'd have needed days to do this, if she could have done it at all. She could read people's minds, but afterwards people knew something had been done to them. "Got him." Aurora was quiet for a while. "Get us out! Fast!"

Not waiting for an explanation, Eclipse called the gift she had held poised and waiting. The two girls fell into a cascade of aqua light, leaving behind the faintest sound of a ringing bell. For an instant, they hovered above raging waves, freezing salt spume blowing around them. Then they hovered above lunar craters. A final wash of blue light brought them to a pine grove, to the canopy of a small tent.

"Hmmh?" Aurora said. "Where are we? That was a triple jump."

"What happened?" Eclipse asked. "You said go, so I got."

"That guy I was reading. He was their security. They have little teeny-tiny robot aircraft, like giant dragonflies. They spotted heat sources. Us. I was working through his mind when one found us. We got out before they could check. They get lots of, ummh, the robots see things that aren't there, so he's probably not suspicious, not even about the flash from your teleport. The triple jump?" Aurora asked.

"Oh! Welcome to the Fortress of Evanescent Darkness, Mod 2. If you're scanned with tesdri—they had those motion detectors—and teleport more than yourself, you teleport the tesdri rays. They spread out from where you went. Someone might detect them spreading, and track where you went in your teleport step. So if you need to hide, you don't teleport straight home," Eclipse explained.

"Anyhow, I got all these notes," Aurora said. "I'll write them up. And I read the guy's mind. He's in charge. That list of other bases I wrote down? It's complete, every one. And I learned how they protect themselves against spies sneaking up on their bases, so we can do it more."

"He was a telepath," Eclipse said. "Pickering said there are no telepaths."

Aurora clenched a fist. She should have found out more about that. "The guy I was reading. He went to Peru—the Andes people. They taught him. Remember? When you listened to the currents of the earth, you said there were telepaths in Peru and Tibet?"

"OK," Eclipse answered. "And now one here. Wait. The others?"

"Oh, right," Aurora said. "Didn't get into their minds. But he was in charge. They stayed totally out of sight. They gave orders and kept to themselves. Their minds? They were almost like Lemurians."

Eclipse nodded. Somepalce there was another layer of plotters here, one she hadn't penetrated yet. One layer at a time sounded good for now. Then she realized what Aurora had said. "Wait a moment! This fellow went to Peru? They engifted him? Gave him gifts?"

"No. Not engifted," Aurora explained. "Morgana showed me what engifting looks like, just not how to do it. This was something that ran in complicated circles. It was attached to him. It did telepathy. When he told it to."

"Can you show me? Please?" Eclipse asked. Aurora passed memories to the older girl.

"Drat!" Eclipse finally said. "It's a *structure*."

"What was that word?" Aurora asked. "*Structure*. What language is it?"

"High Goetic. Mum insisted I learn it," Eclipse answered. "A *structure* is like a gift, except it does exactly one thing...sort of.

Structures don't have a lot of power. But if you know how, you can give one to someone who isn't a persona, and they can talk mentalically. Or whatever. You can teach other personas neat tricks to do with their gifts, by sharing a *structure* with them."

"You can teach me how to make them?" Aurora asked.

"No," Eclipse answered. "I can make them, because Mum did something to me, something fourth order or so. I can't teach how to make them. Do you feel up to doing their other bases tonight? You were really chill. But if you're tired, we can wait."

Aurora nodded. "The other places are a lot smaller. It's no big trade. A couple hours should do it."

~~~~~~

A cheery campfire sent shadows radiating across the beach. Cloud and Star perched on driftwood. Comet and Aurora had wrapped themselves in a large blanket. This was a nice island, they decided, not as hot as the tropics. It was also uninhabited. People had lived here, but not any more. Eclipse, having produced reclining lawn chair and quilt, swaddled herself in the cloth and lay back, listening while Aurora talked. After all, she told herself, Aurora had put it all together, assembling the stray facts she'd been given into a solid pattern. That was Aurora's true gift: not chess or stones or territories, but seeing patterns. References that yesterday made no sense were now depressingly clear.

"...The fellows we got this evening put everything together," Aurora said. "Alex's bailiffs can't find money leaving the country because it stays here. The terrorists don't know they get money from medicine smuggling. The medicine smugglers don't know they're giving their money to terrorists. There's people in between them. Tonight we reached the in-between group. We worked up enough levels to find cross-links."

Eclipse pulled the blanket closer around her shoulders. Her dream of the previous night kept coming back to her. She'd been in England, at the Babbage Shrine, the holy of holies of the Order of Applied Logic. There'd been a ceremony, High Programmers and Analysts Supreme from around the world venerating their cult objects to consecrate computations directed against her. In the central sanctum, lurking within the functional Atlanticean gear computer, had been a creature of grey shadows, a creature of immaterial transistors and magnetic bubbles and optrodes: the Ghost of the Machine. The ghost chittered and babbled at its human followers, leading them to new heights of inspiration. Its inspiration had a single focus: Eclipse and her stolen Namestone. The followers heard logic and truth, but Eclipse recognized the voice of the stars echoing the twisted whispers of the Ghost. These were the men and women upon whom the world relied for moral revelation, and they were firmly entangled by the Adversary. Eclipse wondered what her undermind was trying to tell her. It seemed marvelously obscure.

Her attention returned to the present. Aurora had completed her report. Tracking the medicine smugglers brought them to the crazy people with guns. Pickering's bailiffs had no hint that the two groups were linked. This evening they had jumped through several cities, moving from target to target until they penetrated the terrorist network. There weren't that many terrorists, but they had very effective support. From the final visitation, they had learned where terrorists would strike soon.

"This happens tomorrow morning," Cloud said. "We'll be there to stop them. Should we tell the bailiffs?"

"Mayhaps," Star said. "Bailiffs can get bystanders out of the way."

"If bystanders know, troublemakers might, too," Aurora said.

"We could warn people," Star countered. "Shouldn't we?"

"Star, we absolutely positively don't want these people not to show up, do we?" Comet's answer was not a question. "That's why we were so careful not to upset the terrorists Aurora mind read. If they thought we were watching, they'd call everything off. There are always six or eight of these people showing up at a time to cause trouble, and there are five of us, and these people have never ever heard of personas in their lives so they'll be forcemeat as soon as we hit them, but if we tell anyone what's about to happen the secret might get out and these people won't show up at the mall to be arrested."

"But," Star objected.

"Game it out?" Cloud proposed. After all, this was what you learned in school every year. He couldn't tell which side was right, and boys vs. girls wasn't a satisfying answer, especially when Comet was the girl. He needed the right answer, even if it was the girl's answer. He sketched lines in the sand. "First we warn, second we don't. On first, we warn, they still show up. Or first, we warn, they go someplace else. On second, they show up, we swamp them at once. Or they show up, enough there's a big fight, people get hurt."

"On second," Comet added, "They don't show up at all. Say they get lost."

Cloud waited for silence. "That's all choices?"

"Warn, they show up, is very good. We win, no one else is hurt. But unlikely," said Comet. Cloud marked the line ++/0+, thinking as he did: ++ good result with 0+ chance of its happening. "Warn, they don't show is likely."

"That's a plus," Star said. "No one gets hurt."

"Star!" Aurora groaned. "Star! They want trouble, not shooting up a particular mall. If they don't go there, they go someplace else. For sure. Someplace we aren't. And it's like that video news we saw last night. All those dead people. It's terrible. And sure to happen." Star looked at the ground, then shook his head. Cloud marked the line—/1-.

"Don't warn, they show up and get swamped. That's a win, and sure," said Star. "++/1."

"My line's wrong," said Comet. "They don't show up for some other reason, after we warn? That's them getting lost or something that's got nothing to do with us." She moved to rub out her line. Cloud stopped her, instead adding a matching line under 'don't warn'. "Oh! That's a draw, warn or don't warn. Agree?" she asked. Cloud smiled happily. This was Games, not something girls and boys argued about.

"The last one," Star said, "That's six of them beating six of us, isn't it? That's real bad but no chance." Cloud marked the line -/0.

"Everyone agree?" asked Cloud.

"People?" intruded Eclipse. "If they knew who you were, and what you were, and you warned, they might ambush. We've been careful, but the smugglers we arrested were on video news. The places Star wrecked got noticed, even if people thought he used explosives and flame projectors. For sure, if history were where it belonged, and someone knew I was coming, half of the League Peace Police would be waiting for me. Right? I'm not sure these clowns can ambush us. Not first time around, not with weapons that work. But they might have something up their sleeves. Gas. That silly medicine, Body fields up always?" Cloud added another line at the bottom, marking it—/? .

"Call it," directed Cloud. "Warn or not? One finger or two?" Cloud and Star, Comet and Aurora each closed their eyes and brought up a hand. Each had two fingers showing. Eclipse held both palms before her chest, tokening her acquiescence in their decision.

CHAPTER 35 BRINGING TRANQUILITY THROUGH UNRESTRAINED MEGAVIOLENCE

The food court was almost deserted, the breakfast crowd having decamped to their offices while the coffee break population had not yet arrived. The five sat at a table carefully chosen for its inconspicuous location.

"Now what?" Star whispered.

"Sit," Cloud answered. "Be frigid. Don't get noticed."

"Talk," Come answered. "So we look normal."

Cover story? Aurora suggested. *If someone asks, Mommy told us to sit right here while she buys a dress. You two [images of Cloud and Eclipse] came along. Keeping us company. Last time it took her two hours.* Star winced. *THAT WAS PERFECT, STAR! Do it again if someone asks. [Image of Star wincing, four minds chiming in on how and why his wince communicated the pained acceptance of filial duty.]*

Find Mall Security? Eclipse asked. *Aurora does don't-notice on them? So they don't kick us out? I did that to the Food Court tosser—no, different title, same job.*

"Still boring," Cloud said.

Aurora nodded toward a two-man television news team nursing their coffees at a nearby table. *The video cameramen? Their studio puts them in malls weekday mornings, hoping to see terrorists arrested. They've been at it for a month.*

"You guys are out of base ball nines stories? I don't believe it!" Comet managed a straight face.

'Someone could hear us," Star whispered. "We're talking teams and players who don't exist. There isn't even a Winter League. Los Angeles and San Diego and San Francisco play Summer League." He sipped at his soda, the rest taking turns pretending to eat.

"The Zelza Orangemen? Are they still eight-time All-League Series champions?" Eclipse asked, her fragmentary knowledge of the national pastime stretching against its outer limits.

"No Orangemen." Cloud answered. "Not even a Zelza. It's got a different name. The city of Zelza was renamed after a mythical persona. We have to look him up. After all, myths of personas must start someplace. And a New York team - not the Flying Dutchmen - actually won a pennant." All five smiled at the absurdity.

"No Winter League?" Aurora asked. "What do boys watch on video all winter?"

"Football," a puzzled Star answered.

"You mean kickball? Or soccer? They watch a girl's game?" Comet looked perplexed. At home, boys would never watch a girls' game of anything, any more than girls would watch a boys' game like base ball nines.

"Tackle football," said Star. "Guys wearing armor and stuff, like they are personas. Except they aren't. Telzey found a news item. They play soccer in Europe. And it's guys playing, not gals. Except the American National Women's Team is the greatest in the universe. And in America, grass hockey is for girls and ice hockey and lacrosse are mostly for boys."

"Oh, that is simply too strange for words," a tired Comet said. "For sure, I've heard of tackle football, cause President Wilson made Congress agree to ban it, and everyone knows that, because that was the last time a President ever asked Congress for a law, so it's as important as the Constitution of the Fourth Republic and the Bill of Rights. But guys playing soccer? Only girls playing grass hockey?"

"Guys would play soccer well," Eclipse said, "even if it was only fun stories before the change." Cloud nodded and smiled at her.

Gang? Aurora interrupted. *Mall Security! They're in their office. Men are pointing guns at them. One man answers the Bell. The County Marshal thinks everything is great here.* The fivesome gave her their full attention. *There's bunches of other fellows wandering around the Mall, all aware of each other. Like FedCorps Commandos.* Eclipse frowned. FedCorps Commandos, ungifted or not, were not her favorite people.

Burglar alarms? Cloud asked. *Has someone—no. They don't have a local persona league.*

Where are they? Comet chimed in. *What are they doing?*

Walking, Aurora answered. *Trying to have people not see them. Give me a moment? They pulled the mall out of DataLink. Whatever they call DataLink now. No computer links. People are upset. They buy things and their debit cards won't subtract. No, not debit cards. Like debit cards, but inside out. Buy now. Pay later. A very stupid idea. So they stand there. Clerks are running in circles.*

Be frigid, sister. Star tried to be encouraging. *Besides, they've got a persona league here. In place to rescue them.*

? Cloud inserted.

Greater Medford! Us. And we're almost at Medford, Oregon, even. Star looked around the table. *And the world's greatest solo.* He allowed himself a dramatic pause. *Eclipse, the Invincible.*

Invincible? Eclipse said. She managed a grateful smile.

*You took the Maze, right? You told the whole League of Nations to *fire off, right? You blew away Solara. You're going to tell me who changed the world, so I can blow them to dust, right? You must be the greatest!*￼ Star explained.

He didn't say great at, Cloud cut himself off at mid-word, the 'what' passing almost unthought from his mind. *What are they doing?*

They've got places to go, Aurora said. *They're so many! Twenty-plus. We thought six! Okay, found a fellow who knows half the plan. They'll start something there.* She indicated the far end of the Food Court, where three girls scarcely older than Comet were having brunch. *Cause a commotion. Start shooting. When people run, the rest start shooting. Getaway truck is outside.* She marked another point on her mental image of the mall.

Set off fire alarms? Cloud asked. *Clear the building? Now we know who they are?*

Aurora tensed. *I can't. Someone's pulled the plug. No power.*

The fivesome strained not to look except at each other. There came louder voices. A half-dozen juveniles, youths of eighteen or twenty, sauntered across the Court, converging on the three girls.

This is it. Go! Cloud ordered. He rose, moving to follow the juveniles, who had grouped at the extreme end of the Court and begun making loud, crude remarks in the girls' direction. Comet and Aurora flushed at the words. Eclipse widened her steps to keep two paces behind an obviously furious Cloud, leaving Aurora lagging in her wake.

A punk leaned over the table, reached for one of the girls, to be slapped away. The girls looked around, desperate for help, not at all sure that Cloud qualified. Cloud's glare, even directed at the six punks, was less than completely reassuring.

"She told you to leave her alone," a determined Cloud announced. He stepped around the table, blocking the direct path between two of the girls and their assailants.

"Well," asked one of them, "What have we here? Playing hero? How cute!" The punk tugged at his sleeve, pulling from a concealed pocket a half-foot length of black plastic.

"You have a problem with heroes?" Cloud asked, setting his hands firmly on his waist. "Or mayhaps you simply have problems?"

"Oh," the second punk grunted. "Oh. A wise guy. Clever."

Eclipse moved up to Cloud, staying a half-pace back. "I'm left," she whispered. She stood on the balls of her feet, fists open. Aurora was a few yards behind them.

"Oh," continued the second punk. "Two of them. How cute. Or does the real little girl make it two-and-a-half?"

Guys? Aurora's thought came. *There are thirty! All with guns!*

They pulled the Bell cables. That RadioBell lookalike Alex showed us—
*it's jammed.**

*These six have back-up?** Cloud asked.

*Upper balcony.** Aurora flashed an image of the mall, men and
weapons clearly marked.

*Find them all, Aurora,** Cloud directed. *So we take them out fast.**

Star leaned back against a column, legs crossed. Had anyone's
attention not been riveted to Cloud and his opponents, the golden haze of
Star's body shield would have been seen at shirt sleeves and collar.
*Hey,** Star answered cockily, *They start shooting, they're toast!**

The punk closed on Cloud. "Move it, twit!" He pressed a stud on the
plastic, revealing a six-inch switchblade. The knife floated towards
Cloud's face. The three girls squealed in terror and pushed back from
their table. Cloud took a half-step toward the punk, Eclipse fanning out
to his left. *Aurora?** Cloud called. To his relief, she had maintained the
mindlink. *I move, you wall the ungifteds? Yourself, too.**

The punk slashed down. To Cloud's heightened reflexes, the move
was dismally slow. He reached, caught the punk's arm above the wrist,
and twisted sideways, hearing a comforting snap as the punk's elbow
exceeded its biologically-appointed rotation limit.

The remaining hoodlums, not waiting for their leader, began drawing
knives and guns. Cloud released the punk's now-useless arm and made a
short punch, connecting with the hoodlum's chin. Cloud's strength was
behind the blow. The punk's neck snapped before his body began its
upward trajectory. A second punch sent the body backwards, straight at
two followers. They scrambled sideways, desperate to gain a clear field
of fire. Almost too fast to be seen, Cloud vaulted the table, modulation of
gravity giving him an impossibly flat trajectory. An incidental kick
dropped one hoodlum; he body-tackled the second. They sailed
backward for the floor, the punk thinking he had an easy target firmly in
hand, Cloud noting that very soon he would be able to smash the punk's
skull repeatedly into the tile and reinforced concrete of the floor.

Aurora snapped a force wall into position, its gray haze flickering like
an aged fluorescent light, setting a virtually impenetrable barrier across
the Food Court. The girls, shielded but dumbfounded, stood gawking.
Not waiting for Cloud to complete his moves, Eclipse flashed into action,
a double step leading into right pivot kick directed at a hoodlum's kidney
and ribs. In the moment she connected with her target, her hand stabbed
left, fingers lined with the steel of a body screen passing under a second
opponent's rib cage into kidneys and solar plexus. The kick drove her
left. To Comet's eyes, a flicker of blue betrayed Eclipse's screens,
powered to stop knives and small arms. Eclipse's recovery continued

into a second kick, straight ahead, catching the final and by far largest hoodlum off-balance. The crunch was a knee, shattering on contact with force-screen-hardened heel. A left-handed back-swing snapped the second punk's shoulder. The final punk rolled forwards. A final Y-kick, Eclipse fully extended, crashed into the third punk's face.

The slightest hum. Cloud and Eclipse glanced over shoulders, noting where the first hoodlum held half of an Uzi machine pistol. The other half fell floorward, Star having neatly cut the weapon in twain with one shot.

STAR! Aurora called. *MEN on the BALCONIES* She flashed three images, three groups of men bringing automatic weapons to the ready.

"Toast," Star announced. "Toast." *Oops! No lines of fire. [Images of the group he was about to engage, and groups he couldn't reach without demolishing innocent bystanders.]*

Cloud leaped for the balcony and more villains. His jump was accompanied by fog, appearing around the hoodlums, thickening until none save he could see. Eclipse blurred into violet light, the ring of a massive gong marking her reappearance next to the third group of criminals. A hum and whine marked Star's opening shots; the chatter of heavy automatic weapons indicated his lack of perfect aim.

They ducked, noted Star. *But great news! They're all shooting at me.*

Spectators heard crashes and thuds. Unconscious bodies rained from Cloud's fog, sailing over the balcony rail toward the main floor. Eclipse launched a rapid-fire set of blows, reducing the group she had engaged to bodies on the floor, guns scattered in all directions, and a single figure who expertly blocked her first pair of moves and returned a chop and kick in kind. Behind her, shoppers not fleeing for their lives saw lines of tracer rounds bounce harmlessly from Star's clothing. His counterfire, precisely accurate, dropped one felon after the next.

Aurora? Star asked. *The men with guns. They were trying to kill me? Weren't they? I mean, I didn't have time to tell them they're under arrest. That's really bad. It's not a proper duel if I kill them when they aren't trying to kill me.*

Check, his sister confirmed. *They're trying. Well, they were trying. Ones DOWN THERE! Targets are SHOPPERS! [Images of the mall, people with guns precisely marked.]*

Great. Real great. There's even walls in the way. Star groaned.

Hang tight, brother. Comet, swathed in brilliant pastels, zipped across the Food Court, grabbed Star in her flight field, and accelerated two of them down the central arcade. An occasional jink swept her around the decorative banners that filled the atrium. Not quite too late, she reminded herself that she really should not go supersonic inside a building she cared about, no matter how precisely her flight field tried to put back the air molecules after she passed.

Eclipse blocked the chop and kick, then dropped into a purely defensive posture. The elderly African gentleman before her paused. Surely she had only hit three blackshirts? All six hoodlums lay unconscious on the pavement. She smiled and executed a formal bow. "My apologies for this inconvenience," she said. "These persons planned on impoliteness." Apparently Manjukuoan handfighting had survived better than Manjukuo itself.

"Inconvenience?" the gentleman answered. "These men seem to be enjoying their nap." He grinned and returned her bow, bending a shade shallower than she had.

ECLIPSE! Aurora shrieked. *There's NO TIME for GAMES! There's more of them!* Another picture of the Mall, villains, locations marked.

This is not a game, Eclipse countered primly. *This is correct manners. Why don't you stop them?*

I CAN'T! I'd have to MANIFEST! The exchange between Aurora and Eclipse lasted tens of milliseconds.

Aurora, I manifested. Star has. Even Comet has. Besides, you think anyone will notice, there being a full scale battle going on here? Eclipse finished her answer by jumping skywards, flight field engaging as she did. "Pardon me, talk later!" Her apology to her erstwhile foe went heard but unseen. The Master had noted gunfire and was well into a leaping roll through the door of his Dojo. A rear door and fire escape were his urgent target.

The three girls at the restaurant shouted at Aurora. "Run! They're shooting." Aurora ignored them.

One of the girls darted to grab Aurora, a small child who had obviously panicked and frozen, out where she'd be shot by terrorists. The other girls sprinted for the exit. Aurora spread her arms above her head. The space around her faded to gray, then sharpened to a polished-gold pyramidal latticework, within which appeared an unsmiling lidless eye. Around the mall, striking at the speed of thought, bolts of mentalic energy struck down terrorist after terrorist.

"Gleep!" choked Aurora's erstwhile rescuer, suddenly wishing she had not skipped an impromptu field hockey game to walk the mall with East-coast visitors. She turned, almost running down the television cameraman, who stood and filmed, oblivious to personal hazard. Only later did she remember a terrorist, recovering from one of Cloud's kicks, whose surreptitious pistol draw came to a sudden stop when she broke her field hockey stick over his head. Only much later did she remember the little girl's voice, inside her head without her hearing it, telling her where to run.

Star and Comet, having covered a third-mile of mall in a few seconds, finished a hairpin turn and worked back along the Mall, Star's bursts of energy occasionally pausing for a Comet jink to dodge gunfire. Cloud, his charge down the Mall masked by fog, spoke. *Guys? Something started in the Food Court. I had surprise. All along the Mall they started shooting at once. Sure looks familiar? But how'd people down there [Image: Star and Comet's end of the Mall] know what we're doing here?*

Eclipse, screens at high power, flew above the balcony, her trajectory a series of lunate arcs. She approached individual goons from near-vertically above, relying on steel-hard screens, close to a hundred pounds weight, and flight fields that could accelerate her at tens of gravities to knock villains from their feet, concuss skulls, and break miscellaneous bones. Cloud's question evoked her unconcealed astonishment: It was sensible, and she hadn't thought of it before he had.

Aurora concentrated on hoodlums in unseen locations. Mall Security, held at gunpoint in their own office, saw their captors drop weapons, clasp at heads, and fall to the carpet, lapsing into convulsions and unconsciousness.

COMET! STAR! Aurora again shouted. *Men in the center.* [More images, points well-marked.] *Throwing grenades.*

"Too many, Star," said Comet. "What do we do? I can catch them all, but where do I put them?"

Mine! Eclipse answered. **Comet! Clear out!** She gestured at the Mall's center court, where fountains splashed, birds trilled in a huge cage, and a milling swirl of panic-stricken women and children formed a target for the grenadiers. A cacophony of discordant carillons. A wave of blue light rolled over the crowd. The wave receded, revealing an empty promenade into which fell a half-dozen phosphorous grenades. **They're outside now,** explained a dizzy Eclipse. **Mayhaps a mite confused? Timing was tight. [Image: grenades in upwards trajectories, still feet over the crowd when the crowd was teleported.] Comet? You and Star? Outside reconnaissance?**

Check.

HELP ME Aurora suddenly screamed. *HELP!* Her shout carried the brassy taste of unexpected pain. *There's a LEMURIAN. HE'S HURTING ME!* She managed a blurry image of her location, the lattice-pyramid of her gifts crumpling around her. Don't cry, she told herself. Crying is for little boys, and you're a girl.

"Aurora!" Comet shouted. "Where?" Cloud, his next three targets in plain sight, concentrated on his immediate opportunity.

Fight back! Darn it, Aurora! Stop being a scaredy-cat all the time! Eclipse's answer was sharply unforgiving.

I am NOT a SCAREDY-CAT! YOU'RE even MEANER than BRIAN! Aurora, anger distracting her from the pain of the mentalic attack, focused her will on her own defenses. The hostile mentalist had infiltrated her mind, wedged openings in her outer screens, and was trying to inflict lethal damage within. *You STOP THAT!* a furious Aurora shouted. Counterblows fragmented wedges and shattered webs of infiltration. Her foe matched blow for blow, trying to re-establish his positional superiority. Aurora reached within herself, deeper and deeper, desperately calling strength she hoped she had.

Where are they? Eclipse asked. Her objective of angering Aurora having been accomplished, her new thoughts were as flat as unsweetened whipped cream.

There. [Two sharp pictures, points in the Mall's two office wings.] HURRY! They're stronger than me! Aurora said.

Got it. Eclipse? Take left? Cloud said. The boy leaped over sales racks, turning from the main mall into a large men's store. **Behind that wall, I think.**

Check. Eclipse confirmed.

HURRY, Aurora pleaded. *The LEMURIANS are BOTH attacking ME, and THEY'RE WINNING.*

Cloud gestured. The further wall of the Men's Store cracked at a dozen seams, gray concrete dust eddying across the room. A further gesture set up new clouds of dust, sending racks of suits and sport jackets spilling onto the carpet. Row after row of cinder block crumbled, burying good fabric in a sea of gray. Something emerged from the haze. Cloud stopped in his footsteps, gaping in astonishment at the creature in front of him. What was it? Surely nothing like that had walked the world before the change. Was it a giant spider bred with a man, the cross being a creature the height of a horse, but twice as wide? The head was human, on a human neck; the skin, where not covered by polished-blue strap-on armor, was slate gray. Eight limbs, jointed like human arms but dangling vertically from the torso, came in four pairs; the forward-most two waved large-caliber automatic weapons.

Customers screamed in terror. Others stood paralyzed with astonishment. The creature began shooting, systematically killing everyone in its path.

CLOUD! Aurora shouted. *The LEMURIAN. It's right in the room *with you! Can't you see it?*

No problem, Cloud said nonchalantly. He reached within, summoning the full scope of his gifts. Opaque clouds flooded the salesroom. Deafening crashes marked lightning bolts, one after the next striking the creature's armor. The creature fired randomly, lashing out against a foe it could no longer see. Once and again, single rounds hit Cloud, stinging despite the protections of his gifts. He shifted aim, targeting the guns, which detonated with a satisfying staccato crackle of exploding ammunition. The creature bellowed in agony. Its armor, heated by grounding currents, glowed orange-red. Around it the store burst into flames, a dismal hiss marking the unsuccessful effort of the Mall's sprinkler system to compete with Cloud's energy bursts. Cloud redoubled his efforts, lightning rumbling in a near-continuous roar. The creature fell to its elbows, thrashing convulsively, and collapsed in death.

Was that it, Aurora? he asked. *It was real tough. It stood up to a lot. More than a caisson would, even.*

Help Eclipse! The other one! HURRY!

Comet and Star soared around the Mall. To their astonishment, the rear of two eighteen-wheel trailers burst apart, each trailer disgorging a pair of tanks. Was that possible, Star wondered? Wouldn't a tank crush the frame of a moving van? Neither their wheels nor bridge abutments would tolerate such a load. Notwithstanding his unspoken objection that the laws of nature forbade what he saw, the tanks rolled ahead, completed three-foot drops off the rear of their trailers, and advanced on the defenseless mall.

Star spotted the tanks. *Aurora?* he asked. *Friendly?*

NO!!! NO!!! ANTIAIRCRAFT! Aurora shouted.

Across the Mall, Eclipse shot down a hallway, a trajectory near the ceiling allowing her to dodge fleeing salesmen. She winced while she scanned the rooms ahead. There was the Lemurian, right where Aurora had indicated. The walls were concrete brick, but the Lemurian's outline blocked her scan. A force field! Pickering's assurance that his world knew nothing of energy defenses rang hollow, or he was less knowledgeable than he thought.

A doorway was not in sight. Grimly, she brought arms across her face in an X-block, enhanced screens and flight field, and rammed the wall in front of her. Cranking down her levels, quickly, hurt. She had expected a few ungifteds with guns, not full-scale combat. The shock of collision ran up her arms, jarring shoulders and rattling teeth. Fragments of cinder block, shards of concrete filling, and pieces of tie rod sailed in all directions.

The Lemurian, concentration entirely engaged in fighting Aurora, looked confusedly up from its desk. To Eclipse he appeared human, lacking the deformities characteristic of a dedicated Racemaster. A shapeless beige coverall failed to hide heavy body armor. Body screens were marginally visible as edges within which dust-laden air remained crystal clear.

Outside, Comet dipped earthward, skimming inches above the mall roof. At the wall, Star dismounted. Comet turned to soar away, eyes alert for hostile fire.

At the edge of the parking lot, within the lead tank, Commander spoke to gunner. "High explosive. Load. Target main entrance. Driver: active opposition, unspecified. Three, warn the Illuminated Ones. Button up before we hit the entrance."

"Loaded!"

"Fire." The tank resounded to the roar of its main battery as a shell packed with explosives headed for the Mall. Further rumbles were other tanks, also opening fire.

"No way," Star said to himself. "No way you guys do this." He gestured at the rightmost tank. A coruscating blaze of energy struck down, killing the driver and sending the vehicle momentarily out of control. Within the vehicle, crew scrambled to close hatches and extinguish fires set by Star's blast. "Golly, Eclipse was right. Multiple targets would be so frigid right now!"

In the tanks, command radio operator reported to formation leader: "Four is hit! Unknown weapon. Three says weapons installation on mall roof."

"Three!" Formation Leader called. "Where on the roof? I see nothing anomalous."

"The man. That's him! That's him! Laser weapon. Engaging with hull MGs," Three reported. Formation Leader scanned the roof. What was that skywards? A signal flare? Too late to engage it, whatever it was. "No effect," Three reported. "Engage with main battery. High explosive! Fire!"

"One and Two," Team Leader ordered, "continue at Mall. Three, provide overwatch. Four, recover to perimeter overwatch. Forward! Forward! Forward for the Living God!" An explosion to Star's right marked the first shell. He kept his attention on Four, concentrating his will. A searing burst of energy lanced against the hapless tank, lacing the treadwork, destroying an entire side's drive sprockets. Four spun right, immobilized and burning.

Three fired. A direct hit! Star was momentarily blinded by thick smoke. He attacked Four one last time, harder than ever, making a bank shot at the gap between turret and chassis. Brilliant pyrotechnics marked another hit, one welding turret to body.

"No effect!" Three reported. "HE has no effect."

"Correct your aim! Human targets cannot resist high explosive!" Command continued its roll between ranks of parked cars, driving for the mall entrance. Motorists swerved to either side. Command driver skillfully wove left and right, carefully avoiding any impact that would assuredly crush the cars but would risk immobilizing Command.

"Another direct hit!" Three reported to Command. "No effect. Gunner! Switch to APDS! Fire!"

Twenty pounds of depleted uranium smashed into Star's screens, the golden haze deforming as it dissipated the impact. Star sailed backward, his involuntary flight followed by a trail of vaporized metal. He hunched over, trying to recover his breath. Lights swam before his eyes. What was that? Something that hit harder than a strong persona. Don't cry, he told himself. No matter it hurts. Crying is for little girls, and you're a boy.

"Reload!" Three ordered. "Armor piercing."

Within the Mall, Eclipse felt delicate pressure against her mindscreens. Telehypnosis, she recognized, something to persuade her to relax her defenses. Very skillfully done, likely effective against unprepared targets. Her counterplay was more grossly physical. She changed course, altering her flight across the room. The Lemurian began to duck; she rolled sideways so her body screen brushed against his. She rebounded sideways, sending him sprawling. A half roll and more power to her flight field let her follow his trajectory, bouncing him into a steel pillar. The building shook. The Lemurian leaned against the pillar, lips slack, eyes unfocussed. She grabbed for his chest. If his screens weren't protecting him against impact, a few trips through nearby walls, him leading the way, might do wonders to rectify his ethics.

Body armor exploded in a flare of pyrotechnics. Eclipse found herself holding a six-foot column of flaming magnesium, metal burning brilliantly in the near ultraviolet. Her screens soared to higher and higher power, protecting hands and face from eye-searing light and heat. The demand on her gifts left her staggered, arms and legs shaking like the branches of an alder in a gale. Each reinforcement of her defenses, each step deeper in level, had taxed her personal strength. Suddenly she'd taken many unplanned steps with virtually no separation between them. She fought off an attack of nausea.

I think it's dead, Eclipse, a shaky Aurora noted. *All its mind went away.*

A clanging gong; a violet flash. Eclipse was outside, hovering above the pasture beyond the mall. The ground below was an empty field, grass not yet green. She shook her head. Brilliant worms of light crawled across a narrowing field of vision. She pushed away from her former opponent, allowing the incandescent mass to fall harmlessly to earth. Now what? she asked herself. She hurt inside. She'd done too much, too fast, calling on too many different gifts without a proper warmup first. It didn't matter. Star needed her help. Star was in real trouble, with a line of caissons—where had those come from?—crawling across the tarmac. She had to help him. She reached inside, calling the gift that let her alter the metric of space until there and here became one and the same.

Nothing. No all-consuming cerulean waterfall. No cascade of metallic song. Nothing. Vision faded to a reddish haze. Time to bail out, came a terminal coherent thought. Bail out or seriously hurt yourself. Her rapid glide, scarcely more than a half-controlled fall, dropped her into a copse of trees. A stumble and roll left her flat on the ground, face to the sky, a shallow depression masking lines of sight from the nearby battlefield. Eclipse released her gifts, demands on her strength falling virtually to nothingness. She concentrated on trying to breathe, waiting for the cold spring air to revive her. Star needed her help, and she was failing to help him. The levels of power, the Fall of Crystal, the Tomb, the Hall of the Lidless Eye, all waited her call, but the strength to reach them was gone. She'd prepared herself for a few hoodlums with guns, not an army with persona support. Now she'd asked more from her gifts than her fragile physical form, levels not properly summoned, could sustain.

Star let his good sense reassert its presence. Be smart, he told himself. This was not the moment to stay in one place, groaning and moaning. That was for little girls. Comet hadn't done that over Washington, and she'd been hurt a lot worse than he was; he wasn't going to let her show him up. Not in a world that didn't know how incredibly frigid he was. He threw himself to the roof, moving sideways on hands and knees until he reached the parapet. Two caissons were rapidly closing on the Mall entrance. The third's gun was aimed at the roof, its crew obviously looking for him. Pedestrians fled in all directions. It was up to him.

He stood. A cone of golden fire surrounded the third tank, burning off the paint, flaming until exterior fittings glowed orange-red in the heat. The turret wheeled, a desperate gunner trying to bring Star into his sights. Star focused a pencil of energy, playing first over the turret ring and then against the gun mantlet. A dull bang! marked a loaded shell cooking off. The crew bailed out of emergency exits just before the tank burst into flames.

The final pair of tanks rolled up the slope, machineguns blazing at Mall walls. Star called on all of his strength, sending a single needle-sharp blast directly at the first tank. The lance of energy penetrated front armor, crew spaces, engine, and rear armor, sending vaporized metal spraying in all directions. Detonation of the ammunition stores brought the vehicle to a shuddering halt. Seconds later, a similar blow put paid to the final tank and its crew.

Star leaned over, saw what the terrorists had done and wished he hadn't eaten. He'd still won. No matter they'd been a lot stronger than expected. He'd beaten them, practically all by himself—well, Cloud had done a great job, and Aurora had helped a teeny bit, and Comet had gotten him into position fast. But he'd beaten them. He crossed his arms, set one foot on the parapet, and protectively scanned the parking lot. Even the appearance of Eclipse at his shoulder didn't perturb his mood.

"Really good!" she offered. Star glowed at the compliment. Her voice was faint. He wondered where she'd been. Mayhaps she'd actually done something useful for once? Something involving work? Mayhaps even danger to herself? That sounded farfetched, despite the unusual sheen of sweat and deep flush to her cheeks. "Were those guys tough as caissons?" she asked, distracting his thoughts.

"Yeah! Tougher! I had to hit them three or four times before they'd stop." He nodded confidently.

"You stopped them," she said. He hadn't expected her to clap him on the back. It was a real mark of appreciation, one only boys did to each other. Girls, he knew hugged, or even dumber things. Only boys knew how to show appreciation properly. How had she thought to do it? His sisters never would. "We still need to find the real villains."

"You'll get them!" He managed to grin at her. "Soon, right?" He checked his enthusiastic rush of words when he saw how hurt she looked.

"I try, Star. I try. I don't break promises. I haven't done it. I simply can't find their trace." She set hands on hips and turned away from him, her shoulders sagging.

"I know, Eclipse. I believe you." He tried to sound reassuring. She shook her head despondently. "You did great, finding that Rajul creep and this place. I do believe you." He hugged her, just for a moment.

Guys? Aurora said. *I think we ran out of villains.*

Aurora? Cloud spoke. *Find people who are hurt? If we get them in one place, Comet can fly them to hospitals.*

I'll gather, Comet announced, *if Eclipse ports.*

It needs several hospitals. There are lots of wounded. Some dead, Eclipse added. A few minutes recovery would leave her marginally able to invoke her gifts reliably.

A quarter-hour later, the fivesome stood in a distant corner of the parking lot, hidden from sight by parked cars. Eclipse, dazed, leaned back against a van, then shifted which shoulder she was leaning on. Something in her left arm had torn when she hit the tie rods, back when she was taking out the Lemurian, and she wasn't up to healing it at the moment. She didn't want to remember how many teleports she'd just done, one after another without even time to stretch in between. Hospitals weren't set up the way they had been before time was rearranged. They weren't practiced for mass casualties and triaging, not that hospitals had triaged often before the change. Luckily the second hospital she'd used had someone competent, the way she saw competent, someone who'd seen the battle on real-time video, accepted that a wisp of a girl was faster than all the ambulances in the world, and told her where—Portland, Seattle, San Francisco, New York—to take the wounded.

"Guys?" asked Star. "That's Alex's car. Where Alex?" They looked guiltily at each other. They'd all forgotten. Foreseeing no more than a random shooting or two, they'd agreed to let Alex come along, trusting his estimate that he'd be totally safe so long as he was well outside the mall area. Thirty terrorists, a tank platoon, and a pair of monsters was more than the expected guest list.

Aurora pursed her lips, an expectant frown crossing her face. "I can't find him!" she announced. "I can't find him anywhere!"

"He's got to be here," Cloud said. "He's got to be here someplace. He was way outside, not where he'd be in any danger."

"I'm looking. I'm looking!" The others felt an eye-searing brightness. Aurora sagged, her sister supporting her. "Sorry," Aurora eventually continued, "I found him? Three feet behind us. Sorry it got too bright."

"Good morning!" Pickering's perpetually cheery greeting was met by a babble of voices as the fivesome voiced their fears for his safety. "I see you dealt with matters. When the tanks emerged from yonder trailers," his walking stick pointed to the burning vehicles in question, "I decided it was high time to seek protective cover. I trust my absence did not overly alarm you?"

Aurora stared at Pickering. He couldn't have been behind his car, she told herself. He absolutely couldn't have been there. She hadn't made a stupid mistake like that in months and months. What had she done wrong? Her siblings poured out a description of the battle, Pickering listening to four voices at once.

"All finished here?" he asked. "Wounded to hospitals? Prisoners under guard? Leaders telepathically...actually, I don't know that. Aurora?" He focused his attention on the girl. "If they don't want to talk, can you pry facts out of their minds? Their employers' names, for example?"

"I looked," she answered. "The punks were getting a chance to be violent for pay. The tanks, they were backup. They'd never been needed before. They were very surprised to learn there was someone shooting back. They knew how they'd make their getaway, a truck. The two Lemurians knew lots, but they're dead."

"I suppose dying is an obstacle to mind reading," Pickering observed calmly.

"Not exactly," Eclipse answered. "Being in someone's mind when they die is like being in a city, sinking into the ocean, as one by one all the lights are doused. You see all sorts of things, just before they sink into the final shadow."

"But these people were dead too fast," Aurora explained. "Cloud completely zapped one. After Eclipse wrecked his screens, the other, he turned into a torch."

Pickering surveyed fires in the distance. Traffic jams at Mall exits promised a very slow trip home. The thought of departure raised an interesting question. "How did they plan to escape? Is there a local safe house?"

"Oh, no!" Cloud put hands to forehead.

"We forgot!" Star shouted. "Aurora? Quick! Where's the getaway car?"

"Gone," the embarrassed twelve-year-old answered. "There was a truck. They were supposed to pile in and run. I see where it was. Now it's gone."

"Aurora!" the boys whined in unison.

"It could be miles from here," Comet said. "What did it look like?"

"I don't know," Aurora answered. "I heard where it was parked, not its color."

"Eclipse," Cloud said, "I thought you said you don't have super strength. But I saw what happened to the guy you kicked in the face."

"I don't." Eclipse shrugged. "That was force field. Yours is right at your skin. Mine is a bit out to protect my clothes. And I can make my force field rigid, so I'm like a piece of solid steel, close to a hundred pounds and moving fast. When I kicked the guy, it was like hitting him with a hundred-pound sledge hammer."

Pickering looked at the Mall. A Sheriff's vehicle was proceeding in their direction. "I fear we attracted attention," he remarked. "You did fly to this point, Comet. They may wish to speak to Star. There is an interesting legal conundrum as to whether or not State laws discouraging private possession of antitank guns are binding on human beings who do it by waving their hands."

"Do we want to talk to him?" Eclipse asked. "Alex home, then the local authorities?" Seeing only negative responses, she looked inwards, summoning the gift that distorted space until here was there, taking the fivesome, Pickering, and his automobile away from the battlefield.

CHAPTER 36 ASK THE ARMY

"General Marquardt?"

General Benedict Marquardt froze in his tracks. The female voice came from directly behind him. BOQ temporary furnishings were spartan, but since his arrival he'd done little but sleep here, and not much of that. There was no room for someone to be hiding in a near-empty dinette. "Yes?" He turned smartly. "I didn't hear you knock," he said. "Let alone ask permission to enter." He couldn't possible have an aide this stupid, could he? A glance took in two figures in front of him, short, oddly attired. One had to be the girl who rescued the space plane. From her getup, the other was a friend.

Aurora cringed. Now a grownup was about to get mad at her.

"Sorry. Couldn't. Security." Eclipse explained. "You want to catch all the terrorists? You were on video, the man in charge of that."

"Darn right I do. Can you help?" The girls nodded. "Have a seat. I've got soda in the fridge." What were these kids supposed to do? What were they doing here? The kids had snagged a space plane out of orbit, too, much to the relief of American Interplanetary Spaceways. What could they do for him? He heard the report from this morning. At that Oregon mall, they'd finished off more terrorists in ten minutes than his command had seen in three weeks. Terrorists had had tactical surprise, too. Three dozen men, four tanks, and two creatures was off the top of the scale as a terrorist force. The terrorists still lost. "Mayhaps that's: What can you do?"

Thanks and introductions out of the way, Aurora explained. "I'm a telepath. So's Eclipse. She teleports. And breaks things. We tracked down all their secret bases. They're hidden. You had to mindread people to find them." Eclipse pulled maps and a pad of notes from an envelope. General Marquardt decided he couldn't remember a legal restriction on telepathic searches. But he'd be darn sure they had legitimate evidence before he went for search warrants.

"That's very impressive," Marquardt said. "My staff will be fascinated." Marquardt wondered if he should believe these two. "Washington will be truly grateful." The two girls' heads snapped toward each other. What had he just said?

"You shouldn't," Aurora said. "It's...Eclipse, that's what you did. You explain."

"Terrorists have very good electronics. And telepaths. We can tell. They've got your office wormed...ummh...bugged, you'd say. This place and your phone here are OK. They've got one of their—things—across your line of command. Across people who order you," Eclipse said.

"Doing mind control," Aurora said. The disgust in her voice was self-evident. "We almost took the map to Washington. Except Eclipse checked first. And found the Lemurian. Whatever he is. Controlling the people you work for."

The General was briefly thoughtful. "This is a bit much. The HQ compound is carefully swept. My superiors are just as careful. Let's start with getting bugs out of my office." Now, I report to the President, he noted to himself. With asides to the JCS and polite nods towards SoD. If something is compromised up there...well, you were told not to call all the time, just stay on with your job. See what the kids have.

The girls looked at each other again. *This is telepathy,* Eclipse announced. *But I can do pictures, too. I'll show you a salesman I raided.* [A littered apartment, surprised occupant staring at Eclipse. Two guards rushing in, blasting away with machine guns, to be shot by Eclipse. Robot with ray pistol crashing though wall.] *I didn't know you had robots or beam weapons.* [A second pistol, much heavier, the shock of recoil hurting Eclipse's wrists. Burst of light, walls sailing in all directions, Eclipse near the center, unhurt.] *And now I'll show not-quite-mind-control.* "Which hand is your soda in?" she asked. A decidedly right-handed general looked down, finding he had subconsciously switched his glass to his left hand. He switched it back.

"You can do that?" a surprised Aurora asked.

"Smoke and mirrors," she explained. General Marquardt had obviously caught the surprise in Aurora's voice. "And where's the glass now?" Marquardt stared at his glass, again in his left hand. He transferred the glass to his right hand again, gripping it very firmly. "As long as you pay attention, I can't fool you," Eclipse said. "You've got to be real distracted for my trick to work. Like driving a car, and thinking about something else. The Lemurian—whatever—does real mind control, makes people do things they don't want to."

"I don't suppose you have a plan for dealing with these people?" an uncomfortable Marquardt asked. Urban combat, room to room in a building with an opponent who could make your troops shoot each other, sounded problematic.

"When you're ready—your call, your choice—to take care of these bases, I'll fix the one in Washington. He's a persona. Ungifteds like you fight ungifteds. Personae like me deal with personae. Fixing him is our job," she announced matter-of-factly.

"Your job?" Marquardt's tone was decidedly negative. "Aren't you just a bit young for this sort of thing? I caught your TV interviews. If this was before things got changed," Marquardt decided he really did not believe that part, but no matter, "wouldn't I just send each of you home to your parents?"

Aurora, frightened, tried to make peace. "Me. Don't need to shout at me. I'll go. I did my part."

"Actually," Eclipse said, "if this was before the change, I'd do what I want to. When the Aztecan Empire—you don't have one of them— invaded America, I wrecked up their antimissile defenses, and killed their commanding officer. If you had a European officer here, he'd probably try to arrest me. Or kill me." The General's eyebrows rose. "The League of Nations was really fired off at me. No matter. There's isn't even a League, not now. But I'm legally an adult." General Marquardt wondered what would drive men to kill a girl no older than his first grand-daughter. He had more important problems. This enormous cache of supposed information—was it legitimate, or some sort of ruse? His staff would need to confirm what they were being told.

He picked his telephone. "Jim? Ben here. You, Staff Intelligence, Signals, here...no, I'm at my quarters...ASAP. Do not use phones. Yes, there's a very good reason. Fifteen minutes? And bring your T-4s and files." Marquardt turned back to Eclipse. "You'll brief us. Get the bugs out of my office. Help us keep them out. We'll speak up when we're ready, or have more questions."

~~~~~

General Benedict Marquardt and staff stood in their temporary headquarters. They had spent two days checking Aurora's report, confirming everything she had said. Facts they'd known, and she hadn't, confirmed her story. He'd been convinced after the first hour, when the girls had pulled the bugs from his offices. Microphones were one thing. Three-inch machines, shiny steel millipedes that tried to scuttle away from capture, were outside any envelope he knew. Now lights and pins on half a dozen maps marked his forces, carefully and secretly deployed to dozens of assembly points.

Eclipse and Aurora popped out of thin air at the foot of the map table. "All done," Eclipse announced. "Surprise is worth lots. The Lemurians in Washington killed themselves. That shut down the mind controls. The people back in Washington are a mite confused. After they saw the dead Lemurians, they stopped shooting at me. Didn't hurt, but I really had to shout to be heard over machinegun fire. But they remember their mind controls, making them not see Lemurians standing five feet in front of them, telling them what to do, and them doing it. So they believed me when I explained the rest. And I brought this back." She handed General

Marquardt a hand-addressed, neatly-sealed apple-green envelope. "You're cleared to go ahead."

"Eclipse," Marquardt said, staring at the envelope. The stationary, after all, was unique. How had he failed to ask the obvious? "You somehow skipped saying. Exactly where were the other Lemurians hiding?"

Eclipse hesitated. "It's...what was that building called, Aurora?"

"The White House. That's how we could bring you your personal orders from President Poniatowski, sir," the younger girl said.

The silence in the room was broken only by the sound of tearing paper. Marquardt stared at the letter. The handwriting was a bit shaky, but entirely recognizable. The confirmation code at the bottom of the letter matched the mysterious message received a few minutes earlier.

"H minus four," he announced to his staff. "Proceed."

~~~~~~

Four hours later, a silver Chevrolet with government license plates rolled up to the front of the New Liberty ranch. The gates were closed and padlocked. Four Federal agents got out of the car, one with a search warrant and large megaphone.

The first began to read aloud, getting as far as "I am a United States..." before the shooting began. The car's radiator grill was dented once. Other rounds bounced off the air in front of the agents. Oblivious to the gunfire, the first man finished reading his announcement, joined his fellows back in the car, and drove back down the road, entirely grateful that Aurora's wall had protected them from injury.

"I think that counts as resisting service of a warrant," the oldest said. "Not to mention destroying government property. The courts get to decide whether shooting at you is a crime if you're bulletproof."

"We phoned ahead. They knew who we were," the second said.

"Sometimes you can see the virtues of dynamic entry," the youngest said. The three older men rolled their eyes. They all had too-clear memories of the errors of the 1990s, and political groups who never forgot your mistakes. "What would we have done without our invisible magic wall?"

"For one, not found these guys," the senior agent said. "They've got perfect records. The usual list of right-wing suspects, most of whom would momentarily do anything to help us, all think these guys are California tree-huggers. There's no, zero, nada record of any heavy construction, no hires of contractors, no purchases, no one noticing fleets of trucks. What's to suspect?"

357

~~~~~

General Marquardt's command post crackled with activity. The search warrant presentation had gone off substantially as needed, except for the level of the violent response. The expectation had been an armed guard turning the Marshalls back. The heavy machine gun was a surprise.

Aurora and Eclipse had stayed at a safe distance, protecting the Federal agents from mind control. Aurora had personally promised Marquardt and his staff that the two would not let themselves get shot at. Marquardt was sure Aurora would keep that promise. He was equally sure that Eclipse would do what she pleased, no matter how violent things became. He wished he could just tell the girls to go home to their parents, that the U.S. government now had everything under control, but so long as the other side had its own telepaths, he really didn't have a choice. Besides, if the two of them were telling the truth, they couldn't go home, it not being there any more.

The remainder of the operation was three hours behind schedule. Clouds were turning pink with approaching twilight. Unfortunately, the U.S. Marshalls with Aurora and Eclipse running overwatch had passed the last cutoff before the delay was recognized. Belatedly, Signals recognized that, with two mind-readers in support, radio silence was no longer the obstacle it had been historically.

Tanks and armored personnel carriers rolled across the open land covering the eastern part of the New Liberty ranch. Helicopters swarmed ahead, preparing for the envelopment drop. Far above them were Air Force fighter aircraft. His staff had questioned the need, but Marquardt had listened very carefully to Eclipse's description of the aircraft she had encountered over Saint Dominick.

Eclipse, arms folded across chest, stood quietly in one corner of General Marquardt's command tent, listening to the conversation around her. To her ears, the pace of battle was picking up. The airborne envelopment had encountered heavy anti-aircraft defenses, and had had to land two kilometers—a mile and a quarter, she translated—west of plan. Caissons and transporters had found the line of fortified positions, and discovered the hard way that smoke did not give adequate cover for an advance. Nor was their armor good enough that they could ignore the other side's anti-tank weapons. Momentarily she wished she had copied her mother's scripting for running large-scale military operations. Mum, of course, knew more about running battles than anyone else in the world. Eclipse didn't want to tell these Americans what to do. She just wanted to know if things were going badly wrong or just usually wrong.

She wished even more they would let her teleport out the wounded, but these people's minds were too tangled up in Pickering's lifeboat ideas to allow that. The thought of someone her age going into a battlefield was too much for them to stand. They were barely able to cope with Aurora providing mentalic coverage. She hunched her cape over her shoulders. Overhead heaters or no, the Sierra Nevada mountains in early April were cold. Her gifts were readied, not called. She would not let herself get soft, letting gifts do what her body could perfectly well do for itself. After all, she remembered, that's why she'd been able to take the Lesser Maze.

Aurora, she asked. *Are Comet and Cloud OK?*

They're fine, invisible, behind his force wall, making passes over these places, Cloud electrocuting all these tiny insect drones, Aurora said. *There are a whole lot of them, including bunches that were armed until Cloud fried them. Star is still annoyed that they didn't want him to lead an attack, but he's happy to stay on our island and guard all the loot we salvaged.*

Good, a relieved Eclipse said. *I didn't have any way to destroy those drones. Not without slagging down the neighboring countryside. And I'm not sure that would have worked. They could dematerialize.*

Eclipse's ears perked. She focused her attention on one operator and a wall console "...DIVAD from NORAD...incoming bogies now over New Mexico... seven targets at ALT 95 thousand and 4500 knots....Charlie 9 flight intercepting..." She'd paid attention when Comet took pictures of the other aircraft. The time-pirates had wiped out all high-speed, high-performance aircraft; no way 4500 knots was a local aircraft. "...bogies descending now altitude 70 thousand...no radio response from bogies... Charlie 6, Charlie 7 flights to back Charlie 9...radar profile matches Vampire-2 series..."

Eclipse forced herself to pay attention to the rest of the room. The locals had shot down Andesian aircraft before and would again. The other sides' personae were here, not up there. So long as they stayed quiet in their bunkers, and General Marquardt told her to stay out of his battle, this was ungifteds fighting over their own territory, fought the way they wanted to fight it.

"...bogies now passing Interamerica Flight 387...loss of transponder signal, Interamerica 387...Charlie 9 approaching...targets now descending, altitude 22 thousand... Charlie 12 and 13 as high-altitude backup...Charlie 12 confirms Interamerica 387 is down... NORAD: bogies are classified hostile..separation! separation! we have separations from incoming..." Eclipse looked around the room. At some point the console operator had said something about 'incoming air - possibly hostile - Air Force intercepting". After a moment's attention, a flag had appeared on the US map display screen, and attentions had shifted elsewhere. Division of responsibility, she told herself. The Army Air Corps—no, here it's the Air Force—gets flying opponents. These people fight the ground war.

Much louder noises in the near distance were artillery and rocket projectors firing support. General Marquardt's staff had politely questioned if the deployed forces were really necessary for a police operation. The General had quoted a President Eclipse had never heard of, about an invasion of Lebanon, a country she had never heard of, something about 'send a division, not a battalion, because that way no one will think of causing trouble'. This Eisenhower fellow, whoever he was, sounded like someone Mum would really like. General Marquardt had been right after all.

"...No report from Charlie 9...Break! Charlie 7 reports Charlie 9 is down, all are down...Charlie 6 and 7 engaging..." Eclipse stared at the US map. The unknown flag was now well into northwest Arizona. The speed was down, to 2000 knots, but they'd be here soon. Then the flag stopped progressing across the screen, and started flashing. "Charlie 6 and 7...fired full volleys...hostiles off screen, flying nap-of-earth...background noise...Charlie 6 reports many direct hits...No effect! No effect! Air-to-air has no visible effect..."

"General Marquardt, Sir!" The operator spoke up emphatically. "Incoming hostile air. Air Force intercept failed. DIVAD Patriot-X batteries notified. Ready and recommend volley fire." General Marquardt nodded assent. "Force notified of hostile air."

"Charlie 7 will close to cannon range...below line of sight...loss of contact...Charlie 12 reports multiple of Charlie 7 are down..." Eclipse looked inwards. The aircraft over Saint Dominick had been as tough as caissons to damage. "Mike-three, break right. Break right!...Mike three all damaged, still airborne... Mike three reports cannon had visible effect on target..." The console operator chimed in "Mike-3 was A-10s firing GAU-8."

"Bogies entering force DADZ. Charlie 7 survivors pulling clear," the console operator announced. "Patriot batteries engaging." Pause. "Incoming aircraft dispersing. Speed now 500 knots." One display shimmered, overlaying the outputs of several consoles. "Sir, those are ground support trajectories." Pause. "Multiple intercepts by Patriot-X. Multiple hits on each aircraft." Pause. Speak into microphone. "Sir, my observers say Patriot X hit targets, but targets are still incoming. No, sir, they can't tell the damage. Setting imminent air attack warning."

To Eclipse's eyes, tension in the room had skyrocketed. *Aurora? You there? Aircraft about that way?* She pointed.

More Lemurians. A bunch. Mind-screened. Can't get a good count, Aurora said. Her final words were almost lost in a distant unearthly whine and a cacophony of explosions. General Marquardt began shouting into a telephone. Staff members were moving just as fast. Damage reports began flashing onto the map displays, almost too fast to read. She tried to listen carefully. The Lemurian's weapons did not sound that powerful. 'Direct hit, no effect' was a not uncommon outcome for attacks on tanks. Infantry, support vehicles, and supplies were a different case. 'Engaged with APDS. Target burning and fleeing north' 'target has crashed and exploded' was an American tank hitting a Lemurian. Apparently local tank main batteries were effective but not ideal antiaircraft weapons. The enemy had to fly a bit low. Also, it sounded as though the tank had been really lucky in where it hit. She'd watched these people run a practice of this operation. They had seemed unconcerned about what might happen if the other side had flying personae. Or aircraft.

Enough was enough, she decided. These almost-indestructible aircraft counted as persona intervention. "Personae," Eclipse announced to the staff room. "Those aircraft? They're Lemurian. They're personae." Her force fields came to bright life around her. "They're mine." She teleported, forestalling any argument.

~~~~~

Aurora huddled against the side of an armored personnel carrier, her body screen glowing wanly against the brilliant glow of an early evening sky. Eclipse had drawn the mysterious aircraft off to the west. In the first moments, she had destroyed a pair of the attackers. The others had clustered together, then followed her. General Marquardt had stepped outside, seen Eclipse destroy a Lemurian, ignore ray weapons fired at her by two others, then stepped back into his command post.

On the ground, the Army's attack proceeded apace. Tanks and armored personnel carriers rolled across irregular ground. The sharp crack of automatic weapons fire and louder sounds of artillery shells could be heard in the distance. Aurora had dug in her heels, blunting Lemurian efforts to tamper with American minds. She was returning the favor, trying to penetrate their mental defenses, equally without success.

What was Eclipse doing? She'd led the Lemurians out of sight over a line of mountains. Brilliant flashes from their combat were strobes illuminating high cumulus clouds. Aurora reached out mentally for

Eclipse. The link between the two girls, never entirely gone, became totally solid. Eclipse, soaking with sweat, was gasping for breath. Aurora recognized the symptom. A persona who did not need to breathe would still try to breathe when she reached the maximum depth of her powers.

Through Eclipse's eyes Aurora saw bursts of energy, blue spirals of light, sail from Eclipse's hands towards the Lemurian aircraft, strike screens, and explode without doing damage. The Lemurians had reinforced their shields and were shooting back, firing wildly as their ships wove tight spirals around Eclipse. Gamma ray lasers, came the recognition from Eclipse's memories. The Lemurians had wheeled out gamma ray lasers and a half-dozen other exotic weapons against Eclipse. Aurora winced from the ache in Eclipse's bones, warning that Eclipse's screens were at their limits. Explosions rocked Eclipse from side to side, slamming her into her own body screens.

Eclipse was clearly in trouble. How could she help? Aurora felt a mental inquiry from the Army commander. If Eclipse were to lure the aircraft back over the battlefield, and then move away, divisional anti-aircraft weapons could be turned against the aircraft. Aurora and the commander felt Eclipse's gratitude. Eclipse followed with a very fast comparison of her attacks and his anti-aircraft rockets. On the Saint Dominick, the attacks she was using had shattered reinforced concrete buildings. Conventional anti-aircraft weapons were simply not in the same range.

The emotion from Eclipse was reassurance, not fear. Eclipse had had a reason to lure the strange aircraft over the mountains, to a valley that had no current occupants. She was going to have to do something seriously violent to damage the aircraft, and it would be just as well that the Army was not underneath when she did it. Aurora felt a twinge of curiosity from the Army commander: He had seen the explosions when Eclipse took out the first two aircraft. What did Eclipse view to be *seriously* violent?

Eclipse reached within herself. To Aurora, Eclipse's consciousness of her own body, of stressed muscles and aching bones, was replaced by a hollow outline filled by white light. For Eclipse, exhaustion was replaced by joy, exultation flooding through her in an unstoppable torrent. She pivoted to face the Lemurian ships, arms and legs locked outward in a cross. Iridescent violet plasma lashed across the sky, arcing from her body into her opponents, shattering airships like so many eggshells.

Power lanced back through the mentalic bond, flooding Aurora with an emotion she had never before felt, an emotion she realized that she shared with Eclipse. The emotion wasn't the joy of being engifted; it wasn't one of the strange emotions that grown-ups felt when they were alone with each other. It was the glory of power.

Aurora realized that she had penetrated the mind-screens of the Lemurians in the complex. Two Lemurians realized what she was doing to them and instantly committed suicide. The other five were hers, subject to her mental examination. Their memories told her that very soon their superiors someplace else would notice she'd made them forget how to commit suicide; they would then be executed by remote control. Aurora had a few moments to salvage their knowledge. She cast about, looking for volunteers whose minds could hold the memories of a second adult while retaining their own identities. Five officers nodded their ill-informed consent. Working as rapidly as she could, she transferred facts and ideas into the minds of the volunteers.

It was close to sunset, but a sun was rising. Not in the east, but to the west where Eclipse had led the Lemurian airships. A massive fireball rose above the hills. Rippling shadows rolled down the slope towards the command team. Around Aurora, soldiers were throwing themselves to the ground, dropping into foxholes, and otherwise taking cover. Aurora hesitated. What was happening? There came a crashing roar. The shock wave from a huge explosion rolled across the encampment. Aurora heard a loud clang as the armored personnel carrier beside her was tossed sideways, crunched into her force wall, and bounced off. She went flying across the field, finally crashing into a tree. She made herself stand up. She had not been hurt, not through her screens, but she definitely preferred to leave aerial acrobatics to personae who could fly.

Suddenly she was surrounded by soldiers shouting "Medic! Medic!".

"What's wrong?" she shouted. For a moment she was so disconcerted that she spoke aloud rather than checking directly what they were thinking.

"She must have hit that tree head first," one of them screamed.

"I'm OK," Aurora shouted back. "My screens saved me." She pointed at where she had started her flight. "And I'm sorry I dented your caisson. I didn't realize it was about to jump." She pointed. A prominent triangular outline, somewhat taller than Aurora, had been stamped into the vehicle's aluminum armor.

"You're sure you're OK?" She didn't recognize the person speaking to her.

Aurora nodded her head vigorously. This sort of thing happened to personae all the time. If you were good, you didn't get hurt. A month ago, things would have been very different. Eclipse had been very good at showing her how to set up a wall around herself. "I'm scanning as fast as I can; the Lemurians I mind-tapped killed themselves." The regiment medical officer realized he was getting a casualty list. Here a man had a broken arm; there someone lay unconscious.

Aurora asked herself what Eclipse had done. Eclipse had been in the other valley when the detonation took place. That hadn't been Eclipse's attack, had it? Was she still alive? Eclipse was very tough, but that was a huge explosion. Aurora realized their mental link was intact; Eclipse was OK, except her body feelings were still missing. Eclipse perceived herself as a luminous shadow free of pain and exhaustion. Eclipse had levels she didn't want to talk about, let alone use; she was using them now.

Eclipse finally noticed Aurora had subdued the Lemurians. Eclipse's interpretation of Aurora's triumph came as a gleaming smile of approval, followed by an "Oh. Right." That was Eclipse talking to herself. She gave Aurora a gentle reminder: After this was all over, the two of them needed to have a little chat.

The noise of battle returned in the distance. Soldiers and Lemurians had remembered what they were supposed to be doing, and were again going about the task of killing each other. Mental defenses around the Lemurian encampment were gone. Aurora began searching minds of Lemurian soldiers, finding their senior—human—officers, and transferring knowledge of Lemurian positions to the American forces. A combat force stripped of its commanding officers was a poor match for a trained military unit whose officers and NCOs had near-perfect knowledge of their opponent's positions. Once the advance was stalled by a heavily fortified bunker. The position was dug into live rock; it resisted even armor-piercing rounds from a nearby tank. Eclipse swooped to pointblank range from the bunker, ignored antitank rockets fired from inside, and sent plasma bursts into openings in its casements. Secondary explosions followed. No further resistance was observed from the bunker. The mental controls of the Lemurian officers faded. Their men no longer understood clearly why they were fighting, especially when they appeared to be fighting their own country's Army. First in ones and twos and then by the dozens, they laid down their arms.

Eclipse returned to the command post. The battle was reduced to a conventional military operation requiring no further intervention by personae. She was really pleased with how Aurora had handled the Lemurian officers, transferring what they knew to Americans before the Lemurians could finish committing suicide. She'd have to tell Aurora that. Many grownup mentalists would not have had the presence of mind to capture their opponents' memories.

The local military intelligence unit had been quite adaptable when confronted with personae. Presumably they could handle the development that their own officers had gained their opponent's memories. Indeed, the Lieutenant who had been the General's aide-de-camp, and who now had the memories of the chief Lemurian, was already speaking rapidly to an intelligence officer.

"They're New Incans! And they're not human," he shouted. Eclipse decided to filter a few of the more emphatic adjectives from her awareness of the aide-de-camp's remarks. These people were not going to be good for Aurora's vocabulary, she'd decided, no matter how carefully they spoke when they thought Aurora was listening. "They're from another planet! It's like that stupid movie! The one that thought we have only one Armed Force, the Air Force! Hollywood morons! But I have this thing's mind inside mine. I know what it did. Sort of. Not every detail, but it knew it was invading our planet. Those aircraft? That was their whole UFO Force." Eclipse stopped listening. The locals, whoever they really were, now had things under control.

Aurora decided the battle was truly over and done with. No more guns were firing in the distance. She couldn't find any Lemurian soldiers who hadn't surrendered yet. Some might be hiding in sealed bunkers or deep caves out of line of light. Troops on the ground reported only prisoners, dead, and wounded.

Eclipse sat down on a tree stump at the edge of command post, head in her hands, crying quietly to herself. Once and again she disappeared briefly, responding to Aurora's calls to teleport wounded men from California to military hospitals across the United States. After a time, there were no more wounded to transport. Eclipse realized that General Marquardt was sitting next to her, one arm across her shoulder.

"You really shouldn't be here," Marquardt said gently. "It wasn't fair to you. I'm truly grateful for what you did, but a girl your age has no business going through anything like this."

Eclipse dabbed her eyes with a handkerchief and blew her nose. "It's my fault. It was my fault. I should have known. They had gamma-ray lasers. So they had light hydrogen. Or worse. I should have lured them further away." She was talking more to herself than to the General. "I should have known how hard they'd blow up. I made an awful mistake. I could have killed people. Your people, I mean."

"You didn't," he said. "A couple broken arms, that's all." The General decided he should be reassured that she felt responsible about being seriously violent. The alternatives were alarming. How could a world full of children like this possibly function?

She shrugged. "It was nothing as bad as the Maze. I came out smiling from that. This time I made mistakes. Big mistakes. So it's my fault." She explained: "That explosion? The big one? The one that could have killed people? That was them blowing up, not that I wasn't seriously violent."

"General?" General Marquardt's aide, the young man who now had an extra set of Lemurian memories, whispered. "That explosion was antimatter. I have that from them. Eclipse? It can't be your fault. Absolutely no one knew they had atomics until you detonated them." Eclipse essayed a stony smile. The import of the aide's remarks registered on the General.

"That explosion was atomic?" he shouted. "Didn't the CBW unit pick up radiation?"

An officer shook his head, an emphatic No! "No radiation. Not then or now. But I just got the yield estimate. 200 kilotons. That's nuclear."

"X-rays," said Eclipse. "Light hydrogen just gives x-rays. I was behind those mountains. They'd be blocked from here. I was right there." The officer who had shaken his head stared at her intently and approached her carefully, wielding a Geiger counter. The unit reported background radiation when pointed away from Eclipse, but became silent when pressed against her garb. After a moment, Eclipse recognized what was happening. "My screens," she said, "they block radiation. Elsewise I'd be fried. This way, it got a bit loud and a bit bright, no big trade." The conversation had distracted Eclipse from the pangs of her conscience, enough to dry her tears.

A sergeant handed General Marquardt a map with circles drawn on it. "Every one, Sir," he said. "We've captured every one of their positions and safe houses." General Marquardt smiled grimly and returned to his command table. Aurora gave Eclipse a thumbs up. Their part was complete. They had promised to clean out the Lemurians. They'd done it. For sure Lemurians weren't time pirates; they didn't know time was pirated. Now it was up to these people to solve their own problems.

CHAPTER 37 LITTLE CHATS

Eclipse concentrated. The two girls faded into an aquamarine wash of light, withdrawing first to isolated ocean and then to the privacy of Eclipse's tent. At Eclipse's urging, Aurora found the cooler, pre-stocked with raspberry ice cream and a bottle of caramel sauce. She made the snacks. Eclipse toweled herself dry and changed to fresh clothing.

"You wanted to talk about something," Aurora reminded, "something that happened in Colorado. Something about what I did to the Lemurians. Did I do something wrong? I missed that. After a bit, they got awful easy to handle."

"Right. Except they didn't get easy. You got strong," Eclipse said. The younger girl looked puzzled. "You have an extra gift, one you haven't noticed. We were linked, and you used it."

"I do?" Aurora asked. "But I remember. I was totally tired. And then I felt really great, better than anything." She recognized the symptoms. "That was a gift! But what did I get?"

"Drain," Eclipse said. "We were linked, and I had to crank down my levels way deep. I should have been that deep from the beginning, and I wasn't. My mistake. You tapped my levels. So you got a lot stronger. You squoonched the Lemurians like bugs."

"Drain?" a tremulous Aurora asked. Draining, she thought, was not a nice gift. It let you take power from another persona, use it for your own, and weaken the other persona. When Eclipse had emerged from the Maze, a half-dozen of the League's best drains had tried to grab all of Eclipse's power to capture her. They'd failed. Badly. "Why didn't you tell me? I'd've stopped. I could've hurt you."

Eclipse looked away for a moment, then answered, finally looking back at Aurora. "You were OK. Mentalics doesn't use tons of power, not like body screens do. I, like, knew it was you and OK, 'cause I didn't need every scrap of strength. Not even when they all blew up." Aurora nodded glumly, not sure it was really OK. "It's good for you: Borrow power, learn to use it better, learn to go deeper sooner."

"Star would get powerful tetched if I did that to him," Aurora said. "He's never been mean enough to deserve that. Even he's always a boy."

"Some people really hate drains. Better no one learns Aurora does it," Eclipse urged.

"And the other thing," Aurora asked. "Except you said you were OK, so I didn't ask. What happened to you? We were linked, and suddenly it was like you were just a bright shadow inside."

"You saw that?" Eclipse asked. "If you have to tell people what you saw, me being wanted by the League, please say: You saw my gifts, not me. And when you drained, there was lots of power. You'll get headaches tomorrow. I did, the time I linked with someone lots stronger'n me. Not I'm lots stronger than you. I was just way deep in my gifts."

"There's someone lots stronger than you?" Aurora shook her head. She knew what Eclipse had faced in the Tunnels.

"Plenty of people," Eclipse answered. "Plenty of people. 'cept I was lots younger then."

"There's another thing," Aurora said. "I did read the minds of all those Lemurians. The Lemurians are sure. In the end, they are going to win. Kill all the people in the world. Or make them into mindless slaves. Make the world theirs."

Eclipse took another bite of her sundae. The intense sweetness of the caramel sauce enhanced the raspberry flavor, wringing out the last bit of its acidity. "They just lost," she said. "Why did they think they were sure to win?"

"Why? They have force field generators." Aurora answered. "Enough to cover their whole country. Their force fields are strong, strong enough lithium bombs won't break them. That's the strongest weapon these Americans have."

"They didn't have those force fields here," Eclipse said. "Those Lemurian airships were tough, nearly unbreakable. Until I hit them really hard."

"The generators are real big," Aurora said. "They get built under mountains. One protects an entire state."

"That lets them win?" Eclipse asked.

"It's like that failed Star Territories game. You built unbreakable Planetary Force Screens whenever you take a world. After a bit, no one can capture anything, and the game paralyzes. But this time, only one side has screens. Any time one side captures an area, they keep it forever. The other side can't win. These Americans? They're in that boat. The Lemurians are sure. The Lemurians are the Americans' doom."

Eclipse looked off into the distance. "Oh, I see how it works. That's ugly." She frowned. "Then why are they bothering with medicine sales and terrorists and mind control of politicians?"

"They're afraid we're creative," Aurora said. "They're afraid we'll invent a shield breaker. Or they put a force field over an area, and we've hidden an army inside that area to attack them. They figure if we're totally disorganized, the Americans won't figure out how to break their shields or come up with clever strategies or have money to pay for huge armed forces."

"Do they worry about teleporters?" Eclipse asked. "Except no one here can teleport."

"They think they're protected. May I show you some images?" Aurora waited for Eclipse's nod. [Open space with thousands of fine perpendicular lines crissing and crossing it.] "It looks like the FedCorps Washington teleport barrier."

"Agreed," Eclipse said. "Doesn't keep you from leaving, but if you try teleporting into the place your teleport powers up the nearby grid lines. They're inside your force field when you materialize. You get skewered and fried, unless you are really good. It might not work against Victoria's gating, which helps Americans not at all; it would work against me. I could teleport out, except I accidentally draw power from the block so where I end up is totally random, like twenty million miles into outer space."

"So we've found a doom. Except it looks unstoppable," Aurora said.

"When your problem seems unbeatable, you need to use a larger sledge hammer," Eclipse said. "These Americans don't have anything better than lithium bombs. I do. Me. And I'm still powered up from taking out the Lemurian air force. Where were these shield generators?" They shared memories. "We need to reconnoiter, spy out what we're up against."

"Bring Comet along?" Aurora asked. "She can speed me up."

"OK, back to the island," Eclipse agreed.

CHAPTER 38 PRELIMINARY RECONNAISSANCE— ACCEPT NO SUBSTITUTE.

The five sat in a circle, Aurora explaining what she'd learned from the Lemurians. "It's like Star Territories," she insisted, "any area one side grabs, the other can't take back, except only one side can do the grabbing. Eventually the other side runs out of territory."

"We're sure the Americans and Russians and Prussians can't break these shields?" Cloud asked.

"The Lemurians are very sure," Aurora answered, "except Prussia now has almost no army. The Lemurians think our America would need a lithium bomb a thousand times as powerful as anything the Americans have. And they're making their screens stronger all the time."

Cloud turned to Eclipse and Star. "Can you guys break those screens?" Star shook his head.

"If I have to," Eclipse answered. "I'm almost sure. But they might have tricks built into them. The teleport portal that sends your attack someplace else—they might have that—is pretty hard to beat. Not impossible. Hard. I'd rather be clever, not just use brute force."

"That's why you always do reconnaissance first," Aurora said, "just like in Territories. And what you taught us, Eclipse, from your mom. So Eclipse takes me to someplace way above their capital. I read a bunch of minds. And Comet comes with us, to speed me way up so I can read a lot of minds in a big hurry. Then we know where Star and Cloud and Eclipse can best wreck their gadgets."

"Sounds good," Comet said. "I'll be invisible. I think I can cover all three of us that way. I've been practicing invisible a lot. It beats getting shot."

"It has to be tomorrow," Star said. "It's night there by now. Everyone is asleep, or has their shades pulled down."

"Sometime towards noon," Eclipse said, "but not that late. Actually...Aurora, did you find out when people go to work or lunch?"

"Off the wall question," Aurora said. "The Army folks have the memories I transferred. Give me a moment." Her stare lost focus. "General Marquardt says 'hi!' to all of us. He says his people haven't hit anything in North America that they can't handle. It's his other aide who has the useful Andesian memories. She says 'hi!' too." Aurora tapped numbers on her lessoncomp. "About one in the afternoon, just before their lunch, is best. They have a long working morning and a short working afternoon. By not-quite-lunchtime people are staring at the clock, not being alert or working hard."

"I'm good with that," Comet said. "A bit early for us, except we've been sleeping at all these weird hours already." Her lessoncomp showed a time. "Five in the morning here. Let's all go to sleep now, wake up earlier, and be ready. Aurora, I'll give us time acceleration. You two guys can just sleep."

"Just as well," Cloud said, "I know you do your best, but sleeping with superspeed gives me a headache."

"See you all then," Eclipse said as she teleported out.

~~~~~

"Good morning!" Eclipse called into the pre-dawn dark. She'd teleported to the appointed location at the appointed time, well, twenty feet off the ground, and dropped to earth. Where, she wondered, was the rest of the team?

"Over here!" Star's voice came from the other side of the hangar wall. "It got windy, so we moved inside the hangar.

Eclipse walked around the wall, and inhaled. "Waffles?" she asked.

"Pancakes," he answered. "For waffles I'd need a fancy iron, but pancakes are easy. With thanks to my big sister for stirring the batter."

"And whipping the cream and washing the strawberries," Aurora added. "We have extra if you want some."

"I should say 'no' to Star's cooking?" Eclipse asked. "I love pancakes. And we've got time yet."

"Lieutenant Fothergill (she's the General's aide) helped a lot once she understood what I wanted," Aurora said. "The guy who gave lost his memories to her? He was not-quite-a-big-boss. His memories pointed to where I should look. We were lucky. His memories include speaking English well. I can read their minds and understand everything. Oh, and General Marquardt is really worried about the Lemurian plan. He knows time is short, but people who can give him orders want to delay the attack until everything's ready."

"Ask me for anything but time," Eclipse said. "Old Goetic adage. Still true. You're good with 200 miles up, Aurora? Or do we need closer?"

"That's like me and the Space Plane," she answered. "It's fine. It's clear line of light and way above their teleport shields."

"Oh," Star said, "Fresh-squeezed orange juice and cold milk, thanks to Comet flying resupply for us."

"I'll do breakfast cleanup," Cloud announced. "You guys just go. I get to do something useful."

"You were great yesterday, Cloud," Star said. "You toasted all those tiny robots."

"Absolutely," Eclipse agreed. "I couldn't have done that. OK, I'm powered way up, just in case." *Aurora, the time to start a drain is now, so you don't wrong-foot me later.*

Done. The younger girl's brows wrinkled. *Still don't like it.*

Needs must, Eclipse answered.

"Link hands," Comet said. "Force field up around us? OK, we're invisible, aren't we, Star?"

"I don't see you at all," he said, "and I know where to look."

"You're totally gone," Cloud agreed.

"Ready for vacuum?" Eclipse waited for two nods. "Teleporting."

~~~~~

Far below them, the sky was clear. The Empire of the New Inca stretched out along the Andes, its borders invisible from the depths of space. Aurora concentrated on her search, sweeping through mind after mind.

Out! Aurora suddenly shouted. *Get out of my mind!*

Eclipse's screens flared to brilliant life "Yiy!" she screamed, holding her screens solid. Her presets had triggered. She was in the path of an attack. Now she'd dropped through two dozen levels without stopping, all that energy being fed directly into her defenses. . Radiation weapon, she recognized, absurdly powerful. The Straight Circle, the Solid Rainbow, and the Well of Infinity hovered around her. She'd dropped, she realized, straight through them. Below her was the icy construct that marked the Square Circle. She clenched her fists. She very much did not want to visit that place, but perhaps there was no choice. Aurora's drain soared in its demands, enough that she felt it cramping her force fields. What was the attack? She should recognize it, she told herself.

I got what we need, Aurora answered. *He was only in my shallow mind, so I smote him with a levin-bolt. What happened?*

Enough, Eclipse said. She teleported, taking the three of them in a single instant to the back side of the Moon. *Aurora! Are you clear?* she asked.

I'm good, the girl answered.

It got bright. Very bright. Comet observed. *Were those lithium bombs?*

Nothing so harmless, Eclipse answered. *Back to my base.* The ting of crystal stemware struck with a spoon marked their departure.

The sky was now blue. The New Mexico wilderness surrounded them on all sides. Eclipse slumped into her folding chair, leaning forward to cradle her head in her arms. Her eyes refused to focus. Comet, standing at her side, was reduced a green blur. "Just give me a moment," she asked. She squeezed her eyes shut, then looked up again. The world was now almost in focus, so long as she didn't turn her head too quickly.

"Eclipse?" Aurora asked. "What is it?"

"I just need recovery time," Eclipse answered. A lot of recovery time, she added to herself. "The Wizard said some of us might die. We just came real close to being the dead people."

"What was it?" Comet asked. "I thought I was keeping us invisible."

"You did, sister," a downcast Aurora admitted. "They had a good mentalist who backtracked me. And the fellow who knew everything about their defenses? He had something that sees gravity. He knew we were there, and totally invisible, so he shot at us. It was my fault."

"We were lucky," Eclipse said. "I was prepped for serious violence. My presets worked the way they should. That attack...it was a solar coretap ray."

"A what?" Comet asked. Eclipse had this marvelous list of strange facts, she thought. How had Eclipse found them?

"It opened a teleport gate, not quite but sort of similar, very small," Eclipse explained, "with one end pointed at us, and the other end in the core of the sun. I think they just let through light and X-rays. My screens protected us. But with my screens that high, I couldn't have pushed an attack through them. Not with the levels I was tapping." Not, she thought, without an attack that would incinerate the nearest continent.

"You need something to eat," Aurora announced. Eclipse pointed to her cooler. Aurora passed Eclipse a pint of maple ice cream. Eclipse pointed at her two guests, more pints of ice cream, and the side of her bed.

"Even prepped, I had to do a crash drop," Eclipse explained, "all the way down, to keep my screens around the three of us. It worked, but after I get you two back to your island I'll need a nap." For a few days, she added to herself.

"Did it work?" Comet asked. "Or did we almost die for nothing?"

"It worked great," Aurora said. "You keeping me at superspeed, sis, made all the difference. They had a mental list, who gives orders to whom. Most of these people don't do mentalics, so until the end I could move fast. That was important. I had to go through like fifty people to find the one who mattered. I was lucky; they all liked windows with good views. Windows prove how superior they are to their slaves.

"So I found the guy running their defenses. He was an engineer, knew what is wrong with them. He'd been having big arguments that they should keep their heads down, do nothing to upset foreigners until they were ready to conquer the world. He's got months before he's ready. But he set his defenses as good as he can imagine. I'm lucky he's not on our Earth. He'd be a Master of Games blocking my way to the top."

"I'm happy you're still seeing the important things first," Eclipse said. Aurora smiled at the compliment.

"And he had this list of the important targets. Those are the ones we have to wreck up. If we appear even a ways below the top of the teleport screen, the sun ray hits us almost instantly," Aurora continued. "That's as low as he dares point the sun ray. Lower and the air turns hot as the sun and fries the city. Below that, he only has radar and gravity detectors and all sorts of antiaircraft lasers, neutron cannon, and the like."

"I can't break into the city by teleporting through their teleport screen," Eclipse said. "Not without dying on the spot. If I appear way above it, their solar core tap keeps me from shooting at them, not unless I use totally crazy amounts of power. I can't just fly in at low altitude. Those targets are way spread out across the Andes. I have to be way up to zorch all of them in the same few moments." And if I use the obvious cheat, she thought, I duplicate the catastrophe that killed the dinosaurs, after the maiasaurs got bored and almost all died out. No, I can't do that; we're here to save the world, not to become one of the dooms.

"There's this big building, huge spire, that's their weakness. Wreck it up and their defenses mostly stop working." Aurora ate more ice cream. "This solar ray, in particular. I have a complete list of targets, I think. We can talk about those later."

"You did really well, Aurora," Eclipse said, "chasing through these people to see their defenses." Even if I can't see how to break them, she thought, unless I ignore collateral damage.

"I thought Comet could make us invisible," Aurora suggested, "and we could sneak up on this tower of theirs, but they'll see Comet with this gravity detector. And you can't turn off gravity." She ate more ice cream. "I only learned this because my super sister sped us up a couple thousand times, so that the couple of minutes before we ran was like days of searching. And then she fed me all these good questions to search people's brains for. And, finally, you rescued us, Eclipse."

"And now you're so kind to us, Eclipse, giving us something to eat when you want to sleep," Comet said.

"For sure. Thanks! That was like four days inside superspeed for the two of us," Aurora said, "using deep space so we didn't get hungry or whatever." The girls leaned back, happily eating maple, strawberry-caramel, and caramel chunk ice cream.

"No gravity!" Comet exclaimed. "That's it!"

"Yes?" a bemused Eclipse asked. "Flying wasn't good enough? No, he saw us with his gravity detector."

"Cloud," Comet answered. "Cloud. And his seventh-grade science experiment." Eclipse raised her eyebrows. "He and friends did the Cavorite experiment. Something like Cavorite. Cavitation? It was someone's name."

"The what?" Aurora asked.

"Cavorite experiment," Comet explained. "This wire hangs down, attached to the center of a horizontal pole. Little weights at each end of the pole. Then you move two big weights close to the little weights, and the gravity of the big weights moves the little weights sideways. A teeny tiny bit. His friend measured it with a laser. That's the Cavorite experiment. Then, his friend knew he was a persona, Cloud made the two big weights massless, like he did with the space plane, and the little weights swung back, because the big weights didn't have gravity any more."

"Cloud turns off gravity?" Aurora said. "Oh, I see it."

"So we sneak up on this tower," Eclipse said, "zorch it, then I wreck their big machines?"

"Except the tower doesn't run the teleport block. The block stays up when we take down the tower," Aurora said. "The teleport block is behind all sorts of protections. And they've got backup for the tower. We wreck the tower; you've got a few minutes to wreck all their other machines."

"Riddle," Comet said. "Why did these Andesians bother with a teleport block? There are no teleporters here, not that anyone knew about."

Eclipse thought for a few moments, then shrugged. "I don't know. But if I help take out the tower, I can't be in the right place soon enough to do my wrecking."

"Cloud, Star, and I do the tower," Comet said. "You do the wrecking. Aurora can be way off, keeping a mental eye on these people."

"I think it won't work," Aurora said. "They have telepaths. They'll hear Comet thinking when we fly in. Not Star or Cloud (they have screens) but they'll hear Comet's thoughts leaking from her mind when she flies in."

"That's only if they notice me," Comet said. "We could take the chance." Aurora shook her head.

"I can fix that," Eclipse said. "Now, you get away how, after you wreck the tower?"

Aurora projected a mental map. "The tower is here. Those machines are ten, twenty, hundreds of miles away. We wreck the tower, then fly straight up. As soon as Comet is above the teleport screen, you can rescue us."

"You get to talk the boys into it," Eclipse said. "Then we practice a bunch of times. Except you two are done with your ice cream, so grab four more pints and I'll teleport you back to your island. You convince the boys. I need to rest for a couple days."

CHAPTER 39 AN INCAN INTERLUDE

Comet lay back on her hammock. Dawn was swift approaching. Another day and a half, and they'd learn if their plan worked. They'd spent half a week testing all the parts they could, and done dress rehearsals, but attacking a whole country was still frightening. She realized that Eclipse, dressed in a plain white shift, her feet bare, was standing at the foot of her bed. Comet tried to sit up to say hello, and found she couldn't move. Was this a dream?

Not a dream, Eclipse said. *I promised I'd fix people hearing your mind, so I'm here to do that. If you trust me.*

Of course I trust you, Comet answered. *You're the most gift-true person I know. But why can't I move?*

Your body is still asleep, Eclipse answered. *For this you have to be awake and asleep at the same time, and you are. So I'm going to give you mindscreens; a couple other things come with them. Not quite a force field, but it you want to fly close to the surface of the sun you'll be able to. And if you punch someone, it's like wearing brass knuckles. Or hitting them with a wrecking bar. Are you good with that?*

Yes, Comet answered. *But how?*

It's way too complicated to explain, Eclipse answered. *I've actually never done it for real before, but the scripting and rules engine are rock solid. It's absolutely safe. At worst I fail and nothing happens.*

OK. Go ahead. It's to save the world. Comet imagined herself nodding agreement.

Done, Eclipse answered. *It's over in an instant. Please don't tell the others where you got your screens. It would cause all sorts of problems. If you have to, you can tell Star and Aurora that I lent you some screens. They've lent powers to each other. They know about lending. Your mind screens are now solid. Practice punching walls to get the rigid force field right. Now, go back to sleep.*

Comet nodded drowsily. Eclipse faded from sight.

~~~~

"Eclipse," Aurora said. "She'll be here in a moment."

"Right on time," Star mumbled. Cloud nodded not-quite-willing agreement.

Across the amphibian taxiway, a black point of darkness appeared. It opened in almost no time to a black circle yards across, its surface shot with polychrome lightnings that flickered and flared. Eclipse, her body screens the deepest of violets, stepped through. She gestured. The circle closed behind her. When she walked, she trailed behind her evanescent bits of half-called gifts, gifts she'd revealed, gifts she'd never mentioned having, gifts that she'd never had, gifts that had never existed.

"Are you guys ready?" Eclipse asked.

"Good to go," Comet said. "Guys, gather close?" The two boys stepped in front of her. She wrapped her arms around them. Eclipse put one hand on Comet's shoulder.

"No mass, no gravity," Cloud announced.

"Presets up," Star said. "Thanks for the lesson, Eclipse. You made it seem really easy."

"You were a really good student," she answered.

"Invisible," Comet added. "Ready to teleport."

"Destination clear," Aurora announced. "Low waves. No boats in sight. I'm watching their gravity detector guy, He thinks everything is fine. Go!"

To Aurora's eyes, the four of them had vanished from sight. Even listening carefully, their thoughts went unheard.

An almost-unseen blue sphere. A single note, a harpsichord at the top of its highest register. Four persona hovered a few tens of feet above Pacific waves.

Aurora? Eclipse called.

Found you, she answered. *The guy with the gravity detector isn't seeing anything. You're ten miles from this 'Transistor Tower'. What an odd name the Andesians gave it.*

"OK," Eclipse said, "I'm stepping out of your flight field, Comet." She leaned back and returned in half an instant to Aurora's side. Her force field dropped to stand-by.

"Now we wait," Eclipse told Aurora.

~~~~~

Comet glided above the waves, carrying Cloud and her brother. The Pacific coast loomed before them. Aurora's thoughts were a reassuring presence at Comet's shoulder. Very carefully, Aurora was looking over the shoulder of the people—loosely speaking—running the New Incan defenses, not reading their minds, just tapping what they were hearing each other say.

They don't know you're there, Aurora reported. *You're right on target. That red column, the thing that looks like an upside-down golf tee, that's the Transistor Tower. You're headed right at it. The openings half-way up are the air vents and air car landing points. Just don't touch the ground until you're well inside.*

We're good, Cloud answered, *this is exactly per plan. Mayhaps no commentary unless things don't match up right? It's distracting.*

Got it, Aurora said. Boys, she thought, were sometimes less than tactful, but he was right. *We're approaching where we have to lose contact. Too many telepaths nearby.*

"Guys," Comet whispered, "coming in for a fast landing."

Comet! Aurora shouted. *They're seeing your flight field, just a trace, and can't see the air car they think it is. And your invisibility field is bothering something.*

The trio, now two hundred feet off the ground, swept through the entrance into the tower. A stiff, hot breeze blew in their faces. "Landed," Comet announced.

"We've got the balcony," Star announced. "Comet? Perhaps hide between those big vertical pipes?" He was deeply worried about his sister's safety, not that he would frighten her by saying so. At least she had mind screens and a force field now. How had Eclipse managed that? It made no sense. Star dashed ahead to a shoulder-height lattice railing, Cloud slightly ahead of him.

The interior of the tower was polished aluminum, open from bottom to top. Implanted in the walls were bright-white glass jelly-bean shapes, each two stories tall, linked by equally luminous pipes. Power modules, Star thought, those big white things are supposed to be power modules. Other pipes, glowing all the colors of the rainbow, laced the walls between the jelly beans. Spaced around the walls were railings and deep recesses; constellations of half-seen lights hinted at control panels. Down at the bottom, a great horizontal wheel formed of glowing bars rotated slowly.

"Looks just like those memories," Cloud said.

"Starting at the bottom," Star announced. His plasma torch streaked down the intervening space to the wheel. Wherever Star's torch touched its periphery, pipes exploded or blew away from their fasteners. He shifted fire to the hub. The wheel shuddered to a stop. Incandescent plasma flared through the openings Star had made,

"Control interfaces for me," Cloud said. Brilliant bolts of lightning flew the diameter of the tower to strike at the recess opposite. Grids of lights flared brilliantly and went out. Display screens exploded. The doors of locked steel cases melted, revealing spiderwebs of wire that burned with green flames. Sympathetic explosions could be heard from other control stations. Cloud shifted his attack to another control station.

Whistles screeched. Horns blared. Klaxons screamed. Ceiling lights flared teal and violet.

"You think they noticed something?" Star said. He directed his attack against a jelly bean. Its twenty feet of height simply sat there, ignoring his attack. "Drat, that module just absorbs my plasma!"

"Switch targets!" Cloud shouted. He directed lightning bolt after lightning bolt at a module and the glowing pipes feeding it. The smaller pipes exploded under his attack.

Star struck at a control station, far down the tower. Unarmored, its aluminum and plastic paneling evaporated like water on a hot griddle. The wires, optical couplers, and plasma tubes below fared little better. Star shifted to the next station, realizing as he did that he needed next to no time to destroy each of them.

Alien voices shouted. Loudspeakers, Comet thought. Loudspeakers were spread out over the height of the building. Aurora had given her memories of Alien-to-English translating dictionaries. Comet needed the reverse. She concentrated her superspeed. Not safe for studying, she remembered, but I'm just thinking about this. She found an approximate translation. 'Attackers on level fifteen. Attackers on level fifteen. Security to level fifteen. Security to level fifteen. Shoot to kill. Shoot to kill. Multiple control failures. Main power has failed. All transistors, shift to emergency power. All transistors, shift to emergency power.'

"They're sending security folks here!" Comet shouted. "Remember your force fields!"

How thick are these walls, Star asked himself? He targeted another control area, then continued to blast away at its rear wall. Flames and molten metal flared back toward him. These walls were weak, he thought, not at all like the tanks he'd destroyed. In a few moments, the backflare stopped. I'm all the way through, he realized. He swung the direction of his torch sideways, slowing whenever there was backflare from a major support girder.

Comet had wedged herself between two translucent pipes. She heard a sharp hum at each shoulder. Something, she couldn't see what through the translucency of the pipes, was rapidly coming down the inside of each pipe. "Cloud! Star!" she shouted. A pair of New Incan guards jumped out of the tubes. Drat, she thought, those are elevators, not big water pipes. Big error: Hiding back here means I can't use my speed. A glance at the ceiling showed how low the support brace above her was. She was trapped between floor, brace, elevators, and two tall guards. Grab the two with her flight field? The space was too constricted; she'd grab the building at the same time.

Comet heard his sister shout, turned, and realized his position was impossible. Sure, he thought, he could torch them. He'd torch Comet at the same time, and her new force field didn't sound to be up to protecting her. Cloud turned more slowly, stopping in his tracks when he realized the danger.

Guards opened fire. Plasma spheres spewed from their rifles, striking Star's shields, not to great effect. Cloud realized more guards were approaching via elevator. His lightning blasts struck and scored the tube walls, without penetrating. Star copied Cloud's example, melting holes in the elevator walls, spattering white-hot metal across the balcony. Elevator units stopped in mid-flight.

One guard had the presence of mind to jump back under cover, into the space already occupied by Comet. She was slammed back into the wall, her force field protecting her. He shouted something in New Incan and started to turn. Comet executed a blindingly fast pirouette, her force field going rigid just before her fist reached his face. He outweighed her by two-to-one, but she was now moving as a fast, totally rigid object. There was a deep crunch as his forehead caved in. He slumped, enough she could fly over him, grab both guards in her flight field and accelerate. The second guard began to react, but by then he was headed almost straight up at close to Mach One. She released the guards, who continued on their upward trajectories, while she returned to the two boys.

Star and Cloud continued building demolition. Once and again, a power module caught on fire, sending pulses up and down to its neighbors.

"Star," Comet asked, "what are you doing?"

"Cutting a wedge out of the building on one side," he answered, "Almost there. This stuff is really soft."

"That works how? We're short on time!" Comet shouted.

Not really, Aurora answered. *You've been there under a minute.*

Telepathy to you is fine, now, Eclipse added. *For sure, they know you're all there.*

"Once I'm done, that half of the building has no support. The building falls over. See, simple!" Star wondered why his usually brilliant sister didn't understand the obvious. In fact, he could hear creaks and groans, and he could see the tower began to tilt.

"Star! We're inside the building!" Comet screamed. Star was shocked. How many improper adjectives had she used before reaching 'inside'? A whole bunch. Cloud froze.

"Yes. So? Oops!" Star answered. Too late, he saw the error in his plan.

Comet ramped superspeed to absolute maximum, grabbed the two boys in her flight field and turned for the outside landing porch. It had steel doors. They were closed. She glanced straight up. There was a small patch of sky visible. She threw every bit of power she could muster into her flight field. They accelerated straight up. Comet bent her trajectory to match the building's increasing tilt, in what felt to be forever but was actually a few tenths of a second. They were in open air. Comet called invisibility and accelerated sideways, dodging away from their last-seen trajectory. "Cloud? Massless?"

"Oh, right. Done." Cloud answered. Comet changed acceleration directions again. She stared down at the Tower. It slumped to the side, rocked back and collapsed in on itself. It must have been noisy, she thought, but we're way beyond supersonic at this point. Dust and flaming plasma hid everything else from sight.

~~~~~

Two hundred miles above the sky, Eclipse appeared from nowhere. *In place, Aurora,* she thought.

Comet's still under you, Aurora answered.

Be frigid, Comet inserted. *Another fifteen seconds and I'm above you. Another minute to FTL transition.*

Holding for twenty, Eclipse said. She would not take a chance that Comet was still in her line of fire.

Be chill, Aurora said. *The folks running their defenses are still trying to figure out why their automatics think something is wrong with the Invincible Transistor Tower.*

Spotted you, Comet said. *I'm looking down from above.*

Their sunray is disabled, Aurora added. *They're trying to bring it back up.*

Don't look down, Comet! Eclipse warned. *Bright.* She waited until she felt Comet's nod. *Targeting check.* She stared through mountainsides at the hidden caverns beneath, ignoring blinding pain from using her ultravision.

Everything matches, Aurora said. *Except they had no trouble detecting you using ultravision, and are going to 'Attack Incoming' alert. They found videos of Star torching the Tower, seen from outside. They're watching what happened next when they should be doing something.*

Attacking...NOW! Eclipse said. An iridescent violet plasma beam lanced down from Eclipse. Her first target was the regional force screen plant, hidden under thousands of feet of granite. The volume her plasma beam intersected transformed instantaneously from solid rock through superheated gas to highly ionized atoms. The pressure in the column of volatilized rock, vigorously compressed by Eclipse's attack, soared until the gas found an escape, expanding explosively into the vaults that held the force screen generators. Eclipse gradually widened the diameter of her attack, flooding the generator's chambers with white-hot gas. Control panels burst into flame. Signal and power cables softened, glowed white-hot, and melted. Molten solder flowed across integrated circuit boards. Vacuum seals failed under excessive differential expansion. Generator crystals cracked. Flames roared from ventilation shafts.

Shifting to next target, Eclipse said. That was the Incan capital's main power plant. In a world that claimed not to understand how to extract electricity from hydrogen fusion, the plant's array of large fusactors was all too impressive. Once again, Eclipse put paid to the installation.

In a quarter hour, Eclipse had finished with demolitions. Several of the Andesianplants had been shielded by deep water reservoirs. Eclipse transformed each reservoir's water to superheated steam. The resulting explosions were not as impressive as Krakatoa, but entire mountains were still crushed to fine gravel and blown into the stratosphere.

Power plants, all gone. Aurora marched through Eclipse's target list. *Force screen generators, smashed. Sunbeam projectors, gone. Molecular spray systems, blown to flinders. Main air defense centers, explodiated. Arsenals—you got the big ones. The guys running their defenses can't figure out why they haven't been next. *

They'll eventually figure out that you're listening to them, Eclipse said.

Meanwhile the guy in charge—the surviving guy in charge—just decided to cancel their invasion, Aurora said. *'Flee through the universe gates' was his order. He's alternating between that and 'Summon Indiwiwi! Summon Indiwiwi!' The less we now rock the boat, the faster they'll be out of here. General Marquardt agrees, so long as I'm keeping an eye on them and you're stomping on anyone who does not flee. All that's left will be mopping up work. *

Eclipse remembered several of Mum's aphorisms. *Mopping up is so simple, unless you're the guy who dies doing it.*

The General agrees. Aurora announced. *He said nice things about your Mom.*

Headed home. Please tell Comet the same.

CHAPTER 40 AFTERMATHS

"I made dinner," Star announced. "Simple things. Lamb chops. Steamed potatoes. A big salad with artichokes and cucumbers." His teammates all applauded and gathered around the table.

"The Andesians had a few more tricks up their sleeves," Eclipse said. "I flattened them. The Americans and all their friends should be able to take care of the rest, especially with the folks you-all captured having a list of what they were doing in each foreign country around the world."

"Back to finding personas?" Star asked.

"Dead end, Star," Aurora answered. "In Moscow I found a historian. Up after midnight to use his library. I paid him consulting fees, so I could read his mind about history. His Rome is not ours. He thought Horatio and the Bridge was a silly story, not Roman arête in action. Worse, he thought history made sense, so you could write down a history of all the countries found in Massachusetts, in order, ending with some British colonies and this United States of America, like you were writing down someone's biography. But there never have been personae. Around the world, whole countries are missing. I made a list, ancient civilizations that never existed. Most interesting ones are gone. And no personae in past civilizations." No one, she thought, who could fly, read minds, heal damaged leaves, limn a sunset in shades of rose and coral. No one with a gift. "It's some Wizard of Mars trick, but I can't imagine what he did."

"But I hope the Andesians were a doom," Eclipse said. "It almost killed me, enough that—what's the old aviator line—I'm flying on fumes. If the next one is much tougher, well, the Wizard said some of us might die, and here I am, Athena's Spear and Shield, front and center."

"Eclipse," Star asked, "You keep using that line. But what does it mean?"

"Ancient story. From ancient Greece, the place where they built the first computers. Athena was a goddess of the ancient Greeks. The Titans, the Gods before the Greeks, who were killed by the Greek Gods when they took over, rose from the dead. They killed the other Greek Gods. Nothing Athena could do would stop them. She had a magic spear and shield; she was still losing. The Spear and Shield told her what to do, and agreed she should do it. She summoned all the magic in the spear and shield and used it, one final strike, against the Titans. The Spear and The Shield were consumed in magic flame, but they took the Titans with them. When you are the Spear and Shield, you die, but your death guarantees victory."

Cloud looked up from his steak. "The Wizard?" he asked. "He said you mayhaps get to die to save the world?"

"Sometimes, Cloud, victory comes with a price," Eclipse answered. "I'd rather the price not be me, but mayhaps I don't get a choice. Duty, heavier than worlds." Her fork stabbed down. "These are really good potatoes, Star," she continued. "What's the seasoning?"

"Olive oil," he answered. "Rosemary. Lots of garlic. And the lightest dusting of parmesan cheese."

"But he told us what came next," Comet said. "He said we would find the answer, and when we finished our trip, everything would be back exactly where we started, except we would know the answer to our two questions."

"Frigid!" Star's waved his arms in glee.

Eclipse was seriously frightened. "Comet?" Her voice was barely above a whisper. "Did you say two questions?" We'd rehearsed her speaking to the Wizard, Eclipse thought. Asking him questions is powerful dangerous, the questioner getting the answer and the bill in the same breath. I for sure had kept my mouth clamped shut, except speaking to Cloud, even staying outside the Wizard's palace while Comet chatted him up.

"Darn! I hate it when I find memories like that!" Comet followed those words with several pointed phrases Eclipse wouldn't have guessed Comet had in her use vocabulary. "But I agreed. I agreed he could leave me the memory and not the remembering of getting it." That, Eclipse realized, meant the Wizard wanted us to know something, now and not sooner, and Comet agreed to help him by carrying planted memories. Comet repeated what the Wizard had said, using his oddly cadenced speech: "The questions are of the four, and of the one. They are the spoken, and the unspoken, the already-paid from the four, and the to-be-paid, paid in coin more bitter than mortal heart can bear, from the one." Comet repeated the Wizard's words, saying exactly the same thing each time.

"Okay," Star said. "We need to beat these dooms, get the answer to two questions, and we can go home. Eclipse? What was your question?"

"Why mine?" Eclipse asked. "Why not yours? One could be any one of us." For sure, Eclipse thought, she did not want the Eye giving her a bill for services rendered. He charged an arm and a leg. Or more. She grimaced as her comb found one more knot, noting that her curly platinum-white hair might go great with all sorts of different color garb, but sometimes was a real pain.

"One more thing," Comet said. "The StarCompass keeps reminding me about our mission. "Prevent the two dooms, or eight billion people will die. But now it's changed its mind. It says one doom will kill eight billion people, but the other will only kill one billion. That just started this evening."

The five of them looked at each other, baffled.

"Oh," Cloud said. "I know. There was a doom for here and now, killing everyone here and now. We just beat it. These people are now safe from it. That must have been these Andesians. But there's still a big doom left, that would kill everyone, and some other small doom, to kill everyone who+ was alive before time got changed." His companions nodded agreement. "So now we need to buy this island, put a base on it, and find the remaining dooms. Unless the StarCompass will lead us to them?"

"No such luck," Comet said. "It's stopped pointing at anything. It brought us to clues, we now somehow have the clues, so it's stopped leading us by the nose."

"Let's finish dinner," Aurora said. "Snacks or not, I'm still hungry."

~~~~~

Eclipse stood on the western shore of her own island, letting the Pacific breeze fan her silver curls. This wasn't as good a place to live as Comet's island, she decided, it being permanently too warm. That wasn't why she was here. Earlier she'd gone swimming, diving below the waves to spend an hour in the luminescent beauty of the night-time reef. A subsequent pass through the central pond had rinsed salt from her skin and hair. She felt fatigue as a deep glow, her muscles relaxed after prolonged, vigorous physical activity.

Last night, she'd crashed into deep sleep. Tonight she wanted exercise, the chance to swim with a brilliant school of fish until the burn filled arms and legs. She'd gone swimming by herself, relying on her gifts to keep her safe. Being by yourself in a real ocean would have been a risk for an ungifted, she considered. She always changed to a bathing suit and swam. Comet might have flown underwater fully garbed, flight field keeping her dry, and then have stripped down to almost nothing to sunbathe.

She could go back to their island, she told herself. That wasn't what she wanted. She'd spent a week with Pickering and the Four, being polite and considerate ever second of every day. Being a visitor was wearing. After months of living by herself, living as a guest with four chatterboxes was more exhausting than base construction would be. Now she could be by herself, relaxing until she could think sharply again.

She had done what needed to be done. Cloud and Star had been right about gifttruth. Ethics demanded that the five move away from

Pickering, that they not use their gifts to take advantage of an ungifted. That task was accomplished. The funds the four had salvaged from Saint Dominick should fund the Medford Persona League into eternity, or at least until history was restored and the salvage became green, peach, and black toy money. She had acceded by abstention to their action plan, so that money was theirs. She had her share of salvage from other medicine smugglers.

Idly, she wondered if the time pirates could be found, or if they even existed. The Andesians had looked like time pirates, but were space invaders. They could have been a trap by the time pirates. If you were time pirates, you put out space invaders, hoping surviving personae would reveal themselves to fight the space invaders. Then you killed the surviving personae. She had been careful about searching Andesian bases. There were no signs of time pirates. In a few days, there would be no traces of Andesian bases, either.

Of course, real history was full of civilizations that had vanished in the space of minutes or hours, leaving baffled survivors to piece together their lives in a world gone mad. Had it happened again? Was that the challenge she should face? Or was she still looking for the time pirates? The Andesians—the Empire of the New Inca—were many wicked things, but one of them was not 'responsible for stealing history'. Pickering's people could take care of their survivors, if need be with discrete persona support.

Exhaustion was a gentle throb in her skull, a blankness that inhibited thought, dimming the spark of her mind like the wet fog that reduces distant bonfires to liquescent glows. There was no one she could ask to help her. There was no one to rescue the world, no one to restore the true reality, no one except her. The foursome might try to help; they wanted their world back. She would have to find the hints, do the thinking, and do the standing up when it came time to get pounded on. She'd saved the world twice. She'd do it again, if she could find the strength. She squeezed her eyes shut, her face swiftly wet with tears.

And after she saved the world? After she set things right, so that once again the opalescent ruins of eternal Leaviork rose like frost-shattered tulips from the Pacific surf, would most of the world be grateful to her? Not hardly. She would still be the supreme enemy of civilization, her reward when captured the hangman's gibbet or the crucifixioner's spikes. Sometimes that last bit didn't matter. Sometimes the knowledge that every hand was turned against her, that no one would offer her a hand in friendship, was almost too much to endure.

Enough! she said to herself. Enough! She told herself she was too tired to think clearly. The faintest indigo wash, the soft harmonies of a glass harp, marked her disappearance from the island, her final destination a remote piece of New Mexico wilderness. Thick pine trees masked her campsite from the air, though when she looked carefully stars winked though the gaps in the branches. It was not her house, but it was safe and quiet and sheltered from the wind. She dropped out of her clothing and curled under her quilt. Sleep overtook her.

~~~~~

Much later, across the Pacific, the sun had reached the horizon. "Eclipse?" Aurora called. Eclipse had been here earlier. Where as she now? The four of them were alone. Not that they could ever be truly alone while they were shoulder to shoulder, the four standing together. "Eclipse?"

"Eclipse just went away," Cloud said, "not saying a word." He felt puzzled. Eclipse was the enemy of humanity, greed incarnate. The League of Nations had justly ordered that she be tried and crucified. In person, she never acted like a supreme villain was supposed to. Villains were supposed to be cruel and malicious—that was what she was supposed to do, wasn't it?

"She promised she'll be back, Star," Comet said, wishing she hadn't left Eclipse out of their circle. "She always keeps her promises. Close as she can." Eclipse was a wonderful friend, she decided. But sometimes she was so quiet that you forgot she was there until she wasn't there any more. Comet looked hard at the table, trying to hide from her own conscience. She knew Eclipse's secret about her mother. Now she'd gone and rejected Eclipse herself, ignoring Eclipse instead of drawing her into their midst.

In the amphibian hangar, on top of the loot they'd salvaged, they found a note from Eclipse.

Guys!

Happy homebuilding! (:^)) I'm happy to handle the purchase and hauling the prefab. Aurora is welcome to call. Everything always takes three times as long as you'd think. Don't defridge when it does, OK? Remember, measure twice, cut once. Running hot water and edison lamps are the twenty-first century

I'd've said goodbye. You were busy. With something really very important, lots more than goodbyes. I need to think. Or read. Or something. The time pirates must have left hints. I'll find them. I did the Maze. I fought Solara and friends, toe-to-toe. I can do anything, right? (:^((

Cheers,
Eclipse

The note closed with as sketch of her seal, the new moon ascendant over a sun in glory.

###

To be continued in Stand Against the Light.

Thank you for reading my book. Below there's still a Glossary and some notes about your author. If you enjoyed this book, please leave a review at your preferred book-sellers and review sites.

GLOSSARY

action: An Action is a planned use of violent gifts. A Regular Action is a constabulary operation, in which the miscreants are presumed to be criminals subject to arrest, fair trial, and swift execution. A Full Action is open warfare, with no constraints on levels, gifts, or instant consequences for the enemies of all humanity, for example, people who bribe judges.

Adara: A political refugee. Or so she said.

Ambihelicon of Geyer: The Ambihelicon is an artifact, usually represented artistically in the form of a tiara, wearing of which grants a persona unlimited power.

Aurora: Public persona of Jane Caroline Wells, eleven-year-old resident of Arlington, Massachusetts. Her public gifts include telepathy, clairvoyance, clairaudience, and other mentalic techniques. In private life, she aspires to the rank of Mistress of Games, based on attaining the rank of Grandmaster in chess and the equivalent rank in at least three other games. Her games include chess, go, territories, and City of Steel, the last being a prehistoric game of elaborate rules played on a hexagonal grid map which, to a vivid imagination, loosely resembles the westernmost reaches of the Russian Empire.

AutumnLost: A human culture founded millennia ago in another galaxy, allegedly reached by starship or sailing craft. AutumnLost is said to live in a temporal fog, emerging into reality for a day or two in each year.

Atlanticean: Any of several languages of Atlantis (or Atlanticea), an ancient civilization that flourished in the eastern Atlantic several millennia ago.

Book of New Miracles: A portion of the Further Testaments of the Christian Bible, concerned primarily with the passage of the Apostles among such places as Leav'k, Marik, and Sarnath.

Cloud: Public persona of Theodore Chester O'Ryan, a thirteen-year-old resident of the city of Roxbury, Massachusetts, and student at the Marcus Garvey Linguistic Middle School. His gifts are the forms of the cloud, including fog, flight, lightning, masslessness, and the strength of the tornado wind.

Comet: Public persona of Trishaset Jessamine Anson (nee Wells), a thirteen-year-old former resident of Arlington, Massachusetts. She recently divorced her parents. Her most noted gifts are flight, fast conscious response, and sensitivity of vision. Her private persona seeks to imitate her father, one of the world's great scientists, notwithstanding that they cannot stand each other. Her siblings Jane Caroline and Brian Sean also have public personae.

Corinne: Daughter of Solara. Appears to be fourteen or fifteen. Her date of birth lies in prehistory. At some date in the depths of time she took up the Ambihelicon of Geyer against a foe poetically described as "invincible star demons". She won, but was reduced to a near-comatose state from which she emerges for a few days in each generation.

cyborg: A mythical mechanico-human construct having a digital component to its intelligence.

Emperor Roxbury: Emperor Roxbury and his replicants attempted to destroy the city of Boston and burglarize the Federal Reserve Bank as a precursor to sharply reducing the world's population by violent means, the survivors to worship Roxbury as God-Emperor of the Universe. Emperor Roxbury disrupted the city and neutralized the Massachusetts Persona League. He was stopped by Star and Cloud; his henchmen were arrested by Aurora and Comet. Emperor Roxbury's replicants were destroyed by Eclipse.

DreamStorm: Fedcorps' premier illusionist.

Eclipse: By vote of the League of Nations, the Supreme Enemy of All Mankind. A female persona, age twelve. Her private persona name—Gloriana—is known only to a few. She solved the Lesser Maze, liberating and keeping for her own use the Most Glorious Namestone. For refusing to yield up the Namestone, the League declared her guilty of crimes against the future. The League ordered that she be captured and given a fair trial and a slow execution. The price on her head includes a hundred tons of Manjukuoan gold, life loan of the Mona Lisa, and a Roman castle.

Edison Theater: A dramatic establishment in which actors and scenery are replaced by their pre-recorded optical images, using a technical scheme based on the Edison patents.

engift: To grant another the use of a gift. Engifting, turning an ungifted into a persona, is generally albeit incorrectly believed to be solely a power of the Lords of Eternity.

FedCorps: The Federal Corps of Volunteer Personae. FedCorps, composed of persona volunteers and ungifted support staff, is stationed primarily in the area of the Federal Capital. Unlike the Armed Forces, who are sworn to the Constitution with the Speaker of the House as their Commander-in-Chief, or the State Militias, who are sworn to the Constitutions of the Republic and of their respective states with their state governor or state president as their Commander-in-Chief, FedCorps is formally the Sergeants-at-Arms of the Congress, sworn to the Constitution with the Speaker of the House and the President Pro

Tempore of the Senate as their joint Commanders-in-Chief.

garb: A costume, brilliantly colorful, often including a domino (mask) and decorated with a seal, typically worn by a public persona. The custom of wearing garb has transmitted itself to public life: would the Senate of the Republic be nearly so imposing if the Senators wore morning suits or opera capes rather than violet togas? Would the officers of the Army Air Corps be nearly so impressive without their feather capes? How would university students recognize their professors if the faculty did not routinely dress in robe and mortarboard, cape and stole and staff?

gift: Gifts are the powers that let one fly, become invisible, or read another's mind. Most people have at least some very feeble gifts. The true physical source of gifts is unknown. There is no evidence that they are hereditary or a result of mutation, training, or surgical intervention. Pasteur's hypothesis that gifts are contagious has statistical confirmation, but no causative agent has been identified. Gifts have always existed, though typical gifts have varied from epoch to epoch.

gifttrue: A persona is gifttrue if he uses his gifts morally, in the service of his chosen community.

Goetic Knights: A globe-spanning secret society and sometimes-dominant governing structure, dedicated to the belief that the best government is government of, by, and for the deeply gifted.

Greater Maze: A structure, traversal of which allegedly gives one the opportunity to reweave the fabric of time.

hittile: An internally-guided "smart projectile", the aiming mechanism being sufficiently accurate that the projectile is expected to strike its target aircraft and do kinetic energy damage.

Holmgren, Lars: Former Secretary-General of the League of Nations, Defender of the Peace of Mankind, Lawful Holder of the Heavensgate, the Most Glorious Namestone, and several paragraphs of additional titles. Argued that the Supreme Enemy should be flayed and burned alive, as opposed to being crucified, as had been recommended by the Special League Subcommittee for the Resolution of the Mode Question.

league: A collective voluntary organization of personae who agree to support each other and work to common objectives. Aurora, Cloud, Comet, and Star are members of the Greater Medford Persona League.

League of Terran Justice (League of Terror and Injustice): A globe-spanning conspiracy of terrorists, bandits, and political malcontents, supposedly dedicated to world government for, by, and of the deeply gifted. There is no actual evidence as to their objectives.

Leaviork: A civilization of several millennia ago, its focus being individual achievement and the enjoyment of beauty. "Better a small frog in a smaller pond" characterizes its worldly attitude. Leaviork's technology was advanced but oddly focused. Its boats had gold fittings while its homes used synthetic diamond and emerald windows. It is said that no Leaviorkianu ever voluntarily travelled more than fifty miles from the homeland.

Lemuria: Any of several militaristic cultures believed to exist under the Pacific and Indian oceans. Lemurian incursions onto the land continents provoke regular and bloody wars. Some authorities believe that Lemuria actually exists elsewhere, only gates to elsewhere existing under the oceans. The Lemurian language, which uses four different syllabic and hieroglyphic alphabets simultaneously, is among the most difficult in the world to learn.

Lesser Maze: A puzzle palace on St. Brendan's Isle, hiding and protecting the Namestone and the Tomb of the Bearer. The Lesser Maze and its defenders are the Namestone's creation. The Defenders are keyed so that they are always just weak enough that they can in principle be defeated by their opponents, if only the opponents use sufficient wit as well as brute force. The Lesser Maze creates a world-wide partial eclipse during serious attempts to traverse its obstacles. The eclipse became total when the Lesser Maze was solved by Eclipse. Descriptions of failed attempts to traverse the Lesser Maze are widely distributed by unseen methods, so that all may know and fear the Lesser Maze.

Lords of Eternity: A group of immortal personae of great age (most are said to predate all recorded civilizations) and power, supposedly including the ability to engift normal mortals. The existence of the Lords (they do not use this title among themselves) as an organized group is open to some question; they do not ordinarily concern themselves with issues of concern to mortals. Well-known Lords include Solara, Prince Mong-Ku, the Screaming Skull, and Plasmatrix-the-Desolation-of-the-Goddess.

Manjukuo: One of the great powers of the modern world, ranking in importance with Russia, Austria-Hungary, France, The Celestial Republic, and Brazil. Its borders extend northwest through Mongolia, north to the Arctic Sea, and southwest as far as the Holy Lamanate of Tibet.

Marik: A technically advanced civilization of several millennia ago, located notably in the western Americas. Marik was given over entirely to public spectacle, its most eminent government officials being Parademasters and Grand Marshals. Virtually its entire population supposedly perished in the space of a few minutes by marching en masse into the Pacific Ocean.

Master of Airships: An eccentric public persona who plotted to make the rigid airship the dominant form of air travel. To accomplish this end, he planned to transmute much of the Indian Ocean to krypton gas, thereby increasing ten-fold the density of air, eliminate both polar caps by changing oceanic currents and deleting the Tibetan plateau, so as to eliminate major storms and severe seasonal weather, and infect all living things with a series of plagues to protect them from the biological consequences of the Earth's new atmosphere. Efforts to render him deceased are believed to have been successful.

mind: A non-physical construct corresponding to the ability to process information. Telepathic testimony shows that minds are possessed by essentially all animals, and by the more complex calculating machines. It is not agreed whether the mentalic memories of the deep rocks—the Currents of the Earth—are symptomatic of a planetary mentation.

mindlock: A forbidden gift, possession of which is punishable in many civilized lands by death, that allows one to dominate the mental processes of another.

Modern English: The dialect of English spoken by our five personae, to be distinguished from Historic English as spoken in Leaviork, and Standard Edited English as spoken by the reader. Modern English draws more heavily on German than does Standard Edited English. Modern English has such constructions as mayhaps, for sure, gifttrue, and mindblitz.

Namestone: The Most Glorious Namestone, the Gate of Heaven, the Holy Key to Utopia, is an artifact of great age and supernal power. In addition to enhancing the gifts of the persona who wields it, the Namestone has intrinsic abilities of its own, notably Rationalization and Material Transmutation. By use of Rationalization, a persona may supposedly purge men's hearts of fear, evil, and all other disorder. The power of Material Transmutation allows the wielder to transform arbitrary objects into other objects. Moving the Namestone to the possession of a qualified user, thereby transforming the world into the kingdom of heaven on earth, has been a primary goal of most human cultures for thousands of years. The Namestone was brought to this Earth by the Bearer, as described in the Atlanticean Sacred Ode to the Most Glorious Namestone, the translation of Tennyson being authoritative, however much Tennyson apologized for the meter and structure of his translation.

persona: (pl. personae, personas) The identity assumed by a person. Public personae are usually persons with gifts, using their gifts to public or private benefit, often while brilliantly dressed. Many public personae also have a private persona with orthodox dress and occupation but no sign of gifts. An open persona is a gifted person whose public and private identities are the same.

Pickering, Alexander Humboldt von: "The State's Greatest Scientist" is perhaps an exaggeration. His ingenious (or perhaps eccentric) theories and inventions have earned him great wealth, if not the uniform respect of all of his peers. The "von" is a self-awarded honorific.

Plasmatrix, or Plasmatrix-the-Desolation-of-the-Goddess: A Lord of Eternity, whose somewhat scanty garb appears to be composed entirely of incandescent gas. Her gifts lie in the field of material obliteration.

Prince Mong-Ku: A Lord of Eternity, a being whose existence predates recorded civilization. While some would see him as the personification of a European interpretation of 18th century Manjukuoan culture, the relative ages of Mong-ku and Manjukuo imply that he shaped Manjukuo in his image. Certainly, without his influence the Empire would not have forestalled Russian expansion into Mongolia and Siberia by seizing the territories first.

privileged bands: In the structuralist unified theory of physics, each point or quantized volume in the universe has associated with it a list of attributes that determine what objects and fields are present (at least in part) at that point. The privileged bands are claimed to communicate directly with the attribute list of each point, allowing one, e.g., to create matter out of nothing by redefining the attribute list in a region from "vacuum" to "solid gold", or, e.g. to change the structure of space to alter the laws of arithmetic.

Rationalism: The discredited Rationalist School of History asserted that human motives and behaviors in distant cultures were basically the same as our own, so that if one understood what a culture valued one could understand the behavior of the culture's members. Irrational behavior of members of foreign cultures was interpreted by the rationalists as a rational striving for a differently ordered sets of goals. Efforts to apply Rationalism to the ancient historical record are a total failure. Most modern historians instead understand that ancient men are fundamentally incomprehensible, so that the primary purpose of history is the presentation of morally educatory tales, such as Leonidas and the Three Hundred. The Temporal Rationalists proposed to eliminate certain inconsistencies encountered by the rationalist school by claiming that, contrary to the physicists, time is not well-ordered, so that different observers need not agree on the order in which historical events occurred.

RTI: Roger's Technological Institution. A scientific school located in Cambridge, Massachusetts on the northern bank of the Carolus Fluvius.

Sarnath: A world-spanning technically advanced trading empire of some millennia ago, its culture being given over entirely to trade, commerce, and personal enrichment. The causes of its disappearance are unknown. It is difficult for moderns to credit the traveler's report that a single Sarnathi speculator managed to corner the entire food supply of the country, then allowed the population to starve to death in order to maximize his profits.

The Screaming Skull: A Lord of Eternity, a being whose existence predates recorded civilization. The Skull is urbane, witty, and polite; he dresses entirely in black. He is widely viewed as being less than bright. His primary gift is the ability to order people to drop dead.

Seal: An ornamental pattern or mark, identifying a public persona, featured on garb or other clothing. Seals seen here include: Cloud: a thunderhead, Comet: a comet, Star: a four-point rayed star, Aurora: the radiant eye and pyramid, and Eclipse: the new moon triumphant over a sun in glory.

The Silver General: Not a Lord of Eternity, though of similar age and power. The cycle of rise and fall of each civilization is said to follow from a struggle between the Silver General and Solara.

Solara: A Lord of Eternity, whose existence predates modern civilization. Her garb features a golden sun mask, eye sockets bejeweled. Scholars infer that she is primus unter pares among the Lords of Eternity. Eclipse's claim to have stood up toe-to-toe against Solara, as opposed to having created for her own purposes the illusion of this act, implies an exceedingly deep ability to call on her gifts.

Star: Public persona of Brian Sean Wells, twelve-year old brother of Comet and Aurora. His most notable gifts are an effective body screen and an extremely potent energy attack. An good student, he is more interested in traditional boyish pursuits: base ball nines and model building. He knows that his sisters will solve puzzles before he does, but becomes bored while waiting for them to do so.

StarCompass: A quadridimensional set of metal sheaves, programmed to lead the holder to predetermined objectives. A loan to Comet from the Eye of Mars.

SDIO: Strategic Defense Initiative Organization. Ronald Reagan's Wall in the Air, given material form.

Supreme Illusionist: A public prankster and rogue persona, whose masterwork was the transformation of Harvard Square into the Piazza Leprecano. He was captured by the Greater Medford Persona League. His urban reconstruction of central Cambridge has been left intact, except that the statue of John Harvard in the yards of the Massachusetts Institution for Theology no longer glows kelly green.

Telzey: A primitive artificial intelligence responsible for Pickering's housekeeping and computer operations.

tesdri: Tesla Detection, Ranging, and Identification; radar.

Transitivity: (Einstein's Theory of Transitivity). In 1922 Solara appeared to Einstein, transporting him in the space of hours to AutumnLost. Based on his observations of certain peculiar phenomena seen at exceeding large velocities, Einstein replaced Relativity with Transitivity, of which General Relativity is a limiting case. The theory of Transitivity explains faster-than-light travel, and indicates conditions under which travel through time is possible, the concept of causality being generalized via replacement of the familiar time t with three time dimensions: t, u, and v. According to Transitivity, one may use time travel to proceed to the past, alter past events, and return to a present not resembling the present that one remembers.

Tunnels: A shifting pattern of holes in an enormous block of volcanic rock located across the universe from the Earth. The block is claimed by some to be an edge of the universe. Passage through the Tunnels without leave of the Guardian of the Tunnels is problematic. The Guardian's price is high, though often the price benefits the giver out of proportion to its cost.

Victoria Britomart Wilson: A human female, age 12. A true heroine, who stood with wit and courage by a friend during terrible danger.

Wizard of Mars: An immortal, seemingly all-knowing, being resident in the Scarlet Castle, the Temple of the Wizard, a vast structure that began life as the volcano Mons Olympus. The Wizard enjoys friendly conversation. It reveals its knowledge to others for a price often too great to pay. The Wizard is neither omnipotent nor omnicompetent: it can be outsmarted.

XO: Executive Officer; the second-in-command of a warship.

ABOUT GEORGE PHILLIES

George Phillies is a retired Professor of Physics living in Worcester, Massachusetts.. He has written more than 160 technical papers and nearly two dozen books. *Airy Castles All Ablaze* will be his seventh novel. His other hobbies include physics research, gardening, and science fiction fandom. He is President of the National Fantasy Fan Federation (founded 1941), the world's oldest non-local SF club. He had been active in politics, and was on the ballot for Federal office twice.

A complete list of his books includes

Novels and Short Story Collections

George D. J. Phillies, This Shining Sea (2000)
George D. J. Phillies, Nine Gees. (2000) [Short Story Collection]
George D. J. Phillies, The Minutegirls (2006)
George Phillies, Mistress of the Waves (2012)
George Phillies, The One World (2012)
George Phillies and Jefferson Swycaffer, Editors,
    A Sea of Stars Like Diamonds (2016) [Short Story Collection]
George Phillies, MinuteGirls, Second Edition. (2017)
George Phillies, Against Three Lands (2018)
George Phillies, Eclipse: The Girl Who Saved the World (2019)
George Phillies, Airy Castles All Ablaze (2019)

Technical Books

George D. J. Phillies, Elementary Lectures in Statistical Mechanics, Springer-Verlag: New York (2000).
George D. J. Phillies, Phenomenology of Polymer Solution Dynamics, Cambridge University Press, Cambridge, U.K. (2011).
George D. J. Phillies, Complete Numerical Tables for Phillies' Phenomenology of Polymer Solution Dynamics (2011).

Game Design

George D. J. Phillies and Tom Vasel, Contemporary Perspectives on Game Design. (2006)
George D. J. Phillies and Tom Vasel, Design Elements of Contemporary Strategy Games. (2006)
George Phillies and Tom Vasel, Designing Modern Strategy Games

(2012) [second edition of ``Design Elements of Contemporary Strategy Games``].

George Phillies and Tom Vasel, Modern Perspectives on Game Design. (2012) [second edition of ``Contemporary Perspectives in Game Design``].

George Phillies, Stalingrad for Beginners (Studies in Game Design - 3) (2013)

George Phillies, Stalingrad Replayed (Studies in Game Design - 4) (2013)

George Phillies, Designing Wargames - Introduction (Studies in Game Design - 5) (2014).

Political Books

George D. J. Phillies, Stand Up for Liberty! (2000)
George D. J. Phillies, Funding Liberty (2003)
George Phillies, Libertarian Renaissance. (2014).
George Phillies, Surely We Can Do Better (2016).

###

CPSIA information can be obtained
at www.ICGtesting.com
Printed in the USA
LVHW040713181119
637663LV00001B/65

9 781695 886247